Leaving Bethany

SUSAN SUTHERLAND

© Susan Sutherland 2020

Published by Susan Sutherland

A CIP catalogue record for this book is available from the British Library.

ISBN 978-1-9989904-0-5 (mobi)
ISBN 978-1-9989904-1-2 (epub)
ISBN 978-1-9989904-2-9 (Paperback)

Book layout and cover design by Clare Brayshaw

Cover image © Maryna Kriuchenko | Dreamstime.com

Prepared by:

York Publishing Services Ltd
64 Hallfield Road
Layerthorpe
York
YO31 7ZQ

Tel: 01904 431213

Website: www.yps-publishing.co.uk

CHAPTER 1

The pot hit the floor with a resounding crash. Loud enough for everyone in the courtyard to hear. Even as I picked up a cloth, I knew it was my fault. After wiping the spilt olive oil from my robe, I bent down to pick up the olives. Mother always said I had a temper, especially with my sister. As usual, I was in the cooking area preparing the meal while she found another way to escape. She knew what I had to do, but she was such a scatterbrain and unable to concentrate on one job long enough to finish it. Who was it who invited him into our home for a meal? It was me and I should have been the one listening to him, not her.

That momentous day began very much as it always had. I awoke before dawn, drew water from the well, ground corn to make flour for the day's bread, fed the chickens, collected the eggs and made breakfast. The sun was almost at its height when I picked up the broom to sweep the ashes from around the oven. I opened the gate and swept the dust out into the street as two boys ran past.

"He's here!" one boy shouted.

"He's come to our village." The other boy turned around to call before he too ran towards the crowds.

The usual sleepiness of Bethany was shattered by cheering and shouting villagers. I leaned the broom by the gate and there he was, standing in front of me. His deep brown eyes looked directly into my own.

"It's nearly the hottest part of the day, you're welcome to come into my home where it's cool. You may rest while I will make you some refreshments." My words took me by surprise, being spoken before I thought them.

"Thank you, Martha," he replied. I wondered how he knew my name when I hadn't not told him. Ashamed that he might see the broom leaning on the gate, I picked it up, and he smiled as I hid it behind my back. Then for the first time, Rabbi Jesus walked into my house, followed by a group of men who were his closest followers and disciples.

"Please sit and rest," I said, showing him the shady spot under the vines where my husband used to sit. Before anyone else noticed, I hid the broom behind the gate. Rabbi Jesus turned as two young people walked into the courtyard.

"May I introduce my brother, Lazarus, and our sister, Mary," I said.

Jesus greeted them before finding a place to sit and I turned to the cooking area to prepare the meal. Mary stood by Jesus's side looking up at him.

She moved away when I tugged her arm and we left Lazarus, normally such a shy young man, talking to Jesus about our home and life in Bethany.

"Get the bread dough I made earlier and make enough flatbreads for everyone," I said turning away to light the oven.

Blowing on a spark, I added straw and twigs until it was alight. Jesus called his friends together and Lazarus joined them, sitting cross-legged on the floor. Sunlight streamed through the vine leaves covering the courtyard. It dappled each head and shimmered as the leaves fluttered in the breeze. Still watching Jesus, Mary picked up the dough.

2

"Are you going to do anything with that dough?" I asked.

"Can I join them?" She muttered.

"No! You'll stay here," I said cutting the leeks. "They can't eat the stew without those flatbreads."

Mary separated the dough into balls and flattened them between her hands. Her scowl was enough to kill the yeast. Needing olives to go with the flatbreads I went to the storeroom and spooned some into a bowl from one of the large storage jars. When I returned Mary had left the cooking area and was standing at the back of the group.

"Come here," I whispered.

Without a word, she pulled a face and came back. She picked up a small ball of dough and squeezed it in her hands until it burst out between her fingers.

"Why can't I listen?"

"You are needed here. Besides, it's not right for a young woman to listen to a rabbi."

"I don't see why not." She smacked the dough ball between her hands.

"Because that's the way it's always been, and no amount of sulking will change anything."

By this time, the stew was bubbling. I stirred it and picking up a bowl, went back to the storeroom to collect figs. When I came back, Mary had vanished again. This time, she had not only joined the men but was at the front and sitting at Jesus's feet, gazing up at him. With flour-splattered hands she hugged her knees, leaving white marks on her robe.

"Mary! Mary!" I said in more of a shout than a whisper.

She ignored me, so I returned to prepare the flatbreads myself. That was the reason I was so irate that I dropped the pot. Not believing what she had done, my anger and shame were tinged with jealousy. How I wished I could drop everything to sit and listen like Mary, and to learn more than I was permitted as a woman. Fear also stopped me. I didn't even know how I dared invite him inside, let alone sit at his feet like a male disciple.

Jesus became quiet, and I approached the back of the group. "Teacher, I see my sister is sitting with your male companions. This is most improper as I am sure you will agree. Please tell Mary to get off her backside and come and help prepare your lunch."

Mary bent her head and stared at the ground. What happened next took me so much by surprise I could never have dreamed it. This was to be the pivotal point in my life. There was my life before that moment, and now there is my life after that moment. Jesus stood and looked at me with those penetrating brown eyes.

"My dear Martha," he said, "you're worried and upset about the work you consider necessary. Do you know what's important in life? There's only one thing, and Mary has found it. So, I will not take it away from her."

If that was not surprising enough, he held out his hand. "Why don't you come and join us?"

A broad smile wrinkled the skin around his eyes, and as I reached out to take his calloused hand, the men made space for me next to Mary. With tears in her eyes and no longer embarrassed, she took my hand and squeezed it. I'm unsure of how long we sat there, and I cannot remember what he said that day, but I felt an overwhelming sense of belonging and acceptance. Even after Jesus had finished speaking, I sat captivated and absorbed.

Lazarus and Mary organised two of Jesus's followers to bring the food to the table. Then Jesus broke a flatbread in half and prayed. "Blessed are you Lord, our God, King of the universe who brings forth bread from the earth."

After the blessing, he turned and said, "Thank you, Martha, for inviting us into your home, and for preparing this meal."

I stared at him, amazed that he should thank me. Just to be in their presence sharing food together was a brand-new experience for us. As women, to sit as equals with a rabbi and his male followers was not a common practice. Too soon, it was time for them to leave.

Jesus paused by the street and turning said, "I'll call on you again soon."

With a dry mouth and unable to speak, my smile gave my agreement for him to return. He turned and caught up with his companions. I closed the gate behind them and leaned against it.

"I've never eaten a meal with such interesting people. Who are they?"

"How come you invited them for lunch?" Lazarus asked as he sat on the seat vacated by Jesus.

"The rabbi appeared in front of me and before I knew what I'd said, they were inside the courtyard. Then I panicked I wouldn't have enough food."

"Martha, you could feed half of Bethany with what we have in our storeroom," Mary joked.

Lazarus turned to Mary. "A smile has been on your face since Jesus stepped through the gate."

Mary sat next to her brother and leaned on his shoulder. "Isn't it wonderful! Such amazing things we've heard today. I can't wait to see him again."

With a sigh, I remembered the broken pot, but when I walked into the cooking area, someone had swept the pieces away. The broom was leaning on the wall by the oven, and plates and dishes lay clean on the table.

"Who did the tidying?" I asked.

"Two of the men offered to help while you were talking to Jesus," Mary said.

"Oh, they shouldn't have done that. It would've been a privilege to tidy up after what they've given us today."

Pleased to rest, I sat on a stool and leaned back on the wall. Watching wispy clouds drifting across a clear sky, I tried to make sense of what I'd seen.

"Mary, how come you sat in front of Jesus?" I asked.

She smiled. "I wanted to hear what he had to say and crept closer until a man nodded to a space. Then it was just a matter of wriggling forward until I was at the front."

"Can't you remember what father used to say about women studying? What would he say if he was alive today?"

Scowling, she pointed her finger and dropped her voice. "There is an old saying that if a man gives his daughter knowledge of the law and scripture, it's as though he taught her debauchery. Now shoo girls, go and help your mother."

We laughed at her impersonation of our father, but it was true. Lazarus attended the religious school to learn the law and the scriptures. However, our father and mother only gave their daughters enough understanding of our laws to run a proper home. Just the minimum to be a good wife and mother.

"Father never realised that we met on the roof after school," Lazarus said. "Do you remember how we used to hide behind mother's washing, and I would teach you what I'd learned?" He laughed until it brought on one of his coughing fits.

Mary folded her arms. "It's not fair. I always wanted to go to school with Lazarus."

I had to agree. As a child, I would have given anything to go with him to school. But that was impossible; his teachers would never allow me, a mere girl, through the door.

Mary continued, "At least father taught us to read and write, which is more than most girls in the village."

"I appreciate that," I sighed, "but it's frustrating I can't read what I want to."

When Lazarus finished coughing again, he said, "This rabbi seems different from those who only let certain people study the scriptures. One of the men said many women follow Jesus."

I put my hand on his shoulder. "Why don't you lie down and rest? It's been an exciting day."

The day had taken its toll on Lazarus and there was no complaint from him. With a deep sigh, he stood and walked away. His coughing echoing inside the house.

Mary agreed with her brother. "One of them told me women disciples sit with them and learn." She grabbed my hand. "Oh, Martha, wouldn't it be wonderful to follow Jesus like that?"

"That's not possible, you are too young, and we have responsibilities. However, I'm interested to meet the other women. I've never heard of a rabbi who allows women to sit alongside the men as disciples. This man is intriguing, he is so different from anyone I've ever known."

Most of the time I enjoyed the role handed to me by God – to look after my two younger siblings after our parents died and after I became a widow. But I felt the weight of responsibility at such a young age, wondering whether I could do as good a job at raising them as my mother. I often asked myself if she would approve of how I was caring for them.

Mary stared into the sky. "Do you think he'll come back? Will he remember us and return?"

"I hope he will because I want to know more about him." Closing my eyes, I whispered, "Please return soon."

* * *

The early spring sun had yet to warm the land and, shivering, I wrapped my scarf around my head. Unable to make sense of the world glimpsed through the rabbi's visit the day before, I strode out to the village well. It was as if he had opened the shutters to let a chink of light into a dark room, only to slam them shut again. Musing upon these thoughts, I placed the pitcher on the edge of the well and poured water into it.

"So?" A voice called out.

The pitcher slipped from my hand, splashing my feet with cold water, but I caught it in time before it dropped down the well and broke. Absorbed in my thoughts, I hadn't heard Rebekah, my neighbour, creep up behind me. Like a spider, she peered out of her shutters, waiting to catch her next victim as they walked past, often appearing with her pitcher or broom at the most inconvenient moment.

"So?" Still waiting for an answer, she stood with one hand holding the pitcher on her shoulder, the other on her hip.

"So, what happened yesterday?" She placed the cracked pitcher on the dusty ground by the side of the well and folded her arms.

Not wanting to talk I looked away. "Good morning, Rebekah. The weather is a little cold this morning, but it should warm up soon."

The early morning sun cast a long shadow, and she covered her unruly hair with a dirty scarf. "Tell me about the rabbi. The one who is been wandering around with that scruffy crowd, doing all sorts of weird things. What were you thinking by asking him inside your home? I said to my husband, 'Jonas, you'll never guess what Martha's just done. Only invited that strange rabbi in for lunch.' Go on, what happened?"

All the village knew of her perseverance for any scrap of gossip, and I had been the victim many times. Blocking my escape, she rubbed her hands in anticipation.

"Was he angry?"

"Why do you say that?" I picked up the full pitcher and slung it on my shoulder.

"I heard a pot smash."

Rebekah was enjoying this conversation more than I was. How could I explain something I didn't understand myself? There were no words to describe the jumble of thoughts and emotions circulating in my head.

Making my excuse, I said, "The breakfast needs making so I've no time to stand and gossip."

"If he comes again," she shouted as I strode past, "let me know and I'll help prepare something. I can come with one of my pots."

Her laughter echoed around the courtyard and my head, even after I closed the gate.

'If he comes again.'

There was nothing special about us or our home in the small village of Bethany that would make Jesus return. I thought he had already forgotten us.

* * *

I thought life would never be the same, but that was the lie I told myself. Each dawn brought the same dull routine, and I carried on as if nothing had happened. One week later, I was sorting pots ready for planting herbs and trying to ignore my brother and sister arguing.

"Be careful with that broom," Lazarus shouted at his sister. "Can't you see I'm holding a chicken?"

Mary swept around his feet. "Just clearing out the rubbish!"

He chased her around the courtyard making clucking noises and pretending to make the chicken peck her. Alarmed, the other chickens scattered, clucking loudly. Lazarus's mop of black curly hair flopped over his eyes as he forced Mary into a corner. Only eighteen months separated them, with Lazarus being eighteen and Mary sixteen, but because of his illness Lazarus was short for his age and Mary matched his height. They had played together from childhood as Lazarus had spent most of the time at home, having few friends his age. Mary swept her long curly hair off her face, and with the broom in front of her, tried to push Lazarus away. The more she screamed, the louder the chicken clucked.

Separating them, I hollered, "Stop it! The sweeping needs doing, and I need you to clean the chicken coop before the evening meal."

"Martha, are you home?" A voice cried from the street.

Breathless, Mary rushed to open the gate and Jesus entered with four of his companions. Seeing him I let out a sigh, without realising that I'd held my breath.

"I told you I'd return," he said, knowing what I was thinking.

The chicken stopped clucking as Jesus took it from Lazarus and stroked its feathers. Though pleased to see them again, it upset me they arrived at the moment I shouted at Lazarus and Mary. I turned to walk to the cooking area.

"Martha!" Jesus called. "Just some bread, olives and fruit with wine will be enough. Don't take long preparing our food because I've things to say and want you here with us." I turned in surprise and he nodded. One of his disciples followed as I walked into the cooking area.

"Can I help?" He asked. "Jesus has often mentioned coming back to Bethany, and we're pleased to be here. I'm

John, and with my brother, James, have followed Jesus for two years now, along with Simon and Andrew."

Unsure how to answer his friendliness and an unusual offer of help from a man, I smiled and showed him the storage area. He spooned olives into a dish and carried it through with a bowl of dates. When the meal was ready, Jesus put the chicken down before blessing the bread. Mary carried her plate and sat in a place next to Jesus, pushing John aside. He looked up and smiled, making way for her. Lazarus poured the wine, and we ate a family meal together as we had on Jesus's first visit. This was something that had been missing from our home for a long time. I had relaxed and begun to enjoy myself when the inevitable happened.

"Hello, Martha, how are you?" It was Rebekah. "I thought I'd call and see you today. Oh, it looks like you've visitors."

What would Jesus think of my neighbour? To hide my embarrassment, I collected the empty plates. Even though he met hundreds of people, at that moment he was a guest in my home. Rebekah could find her own rabbi. Jesus was ours, and I wasn't sharing him with anyone in Bethany. Lazarus steered her back towards the gate, mumbling how nice it was for her to visit but now was not the time. Jesus didn't seem to mind. He didn't comment and carried on talking.

What a privilege to sit and listen, and this time I paid careful attention. He said God is our Father, even calling him Abba, which in our language means 'daddy', the same word we called our father as young children. How can we call God a word so familiar as Abba and get away with it? I stared at Jesus.

"Yes, Martha, you can call God Father, and you can call him Abba." How would I ever be brave enough to do this?

Jesus's second visit was brief and though saddened by their departure, I knew it was wise because bands of robbers often roamed the hills. Jerusalem was only forty minutes' walk away, but it could still be a dangerous journey after dark.

As he left, he said, "I'll see you soon, and you can now believe I'll return when I'm able."

Summer brought with it a sense of anticipation and we eagerly awaited each visit, filling us with wonder and hope that we were at the start of something new. Jesus filled our house with his presence, and whenever he left, it felt smaller as if a room was missing. Afterwards, we'd sit and discuss his marvellous words, capturing them in our memory.

CHAPTER 2

Shifting the heavy bag, I rubbed my shoulder. Jesus was due later that day, and I was returning home from the market. A shadow passed over me and when I looked around, Rebekah and her husband, Jonas, were standing at my elbow.

"Good morning, neighbour," Jonas said and, repositioning the bag, I returned his greeting.

Rebekah sighed, put her large bag on the ground and laughed. "These vegetables get no lighter."

Jonas scratched his head. "I'm pleased we met this morning. There's something I need to say and have been looking for a suitable opportunity." He liked to speak and expected everyone to listen.

Rebekah nodded. "Yes, we're worried for your safety and don't want any harm to come to you."

"What harm?" I asked.

"There are disturbing reports you are entertaining disreputable people in your home," Jonas said.

"Who are you referring to?"

"Oh, Martha," Jonas leaned forward, "you know I mean the travelling rabbi from Nazareth."

"Jesus has never hurt us?"

Rebekah grabbed my arm. "It's not what he might do but …"

"But what could happen to you by association," Jonas interrupted his wife.

I shook my head. "I don't understand what you mean."

"My poor neighbour. It's good we are here, isn't it Rebekah?"

"It's in your best interests," she nodded.

"Yes, we are only thinking of you. Who knows where this seditious talk will lead? Jesus has spoken out against the Temple and the law."

"No, he hasn't. He's always talked about a renewing of our faith and defending the law."

Jonas shook his head. "What a pity you are so naïve, and don't have the wealth of experience I do. My many influential friends and I are wise enough to understand these things and you ought to listen to us not him."

I turned to walk away and said, "If you listened to his teaching and didn't gossip about what someone reports he said, then you'd understand. Why don't you come in and talk to him later today?"

Other people at the market looked around when Jonas laughed. "I knew your father well, and he would be very disappointed that you have invited danger into your home which threatens Lazarus and Mary."

"Who I entertain in my home is of no concern of yours."

Rebekah wrung her hands. "Oh, please be careful, Martha, I'm worried about Mary, she's …"

Jonas pushed Rebekah away. "She's unmarried, and it will harm her chances of a successful engagement by mixing with such a person as Jesus. What would your mother say if she knew? If the Temple authorities should hear about the activities in your home, there may be a danger to Lazarus too."

Rebekah moved to hug me, but I pushed her away. She fiddled with her scarf. "It's upsetting, but I know you'll make the right choice for the safety of your family."

"Come, Rebekah, we've done our duty to our neighbour. It's in her hands now."

Rebekah picked up the bag and walked behind Jonas. Standing tall, I wiped my eyes and followed at a distance. There was a decision I had to make: to continue seeing Jesus or do as my neighbours advised.

Mary ran into the courtyard. "Martha, I've done the work you asked me to do. The rooms are ready, and the bedding put out for everyone. Are you all right? Your eyes are red."

"It was windy by the market and dust flew into my eye, that's all." Jesus was coming in a few hours and I intended to welcome him as always.

* * *

When Jesus arrived later that afternoon, I pushed all thoughts of Jonas and Rebekah from my mind. I wouldn't let them spoil what we had; it was becoming too precious. Besides, I enjoyed playing the hostess and having company, especially people like Jesus and his friends who gave me far more than I could repay.

The following morning Jesus said they were leaving for Galilee but asked if we would walk with him before he left. Quick to grab her travelling cloak, Mary waited for us by the gate. We walked out of the village, past white stone walls and up into the olive groves. Only two miles away to the west lay the bustling city of Jerusalem, but here on the eastern slopes of the Mount of Olives lay the peaceful village of Bethany. Spring had turned into early summer and we followed the path, edged with the yellow, white and pink flowers of the wild broom. Up, to the silent and deserted olive presses. At harvest time, the area would be noisy with busy farm labourers collecting the olives and pressing them into valuable olive oil.

Jesus sat on a rock underneath an olive tree, its small white blossom hanging overhead, and nodded to me. This was where my husband, Nathan, and I ate our last lunch together just hours before his death. I often revisited this spot to sit and reflect upon my life and my loss. Sighing, I knew Jesus had chosen it deliberately, and we settled down on the surrounding ground.

"Can you tell us a story?" Mary asked.

He leaned forward and began. "There was once a businessman who had to travel on the long and hazardous journey from Jerusalem to Jericho. He arrived at the most dangerous part of the journey and, frightened, he looked around the rocky canyon. Without warning, a gang of notorious robbers jumped out from behind a rock. They attacked him, took all his money and belongings and even stripped him of his clothes."

"That's terrible. The poor man!" Mary looked at Jesus. "Did anyone help?"

"The first person along the road was a priest who saw the man injured and bleeding to death. Do you know what he did?"

"He helped him," said Mary.

"Well, he was on his way to Jerusalem and worried in case the man died. If he touched a dead person, he would be ritually unclean and unable to worship in the Temple. So, he tried to get as far away as possible as he walked past."

Lazarus shook his head. "That's not very nice."

"The dying man summoned enough strength to open his eyes and saw another religious man. 'Help me,' he groaned.

But being in a hurry, this man didn't want to delay his journey to Jerusalem and pretended he hadn't heard the cries for help. Ignoring the man, he ran past quickly in case the robbers were still hiding nearby.

"Now a third man was travelling to Jericho to sell blankets which he carried on his donkey. When he entered the canyon, he saw the injured man lying unconscious in the road. Without considering his safety, he ran to him and gave emergency first aid. He bandaged his wounds and put a new blanket around him. Carefully he placed him on the donkey and took him to the nearest inn, even giving the innkeeper money to look after him with a promise of extra if needed when he returned."

"What a good and generous man to help a fellow traveller," I said. "Who was he?"

Jesus leaned in towards us. "He was a Samaritan."

Open-mouthed, Lazarus sat up. "A Samaritan? No! Samaritans and Jews have nothing to do with each other."

"This Samaritan knew we are to love our neighbour as much as we love ourselves."

"We live in separate villages, so he can't have been his neighbour," Mary remarked.

"What do you think, Martha?"

"I suppose he acted as if the injured man was his neighbour. We're to help anyone in need, and it should be regardless of who they are," I replied.

"That's right. Regardless of who they are and where they live."

I looked away from him. It might be easier to love a Samaritan than my actual neighbours. Without telling him, he understood my attitude towards Rebekah and Jonas. But that was their fault, not mine. I didn't want to spend time with people like them. Walking home, I held Mary back so Lazarus could be with Jesus on his own. Since they met, they had become good friends and chatted together as they walked back along the path. Lazarus enjoyed Jesus's company and was now more open and friendlier with strangers than before. I couldn't deny my brother this friendship. Jesus was not dangerous. He was just a rabbi, and I felt sure no harm would come to him or us.

Despite Jesus's words, I still tried to avoid Rebekah, but that was not always possible. Whenever we spoke, she was more interested in sensational gossip than his teachings. At first, I wanted to keep Jesus to myself, but gradually I told my neighbours about him. I considered ourselves to be his special friends in Bethany, and I confess pride often coloured what I said.

* * *

As summer progressed, we became friends with Jesus's closest disciples and followers. Sometimes he arrived with a few and at other times the wider group accompanied him. In partnership with Simon and Andrew, brothers John and James used to own a fishing business on Lake Galilee to the north. They gave it up to follow Jesus. John was the more serious of the two whereas we often heard James laughing or at the centre of a joke. Andrew and Simon were close and had similar temperaments, but Andrew was quieter than his more boisterous brother. Often in the middle of a discussion or loud conversation, Simon's booming voice and laughter echoed around the courtyard. The disciples looked up to Simon as the leader of the group.

There were others in the wider group including Matthew, who had been a much-reviled tax collector. Not only did tax collectors collect the taxes for the despised Romans, but they also embezzled money for themselves. When Matthew met

Jesus, he gave up his lucrative job and returned any money he had taken for himself. Judas, a quiet man, often sitting on his own, took care of the money given to the group to fund their journeys and buy food. Thomas was cheerful and liked to help around the house whenever he visited. We welcomed each one, and they soon became our friends.

After one of their overnight visits, I was folding and storing the bedding and noticed the parcel lying at the bottom of the bedding chest. Wrapped in a piece of plain linen was a small wooden box. Tracing the delicate patterns of the mother-of-pearl and coloured wood inlay, I remembered the evening my new husband Nathan gave it to me. He had bought it on his first visit to Jerusalem after our marriage and kissed me as he saw my delight as I held it for the first time.

I slipped a gold and opal ring on my finger. Flashes of green, red and blue dazzled brightly within as I raised it into a beam of light. Reminiscent of happier times, the ring was an engagement gift and once worn with pride. Now its beauty was marred by dry and calloused fingers. I replaced it with the necklaces and bracelets, now no longer worn. Closing the lid with a snap, I put the box back into the chest hidden amongst the bedding.

* * *

"He's here." Mary leaned over the edge of the roof. "Martha, Jesus is coming." Supposedly on the roof to spin wool, I knew Mary went there to spot Jesus arriving because I did so myself. "There's a woman with them!" Staring into the distance she shielded her eyes from the glare of the sun with her hand. "I can see Jesus, John, James, Simon and a woman. They're at the village."

Lazarus opened the gate as Mary ran downstairs and into the street. Wiping my hands on a cloth I met Jesus as he walked in, followed by the woman Mary had seen.

She grabbed my hands. "You must be Martha. Jesus has told me so much about you, and I've wanted to come to Bethany for a long time." Her soft hands shamed mine.

Jesus laid a hand on her shoulder. "This is Johanna."

Trying to pull away, I said, "Please excuse my hands, I'm preparing garlic for storage." Johanna gripped tighter, ignoring the smell.

"James tells everyone of the wonderful meals you prepare. I am looking forward to helping and taking new cooking tips home."

Showing her a seat, I said, "Please sit and rest after your journey."

The men made themselves comfortable, having grown accustomed to our home as much as we had become used to them. Lazarus brought out a jug of wine and water, followed by Mary with the cups. Johanna sipped her drink and looked around the courtyard. She was a tall woman of slender build whose grace and poise marked her as a well-bred lady that no dressing in a rough travelling cloak could hide.

"Martha, what a lovely house, and your courtyard is beautiful. It reminds me of my grandparents' home." Johanna stood and walked towards the herb garden. "Your herbs are growing much better than mine." Picking a mint leaf, she rubbed it between her fingers before smelling it.

Mary joined us. "They have grown since the weather became warmer and we now water them every day. I re-potted the marjoram last week."

"Is it still alive?" Lazarus shouted from across the courtyard.

Mary tutted. "It's growing better than the radishes you planted!"

"That was last year, and she still brings it up," Lazarus said to Jesus who laughed. "I asked Mary to water them and she forgot."

"They were your radishes and you should've watered them yourself. I haven't asked you to water the marjoram."

Johanna laughed at my bickering siblings, and I wondered whether her children were the same but imagined they were well behaved. After Johanna had rested, and despite asking her not to, she helped prepare the evening meal. Before long we were eating a stew of lentils and beans with flatbreads. Lazarus coughed and held onto his chest. I considered suggesting he lay down to rest but didn't want to embarrass him in front of Jesus and the others.

"Did you know Johanna lives in Herod's Palace?" Simon said with a mouthful of food. I'd heard of her connection with Herod Antipas, who was our king in name only. We all knew it was the Romans who held the power, not Herod.

"I do not live in the palace," Johanna replied.

James laughed as he placed a piece of flatbread into his mouth. "Well you live next door!"

"Chuza, my husband, is Herod's servant," she tried to explain.

"Some servant, only his chief steward," James continued to laugh.

"Johanna, you'd better explain everything to Martha," John said to her.

"Chuza oversees Herod's household and staff. We live near the palace in Caesarea on the Mediterranean coast, and he often travels to Jerusalem with him. But, where we live is not important, because it is Jesus to whom we are indebted and willing to support in any way we can."

Simon leaned across. "Tell Martha about the first time we met."

"I had been ill for several days, and no matter how many doctors we saw, including Herod's own physician, they could not help or even make me comfortable. Chuza suggested going to see a travelling rabbi who was healing people of various diseases. The children cried when we said goodbye and I feared I would never return home. By the time we reached the crowds around Jesus, I was sweating, my throat had swelled, and I was struggling to breathe. Finally, I lost consciousness and Chuza had to carry me. Pushing people out of the way he screamed to catch Jesus's attention."

James interrupted. "Chuza has such a cultured educated voice that I noticed him at once. 'Rabbi, please heal my wife. For the sake of our children, heal their mother,' he cried and pleaded with Jesus."

"Jesus found me," Johanna continued, "and even unconscious, I felt a warmth spreading from my shoulder where he touched me. The sound of his voice calling my name drew me back into life and when I opened my eyes, he was looking down at me."

Johanna became quiet remembering that day, and Simon took up the story. "Chuza would never have believed without seeing. His mouth moved, but no sound came out."

"Then Chuza grasped me so tight, I could not breathe again. Since then, it has been our privilege and honour to serve Jesus."

"Is it dangerous with Chuza working for Herod and you following Jesus?" Mary asked.

"Herod's household is a perilous place for many reasons." She leaned forward and whispered, "He has even had members of his own family murdered. Chuza has worked for him for a long time and knows his mood swings but is careful around him and his household."

"You're so brave!" Mary leaned across the table to touch her hand.

"No, we are not brave, just passionate about Jesus's ministry. When travelling with Jesus, I miss Chuza and the children, but without him, I would now be dead, and they would be without their wife and mother."

Johanna's story was compelling, and I wanted to know more about her life. Mary made up a bed for her in the room we shared, and we continued to talk after we retired for the night.

"Is Chuza handsome?"

I turned in horror. "Mary, you can't ask Johanna that question!"

Johanna laughed and, sitting on the bed, brushed her long black hair. Ignoring Mary's question, she asked one of her own. "Is this Nathan's family's house?"

"Yes, this is the home we shared, and our childhood home is nearby. There are tenants in now, and Lazarus will move back there when he marries."

"Did you meet Nathan before the marriage?" She asked.

"I often saw him in the village or at the market talking to other men. Sometimes I felt him watching me, but this didn't make me uncomfortable, just the opposite." I raised my eyebrows remembering my younger self. "I used to find excuses to walk past him, especially if he was alone. One day I saw him standing by his gate as I was walking to the market."

Mary looked puzzled. "The market is in the other direction from our old home."

"I must have decided to walk the long way around for a little exercise." Johanna and I looked at each other and sniggered. "Even though I knew it was inappropriate, I looked up into his face and our eyes met. Brown hair tumbled onto his shoulders framing his face, and hints of green flashed in his hazel eyes looking into my own. No one had ever looked at me in that way before and turning aside, my heart jerked in my chest. I didn't tell anyone because I had to keep my longing for him a secret."

"Yes, women have little say in who we will marry, and cannot be open with our feelings." Johanna shook her head.

"Fortunately, he felt the same, and only a few days later, father and mother asked me to speak with them. Both of Nathan's parents were dead, and he himself approached with a marriage proposal. This pleased my father as he and Nathan's father had been prominent men in the local synagogue and had known each other well. Having only heard good reports about Nathan, I willingly accepted his proposal."

"It's so romantic," Mary sighed. "I hope that will happen for me one day soon. Promise me you won't make me marry someone I don't love?"

Patting her hand, I reassured her. "I promise I will never make you marry anyone who isn't good enough for you. We had a spring wedding and everyone cheered as the procession made its way through the streets to my new home. Dressed in my finest clothes and jewels, I kept looking at the handsome husband by my side and felt like the most fortunate girl in the whole of Judea. The festivities lasted a week, with music, singing and dancing each day." These bittersweet memories made me smile.

"She was beautiful, and I've never seen her so happy. There was no need to light any lamps in the evening because her face shone so brightly."

I cuffed Mary on the arm. "Don't exaggerate!"

"By the way you talk about your husband, I can tell your marriage was a happy one," Johanna commented.

"Every young bride worries about her marriage and what her husband will be like," I replied.

"That is true," Johanna nodded. "Even the most eligible bridegroom can turn into a tyrant when alone with his wife. From marriage to a farm labourer or a prominent and religious man, a woman can never be sure until it is too late."

"But I needn't have been anxious. As each day progressed, we learned to love each other more, and what a joy it was to spend time together."

"We have both been fortunate with our husbands."

"Each day I looked forward to him coming home from the fields, and sitting together, we'd talk over the evening meal. He often asked my advice concerning matters of the farm or his labourers, and he listened as I talked about my day. Just after our marriage, he took me to see the farm, and I'd often visit him for a summer lunch in the olive groves where it was cool. We imagined a life full of children filling our home with joy and laughter, and we thought it would last for ever."

Mary hugged my shoulders and gently brushed my hair, smoothing it out behind my back with her hand.

I sighed and continued. "The sadness of losing both my parents within twelve months of each other marred our happiness. This was only matched with my other terrible anguish. As each month passed, I was further disappointed and under the weight of expectation to produce a child, preferably a son, as my husband's heir. Nathan assured me we had plenty of time, but it was time we would run out of. The stigma of being both a widow and childless is overwhelming. As if by some reason I'm to blame. Everyone in the village believes this to be true, and I've heard them say so many times."

"Rebekah is the worst," Mary tutted, "but she has no children either, so why gossip about Martha so much?"

"People can be cruel and often blame others to detract from their own problems." Johanna reached out and patted my hand. "It is unusual for a widow to live in her husband's home with her brother and sister."

"Nathan was the only surviving child of his parents, and there was a distant cousin whom I assumed would inherit the property. The day after the funeral, I was packing my belongings to return to our childhood home when his cousin called. Unknown to me, Nathan had planned for my well-being in case of his death. The deed of inheritance named me as the owner of not only the house but also the farm. Widows rarely inherit outright, but his cousin accepted this as Nathan's wish. I stayed in the house and appointed the farm manager to run the estate."

"You are very fortunate. There are stories of widows having to live in their own home as little more than an unpaid servant."

"I'm very thankful for what Nathan did for me, even after his death. With Lazarus inheriting our parent's home and land, we have a good living and are financially secure," I replied. "But Johanna, you have not answered Mary's question."

"What was that?" she asked looking puzzled.

"Is Chuza handsome?"

We talked long into the night, and despite Mary's questioning about the palace and the details of their life, Johanna preferred to talk about Jesus. It was late when we blew out the lamps and, after everyone was asleep, I lay in the dark and thought of my life. Rich and educated women often left me feeling insecure, considering that my lack of knowledge of the world was inadequate and held me back. But Johanna differed from what I imagined.

Having never been far from home I couldn't imagine a life following Jesus like she did. I was a bird that liked my own garden and lacked the confidence to fly away to new places. I wondered whether I'd ever have the courage to leave Bethany.

* * *

Neatly tucking her hair into her headscarf, Johanna stretched and yawned. She had offered to grind the corn to make flour for the morning bread and knelt by the grinding stones. Upon opening the gate, I entered the deserted streets and walked towards the well. The night sky gave way to dawn, and a line of faint yellow light seeped over the horizon. When I returned, Jesus had knelt next to Johanna to turn the handle of the top stone while she poured in the corn. I stood in amazement and put the pitcher on the ground.

"Jesus, what are you doing?"

"Helping Johanna," he replied.

"But you can't do that."

He continued to turn the top stone. "Why not?" He asked, and when I didn't answer he continued. "I awoke early and was praying on the roof when I saw Johanna grinding the corn. So, I offered to help."

"That's a woman's job," I exclaimed.

He laughed. "You know how little attention I pay to expectations and conventions."

There was no answer I could give, so I picked up an empty pitcher and went back to the well. When I returned there was enough flour to make the bread, and Jesus blew into the oven to light it. Mary appeared, rubbing her eyes, and together we sat listening to Jesus as he put the flour into a bowl, poured water in and kneaded it.

"Bread is important and eaten with every meal. But, no matter how much you eat, you cannot live by just eating bread, there's more to life than this. This bread," he lifted the dough, "is a symbol for me. I am the bread that gives life and once you have tasted the bread I give, you'll never go hungry again."

He covered the bowl with a cloth and, leaving it to prove, sat with us. Jesus had described me perfectly, starved and hungry, not for the bread he was making, but for the bread he was. Noises from the house reminded me that others were rising and would want their breakfast. I stood and Jesus held onto my arm.

"Martha, you have plenty of time to be busy, but not much time to spend with me. I know how anxious you are but worrying achieves nothing." He steered me back to my seat.

"I worry about my children when I am away from home," Johanna said looking away.

Mary added, "I worry about my future. Who will I marry? Will I have children?"

Unable to voice my worries, I stayed silent.

After a pause, Jesus continued. "Don't worry about your life, what you'll eat or drink, or what you'll wear. Life is more important than these things." A sparrow flew down and hopped onto the wall next to him. "This sparrow doesn't fret about where his next meal will come from. God provides food for him even though he's small. Tell me, Johanna, are you more important than this sparrow?"

"Yes, Jesus," she replied.

"Yes, you are. God who feeds this sparrow will look after you and your family." The sparrow flew off over the wall. "Do flowers stay awake worrying about what they look like? Mary, tell me, are you more beautiful than a flower?"

"Yes, Jesus." She grinned.

"Yes, you are. Flowers don't spin, weave or sew, yet are beautifully exquisite. So, don't worry about what you'll wear. What's most important?"

Silent for a moment, I thought of all the times we spent together. "God's kingdom and doing what's right," I replied.

"Yes, Martha, you are right. Do what's most important, and don't fret about tomorrow, let tomorrow worry about itself."

A silent tear slipped down my cheek as the worries and secret fears long kept hidden surfaced. "I worry about Lazarus. He continues to cough and isn't well. I worry about Mary and her future. When mother lay dying, I promised I would take care of them and I worry I won't be good enough."

Each word a stone I'd carried far too long slipped from my heart into Jesus's hands and I felt my burden become lighter.

"Now, shall we get the bread baked?" Jesus picked up the bowl of dough, now risen. Mary hummed as she fashioned it into flatbreads and placed them in the oven.

CHAPTER 3

"Lazarus, you're in no position to argue and I'm writing to Jesus." I nodded to Mary, who ran to fetch my wax tablet and stylus.

Lazarus shivered. "It's all right." Holding his chest, he took another deep breath. "I'll be fine."

Mary placed a blanket around his shoulders. "Jesus will come as soon as he knows you're ill."

Lazarus coughed once more. "There's no need to bother him because he's busy helping others."

Ignoring Lazarus, I wrote: *"Rabbi, our brother and your dear friend, Lazarus, is gravely ill, please come to Bethany as soon as possible. Mary and I know that if you come at once, he will live. Martha."*

Leaving Mary to warm a little wine with spices, I collected a few coins, walked out to the farm and instructed a labourer to deliver the letter to Jesus. Certain he would help Lazarus as he'd helped so many others, I sighed with relief as the labourer ran down the road. Throughout that day, Lazarus continued to worsen, and we felt helpless as he alternated between shivering and sweating. Each coughing fit wracked his whole body, weakening him further. We took turns to sit with him, convinced that Jesus would soon arrive.

The following morning, I was lighting the oven in the cold light of a winter's dawn, when Mary screamed. Lazarus had coughed up blood. Over that fateful day, he became weaker, and Mary often went into the street or up to the roof, longing to see Jesus. Jesus had continued to visit regularly throughout the summer and into the winter, but now when I needed him, he was absent.

Time passed unnoticed until darkness fell and the lamps were lit. Heavy with lack of sleep, my head drooped, while Mary held our brother's hand and mopped his head with cold water. Fear in her voice startled me to wake from a shallow sleep.

"Martha, his breathing is getting worse. Why has Jesus not come?"

Knowing this was the end, I smiled as best as I was able and kissed his forehead. Each gasping breath was now a trial for Lazarus.

"Martha," his breath rasping and his voice now weak, "Mary."

"I'm here," Mary whispered as she smoothed his damp hair out of his eyes.

"Mother?"

My mouth was dry, and I tried to swallow. "She's here."

He calmed as I took his hand, now clammy and cold with sweat, and sang one of her lullabies, reminding me of the day of his birth when mother allowed me to touch him and his tiny hand squeezed over my finger. She told me he was my baby brother, and I was to take special care of him.

"Is Jesus here?"

Unable to utter the words that Jesus had let him down, I said, "He'll be here soon."

Lazarus closed his eyes and stopped breathing. A thousand sensations shattered the silence. The hiss of the oil burning in the lamps, the shadows flickering on the wall, the pain inside my abdomen as if kicked by a donkey. All intensified the silence of Lazarus. Silent tears flowed as we sat motionless before being overtaken by grief. Sobbing, we clung to each other, our world destroyed.

Even if I had wanted help, there were only the two of us to prepare Lazarus for burial. Unmoving, Mary sat holding her brother's hand, until I took it and placed it upon his still chest. In silence, we washed his body with warm water before wrapping him in strips of linen, enclosing aloes and sweet-smelling spices. Each strip wrapped itself around my broken heart and pulled tight in a shroud of grief.

"Forgive me, mother. I promised to take good care of Lazarus, but I've failed," I sobbed.

I'd performed this ritual too many times for those I loved. First for my father, mother and husband, and now for my dear brother. An intense aroma of spices filled the house and, unbidden, despondent memories engulfed my mind. I was married just two short years, to a man I loved and respected, and I'd been more fortunate than many women to be loved and adored in return. Nathan was my friend and my light, and my world came crashing down in one afternoon. Even after two years, I couldn't believe he was no longer there. His absence filled every room, and I still expected to hear his voice calling my name.

Nathan died in an accident without a chance to say goodbye. It was harvest time, and he slipped on the road while driving the ox and cart. The large ox bolted, knocked Nathan to the ground and then ran over him. Farm labourers, crying and wailing, carried his broken and bloody body back from the farm into the house. How could we have lunch under the olive trees heavy with fruit at midday, and my love be dead by nightfall? Only vague memories survive of that day, but the one thing I remember is that I didn't want any help to wash and prepare his body for burial. This was our final private parting. I washed his hands, remembering the tender caress of his fingers and, recalling how pleasant it was to touch and caress him, I kissed him one last time. Here I was again, performing the same ritual, and I wept for my loss.

Too soon, mourners came to take Lazarus away. They placed his body upon a funeral bier, and following, we wound our way up the hill towards the tombs on the Mount of Olives. Leaves swirled across the path, causing us to wrap our scarves tighter around our heads. We placed him in the family tomb beside our parents, to shut him away forever. Mary dropped to the ground as the large round stone slammed closed and I knelt beside her.

"I want Jesus," she cried into my shoulder. "What will happen to us now?"

Mourners helped us home, and we collapsed in fatigue on our beds. The farm labourer returned and said he placed the letter into Jesus's hand. If we were his friends and if he truly loved us, he would have come. Why could he heal others, but not be here to help us? He had abandoned us, and we were alone.

The night was unusually cold, and despite the blanket wrapped around my shoulders, I shivered, unable to get warm. I peered through the shutters at a Bethany, dark and still, matching the quiet of our grief. Even the stray dogs were silent as if in sympathy.

"Where are you, Jesus?" I asked aloud for the hundredth time. "Why have you not come when I need you most?"

A cry from Mary made me turn around. Mumbling in her sleep she kicked her blanket onto the floor. I covered her again, and she quietened as I smoothed her hair out of

33

her eyes. Unable to sleep, I stared out of the window again, feeling abandoned, drained, and utterly alone. The sky in the east was turning pink with the dawn of a new day. But there was to be no joy in it for us. Mary only had me to rely on and I had no one.

* * *

A discord of wailing women surged through the gate to mourn with us. Lazarus was well-loved and respected in Bethany, and many came to share our grief. Mary still looked up every time the door opened, further disappointed when yet another neighbour walked through. Unlike me, she never gave up hope that Jesus would return. Despite being surrounded by people, I felt each hour blurring into one long, empty and lonely moment.

Escaping the oppressive air full of the crying and wailing of mourners, I ran into the courtyard. With a throbbing head, I leaned against the wall to steady myself and breathed in the cool air. Winter rains had arrived, flooding the courtyard and dripping from the roof. As a child, Lazarus loved the rain and would laugh as he danced and jumped in the puddles with Mary. The rain running in rivulets down his back straightened his curly hair. Mother shouted at him to go inside saying the cold rainwater would make him ill, but I enjoyed seeing him having fun.

Rebekah came down the stairs and put her arm around me, and I wondered what she had been doing on our roof. "I'm sorry to hear about Lazarus's death, but Martha, it's a blessing, because he'll be in no more pain. Poor boy, it must've been terrible," she said with false sympathy and another pitying smile.

"No," I shrugged her arm away. "It's not a blessing, and I'd give anything to have him back."

Ignoring me she continued, "You've no male guardian to lead your household now, and you know that's not right. Besides, it's time you moved on and remarried. Both of you are in a risky position, you could lose your home." There was no need to remind me. I knew how dangerous our situation was, especially for Mary as a young unmarried woman. "Jonas's brother is a widower; he can ask if he's interested in you. It won't be a problem for Mary, she's young and pretty."

"Not now, Rebekah."

"Where's that weird rabbi of yours? I thought he would've helped by now. Some of his followers must be single," she sneered. "Besides, it's not right all those women following him around, and he even allows those of bad character to talk to him. Who knows what goes on when they're together? As Jonas said only the other day, 'It's downright immoral'. If you want to improve yours and Mary's chances of finding a good husband, you'd better stay away from him."

That was enough. I pushed past her to run up the stairs, and with a racing heart, fell sobbing on the bed. I was angry, partly because I saw the truth in what she said.

* * *

Sitting around was never one of my favourite activities, and I needed to keep my hands and mind busy. I escaped the wailing women and stood alone in the cooking area kneading dough. A knock on the gate announced another visitor and, not wanting to meet anyone, I turned away.

"Excuse me, Martha, there's someone to see you." A neighbour tried to introduce a man who stood in the courtyard. Without turning around, I continued to knead.

He coughed. "I represent your Uncle Ephraim, who sends sincere condolences upon the death of your brother."

35

I whipped around to see my uncle's agent. Father had mentioned this man, but we had never met. Drooping eyelids shrouded dark eyes, forcing him to tilt his head up to see through narrow slits.

"I understand your father taught you to read." I nodded as he handed me a letter. "Ephraim considers teaching girls a waste of time, but I suppose it's useful in these circumstances. Send refreshment through for me while I await your reply." He walked inside the house, but as far as I was concerned, he could die of thirst.

Ephraim, father's younger brother, hadn't visited Bethany for fifteen years. As a young child, I remember father and Uncle Ephraim arguing as we cowered upstairs. Lazarus held tightly onto my hand while mother held a crying Mary. He had spent his share of our grandparent's inheritance and wanted more money, which father refused. Estranged from the family since that day, he didn't even attend father's funeral. Death and inheritance bring many kinds of vermin into the light.

With stiff fingers, I fumbled with the seal, dreading its contents. *"The news of the death of Lazarus is very sad, and I am grieved at the loss of such a fine young man. As Lazarus's nearest male relative, I will inherit my parent's house. You and your sister now come under my guardianship, and you will sign your current home over to me. Upon returning to Bethany in two days, I expect the existing tenants to have left."* Terse and precise, that was Uncle Ephraim.

"Tell my uncle I expect him in two days," I said to the agent who left with no food or drink. I was still mistress of this house even if not for long.

With his hand on the gate, he turned. "There may come a time when you want me on your side, you don't have many friends."

There was nothing I could do to stop Uncle Ephraim coming to Bethany. To keep my hands busy, I picked up the dough again. This bread would be inedible, I had kneaded it too long. A shadow passed over the bowl and Jonas, with his usual dishevelled cloak and receding hair, approached. Rebekah stayed by the gate, fiddling with her scarf. He smiled with his lips together and said how sorry he was, and how he liked Lazarus though he hardly spoke to him. I wished he'd get to the point; I knew why he had come. With his arms folded he looked around the courtyard as if taking a mental inventory of everything we owned and a note of how much it was worth.

He licked his lips. "I'm sure you agree with me, that it will be better in your current circumstance to remarry. You and Mary are now alone with no male guardian, and as valued neighbours, it's our duty to support and protect you. My brother has been a widower for six months and will take you. He's even prepared to overlook that you failed to produce a child in your first marriage. To save you the inconvenience of moving, he will live here with his five children and mother. It's the perfect solution. If you're not interested, he can have Mary instead, who will then become the mistress of the house."

"Give me two days," I said.

"I need your answer now. He has already approached another widow."

"Does she own a house?" I slammed the dough into the bowl.

"What difference does that make?"

"A widow with property is more desirable than the one without. Two days, and then I'll consider meeting with him."

Jonas didn't like my answer, but I no longer cared. With a curt nod, he walked away. I bent to put the dough by the oven as he spoke to Rebekah.

"Make sure one of them agrees to marry him."

"I'll try," she answered, looking at the ground and rubbing her hands together.

Jonas grabbed her arm. "You'll do more than try, woman. Make certain you do."

Overwhelmed with everything falling out of control, I strode past them, out of the village and towards the Mount of Olives. Needing to be alone and without noticing where I was going, I arrived at the tomb. Breathless and with a chest pain, I sat on a rock beneath an olive tree. With a stab to my heart, I realised it was the rock on which Jesus had sat in the spring. Life would never be the same, because everyone I loved, except Mary, had left. The olive tree was sleeping now but would blossom once more in the spring. Would Mary and I survive and, like the olive tree, become fruitful again?

Crying tears, not only for Lazarus but for myself and Mary, I sobbed. Our cheerful and carefree life was over, and I had to consider which of the two options was the least horrific. To come under the care of Uncle Ephraim, who beyond all his expectations had the good fortune to outlive his nephew to gain two homes and two farms. He would now consider myself and Mary as chattels to be disposed of to the men who paid the most. Or become Jonas's sister-in-law and wife to his dreadful brother. Ending up as little more than a domestic servant to his mother and children in my own home.

There was no way out, and I had to protect Mary from a hasty and unhappy marriage made for the benefit of a man. But I resolved to do whatever it took to safeguard her future even at the expense of my own happiness. Musing over our problems, I tried to find a solution until Mary found me and, putting a cloak around my shoulders, steered me home. She was unaware of the dangers we were facing, but I would have to tell her soon.

* * *

Ever since Nathan's death, I've craved solitude, but it's expected that grieving women mourn together. Mary sat inside the house surrounded by neighbours, who wiped her eyes and smoothed her hair. They wanted to do this for me, but I shook them away, and unable to keep still, preferred to pace the courtyard on my own. Closing my eyes, I felt myself rocking with exhaustion and quickly opened them in case I fainted.

Over another endless and sleep-deprived night, I decided to contact Nathan's cousin. His family had always treated me well, even accepting my inheritance of the farm. Perhaps there was a way to keep it in Nathan's family? That would be preferable to it becoming the property of Uncle Ephraim or Jonas's brother. Throughout the night I'd tried to figure out a solution in a dispassionate cold-blooded way. But I was far from that. I was hot and angry at my limited choices and how life was changing for the worse. Pecking at my foot made me look down; it was a chicken scratching around my sandal.

"I'm sorry, chickens, we forgot to feed you. That was always Lazarus's job. How sad you are scratching in the dust with your heads down. You must miss him too." Noisily, they gobbled their food which I scattered. "You don't have many worries. If you're fed, then you'll be happy and lay our eggs. Do you have any advice?"

"Martha." A whisper made me turn around. "Excuse me." The farm labourer who took my letter to Jesus stood by the gate beckoning me. With embarrassment, I realised I'd been talking to the chickens. He drew me to one side and whispered, "Jesus is here at the Mount of Olives nearby Lazarus's tomb. He asked me to fetch you and said to tell only you."

There was a moment of indecision. I was still angry, but more than anything needed to be with him. I wanted to run, but then everyone might follow. Making sure no one was watching, I slipped out.

"Where are you going?" A booming voice stopped me before I had taken two steps. Dressed in smart new clothes and looking like the rich farmer he now imagined himself to be was Uncle Ephraim. "Are you Martha?" He asked. "Inside, now!"

I followed and stood by the wall as Uncle Ephraim and his agent talked about the house and its value.

"Where's Mary?" My Uncle asked and, I pointed inside. "Sit with her while I audit the house."

I hesitated. "I need to be somewhere."

He nodded towards the indoor room. "You'll go nowhere unless you ask me first."

Expecting me to obey, they moved to the stairs, and the agent opened his bag and took out a wax tablet. Jesus was waiting, but how could he help me now I was someone else's property? It might be dangerous for Mary if I left, but I had to see Jesus. As they disappeared up the stairs, I made a decision and ran out of the courtyard.

I ran as if chased by a wild animal towards the only safe place I knew. Not stopping until I reached the Mount of Olives, I met Jesus, sitting on the rock where I'd sat the day before. His friends sat on the ground a little way from him. He held an olive branch and was turning it over, examined the yellowing leaves. Over the past four days, I imagined what I'd say to him, but at that moment I stood mute. A mixture of emotions surged through my head and body. In silence, we faced one another, until I walked up to him, my mouth dry.

"Jesus," I said, my heart pounding. Of all the emotions present, anger spoke first. "If you'd come when I asked, Lazarus would now be alive. Are we not important to you?"

Jesus remained silent, and I wanted to ask why he'd delayed but didn't dare. Tears spilt down one cheek as he blinked and held my stare. He loved Lazarus like a brother, but I needed to understand why he let this tragic death happen when he could have prevented it. With a deep breath, I relaxed in his presence, even my anger dissipated, because now there was a flicker of hope.

"Even now, I know whatever you ask the Father, he'll give you," I said at last.

Jesus stood and held out the olive branch which I took from him. "Your brother will rise and live again."

"Yes Jesus." Many had told us this and I sighed. "Mary and I know he will rise again, along with everyone else."

"You don't have to wait until then, because I am the resurrection and I am life. Even in death if anyone believes in me, they'll live. So, if you live trusting in me, you'll never die." He held out his hand as he had on our first meeting. "Martha, do you believe me?"

When he held my hand in both of his, everything crystallised into a single thought and the realisation of who this man was. There came a moment of clarity through the mist which had surrounded me.

"Yes, since you first walked into my home, I've believed you, and now I realise who you are. You're the Messiah, our Saviour, who we are waiting for." The disciples remained silent as they took in the enormity of what I uttered.

"Can you get Mary?" He asked. I handed the olive branch back and ran home.

Not knowing how Uncle Ephraim would react to not being obeyed, I opened the gate a crack and looked inside.

He wasn't there, so I crept towards Mary. Trying to keep calm I took a deep breath and, hoping no one noticed, tapped her on the shoulder.

"Jesus has come, he's by the tomb and wants to see you," I whispered. Without a moment's hesitation, she rushed out of the house, and I ran after her. The women followed but there was nothing I could do.

"Come back!" A voice shouted behind me. "Come back at once!" screeched Uncle Ephraim.

If I turned back now, I would be under his control forever. I had to run forward with Mary, who didn't slow down until she reached Jesus and fell sobbing at his feet.

"Jesus, if only you'd come earlier Lazarus wouldn't be dead," she cried in despair. With tear-filled eyes, Jesus raised her and drew us both to him. Many had tried to console us since Lazarus died, but nothing came close to a touch from him.

"Don't consider for one moment, that just because I didn't come when you asked, that I'd abandoned you. Everything I do is for a purpose," he whispered.

The women who had followed us, stood at the tomb beating their chests and wailing.

With a voice like a flint, he asked them, "Where have you put him?"

Rebekah approached. "Rabbi, the tomb is over here." This was the first and only time she spoke to him. His face crumpled, and he sobbed.

"Jesus is crying, he must have loved him," a voice behind me said.

Rebekah replied in what she considered a whisper, but she may as well have shouted. "Well, if he loved him, he would've been here sooner. If Jesus can heal a blind man, he should've helped Lazarus."

I raised my hand to slap her face, and it was only because we were by Lazarus's tomb that stopped me. Jesus either didn't hear or chose to ignore her. He walked up the slope towards the tomb.

"Roll the stone aside," he ordered. After following him for so long, his followers were used to strange requests, and four men heaved it away.

"No Jesus! He's been dead four days," I shouted and ran up the hill. "Please don't open the tomb. There will be the smell of decay by now, and I want to remember him as he was in life, not with the stench of death."

Jesus touched my shoulder. "Martha, you've just told me you believe me, haven't you?" I nodded. "Then you'll see the glory of God." He looked towards the crowd and, making sure he had everyone's attention, raised his arms and prayed in a thunderous voice. "Father, thank you for listening. I'm praying this out loud for those here today. This is so they will know that it's you who sent me." I stared at him open-mouthed.

"Lazarus come out!" he roared, his words echoing around the tombs.

No one dared move or breathe and the only sound was the rustling of the leaves. Even the birds remained silent. The white of the tomb was stark against the blue sky. It seemed a lifetime, as surely it was for Lazarus. There was a sharp intake of breath as a body covered in strips of linen with a cloth over its face, emerged from the dark into the light. I hardly dared to hope. Lazarus was dead when placed inside the tomb; we'd seen enough of death to know when someone has passed from this life.

John ran to the body and removed the face cloth to show the fresh and alive face of Lazarus with no hint of decay. This was too much for Mary, who collapsed to the floor. I stood, unable to breathe, my legs refusing to move, and my hands bound to my sides. Lazarus blinked rapidly, unaccustomed to the light of life after the dark of death. John and Judas laughed as they unwrapped the trappings of death from around the rest of his body.

"Look!" John exclaimed. "Look at his body."

Judas laughed. "Martha, Mary, come and see. Your brother is alive."

No one moved except John and Judas, who touched and showed us the living and perfect flesh. Judas took off his outer cloak to cover Lazarus's naked body, and Jesus brought him to us. Not believing what my eyes told me, I raised a shaking hand and brushed my brother's face. His flesh was warm.

CHAPTER 4

"How did I get here?" Lazarus's face mirrored the shocked faces of the onlookers. "Martha, what's happening?"

When she heard his voice, Mary jumped up and, sobbing, grabbed his neck. "Lazarus, Lazarus, Lazarus," she shrieked between kisses.

Unable to speak I stood mute, holding my breath until Jesus touched my shoulder. "Yes, you can believe. Lazarus was dead but now he's alive."

I gripped his arm tightly and bending over in pain gulped for air, screaming and crying with relief. Finding their voice, the crowd shouted all at once. Jesus ushered us down the hill as they pressed around shoving each other out of the way to touch Lazarus, wanting to check that he was no ghost. News spread, and by the time we reached the village crowds lined the road. Everyone was cheering and shouting the names of Lazarus and Jesus in equal measure.

My elation at seeing Lazarus alive evaporated when I arrived home. Three men stood around a mound of our furniture in the courtyard. Jonas and the agent tussled over a box of my husband's clothes.

"She's marrying my brother, and these belong to him," Jonas screeched.

"I'm Lazarus's uncle and so the inheritance is mine. Don't you know the law, that if a man dies without sons and brothers, then the inheritance passes to his father's brother? That foolish boy was always ill, and I've been waiting for him to die. And Martha is mine, she'll keep house for me. If you want Mary, make me an offer. A virgin fetches a higher price than a childless widow."

"Be quiet!" A voice echoed around the walls, and at once the argument ceased. No one could disobey such a voice as that. A voice which brought the dead back to life.

"Who are you?" Uncle Ephraim swallowed; his voice no longer confident. "Who gave you permission to enter my house?"

"This house belongs to Martha and the family home is Lazarus's," Jesus replied.

Uncle Ephraim laughed. "You're too late. Haven't you heard that Lazarus is dead? Martha and Mary belong to me along with the house and contents."

"You're mistaken, for Lazarus is very much alive."

Three stunned faces greeted Lazarus as Jesus brought him forward. Jesus took the box from a mute agent and gave it to Andrew who returned it inside the house. The disciples picked up the rest of the furniture and replaced it where it belonged. Jonas, Uncle Ephraim and the agent were powerless to resist because they had seen Lazarus alive and their arguments about inheritance no longer applied. Grabbing Uncle Ephraim by the collar of his new cloak, Jesus pushed him towards the gate.

"You can leave now, because Lazarus, Martha and Mary are not without friends, and they have our protection."

Without Jesus's intervention, this would have been our fate: haggled over and divided between men like a piece of furniture and given to the highest bidder, our worth dependent on what a man was prepared to pay. Jesus held onto my trembling shoulders.

"You're safe now. Go inside with your brother," he said.

Neighbours and strangers tried to invade our home until Simon and Andrew pushed everyone out and barred the gate. Carrying on their argument in the street, Jonas and Uncle Ephraim shouted and blamed each other for what happened. A locked gate didn't deter others from trying to peer through the windows until we slammed the shutters closed. Still, in Judas's cloak, Lazarus sat shaking in a state of confusion. He looked around the room.

"Will someone please tell me what's happening?" He said.

Mary hadn't let go of her brother and sat next to him, holding his hand. "Lazarus, it's fantastic. You died four days ago, but now you're alive!" She shouted, torn between crying and laughing.

Lazarus shook his head in disbelief as Jesus took him through the events of the last few days.

"What do you remember?" John asked.

"Not much. I remember becoming ill and worrying when I coughed up blood. A strange coldness filled my body, and then weakness overtook me until I could no longer move."

"You faded away from us and then you died. Yes, you died," I whispered.

"I can't remember anything from lying here until I heard a voice like thunder. It was dark, and the only thing I knew was that I must move towards the sound of the voice. That was you, Jesus, wasn't it?" Jesus smiled and nodded.

Simon dared ask what was in all our minds. "Did you see anything when you were dead?" This one question would follow Lazarus throughout his life.

He shook his head. "No, there was nothing until the voice. I'm hungry. What is there to eat?" I laughed and until that moment hadn't entirely believed that my eyes were telling me the truth.

Jesus said, "It has been a tiring few days. Go upstairs and rest, and I'll send food up to you. Don't worry, we'll make sure no one disturbs you."

As I passed him, I stopped, and through my tears wanted to say 'Thank you' but my voice broke and I mouthed the words.

Jesus nodded. "Get some sleep."

* * *

Stretching after a refreshing sleep, I lay in the dark, closed my eyes and listened to the familiar sounds of the night. Someone had left a lamp burning and with its light, I looked over to a sleeping Lazarus to check his breathing as I had done when he was a baby. Mary slept next to him, and I wondered whether she would ever leave his side again. The house was still, and the crowd outside had dispersed. Putting a blanket around my shoulders and picking up the lamp, I wandered past the sleeping bodies until I found Jesus asleep facing the wall.

"Thank you," I whispered, and not expecting an answer continued, "you have returned our brother and saved our lives too. How can we ever repay you?"

He turned over. "You have Martha, with your love and kindness."

"I'm sorry I lost my trust in you."

He turned to face the wall again and went back to sleep. With the lamp still burning I walked onto the roof and looking across the valley towards Jerusalem, saw the moon reflected in its buildings. The night was peaceful, and

I breathed deeply, enjoying the quietness and considering our good fortune in knowing Jesus.

* * *

The following morning, I was clearing away the breakfast plates when Jesus told me they were leaving again. But I needed to know something first and followed John onto the roof.

"Why did Jesus delay in coming after he received my letter?" I asked.

John leaned on the wall and said, "It's impossible to second-guess Jesus, he often does what I least expect. After reading your letter, he said Lazarus's illness wouldn't end in death. Frankly, it was a relief to stay in safety on the far bank of the River Jordan. The Temple authorities are aware of what he's doing and saying and it's getting increasingly dangerous here. Then two days ago, he said we needed to return to Bethany. But when we reminded him of the danger, he said it was not his time to die yet. He knew Lazarus was dead by then and told us the real reason for the delay was that we would believe."

"That's what he said at the tomb. That it was for God's glory, and I should only believe."

"Yes, there's a purpose behind everything he does, even if it's difficult to understand. I'm sorry Martha, we were anxious when he suggested coming back, but I'm glad we did."

John sat on a chair we used for sewing and I joined him. "A few months ago Jesus asked who we considered him to be. After a moment of silence, Simon said he understood Jesus to be the Messiah and Saviour. You can't imagine how shocking that sounded at first, and Jesus said he was right, but we are to keep this a secret for the time being. I've only mentioned it because you've worked it out for yourself."

"In that instant everything became clear, and I realised who he is. He's the Messiah. Who else can he be?" I said with a laugh.

"John!" James shouted from the bottom of the stairs. "We're going soon."

John stood and turned to face me. "It's a bold statement to make. Only Simon and you have ever been brave enough." Feeling anything but brave I followed him down the stairs to see Lazarus eating another breakfast.

"Are you eating again?" I asked.

"Leave him alone," Mary as always quick to defend her brother. "He can eat as much as he likes."

"Being dead gives you an appetite, and I've got a lot of eating to catch up with," Lazarus said between mouthfuls.

"He's well enough for me to leave now," Jesus said with a smile, then became serious. "If you could prepare food to take with us, we'd be grateful. We need to go back into the desert because it's too dangerous to stay here for now. There are many people here in Bethany who are pleased that Lazarus is home again, but not everyone. While some of your neighbours are celebrating with you, others have already gone to the authorities in Jerusalem. The Sanhedrin is meeting right now to discuss us."

"The Sanhedrin know about us?"

Jesus nodded. "The present Chief Priest and ruler of the council is Caiaphas, who doesn't accept that there's a life after death. So, you can imagine how angry he'll be at the news of Lazarus's return to life."

Laughing together, Lazarus and Mary were oblivious to the danger we were still in, and I wanted them to stay that way. The thought that the Sanhedrin was talking about us filled me with dread. As our powerful ruling council, it controlled all aspects of our lives. Their authority was only limited by the Roman Governor.

As Jesus left, he paused and squeezed my hand. "I plan to return in a few weeks for the Passover festival. Be careful. People are watching you, but don't worry, I'll be with you soon."

Like the olive branch Jesus gave me, he had returned our lives to us, along with our brother's. Our lives were now his, whatever should befall him would be our fate likewise.

* * *

Mary pulled the bedcovers over her legs. "How can we thank Jesus for what he's done for us?"

I agreed. "Whatever we do will never be enough. Lazarus has been back a week, and it's like he never went away, but I'll never forget how terrible it was to lose him." Restless, Mary fidgeted with her blanket. "What do you have in mind?" I asked, knowing her moods well.

Turning onto her side, Mary rested her head on her hand. "Even before Lazarus died, I wanted to do something special. Now I know what I want to do."

Too tired for a conversation, I blew out the lamp. "I'm sure that whatever you do will be out of love and thankfulness."

After breakfast the following morning, Mary ran down the stairs holding a parcel wrapped in a cloth, which she placed in a bag and slung over her shoulder.

"Lazarus and I are going into Jerusalem," she said.

"What are you both up to?"

Mary gave her brother a furtive look and a slight shake of the head. "It's a surprise, and you'll find out soon." She kissed me on the cheek.

"Mary, stay with Lazarus. Don't wander off or get distracted at the market."

"I promise!"

She skipped after Lazarus, they linked arms and walked down the street in the morning sunshine, laughing together as usual. There was a great deal of work to do in the house and a few hours later I opened the gate to sweep the dust out of the courtyard. Smiling, I remembered hiding the broom behind my back the first time I met Jesus.

"Well, I'm glad someone's happy!" I flinched at the sound of Jonas's voice. With a scowl, he leaned on the wall. "I hope you'll not break the agreement we have." With no wish to speak with him, I'd avoided the confrontation I knew was coming. "There's a verbal marriage contract in place."

My knuckles holding the broom whitened. "There was no marriage contract, verbal or otherwise."

Jonas stood so close I could smell what he had had for breakfast. "You made a promise, and now Lazarus is back, he can make the proper arrangements."

Trying to sound more assured than I felt, I said, "You'll do no such thing, Jonas. There was only a promise to consider meeting with your brother. Which I have now decided not to do."

"In that case, you've broken the contract and we expect compensation."

Though afraid, I stood my ground and met his eyes. "Whatever you have to say, you can say to Jesus. But there will be no compensation."

"Just like your husband!" he shouted in my face. "He swindled me, and now you're doing the same. Besides, what good is Jesus? Here's one piece of advice for free," he laughed, thinking this was amusing. "You'd be wise not to invite him to your house anymore. His days as a wandering preacher are nearly over and he'll get what's coming to him."

Annoyed that he should speak of Jesus like that, I spun around and walked back into the house.

"Then where will you be without his protection? I'll get what I deserve. Just you wait and see."

Unable to relax and settle on any occupation, I walked around the house, angry at his words, but also afraid. How could I admit to Jesus that rather than trust him, I'd considered a hasty marriage to secure Mary's future? The gate was flung open and in walked Mary and Lazarus laughing and talking so loudly I heard them from inside the house. Not wanting them to see me upset, I wiped my face on a cloth.

"Whatever were you up to in Jerusalem all this time?"

"You'll find out later." Mary walked past holding her bag, like a chicken, tucked under her arm.

Lazarus hung back by the gate. "Whatever is the matter, Lazarus?" I asked. "You look like you did as a child when you broke one of our mother's pots."

He took his coat off. "I'm sorry, Martha, but my cloak ripped." He poked his finger through the hole in the side of his cloak. "It wasn't my fault."

"Well, whose fault was it then?" I took it from him and examined the tear.

"There was a nail sticking out from one of the market stalls and I snagged it when I passed. Can you mend it?"

I tutted. "I can, but you always create more work."

Lazarus hung his head. "I'm sorry."

Far too concerned about the conversation with Jonas to worry about Mary's parcel and Lazarus's cloak, I went to prepare the evening meal. Afterwards, Mary retrieved the bundle and, sitting in front of me, carefully unwrapped it. Astonished, I reached out to touch a small glass phial, its iridescent blues and greens shimmered in the light of the lamps. It was beautiful.

"What's this, Mary?" I gasped.

"Pure spikenard," she whispered. "I've been thinking about how to show Jesus that I'm thankful, and this will be my gift. I'm planning something special when he returns."

"How did you get this?" I looked at Lazarus to explain, but he looked at Mary. "Mary, where did you get this expensive oil?"

Leaning over, she took the phial and mumbled, "I've sold the jewellery mother and father gave me before they died."

"That's your dowry, and you'll need that to get married," I exclaimed and hoped Lazarus would bring clarity to the situation.

"I wanted to share the cost and sell a piece of my jewellery because I owe Jesus my life," he said.

"This gift is from me, and no one else." Mary wanted to make it clear, this was her idea alone. "Lazarus is back now so I won't need a dowry because I don't want to make a man marry me for money. Besides, when I'm older, I'll follow Jesus like Johanna. When I marry, it will be to someone who loves and follows Jesus too."

Not understanding her, I shook my head. "What good is expensive perfume to Jesus? He's never asked for anything and cares little for material possessions. Whatever are you planning to do? Jesus already knows how much you love him and how thankful we are."

Gently wrapping the phial back in the cloth, she said, "You'll understand when Jesus comes."

CHAPTER 5

I have known no one become healthier by dying. Lazarus was full of energy and set about the neglected jobs, mending doors, hinges and shelves. He even repaired the grapevine arbour of the courtyard. This had long been a concern of mine, imagining it falling on Jesus's head while he sat under it. Glad to have it mended, I was even more pleased to see Lazarus fit, healthy and busy. After almost losing him there was joy in spending time together and the house resounded to the sounds of laughter. Passover approached, and the winter turned into spring. The almond trees on the outskirts of Bethany came into blossom, and their pink buds opened revealing delicate white flowers.

Mary became more excited as the day for Jesus's return neared, and I continually distracted her by giving her household chores. We cooked, baked, cleaned and prepared for his visit. At last, Friday arrived, and Lazarus and Mary ran outside the village to meet our guests. Most of the villagers were as happy to see Jesus and his followers as we were and shouted out in greeting. Children joined in as if it was a festival, running after them, singing and cheering.

Despite the excitement, Jonas leaned on the wall in his usual spot with arms folded and a sour expression as if he had swallowed half a lemon. Rebekah caught my eye before looking away and covering her face with a scarf. Before entering my house, Jesus stopped and turned to face Jonas, who tried to hold his gaze. But it was Jonas who had to look away. He spun around and pushed through the crowds to walk toward Jerusalem. Upon entering through the gate, Jesus and the disciples sat in their usual places as we brought out refreshments and they relaxed in the quiet of our courtyard. Jesus sat in the shade, underneath the arbour and closed his eyes, content to rest awhile in the peace of our home.

A little later Jesus stood and stretched. "Someone has mended the arbour," he said, touching the supports. "Was that you Lazarus? I worked as a carpenter for many years and I can see you've done a good job."

Lazarus, his smile broad, pointed out where he had replaced the old wood and fixed the joints. John leaned forward and sat with his elbows on knees, staring into his cup.

"Are you all right?" I asked.

"Can I have a quiet word with you?" He nodded to the roof.

I followed him upstairs, and he stood silent looking into the distance towards Jerusalem.

"You don't seem your usual self," I said.

"It's what Jesus has been saying recently." I waited for him to continue. "I don't want to worry you, but you should be prepared. Three times he has spoken about this, and the last time was only this morning. The first time he mentioned it, Simon told him not to say those things and Jesus was furious with him. Since then none of us has dared say anything." John paused and breathed out a troubled sigh, the tension showing in his shoulders. "He said this will be his final journey to Jerusalem, where he will be arrested and killed. Then three days later he will come to life again."

Shocked by this news, I replied, "Do you believe him?"

"I've never had a reason to doubt, so why start now?"

We were both quiet for a while until I said, "We know that Jesus can make the dead alive again, there's living proof walking and talking downstairs. If he can do it for Lazarus, why not for himself?"

"Well, I suppose he could, but I don't like this uncertainty."

"Those three days between my brother dying and Jesus returning him to us were the worst in my life. I never want to go through that again."

"I saw the ugly argument between your uncle and Jonas over your possessions."

"That they were arguing over who would have me and Mary was even more horrendous. I've still not admitted to Jesus that instead of trusting him, I contemplated remarrying just to secure Mary's future. Through the whole experience, I learned we should trust that whatever happens, does so because Jesus allows it."

"Thank you, Martha, it's always good to talk with you. I appreciate your understanding and wisdom." Overwhelmed by his statement, I wondered why a disciple such as John who walked with Jesus every day should seek my wisdom. "Come, less of this pessimistic talk, let's join the others," he said, turning to go downstairs.

* * *

The last of the sun's rays shone through the grapevine arbour, casting an orange glow onto the head of Jesus and everyone underneath. I sat by Jesus's feet captivated by every word he said, but Mary seemed distracted, fidgeting with her scarf or sandals. Jesus reached out to touch the trunk of the vine growing over the supports of the arbour.

"Martha looks after this vine well and we have enjoyed its grapes many times. How do you get it to be so fruitful?"

"My father-in-law planted it many years ago. When I married and moved here, Nathan showed me how to take the pliable new branches and wind them around the arbour. This encourages them to grow where we can easily reach out to pick the grapes," I replied.

"Do you prune the vine?"

"Yes, when the vine is resting in the winter, I cut off the old branches. This encourages the vine to grow new ones where the best bunches of grapes will be in the summer."

"Would a branch you cut off, grow grapes?" he asked.

"Of course not." I laughed at the absurdity of this. "Every branch must be connected to the vine to grow grapes. I use the cut-off branches for firewood."

Jesus stood and showed us the buds shooting out of the branches. "At this time of the year, the buds are forming on the vine. It is not until later in the year that the grapes will be ready for harvest. I am this vine, and the gardener is my Father. Like Martha, he looks after the vine, and prunes branches that don't have grapes, so that the following summer they may be more fruitful. If I am the vine, then you are the branches. If you want to produce fruit, you must stay connected to the vine. It's my Father's wish that each one of you produces as much fruit as you are able."

I considered the olive branch Jesus had given me by the tomb, pleased that now I could look forward to a productive and fruitful life.

Jesus continued, "I love each one of you as much as the Father loves me. Just as the branches must stay connected to the vine to be fruitful, then you must stay nourished in my love. I'm saying this so you might have the same joy that my Father and I share. This is my new commandment that you should love one another in the same way you have seen me love you. The greatest love is one which sacrifices everything and is even prepared to die for one's friends. Each one of you is my friend, and I have always considered you as such. This is my command in three words. Love each other."

By this time it was dusk, so Lazarus and I lit lamps and placed them around the courtyard. This was my favourite time, listening to Jesus by the light of the lamps, enjoying being in his presence and learning much about God. I looked for Mary, but she had disappeared, unusual when Jesus was at home. She had been in a strange mood all evening and I wondered what was distracting her.

No longer nervous, she returned with the phial of spikenard held in both hands. Her presence caused everybody to stop talking, and the room quietened as we all looked at her. With slow and deliberate steps, she walked towards Jesus. Every eye was on her as the phial's iridescent colours flickered in the lamplight, creating blue and green flashes. Bending down in front of Jesus she removed the phial's stopper, and at once the smell of the spikenard struck everyone's nostrils.

She lifted one of his feet and pouring on the spikenard, washed and massaged his foot before removing her headscarf and drying the foot with her hair. Taking up the other foot, she poured the remaining contents of the phial to the last drop, before drying that one too with her hair. Everyone was still, and I dared not breath, in case I spoiled the moment. Tears in Jesus's eyes mirrored the ones in mine. There was a quiet simplicity in Mary's act, which shouted of her devotion and love.

He placed his hands on her oil-streaked hair and kissed the top of her head. As I watched, I finally understood why it was necessary to sell her dowry to show the depth of her love for Jesus, and I blessed her for it. There was quiet for what seemed a long time until one discordant voice broke the silence.

"What an utter waste of money. This amount of spikenard must be worth at least a farm labourer's wages for a whole year. This could've helped many poor people." It was Judas.

Jesus whipped his head around and glared at him. "Be quiet, Judas!" he ordered. "Leave Mary alone. She has performed an act of worship which is neither a waste of time nor money. There will always be poor people around you, but you'll not always have me. What she has done is to prepare my body for burial while I'm still alive." I looked at John, and he nodded. Jesus was talking about his death again.

Jesus stood up. "Everyone will remember Mary's complete act of love, devotion and worship and will tell her story to every generation. No one will forget her."

He took her hand and raised her to sit on the chair he had vacated and patted her cheek. Sitting serene and regal, her face shone in reflection of his. The aroma of the spikenard filled the entire house; our clothes, possessions, everything suffused by the love of Mary.

Since Jesus's arrival, a small group had congregated outside, and more had continued to arrive. Those outside the house now smelled the spikenard permeating even through the walls, and the sound of their shouting spoiled this wonderful moment. Lazarus opened the shutters to see a large group of people clamouring to look inside.

"Are you Lazarus?" one man shouted. "What was it like to be dead?"

Lazarus stood open-mouthed looking out of the window until I pushed him aside. At the back of the group, stood Jonas and Rebekah, their faces lit by the lamp Jonas carried. Heads together, they talked to a Temple priest, who nodded when Rebekah pointed to our house. Even though I couldn't hear what they said, their menacing faces showed their intent. With a bang, I closed the shutters and turned a frightened face towards Jesus. He suggested we should go to bed and that the crowds would soon disperse. They remained there well into the night, and I would have been afraid, except for the reassuring presence of Jesus.

Afraid of what I'd seen, I told no one. It unnerved me and only compounded the things John spoke of. Jesus's words that he would give up his life for his friends and Mary anointing him for his burial only added to it. Despite my fears, I relaxed with the aroma still on Mary's hair and, as I lay on my bed, my words to John came back to my mind. "We should trust that whatever happens does so because he allows it."

* * *

The pungent smell of the spikenard hit me the moment I awoke, pervading my senses and reminding me of the previous evening. Permeating everything in the house, it hung in the air. It was Sunday, the day after the Sabbath, and Jesus planned to go to the Temple. As he prepared to leave, Mary, Lazarus, and I collected our cloaks.

Jesus stopped us saying, "You need to stay behind today. That includes you, Lazarus. Some people want to harm you, and I want to make sure you're safe at home."

"I want to go to the Temple with you," Lazarus pleaded.

Jesus held onto his shoulders and said, "Lazarus, you need to remain inside today. Promise me you'll stay here."

"All right, I promise to stay at home and be careful," he looked away and whispered, "and be bored."

Disappointed, but without a word, we replaced the cloaks on the hangers and watched them leave the house. Two village women chatted by the well, and several bystanders stood in small groups looking at our home. They would have a frustrating wait for something interesting to happen in Bethany that day. Jesus and his companions set off on the dusty road leading to Jerusalem.

"Where are they off to then?" I jumped at Jonas's voice and wondered whether he had lain in wait. Rebekah stared down from an upstairs window.

"Just off to Jerusalem," I said, trying to sound aloof.

"Are you not going with them?"

Not wanting to get into a conversation, I shook my head. "No, I have things to do today."

As I returned inside, a plan formed in my mind. It wasn't me who had promised to stay home. Never having seen Jesus outside Bethany, I thought I would follow at a distance and watch. A short time later I collected my cloak for the second time that morning.

"I'm going out for a while," I said, hoping to sound casual. But I couldn't fool Mary and Lazarus, they guessed where I was going.

"You can't go out, you promised Jesus to stay here," Mary protested.

"It was Lazarus who promised," I pointed out.

Mary dashed passed me towards the door. "I'm coming with you."

"No!" I grabbed her arm more forcefully than intended. "Jerusalem will be even more busy and crowded than usual."

"But Martha, I want to come with you." When I wouldn't answer she continued, "I promise I'll stay next to you the whole time."

"Mary, promise you will stay here today?"

"But …"

"You will stay here with Lazarus."

Mary folded her arms and pouted her lips. "I promise to stay at home, while you follow Jesus and have all the fun."

"It's not fair," Lazarus complained.

"Don't act like a child," I said.

"You treat me like one, but I'm eighteen years old now."

"In that case, you should be more responsible. Jesus specifically asked you to stay home, so stay here and look after your sister."

Angry, I picked up my cloak and strode out of the house. I hated arguing with my brother and sister and I knew that Jesus had meant that we should all stay in Bethany, but I wanted to see him in Jerusalem. The aroma of the spikenard lingered on my cloak as I slung it around my shoulders. With a mixture of emotions, I walked out towards Jerusalem. I was excited, and wondered what I would experience that day, and also apprehensive after Jesus's words the day before. I planned to stay well out of Jesus's way, to watch from a distance and get home before them. Jesus would never know I'd followed him.

CHAPTER 6

The hot, dusty narrow streets bustled with pilgrims. Everyone pushed and jostled, all heading in the same direction. From out of every district of the Roman Empire, Jewish people came to worship at the Temple in Jerusalem for Passover. The city was more crowded than usual, and a crush of people surged forward.

"Hosanna, blessings on the one who comes in the name of the Lord! Hail to the King of Israel!"

Pilgrims were singing psalms and songs with more exuberance than normal. 'Hosanna', a shout of praise to our God.

"Do you think he's the Messiah?" A young man asked another next to him.

"I hope so because we need one," his friend answered. "Jesus performed a miracle once, right in front of me. He healed a young woman, unable to walk from birth. The last I saw of her she was running down the street shouting and singing."

"I guess he must be a special person and close to God then," the first man answered.

Others standing nearby joined in the conversation. "We need a strong warrior to raise an army against the Romans and liberate us from their tyranny."

"Yes, we need a man like King David, the most famous, strong and brave king in the history of our people."

"Or Moses who freed us from slavery."

"And Joshua who led us into Judea."

"We need a Saviour!"

"Saviour, Saviour," they cried with great fervour.

The back of a head, so familiar to me, came into view, and I sighed, relieved that I had found Jesus, at last. He was riding a grey donkey surrounded by his disciples who struggled to make a way for him through the mass of people. The crowd, ecstatic in their praise, shouted out his name and hoped he would turn towards them. Others cut palm branches and waved them above their heads or laid them on the ground, along with cloaks and blankets for the donkey to walk over. Children sat on the shoulders of their fathers to get a better view and protect them from the pressing multitudes. Everybody was waving and shouting at Jesus.

A group of men stood at an open window, their demeanour in contrast to everyone else. Where the people shouted, sang, laughed and smiled, they wore grim faces with folded arms and sour expressions. They were not enjoying the spectacle below them. As I stood looking at them, the pressing of the crowd caused me to knock into a man underneath the window. His pristine white linen clothes and white turban showed that he was one of the group above, a priest from the Temple.

He glared at me. "Woman, you have knocked into me."

"I … I'm sorry, it's not my fault. Everyone is pushing me," I tried to explain.

He brushed his clothes, paying me no more attention than he would to a hen scratching in the dust. Tears filled my eyes at his cruel offhanded treatment. To him, I was worthless and of no significance. These were our religious leaders and teachers but how different they were from Jesus.

"Have you heard about a young man called Lazarus from Bethany?" At the sound of my brother's name, I spun around and breathed out in relief when I didn't recognise who had spoken.

"Yes, they say he died, but Jesus turned up and made him come alive again," someone added.

"My wife's cousin's mother-in-law's sister was there. She said he came out of his tomb in his grave bandages, and his sisters fainted," another man said.

"I'm not surprised they fainted, I would too," his wife cackled.

"Wouldn't it be great to see a miracle today? It'll be a good tale to take home," the man said.

Trying to move away in case someone recognised me, I lost my footing and slipped to the ground. Frightened of being stepped upon I curled into a ball and could only see legs and feet. Panicking, I tried to stand, but my feet kept slipping until hands grabbed my arms and lifted me into the air.

"Martha! Are you all right?" I opened my eyes, to see the concerned faces of Simon and John shouting my name and bringing me to my feet.

"Are you injured?" Simon asked, and I shook my head. "Come on, Martha, let's get you nearer to Jesus where you'll be safe."

I controlled my breathing and trembling enough to ask, "How did you know I'd fallen?"

"Jesus noticed you a while back and asked us to keep a lookout for you. Which I tell you, is difficult in this throng," John replied.

Though grateful that Jesus had seen me, I was alarmed that he now knew I'd followed him. As we came closer to Jesus, Simon went up to him and shouted into his ear to make himself heard over the noise. Jesus turned around, and my eyes met his before I turned away in shame. John led me to the disciples, and I followed behind Jesus.

Making slow progress, we headed towards the Temple. As we entered a narrow alley, the same group of priests I'd seen earlier blocked our way. At the front was the man I'd knocked into, his scowl for Jesus much worse than the one he had given me. He dismissed me as irrelevant, but he recognised the significance of the crowds chanting, and Jesus's response.

"Rabbi!" he tried to shout over the praise of the people. If he was waiting for silence, he got none because the crowds never stopped shouting and singing.

He shouted louder. "Rebuke these people. They do not realise what they are singing, but you do." Jesus remained quiet and refused to move aside. Used to being obeyed, the priest's face flushed as anger rose within him. "You must stop them, this instant."

Jesus replied, "Do you see these stones at the side of the road? If the people keep quiet now, these same stones will shout out in praise. You cannot stop this." With that, he moved the donkey forward, and the priest, red-faced, moved aside, powerless.

The people continued their songs to Jesus as the King of Israel. He couldn't have looked more regal, even if he'd ridden a white charger instead of the humble donkey. His humility was so different from the pride of others. Jesus is a King, but a king like no other. People in the crowd were seeing what I'd seen, that he is our long-expected Messiah, come to bring in God's kingdom.

High on a parapet above the street, a squadron of Roman soldiers stood alert, watching the crowds, the sunlight flashing off their spears and shields. Glaring at the procession as it wove its way around the narrow streets, a battle-worn centurion with a scar across his face fingered his sword nervously. Turning to the group of soldiers he spoke to one who saluted and ran off. I wondered where he was going and if there was a message sent with him. At that moment I understood that the Roman authorities were as frightened as the Temple priests. Despite the hot and oppressive crowds, I felt a chill as I recalled Jesus's recent words about his death.

* * *

We shielded our eyes against the sudden brilliance of the sun glinting off the Temple's white marble and gold. Jesus dismounted from the donkey and climbed the wide flight of stairs up to the entrance. As he hadn't asked me to leave, I followed up the steps worn smooth by the feet of countless worshippers. On we went through the triple gates leading into the hot and airless tunnel, where it took a moment for my eyes to adjust to the abrupt darkness. John placed his arm around my shoulder guiding me through, and we emerged blinking into the Temple courts.

No matter how many times I visited, I never became accustomed to the overwhelming smells. The burning sacrifices, mixed with sweat, animals and manure all pervaded the Court of the Gentiles. Stallholders sold their wares to pilgrims who could buy anything from refreshments to souvenirs to take home. The shouts of the stallholders and sounds of debating and arguing drowned out the chants of the priests. This, added to the baying of the animals ready for slaughter, made the Court of the Gentiles the busiest and noisiest place in the whole Temple, resembling a bazaar rather than a place of worship.

Whenever I visited with my family, we always bought our sacrifices and went straight through to the relative quiet of the Court of the Women where only Jews were allowed. Mother, Mary and I remained there as our father, Lazarus and Nathan went up a small flight of steps into the Court of the Israelites. Reserved for men only, this was not a place for me. Even as a child, I argued with my mother at the unfairness of this, but she said I should accept it. As a female, the law refused me admittance. But God was my God too, and I wanted to worship him in the same way as my brother and father. With Jesus, things were different; he never excluded his female disciples. We sat together with the men, learning together at his feet.

Nathan described how they offered our sacrifice of a bird or young lamb to the priests. They would stand and watch as the priests slaughtered it and collected its blood to sprinkle onto the altar. Jesus told us that in the centre of the Temple was the Holy Place where God himself lived. A heavy curtain separated this Holy Place from everyone. Decorated in blue, purple and scarlet, with angels embroidered in gold thread, it must be beautiful. But neither I, nor anyone else I knew, would ever see it. Only once a year, on the day of atonement, could the High Priest enter and, in order to take away the sin and wrongdoing of the whole nation, he would scatter the blood of the sacrificed lamb.

To my right, the Antonia Fortress loomed over the Temple precinct. This was the power base of the Romans, and the seat of the Roman Governor, Pontius Pilate. With an air of menace, soldiers observed the proceedings in the courts below, on the alert for any incidents and threats of insurrection. Passover was a good time for trouble, with the Temple the usual flashpoint. I shuddered as the ominous feeling returned, reminding me of the Roman centurion and the soldier he had sent away.

Next to the stalls selling the sacrificial animals were the tables of the much-despised money changers. Behind the tables piled high with money bags and coins, they sat to conduct their business. Nathan called them corrupt and dishonest, and together with the priests, they made large sums of money. As worshippers, we had no choice; we had to use them. Our Roman coins, in everyday use, had the Emperor's head stamped on, making them offensive and unworthy to buy the sacrifice. We needed to exchange these for Temple coins, but at a high rate of interest, fixed between the money lenders and the Temple. This and the extortionate cost of the sacrificial animals, made buying them an expensive duty that many people could ill afford. No one liked this practice but what could we do? We were powerless, and no one had ever confronted this until that day.

Judas, who kept the purse, approached the money changers to exchange the coins, until Jesus held out his hand to stop him. He stood in front of the tables to gaze at the money changers, and his expression changed into one which I'd never seen on his face until that day. The usual open friendly expression turned into one more determined and outraged. Some might say angry, but Jesus was never a man out of control, this was controlled anger. He knew what he was doing and why. Not one of them could hold his gaze and they wilted under his stare. Silence descended upon the Temple court as everyone became quiet, wanting to see Jesus in action.

Erupting as a bull let out of a gate, he charged at a table and overturned it. Coins rolled over the paving slabs as it crashed to the floor. With a shout, he rushed to another table and overturned that one and then another, until the ground was full of coins. The money changers shouted at him and scrabbled around on the ground trying to collect the coins. Children scurried between the tables and legs of the money changers and pocketed what they found, many at the instigation of their parents who recognised an opportunity when they saw one. Within a minute the Temple guards appeared, but none dared arrest Jesus. With the screams of the money changers echoing around the courts, he knocked over the table where the doves were for sale. Their flimsy cages broke open, and they flew away, squawking in freedom, released from certain death.

With a voice, loud enough to crack the stones of the Temple, Jesus shouted, "Our scriptures say God's house should be a house of prayer, but you have turned it into a den of robbers. It's a bandits' kitchen."

The people and the pilgrims cheered, but the Temple guards stood grim-faced, not daring to approach. Jesus's reputation as a healer preceded him, and within a few minutes, we were surrounded by an expectant crowd. Children who followed us up the hill ran around with palm branches and a few coins jingling in their pockets, singing the same songs they had during the procession.

"Hosanna, Hosanna to the Son of David," they sang.

The only miracle I had seen Jesus perform was when he raised Lazarus from the dead, and I was eager to see more. Witnessing so many people wanting to speak to him was humbling knowing that he stayed at our home as a friend. Unsure of what to do, I watched John go through the crowd and take people who needed healing to Jesus. Being shy, I considered this too hard for me, so I remained to one side with the crowds.

"Mum, do you think Jesus would heal me?" A boy of about sixteen years held onto his mother's arm.

"Every time we try, we can't get near him. There are too many people," his mother replied.

"I don't want to go home again without at least trying." The boy outstretched his hand and pushed the back of the person in front.

The man turned around and shouted, "Hey, watch what you're are doing. Wait your turn."

"David, be careful." His mother grabbed hold of him. Turning to the man she tried to explain. "I'm sorry, my son is blind and can't see where he's going."

"Excuse me," I said to her, "do you want to meet Jesus?"

"Yes, we've tried twice before, but never get near him." She wiped her eyes with her scarf.

"I'm Martha, one of Jesus's disciples." This took me by surprise. I'd never called myself a disciple. "Would you like me to take you to him?"

"Yes, please," David touched my arm. "I want to see because I have to rely on mum and my brothers to look after me, and I want to be useful at home and in the family business." Holding onto David's arm, I helped him and his mother through the crowd to get next to Jesus.

"Jesus, this is David."

Jesus held David's head in his hands. "Hello David, what can I do for you?"

"I'm blind, but I want to see." David's voice was quiet, almost a whisper.

Jesus put his hand over David's eyes and prayed, then asked, "What can you see?"

David squinted and looked around himself. "I can see people." His mother gasped. "But they look like trees moving."

Tears slid from his eyes, whether out of emotion or healing I couldn't say. Again, Jesus placed his hand over David's eyes and prayed.

"Open your eyes."

David blinked and looked at his mother. He giggled and then laughed out loud.

"Mum! I can see you! I can see!" He grabbed his mother until she pulled herself away.

"Thank you," she cried and held onto Jesus. Thrilled at what I'd seen, I clapped my hands, pleased to have played my small part in David's healing.

"Martha, sit with David and his mum, and tell them the things I've taught you."

"Would it be better if someone else does it?" I asked, feeling unconfident.

"You're capable and can do it." He turned to the next person who needed help.

Apprehensive at first, I drew them aside and told them the things Jesus had taught me. Soon gaining confidence, I surprised myself at how much I had to say. We embraced as they left and I returned to Jesus, who by then was sitting teaching the crowds with a small child on his knee. This was too much for the pompous Temple authorities. Overcome with indignation and with the same churlish expression as the priests, they walked up to Jesus.

"Do you hear what these children are singing?" the leader cried, his eyes glaring.

"Yes, I do," Jesus's voice was placid as he stroked the child's head, "and have you read in our scriptures the psalm that says God has taught children and toddlers to give him praise?"

Incensed, the leader shouted, "Who authorises you to say these things? Show us a miraculous sign to prove you have God's authority."

I may not have received an education in religious studies, but even I recognised that Jesus had just performed many miracles under their contemptuous gaze. Jesus stood, and returning the child to his mother, opened his arms wide.

"Destroy this Temple and I'll rebuild it in three days."

Incredulous at this statement, they sniggered and derided him. "Don't you know it has taken forty-six years to build this Temple? Who do you think you are in saying you can rebuild it in three days?"

Ignoring them, he turned and said it was time to leave. Already trading again, the money changers glared sideways as we passed. The streets were quieter on the return journey and we soon walked through the stillness of the Mount of Olives. I knew I had to face Jesus sometime about leaving Bethany that morning. Yet I became nervous as he came up beside me.

"Come, Martha, walk with me," he said.

My heart leapt and pulsed as I wiped my clammy hands on my cloak. "I'm sorry Jesus," I blurted out, trying to justify my actions. "It wasn't me who promised to stay at home this morning, that was Lazarus."

"I knew how crowded and dangerous Jerusalem would be today."

"Thank you for sending John and Simon to help when I fell."

"Do you understand the things you saw today?" He asked.

"Not everything, but there was no mistaking how the priests and Temple authorities reacted towards you. The Roman soldiers were watching too from the fortress and on the streets. You've made dangerous enemies today. Is it time for you to go back into the safety of the desert again?"

"No, not this time. I'm right where I need to be."

"When you mentioned destroying the Temple, did you mean something other than the Temple made of stone?" I asked.

"You are right, and your understanding is more than most. Yes, I meant my body, and what did I say would happen after three days?"

"That you would rebuild it again," I replied.

"Don't forget that." He stopped and looked at me. "Martha, do you believe me?"

I met his eyes. "Yes, I believe." At that moment, I believed anything was possible.

"Do you remember what I asked you just before I raised Lazarus to life again?"

"You asked whether I believed you."

"Now more than ever, I need you to believe and trust me. The events of the next few days will rock and shake each one of you. I need you to be strong and look after everyone. You can do this for me, Martha, I know you can. Don't be alarmed because you won't be alone. I'm sending others to help you."

He had more faith in me than I had in myself.

CHAPTER 7

For the moment the house was quiet, but we were expecting guests and by evening every room would be full. It was the day after our visit to the Temple and Jesus had returned to Jerusalem for the day. Lazarus swept the upstairs bedrooms and carried up blankets and mattresses, while Mary made up more beds. Later that afternoon, I did a last-minute check that the preparations were in order and the evening meal prepared. Taking a moment to rest, I was dozing under the arbour when a deep booming voice came from outside, followed by the laughter of a young man. These voices belonged to strangers and a knock on the gate caused me to sit up straight.

"Martha!" I jumped up at the sound of a familiar voice and, running to the gate, embraced my friend.

"Johanna, how good to see you again. It has been too long since we were together."

From upstairs, Mary and Lazarus bounded into the courtyard to greet our guests. Two women and two men followed Johanna, including the largest man I had ever seen.

"Hello, you must be Martha," he shouted and grabbed my hand in an eager grip until my fingers hurt. His presence alone filled the courtyard and, being level with his chest, I had to look up into his face. With a broad smile to match his thunderous voice, he took it upon himself to introduce the guests. "You know Johanna of course, then we have Miriam, and it has been our pleasure to escort Jesus's mother herself, Mary."

A face peeped from behind the large man. "He should introduce himself, but seeing he hasn't, I'll do it. This is Barnabas, and I'm Stefanos. For the past year, we've followed Jesus together through Galilee and are now returning to Jerusalem."

"Lazarus, the man himself!" Barnabas moved quicker than I expected, squashing Lazarus in the enthusiasm of his greeting. "Jesus has told me so much about you that I'm keen to find out more."

With an effort, Lazarus pulled away from Barnabas to be greeted by Stefanos. They stood talking to one another, and I noticed the similarity in the two young men. Since his miraculous return to life, Lazarus had grown and was developing into a fine young man. Stefanos, a little older and slightly taller than Lazarus, had a similar mop of lighter-coloured curly hair. Wispy strands of sandy hair protruded from his chin as he tried to grow a man's beard.

Mary moved to stand next to Stefanos. "I'm Mary," she said.

He smiled in greeting and Mary returning his contagious smile.

"Barnabas, are you staying here with us?" I asked, wondering where he would sleep.

"Despite all I've heard of your cooking we must decline. The plan is to meet with Jesus in the Temple and then stay with Stefanos's family." I wondered if the family across the street could hear Barnabas.

Stefanos continued. "My family live in Jerusalem, and I wouldn't like to explain to my mother I'd stayed anywhere else. Besides, she's looking forward to seeing me and I can't wait to be home again." After a short rest, they left us, and I caught up with Johanna's news and talked to Miriam and Jesus's mother.

When Jesus returned, he embraced his mother and picked her slight body up into the air. She laughed and kissed him on the cheek. After dinner, they walked out alone to the Mount of Olives.

* * *

Meeting Jesus's mother, Mary, had long been a desire of mine, and the next morning we sat on the roof together. We talked about how hard life was for a widow, and how much we still missed our husbands. Her quiet spirit and faith made an immense impression, and she was a great comfort to my still-raw grief. Mary had a unique ability to make those who met her feel loved and secure and she had the energy and vigour of a much younger woman; she still walked upright without the need for a stick for support. Her husband, Joseph, had died several years before, and after his death, Jesus took over the care of the family and the carpentry business until he left to become a travelling teacher. None of her other children understood Jesus, and Jacob, next in age, blamed him for abandoning his family, even accusing him of being insane. This upset Mary, and she prayed that one day they would understand and come to believe in him as she did.

Later that day, as we prepared the evening meal, Miriam told us her story. She was grinding cumin seeds to flavour the meat and to this day, the aroma of cumin reminds me of her.

"The day I met Jesus was the turning point of my life. That was the day I became re-born to live it again from the beginning, but this time the life I was meant to live. I come from a town on the shores of Lake Galilee called Magdala, which explains why people call me Miriam Magdalene. As a child, I always felt different from other children and they never let me join in their games. Everyone said I would get better as I grew up, but I never did. By my eighteenth birthday, I couldn't leave the house and became terrified if I stepped out into the street, often lying in bed for days without sleep.

"If the days were bad, the nights were worse. Voices, that no one else could hear, whispered and shouted from out of the dark. Sometimes their screams sounded so loud that I awoke my mother in terror, thinking there must be an intruder in the house. At night, I wandered the house searching for knives or anything to cut myself. My parents tried to hide them, but I was cunning and always found their hiding places. After each cut, the soothing blood trickled down my arm, bringing relief for a few minutes until the grim feelings returned. It was the only thing which helped, and I couldn't stop. I was in a constant state of terror and confusion. Unable to think straight, my thoughts coiled together like a twisted skein of yarn.

"Our neighbours claimed a demon had possessed me, and they would hurry past my family in the street, only adding to the shame and guilt which my parents felt because they were powerless to help me. They had long given up hope of a cure, but one day they heard Jesus was visiting Magdala and saw this as my final chance. How much they must love me to have endured my behaviour all those years and still want to help. When they said I had to leave the house, I panicked that they were going to kill me. In shock, I screamed and shouted, biting, scratching and kicking out in fear. By the time they dragged me to Jesus, I fell on the ground exhausted and unable to move. Whimpering, I curled up with my knees to my chest.

"At sunset, Jesus spotted me in the crowd, and my mother cried out to him to help her daughter. Mercifully, he came over and saw me, dirty and dishevelled, kneeling on the floor with my head on the ground, moaning and rocking from side to side. Placing his hands on my head, he prayed that I would be healed and made whole. Warmth spread from his hands into my body, and each angry and unpleasant thought untangled itself and into my muddled and dark mind came a light of peace.

"The first thing I remember is taking a deep breath which relaxed my body and I looked up to see Jesus bending over me. He looked me in the eyes, and at that moment no one else mattered. 'My daughter, you are now well. Go home with your parents and live your new life,' he said. Turning to my parents he said, 'Look after her, she's precious'. My father lifted me up, and for the first time in years, I looked back and smiled. That was too much for them and they broke down in tears. Overwhelmed with gratitude they couldn't speak.

"People stood in the streets of Magdala calling out to one another to come and see the change in me. I walked up the street with my hair brushed, wearing clean clothes, and holding the hands of my mother and father. They cannot stop telling everyone they meet about how Jesus healed me. Since that day I help in any way I can and travel with him throughout Judea."

There was silence as Miriam finished, then, with tears in her eyes, my sister embraced her. "We have so much to be thankful for," she said on my behalf.

This smart, assured woman seemed at odds from the one she had been. She told her story with an honesty and integrity that I had never heard before and my heart warmed towards her.

* * *

"But Martha, I want to go into Jerusalem with Jesus. Miriam said she'll look after me and Johanna is going as well." It was Wednesday morning and my sister stood with her arms folded and repeated her request.

"We'll take care of Mary, and I'm sure she'll be good." Miriam smiled at her.

"I promise to stay with them," Mary pleaded.

"What about me? I want to go too." Lazarus hated being left out especially from something concerning his younger sister.

"No!" I said. "The Temple authorities are on the lookout for you. Lazarus, you're not going anywhere near there."

"It's not fair, I'm older than she is. Stefanos will be there; I can stay with him and Barnabas." Lazarus looked over to Jesus for help, but he shook his head. "What's the point of coming back to life if I have to stay at home all the time?" Lazarus pushed past, slamming the door.

Hiding my face in my hands I said, "I apologise for Lazarus's behaviour."

Jesus put his hand on my shoulder. "He'll be all right Martha, and you'll know when the time is right to let him go."

Mary was the first to collect her travelling cloak and waited at the gate until everyone was ready. Before she left, she looked back at Lazarus and pulled a face. She then put her arm in Miriam's and skipped down the street. Lazarus brooded and complained about being left behind for the entire morning, and it was difficult to find jobs to distract him from sulking. Jesus's mother insisted on helping me with the morning chores, but she tired easily, so I left her resting in the shade. Lazarus cleaned out the chicken coop while I tidied the upstairs sleeping areas.

Upon returning to the courtyard, Mary wasn't there, and Lazarus didn't know where she had gone. There was no answer when I called her name, so I went to the roof to see if she was there. I caught sight of her sitting by the well with Rebekah. They sat so close to one another that their heads touched. Rebekah nodded before wiping her eyes on her scarf, then kissed Mary on the cheek. Mary was closing the gate when I came down the stairs.

"Mary, I've just seen you talking to my neighbour." Worried that Rebekah might listen, I steered Mary inside the house. "I need to warn you what she's like. She spies on us and told the Temple authorities after Jesus raised Lazarus from the dead. When Jesus arrived a few days ago, I saw her and Jonas with a Temple priest pointing to our house. It's not wise to talk with her so freely."

Dismissing what I said, Mary asked, "When did you last talk to Rebekah?"

"Only when I can't avoid her! She's such a busybody and makes it her business to know every shred of gossip about everyone."

Mary took my hand. "Are you aware of how hard her life is? She has said many things in confidence which I cannot repeat. Except to say a little understanding would help."

It never occurred to me that Rebekah would have problems of her own. Perhaps this was the reason she concerned herself in other people's business, to stop worrying about her own life.

Mary continued, "Jesus has said many times to forgive others when they hurt us."

"But she has harmed Lazarus and may harm Jesus too."

"Simon once asked Jesus how many times we should forgive someone, asking whether seven times would be enough. Jesus's response astonished him. He said we are to forgive seventy times seven occasions."

"I'm finding it hard to forgive once."

"Try to change your thinking and pray for her. That will help, and when the time comes, you will find forgiveness."

"I'll try," was all I could say, without considering it would ever be possible to do so.

There was a quality and an aspect of Jesus's mother's life that others respected, and I wished I could be more like her. People wanted to speak to her, and she had time for everyone.

* * *

The gate crashed open, banging against the wall and rattling the hinges. My sister tumbled through, breathless, with her headscarf around her shoulders and her face shining.

"Oh, Martha, it's been such a wonderful day, you'll never guess the things I've seen, there's so much I need to tell you. These men came to talk to Jesus and asked him very difficult questions, but he answered them all. Where's Lazarus?" She didn't pause for breath.

Lazarus peered over the edge of the roof and looked down on his sister. Mary glanced up and, ignoring his frown, continued. "Lazarus, come down; I need to tell you something." Without answering, her brother ambled into the courtyard and leaned on the wall with arms folded as the rest of the group arrived.

"Mary, you can tell us after we've eaten. Everyone is tired and hungry. Let's eat first," I said to her.

After we cleared away the remains of the meal and lit the lamps, my sister brought more wine. "Martha, can I tell you what happened at the Temple? There's so much to tell, I'm not sure where to start."

As I nodded, she put the jug of wine on the table and, making sure she was the centre of attention, began her story. "It was so amazing. Everyone stopped what they were doing and pointed to us as we walked into the Temple. The men changing the money gave Jesus such dirty looks, and I laughed when he looked at them and they backed away. People were expecting Jesus and at once surrounded us. Jesus asked them to sit on the ground and began teaching. A woman with a baby asked me if I was with him, and I felt proud to say I was and that he stays at our house.

"You'll never guess what happened? A group of Pharisees tried to trick Jesus, but he's far too clever." She looked in my direction. "They interpret the law and are very strict." I nodded as if I didn't already know. "They walked up to us, looking superior, but they are only jealous that Jesus is more popular than they are."

She coughed, straightened her clothes and, pursing her lips, mimicked their manners and in a deep voice continued, "'Oh, teacher, you are a man of integrity and always teach the truth.' They don't really believe this but thought they might trip him up if they flattered him first. 'You are not swayed by other people's opinions, so tell us, should we pay taxes to the Emperor?' They thought they were being clever, but not clever enough. Jesus asked for a coin and showing it to the crowd, asked whose face was pressed into it. It was the Emperor, of course, so Jesus said to them … What did you say, Jesus? I want to get the right words."

"Give to the Emperor what belongs to him and give to God what's God's," Jesus answered.

"That's right! To give to the Emperor what belongs to him and to give to God what's God's," Mary repeated. "Well done, Jesus."

Jesus smiled at her. "Thank you, Mary."

Mary waited for us to stop laughing before continuing. "Pretending they were interested, they then asked, 'Which is the most important commandment in our law?' Jesus told them straight and said the most important one is to love God with everything in your heart, all that is within your mind and your entire soul. That's right, isn't it?"

"Yes, Mary, well remembered. Can you remember what's the second most important?"

"Yes, to love your neighbour as much as you love yourself."

"Well done Mary. Don't forget these things."

Mary beamed. "I'll never forget them."

She sat down on the floor next to Lazarus and put her head on his shoulder. After his disappointment, Lazarus had made friends with her again. They could never stay angry with each other for long. I remembered Jesus's mother's words that afternoon, and though difficult, vowed to at least try to understand Rebekah even if I couldn't love her.

As usual, when I had guests I made sure that everyone was comfortable and settled in their beds before retiring myself. Holding a lamp, I checked the gate was secure and the shutters closed. With a smile, I remembered Mary's impersonation of the priests and Pharisees and the good time we had spent together. The evenings with Jesus in my home were the happiest.

* * *

Pitcher in hand, I walked into the street to see Rebekah bending over the well, the early morning light casting a long shadow. Dashing back inside I hid behind the gate, thankful that she hadn't seen me. The previous evening, I'd determined to understand Rebekah more, even if I couldn't love her. With resignation and taking a deep breath, I reopened the gate.

"Good morning Rebekah," I tried to sound cheerful.

Startled, she spun around and replied, "Good morning."

"What a lovely spring morning," I said trying hard to make conversation. Avoiding my eyes, she looked down at her pitcher, covering the side of her face with her scarf.

"Is everything all right?"

"Nothing different today than from any other day. Just the usual," she mumbled into her scarf. "The older lady is nice, and we had a good talk yesterday. She said she's Jesus's mother. Will she be staying long?" For the first time, she said nothing derogatory about Jesus.

"Just for Passover," I said, pouring water into the pitcher.

Even though I'd approached her, I didn't want to let slip any information Rebekah and Jonas might use against us. Picking up the full pitchers, we walked back alongside each other. Upon returning home I continued to make breakfast for my guests.

Jesus finished his breakfast and said, "I've arranged for a room in Jerusalem for us to stay for the Passover festival."

I looked at him. "Oh, I was expecting you to remain here."

"Don't be disappointed Martha, there are events happening and I must be there. Before I leave, I want to spend time with each of you because there are important things I need to say."

After speaking to Mary and Lazarus, he asked me to sit with him in the courtyard. "Would you look after my mother for me?" He asked.

"I'd be delighted to, and she can stay as long as she likes," I replied.

"Thank you for everything, I'm grateful for your kindness."

"Oh, it's nothing compared with what you've given us. We like to contribute to your work in our small way."

"Don't underestimate your contribution, Martha, or what you'll achieve in the future. Do you believe me?"

Upset he should ask again, I nodded. "Yes, Jesus, you know I believe you. You asked me the same question four days ago." This was the third time he had asked whether I believed him, and for the third time, I said yes.

He enclosed my hands in his. "It's important that you believe the things which I've said." Staring into my eyes, he whispered, "The time is coming when the shepherd will be taken away, and the sheep will scatter. I need you to take care of my friends, and they'll need you as never before. Will you do this for me, Martha?" Though I didn't understand what he meant, I nodded. "Don't forget the things I've said. There's a time coming soon when you'll pass them on to others."

"Yes Jesus," I replied, willing to do whatever it took.

Under a pale blue sky, the group assembled in the courtyard, ready to leave. As usual, I'd prepared far too much food, and gave Andrew and Judas the wrapped food parcels to take with them. Jesus was the last to leave and gave his mother a fond kiss on her cheek.

"Goodbye, Mother."

Mary stroked her son's face. "Goodbye, Jesus."

He turned and left. Standing together, we watched him walk down the street to join the others. At the corner, he stopped and waved before disappearing. Miriam put her arm around Jesus's mother and brought her back inside. She laid her head on Miriam's shoulders and sobbed.

CHAPTER 8

"Have you seen Lazarus? I can't find him anywhere." I wandered onto the roof where Johanna and my sister were sewing.

"No, we have been here all afternoon, since Jesus left this morning," Johanna replied, folding her sewing away. "It is getting too dark to work, so we are coming downstairs now."

"Mary, have you seen him?" I asked.

She turned away and mumbled into her sewing.

"What did you say?"

"Lazarus isn't here."

"Where is he?"

"He's gone out."

"What do you mean? Gone where?" My voice rose.

"Don't shout Martha, it was his idea. He's gone back into Jerusalem to find Jesus."

I grabbed her arm. "Why didn't you say something?"

She shook her arm away. "He said he'd be back before you noticed him missing."

"After almost losing him once, I don't want to go through that again. It'll be dark soon and it's too dangerous to walk back alone from Jerusalem in the dark."

Johanna put her hand on my arm. "It will not come to that; I am sure he will be safe."

"Mary, you stupid girl!"

Furious with Lazarus and disappointed with Mary, I ran down the stairs and out of the gate to the end of the street. Having matured and grown recently, their childish behaviour annoyed me.

Earlier in the day, after Jesus left, Lazarus had sneaked out and followed him into Jerusalem. Watching from a distance he had seen them walk to a large upstairs room, to the south of the city. As Jesus entered, he had turned and shouted to Lazarus to stop hiding around a corner. Then Jesus told him to return to Bethany as he wanted to share the meal with his closest disciples.

Embarrassed, Lazarus complained at being sent home and was laughed at by some of the men. Now he had gone out again without telling me. Fires were lit as evening descended and the trees faded into the gathering gloom. I continued to stare down the road, willing Lazarus to appear. A tap on my shoulder made me jump, but it was only Miriam with my cloak which she wrapped around my shoulders.

"Why don't you come home?" She said

"Not until I know he's safe."

"I'm sure he'll be with Jesus now."

"You can go back if you like, but I'm staying here."

Miriam ignored my unkind tone and didn't move. I had only known her a few days, but there was a kinship between us as we stood in silence.

"What's that up ahead?" She pointed into the distance towards Jerusalem. "There are lights along the road."

"There must be at least fifty torches. Come on." I moved forward in the dark up the familiar paths into the Mount of Olives.

"Martha!" Miriam shouted, "Where are you going?"

"Lazarus may be in trouble. I can walk these paths in the dark. Follow close behind me." Miriam and I stumbled up the path which was harder than I expected with no light.

A male voice shouted out ahead of us. "Look at the lights, there's a mob coming, we have to get out of here."

"It's Simon. Jesus must be here too." Miriam took hold of my hand.

"Jesus, don't just stand there, run!" Simon entreated.

Another voice I recognised as John's added, "There's no time to waste Jesus."

Other voices shouted and urged Jesus to run, but I didn't hear Jesus speak. Miriam and I reached the clearing as the first of the mob reached them, their intent showing on their faces in the torchlight. From out of the darkness a hand grabbed my arm, I screamed.

"Martha, shush."

"Lazarus, what are you doing here?"

"Be quiet. Duck down and hide."

"How long have you been here?" Miriam whispered.

"I arrived at the same time as Jesus and hid to watch because I didn't want him to send me home again. They talked for a while, then Jesus took Simon, John and James to one side to pray. I was going to stand up when I saw the lights."

The mob stopped in front of Jesus who stood impassively. The guards at the front were less confident when faced with a man who stared them down. A priest pushed his way to the front, and I recognised him as the priest I had bumped into in Jerusalem a few days earlier. His face now a sneer, he had come with enough men to make sure he would get his way this time.

"Who do you want?" Jesus was the first to speak and his commanding voice echoed around the Mount of Olives. The guards, despite their swords and weapons, flinched back.

"Jesus of Nazareth," the priest shouted into the night trying to sound forceful.

"That's me." Jesus opened his arms wide. "Am I such a dangerous revolutionary that you must send soldiers with swords and daggers to arrest me? And why have you come here in the dark when I've been in the Temple every day?"

The priest made no reply and stood aside as a man with his head covered came forward, walking through the guards to stand in front of Jesus.

"Why are you with them?" Simon screamed.

Ignoring Simon, the man kissed Jesus on the cheek in greeting then slunk back into the darkness.

"Who's that?" Lazarus whispered.

"I can't see," I replied.

Two Temple guards stepped forward with a chain and manacles, and Jesus offered his hands. They looked back at the priest to confirm that he was the one they were to arrest.

The priest shouted, "Do it!" and they approached Jesus who offered no resistance.

With a shout, Simon ran forward and wrestled a guard to the ground. Another guard hauled him off and held a dagger to his throat. Simon looked at Jesus who shook his head.

"Simon," Jesus's voice cut through the clamour. "There'll be no fighting." To the priest, he said, "I'll go with you voluntarily. It's me you want, so let my friends go."

Four Roman soldiers stood around looking bored; this arrest of a travelling preacher held no interest for them. One stood scratching his head in front of the bush where we were hiding. The bush rustled when Lazarus moved his position to get a better look.

"Who's there?" the soldier barked.

I grabbed Lazarus's arm to prevent him from moving. His eyes wide with fear, my brother's body shook under my grip.

"I said, who's there? Come out or I'll poke you with my sword," he laughed and unsheathed his sword.

Lazarus moved to stand. "Don't!" I whispered and gripped his arm tighter.

"Stay here," he insisted and stood to face the soldier.

A second soldier grinned. "Look what we have here, a snivelling little rat."

"Arrest him too, he's one of their gang." My blood drained from my head and I felt dizzy as Jonas strode up to the soldier.

The soldier sniffed. "Who are you to give orders, little snitch?"

He grabbed Lazarus's cloak, which ripped and fell from his shoulders. I said a silent prayer of thanks that I'd been too busy to mend his damaged cloak. Lazarus ran down the hill.

"Don't stand there," Jonas screeched. "After him!"

"I'm not wasting my breath chasing boys."

Jonas pointed towards Bethany. "I know where he lives."

The soldier shrugged. "What do I care?"

He ignored Jonas and flung Lazarus's cloak on the ground. Sheathing his sword, he walked back to the mob, leaving us alone to breathe once more. The mob manhandled Jesus down the path, followed by the guards and soldiers. The disciples stood in a tight group holding onto each other in stunned silence. Simon turned his head when Miriam said his name but didn't register who we were.

"John." I tugged his arm, but he remained silent.

James came to his senses first. "Miriam, Martha, what are we going to do?" Miriam and I looked at one another, as lost as they were.

"The soldiers nearly arrested Lazarus, and he's run away. I need to follow him." I turned to run back home.

"Martha, wait!" shouted Miriam. "Someone should follow to see what they do with Jesus."

"I'll go." Simon set off at once down the hill, following the lights.

"Simon!" He turned to look at me. "Meet up with everyone back at the upstairs room, where you were this evening."

Simon nodded. He was the only one who volunteered to follow Jesus and sprinted down the hill as fast as he could in the dark over unfamiliar ground. The rest stayed stuck where they were.

James put his hand on my shoulder. "John and I will make sure you get back home safely. Who knows who's hanging around." I nodded my thanks.

With leaden steps, the men made their way down the hill back to Jerusalem and we turned to run home.

* * *

A light was still burning in an upstairs window when we returned to the house. I pushed the gate to find it barred, so I knocked gently.

"Who is it?" Johanna's concerned voice asked.

"It's us," I whispered.

When Johanna opened the gate, we rushed in and James quickly barred it behind us. She nodded her head inside where Jesus's mother was attending a sobbing Lazarus. With a cloth, she washed grazes on his face and elbows, showing he had fallen over in his haste to run home.

My sister flung herself on me. "Have soldiers arrested Jesus?" she cried, and when I nodded, she sobbed on my shoulder.

Not knowing what to say, I sank down on a chair before my legs collapsed. I took a cup of wine Johanna held out for me and gulped it down. She placed a cup between John's hands and drops of wine spilt on the floor as, hands shaking, he took a small sip.

"Can you tell us what happened this evening?" Johanna's voice had a calming effect.

James looked over to his brother who stared into his wine. "Jesus took us to the upstairs room, and the evening started the same as any other. Together, we shared a meal as we have done hundreds of times. But it soon became obvious this meal would be different. Jesus stood, and I expected a blessing over the meal as usual. Instead, taking off his outer robe, he wrapped a towel around his waist. Pouring water into a basin, he knelt in front of me, and picking up my foot, washed and dried it with the towel. There was complete silence, no one spoke."

"I couldn't think of anything to say," John interrupted. "He has said so much in the past few weeks about the Messiah and Son of God and then he acts like a slave. He confuses me."

James continued as John became quiet. "He even resembled a slave with a towel wrapped around him. The only one who dared speak was Simon. You know what he's like, he always finds something to say. He wouldn't allow Jesus to wash his feet like a common slave. Kneeling by him, Jesus looked up and said unless he washed his feet, Simon would no longer be his friend. Upset, Simon asked Jesus to wash his face and hands as well, which Jesus refused. He said we were all clean except one, but at the time he refused to tell us who."

John took up the story. "After Jesus had washed everyone's feet, he asked whether we understood what he had done. None of us did. Even Simon was quiet. Jesus said one day we would figure it out."

"I know why he did it," my sister Mary said in a quiet voice.

Lazarus turned to her. "How can you know when no one else does? You weren't even there!"

"I washed his feet because I love him, and he washed your feet because he loves you," Mary said to James.

"I suppose you're right. Jesus said we call him rabbi, teacher or Lord, as we should because this shows how important he is. But it's also important that we serve one another as he's shown us this evening. He said he was giving us a new command, which is to love each other in the same way as he has loved us. This is what it is to be a disciple, and how other people will know we are Jesus's followers."

A sob racked John's entire body. "What have we done? Will we ever understand Jesus?" He wiped the tears from his cheek. "I'm so ashamed of my behaviour, even arguing which of us was the most important. We said terrible things to one another and now Jesus has been taken away and I don't know what to do." He grabbed clumps of his hair and pulled. "What are we going to do now?"

More in control of himself than his brother, James put his arm around John and said, "It wasn't you John, you didn't betray him. We all regret how we argued in front of Jesus, but it wasn't you."

My sister ran over to him. "Tell us who."

John wiped his eyes with the back of his hand. "Nothing took Jesus by surprise, either at the meal or later when they came to arrest him. He said one of us had already betrayed him. Leaning over to Jesus I whispered, 'Who is it?' Jesus said it was the one who shared the food with him. He dipped a chunk of bread in a bowl and passed it to … to

Judas." There was a sharp intake of breath from everyone in the room. "Jesus told him to do what he intended to do. Judas glared at him and walked out."

"Judas was mean to me and complained when I poured the spikenard on Jesus's feet. He didn't understand me, and he doesn't understand Jesus," Mary said in response to this news.

"This is more than being mean, it's an act of betrayal," John said to her. "Who knows why he did it. Judas is one of us, we are brothers and he has turned against his own family." Quietness returned as the men stared into their drinks.

"Can you tell us what else happened?" Miriam asked.

More able to speak now, John continued, "The evening continued in this strange way. We'd finished the meal when Jesus picked up a flatbread and broke it into two pieces and passed it around. He said it is his body which will be broken for us. Later, he lifted the cup of wine and said this is a new promise between God and his people. He'll seal this agreement with his blood, which he will pour out as a sacrifice. Just like the sacrificial lamb, we will eat at the Passover meal tomorrow; he'll sacrifice himself and we won't be able to stop him. He told us to remember his sacrifice and the new promise in this way.

"After that, Jesus wanted to go to the Mount of Olives to pray. Subdued, we walked out of the upstairs room in silence. That is, all of us except Judas who was elsewhere. If I'd known what he intended to do, I would've stopped him, but Jesus didn't. In silence, we walked up the hill and Jesus asked Simon, James and me to follow him a little further and be together while he prayed. We sat under an olive tree a little away from him.

"Falling on his knees he asked God to find another way to carry out what needs to happen. In agony, he prayed and, being crushed, needed us more than ever, but we were tired and fell asleep. Jesus shook my shoulder and asked me to be with him as he prayed again. Guess what I did? I fell asleep once more. Stirring, I heard him say he would do God's will and what God wants, not what he himself wants.

"By this time, it was dark, and my eyes kept closing. With everything that's happened this week, I've been so tired. He woke us a second and even a third time. The last time he said he had now determined to do what God wants and whatever happens from here on in, God has already decided. How I wish I'd stayed awake and been with him when he needed me. Tonight, I failed him after all those times he has supported and comforted me." John cried once more and wiped his face on his sleeve.

"Don't blame yourself, John," James tried to reassure him, "it wasn't only you. We were all there."

Johanna sat next to Jesus's mother, holding her hands. "Mary, your hands are cold." She rubbed both of Mary's hands in hers, and I put a blanket around her shoulders.

Still shaking, John got up to leave and embraced Jesus's mother. "We shouldn't be here. Jesus needs us. But I don't know where to go."

"Go back to the upstairs room as agreed. We'll come early in the morning and find out where Jesus is," I said.

I said goodbye to John and James in the courtyard under the moon. Miriam opened the gate and looked around at the quiet street before letting them out into the night.

"Be careful," she whispered.

Miriam, always the strongest and most practical, suggested that we should try to rest. But there was little sleep that night for us and dawn broke too soon.

CHAPTER 9

This time it would be me who sneaked out of the house before dawn. Johanna, Miriam and I wanted to spare Jesus's mother, Lazarus and Mary the distress of the forthcoming day and agreed to leave them behind in Bethany. But they were waiting for us in their travelling cloaks in the courtyard. Lazarus's shock of escaping arrest just a few hours earlier had changed him. No longer my little brother whom I had to protect, he had grown into a man overnight.

"Martha, you won't leave us behind this time. We'll face today's challenges together because we can't leave Jesus alone without his family around him."

Impressed by his new courage, I said, "We're going to the upstairs room, and Simon and John will decide what happens." They nodded together in agreement.

Darkness was giving way to light coming from the east as I closed the gate behind me. It would be dawn before we entered Jerusalem. Jonas's house was still, and I wondered whether he was at home or in Jerusalem. Pain gripped my stomach, and to steady myself, I leaned on their wall. Lazarus put his arm around my waist, and I was glad he was there.

With her face expressionless, Jesus's mother looked straight ahead and walked with a determined stride between

Johanna and Miriam. She was not a lady to turn away from danger or despair, and her strength gave me the courage to continue. Mary stopped as we approached the place of Jesus's arrest and she looked towards Jerusalem as her son had done. A thin line of yellow light crept over the horizon.

"My new husband and I walked along this road, and I carried my baby son in my arms, excited to present him at the Temple and offer thanks to God for his life." Tears formed in Mary's eyes as she recalled this happier time. "After we had presented the sacrifice, an old man called Simeon asked if he might hold Jesus. At first, protective of the baby God had given us, Joseph refused, but I handed him over to Simeon. Jesus gazed at him the way babies do, and Simeon laughed. He told us he could die in peace because he'd seen God's light, but many would oppose Jesus and a sword would pierce my heart and soul. This is happening now. There's a soldier thrusting his sword into my heart, and it's crumbling."

Miriam put an arm around her. There were no words to say, only the comfort of our presence. Summoning strength Mary continued, "An old lady, called Anna, saw Simeon holding Jesus, and after taking him from Simeon, held him close. Many people viewed her as a nuisance, but others said she was a prophetess. Jesus returned her smile, reaching up to touch her face, as she sang and praised God. Anna was old and frail, and Joseph, worried that she might drop the baby, took him from her. I heard that both Simeon and Anna died soon afterwards."

Above the noise of the birds welcoming the dawn, I strained to hear her quiet voice. "God gave the baby to us and we watched him grow into the man he has become. Every mother thinks her son is special, but I know my son is truly special. He's God's son, his anointed, and the events of today are part of God's plan, but it doesn't make this easier for any of us."

Taking a deep breath, and with her voice faltering, Mary continued. "God will be with us today, even though it will appear he has abandoned us."

Jesus's last words before he left the day before came to mind. He asked whether I believed him, and I had said yes. Today would be a test whether I did, and I hoped I would be equal to the challenge.

* * *

Lazarus led us towards the room Jesus had prepared the day before. At the side of a street in the south of the city was a narrow passageway with a steep flight of stairs. At the foot of the stairs we paused and heard sounds of arguing coming from the room upstairs. We climbed the stairs and the arguing ceased when Lazarus knocked. James opened the door with hair dishevelled and dark skin under his eyes; he hadn't slept. Remains of the evening's meal were still on the table, with overturned cups and dried wine and food stains. The air was stale with sweat and fear. John breathed out and tears spilt from his eyes as he nodded to a figure lying on the floor in the corner, resembling a pile of discarded clothes.

"It's Simon," he mouthed.

Simon lay curled up on the floor facing the wall. I knelt and touched his shoulder. "Simon, it's Martha."

He turned towards me, hurt and despair imprinted on his face.

"Go away!" he shouted and returned to face the wall. Hair was matted on his face where tears had dried, his eyes were wild and his breath stale.

Andrew looked up from his place next to his brother. "He won't speak to anyone. Last night, he followed Jesus to

Caiaphas, the High Priest's house, and he's been like that since he returned."

My sister poured wine into a cup and, without a word, placed it next to Simon. She slid down the wall and leant against it, with her chin on her knees. The men looked at us with tired and glazed eyes, silent, lost and desperate.

Miriam held my hand and sighed. "Martha, what shall we do?"

Everyone looked at me and, hoping I sounded more confident than I felt, I said, "The first thing is to find out is where Jesus is."

"A guard said they were taking him to the Romans." This made us turn around as it was Simon who spoke. Talking to the wall he said, "Jesus saw me."

"Good, he knew you were there." Andrew tried to offer a grain of comfort to Simon.

"It's not good!" Andrew recoiled from Simon's stinging words. "I thought I was better than all of you, but I'm nothing and now Jesus knows it." He sat up and drained the cup of wine, wiping his mouth on his sleeve. "What did Jesus say about me last night?" No one answered. "If you don't remember, I do. He said three times I would say I don't know him. Three times before the cock crows at the start of the new day I would deny him. Confident and cocky as always, I said I'd rather die than disown him. Keeping to the shadows, I followed the soldiers to Caiaphas's house and stood by the fire in the courtyard.

"A young servant girl walked past and said she had seen me with Jesus. Afraid of a fourteen-year-old girl, I told her to shut up as she hadn't. Five minutes later a man asked whether I knew Jesus, and again I denied it. Just before dawn, another servant said he could tell I'm from Galilee by my accent and I must be with Jesus, but I swore and cursed that I didn't know him.

"A door opened, and Temple guards manhandled Jesus out, saying they were going to the Romans. Jesus heard every vile and disgusting word I called him. The cock crowed, and I looked at him in horror, realising what I'd done. His eyes filled with sadness and the soldiers pushed him away. I ran back here because I've nowhere else to go."

John knelt in front of Simon and put his arm around his shoulders. This time Simon didn't back away from touch. "I remember what Jesus said last night, but it's you who've forgotten something. Jesus said afterwards that you will turn back and that you are to be a strength to your brothers. We need you to be strong, and I need your faith now. You've not let us or Jesus down." Finally, Simon gave way to tears and sobbed on his friend's shoulder. His cries filled me with sadness, but it was better than facing the wall in mute silence.

"Pilate, the Roman Governor, is stationed in Herod's Palace," Johanna said.

"Some of us should go there now," I said.

Miriam agreed. "It will be safer for us women to go alone. That includes you, Lazarus."

Lazarus, his new maturity showing, did not object. "You're right, it would be more dangerous if I went along."

John shook his head. "I don't like the idea, but I agree you will be safer on your own."

James stood next to Jesus's mother and asked her, "Would you rather stay here with us?"

"No, I want to see Jesus. He needs me now," Mary replied.

Johanna put her hand on Mary's arm. "We'll look after her."

* * *

Raucous jeers increased in volume the nearer we approached Herod's Palace. Unusual for so early in the day, we had to push our way through a crowd into the courtyard. Afraid of being recognised as the wife of Herod's steward, Johanna hid her face in her scarf. She held onto Jesus's mother as Miriam and I shielded my sister from the crush of bodies. These were different people from the ordinary families we passed in the city. There were few women and no children in this crowd which resembled a baying mob. The first real stirrings of apprehension surfaced, and I asked someone who looked the least frightening why they were there.

"Don't you know?" he laughed. "That wandering preacher from Galilee is in there being interrogated by the Roman Governor. We know what that means don't we?" He looked at the five of us. "Why do you ask? Do you know him?"

Remembering how wretched Simon felt after saying he didn't know Jesus, I swallowed and replied, "Yes, we do."

The man pointed us out to his friends, who joined in with his laughter. Uncomfortable, but determined not to show it, I looked away, knowing a mob will pounce on any sign of weakness. A movement behind caught my attention and, with a jolt, my heart lurched inside my chest. It was Jonas. He walked up to a group of priests who stood outside the Palace gates.

Johanna looked towards the gate. "They will not enter the courtyard because the Romans are here. If they did, they could not worship at the Temple later today because they would be ritually unclean. That's Caiaphas, the High Priest, standing at the back."

"Our uncleanliness is clearly no concern of theirs," Miriam noted.

"What do they want with Jonas?" My sister asked.

One of the priest's pack spoke to Jonas and pointed to a balcony, while another dropped a heavy bag into his hand. Jonas then tried to talk to Caiaphas who turned his head away. My neighbour moved through the crowd giving instructions to groups of men and handing out coins.

Simmering in anticipation, the crowd stirred as they saw movement on the Palace balcony. Pilate strode out to face the crowd which erupted into shouts when a soldier pushed Jesus forward to stand at Pilate's side. Standing upright, Jesus stared at Pilate who was the first to look away. Despite appearances, it was Jesus who was in control of the confrontation. Pilate, dressed in the uniform of a Roman soldier, scowled in both anger and fear, trying to prevent a riot. Jesus's face was bloody and swollen and blood on the front of his tunic showed he had already received a beating.

The crowd hushed when Pilate lifted his hand. "After interrogating this prisoner, I have found him not guilty." Jeers from the crowd forced Pilate to speak louder. "However, it is your custom to release a prisoner every Passover."

With a click of his fingers, he commanded a soldier to push another prisoner to stand next to Jesus. His long-matted hair and beard, and dirty bloody clothes, showed he had been a prisoner a long time. Wild eyes blinked as he shuffled into the sunshine and with manacled hands, he tried to shade his eyes.

Pilate tried to reason with the crowd. "Who shall I release today? Shall I acquit this man, your King of the Jews? Or Barabbas, the prisoner guilty of murder?"

The crowd shouted at once. "We want Barabbas! We want Barabbas!" This criminal was a bandit with a deadly reputation. "We want Barabbas!" they shouted louder. With a hand on the shoulder of the man in front, Jonas jumped raising a fist in the air and spitting out his words, encouraging those around him to do the same.

Pilate held up both hands for silence. "Set him free!"

Barabbas, surprised by his unexpected release, shouted and to cheers from the crowd, raised both hands into the air. Pilate summoned the soldiers to take Jesus away and, huddled together, we waited.

"What will happen now?" Mary asked. I shook my head, lost for words.

Miriam held onto Mary's arm. "This mob worries me. They want blood and sense they might get it." She looked towards the entrance. "The priests at the gate have disappeared."

"There is a way around into the Palace. Maybe they have gone to the side door to speak to Pilate or Herod," Johanna said.

"They're back." Miriam had seen them return. "And by the looks on their faces, they have what they wanted."

Betrayed by their scornful smiles, they already knew the outcome. The mob cheered again as Pilate walked onto the balcony and fell silent as he spoke.

"We will now bring the prisoner out, but understand this, I don't find him guilty."

They roared when Jesus appeared, while we gasped in horror as two soldiers brought him onto the balcony. With flesh hanging off his bare back and blood running down his body they placed a purple robe around him. Their torture now turned to mockery and, with scornful cheers, they bowed before him.

A soldier carried a woven crown made from thorns and with a mock bow he approached Jesus before slamming it on his head, causing Jesus to wince. The pain caused him to sway backwards, but he stayed upright. Blood trickled down his face into his eyes. My sister screamed and grabbed hold of my arm, while Johanna held Jesus's mother close. The men around us laughed and jeered, but there was no reason anyone should find this amusing whoever was being tortured.

"Your friend doesn't look too good now, does he?" The man next to me dug his elbow into my ribs. I refused to answer.

Jonas's voice yelled out above the clamour, "Crucify him!"

Pilate had Jesus taken inside and before they took him away, a soldier spat in his face. It was only a matter of a few minutes before they emerged again. Without the purple cloak but with the thorny crown still in place they pushed Jesus to the floor, the tracts of the whip visible on his back. Leaning onto a pillar, he picked himself up, leaving behind bloody handprints. Jesus continued to stare at Pilate, who looked away.

Again, Pilate called for quiet and asked, "What shall I do with your King?"

The mob took up Jonas's chant. "Crucify him! Crucify him!" Everyone apart from us chanted the same.

"Take him away and crucify him." Pilate dismissed Jesus with a callous wave of his hand. We looked at one another with disbelief. Jesus was to be executed.

Jonas appeared by my shoulder, and with his voice hoarse with screaming said, "Got what he deserves. Pretending he's someone special when he's just another upstart from Galilee. Who is he to tell us what to do? He's nothing. Someone else might get what's coming to them soon. I'll personally make sure your dear little brother won't be able to escape next time. And then we'll see what happens to you and darling Mary." He put his head back and laughed.

Miriam turned to say something, but I touched her arm to silence her. It was better to remain quiet. Everyone had what they wanted. The priests were disposing of the man who questioned their authority, and the mob walked away with money in their pockets. Pilate averted a riot without a second thought for Jesus, while getting one over on the priests by calling him King of the Jews. In this cruel dark place, Jesus was alone, apart from the five women who loved him.

CHAPTER 10

News of Jesus's impending execution spread, and a crowd formed outside Herod's Palace. They came either to mourn or to gloat, and they waited with us to follow the procession to the place of execution. Shock reduced us to silence and we clung to each other. Silent tears dropped from my eyes as my sister's hand found mine. With a shout, a detachment of soldiers emerged from the entrance, and pushing people aside, they brought Jesus out. Slung across his shoulders, tied with a rough rope, was the crossbeam of his cross, stained red with the blood of its previous occupants.

Still wearing the thorny crown digging into his forehead, Jesus saw us and, through blood-stained eyes, gave us a weak smile of recognition. I was glad we were there to offer him comfort in this, his final hours of need. I ran forward, grasped his hand and, through my tears, smiled back, trying to be strong for him and his mother. A soldier pushed me away back into the crowd. I prayed for strength for each of us because I knew soon it would get worse, much worse. Behind Jesus, two bruised and bloody men followed, condemned as criminals to die that morning alongside him. Jesus stumbled and fell on the path, the crossbeam knocking him to the floor.

"Get up, pig." A soldier with a whip fell upon him, kicking and whipping him until he struggled to lift the crossbeam to stand on his feet. A few paces later, he fell once more.

"He won't make it," the soldier with the whip said to the Centurion in charge.

The Centurion pulled a man from out of the crowd. "You! Pick it up and carry it for him," he barked his order.

Surprised, the man had no alternative against a soldier with a sword and an inclination to use it. Jesus fell when the soldiers untied the crossbeam and threw it on the floor. The stranger picked it up and followed two soldiers who dragged Jesus between them, his white tunic soon stained blood-red from the crossbeam.

Head down, watching the path under my feet, I trudged out through the city gates. I knew where we were heading, towards Golgotha, the place of execution. There were often crucifixions there, in a place called the skull. Whenever there was trouble in Jerusalem it was always the poor who paid the price of others' rebellion. I had seen people hanging off the crosses but never stayed to watch this horrendous and evil practice until then.

Life was cheap for the Romans, and no life mattered except their own. Of all forms of execution, crucifixion was the worst; cruel and most feared. Reserved for non-Roman slaves and rebels, it was meant to humiliate and shame, as well as kill. Evil was present that day and you could smell it, mixed with the stench of blood, sweat, faeces and fear.

The path rose towards Golgotha, and a look passed between Miriam, Johanna and I. We hung back, not wanting Jesus's mother to witness the moment her son was nailed to the cross. The screams, as soldiers hammered nails through wrists and ankles, hurt as if they were our own. Each excruciating hammer blow struck into our very hearts, shattering them into many pieces. I held my sister tight as she screamed with each strike. The criminals struggled and shouted, but the more they cursed the more the soldiers laughed. Soldiers raised Jesus's cross upright and slotted it into a hole in the ground sending a jolt of pain through his body.

"Father, forgive them because they don't know why they're doing this," Jesus said.

Used to abuse but not forgiveness, the soldiers stopped and looked at him in amazement, before shrugging and continuing their gruesome task. The crowd parted as the priests from outside Herod's Palace arrived to witness the death penalty being carried out. Caiaphas, who would not soil the soles of his shoes by appearing at Golgotha, sent his second-in-command. He looked up at the charge sheet nailed above Jesus's head which read, 'Jesus of Nazareth, King of the Jews'. Red with rage he strode up to the Centurion.

"I insist you change the charge against this man. It should say he claimed to be the King of the Jews. This is an outrage," the priest yelled, pointing to the sign.

With a contemptuous look, the Centurion replied, "The Governor wanted that, and that's what he got." Grinning, he took hold of his sword. "If you insist, you could try to take it down and change it yourself." Grumbling, the priest backed away to a safe distance, and the soldiers sniggered.

After stripping the three men, the soldiers divided their clothing between themselves. An argument arose as to who was to keep Jesus's cloak and appalled, I watched as they threw dice for it, cheering when one of them won. Their mockery showed complete and utter contempt and disregard for the men's suffering and that of their families. At this, I gave way to anguish and despair. All thoughts of staying strong gone, I fell to my knees and sobbed. Jesus's mother fell next to me and beat her chest, wailing until Miriam held her, and inconsolable, we rocked back and forth.

A large group of people gathered around the three crosses. Most were there to see Jesus, and like ourselves were grieving for a man who had spoken about love being cruelly cut down out of jealousy. Many others came out of curiosity, wondering what Jesus would do.

A woman shouted above the noise, "We've seen him do miracles, and only last month he healed my neighbour's baby. I wonder if he'll free himself?"

Her husband agreed. "If he's the Messiah he will because God wouldn't let him die like this."

Someone behind me laughed in contempt, and despite the heat, I shivered.

"He said he could destroy the Temple and rebuild it in three days. That's impossible because he can't even save himself from death." It was Jonas.

Unseen, Jonas had joined the priests, who continued to shout insults. The priest who had confronted the soldiers strode up to Jesus's cross.

Pointing his finger and with spittle flying, he shouted, "If you come down now, everyone will believe you're the Messiah." After waiting a few moments, he turned to the crowd and said, "You see, he's just another insignificant nobody from Galilee."

Jonas joined in the taunts. "No one will ever remember his name."

He put his head near mine, and I closed my eyes so I couldn't see his face. But nothing could protect me from his bad breath or grating voice.

"Now we can forget him and get back to life as it was."

Many in the crowd continued to mock and sneer until it was clear Jesus wouldn't free himself. The criminal on his right side summoned enough strength to join in the taunts. In agony, he turned his body and shouted at Jesus.

"If you were the Messiah, you'd save yourself and us along with you."

On hearing this, the other replied, "Don't you have any fear of God? We are both guilty of the crimes and deserve our punishment. But this man did nothing wrong." Through his tears, he shouted, "Jesus, remember me when you get to heaven."

Jesus turned his head towards him. "I'll tell you the truth." Each shallow rasping breath now took what little strength he had left. "Today, you and I will be together in heaven."

An elderly woman on her knees in front of this man's cross turned to Jesus.

"Thank you, rabbi," she said through her tears.

We were not the only women to lose a cherished one that day.

The two criminals cried, one in derision and the other comforted by Jesus's words.

Startled, I shrieked when a hand appeared on my shoulder and, turning, I saw a hooded figure. The hood was removed to reveal a pale and drawn John who put his arms around Jesus's mother. His arms enclosed her body, and she wept into his shoulder.

"I had to come," he said, looking up at Jesus.

"Where's Lazarus?" I asked.

"He's in the upstairs room."

With an effort Jesus opened his eyes and lifted his head. "John!" His voice barely more than a whisper rasped in his throat, each word difficult as he struggled to breathe.

"Yes Jesus, I'm here."

"Look after my mother." John nodded his agreement.

Mary, shielded by John's arm, looked up at her son. Unable to speak, her lips trembled.

"Mother, John will care for you." Even near death, Jesus needed to know his friend would care for his mother.

A drop of blood seeped onto his pallid skin from under a thorn and into his eye. He blinked, and it trickled down his face and chin. Mixed with sweat and blood, it fell down his chest, onto his legs and dripped off his foot. Suspended in the air it waited until splashing in the dirt like the first drop of rain after the summer drought.

It had only been five days, but it seemed a lifetime since my conversation with Jesus as we returned home from Jerusalem. He had said his body was the Temple, which I could see being destroyed in front of my eyes. After the destruction, he asked me to believe that he would rebuild it after three days. Confident, I had replied that I did, but now my belief, like his lifeblood, was haemorrhaging away and pooling on the ground underneath his body.

Locked in our anguish, we were unaware of time passing, but it had only been three long wretched hours since arriving at Golgotha. By now it was noon and the sun should have been at its height. Instead, darkness descended over Jerusalem and muted blue-black clouds slipped overhead with thunder rumbling among the hills. It was as if a bad storm was threatening. This was no normal storm, but something far deeper, mysterious and foreboding, and we were to be witnesses. The Son of God was about to give up his life.

Small groups gathered together, and a fretful silence settled upon the crowd, more frightening than the jeering and shouting. Removing his helmet, the Centurion looked up at the sky, biting his lip. Experts in war and death, these soldiers were as frightened as the crowd, their mockery finally silenced. The Centurion wiped the sweat from his brow before barking orders to the soldiers. The unnatural darkness lasted three hours, and we watched helplessly as Jesus's life ebbed away. His skin grey with the chill of death, I hoped he wouldn't have to endure much longer.

"I'm thirsty," he rasped, his breathing now shallow.

Someone in the crowd dipped a sponge in wine and, fixing it to a branch, lifted it to his blue lips. With one last effort, he pressed his mangled feet against the nails, straightened his legs and took a final deep, harrowing breath.

"God, my God, why have you abandoned me?" he cried, desperation etched on his face. Then in an unexpected loud voice which shook to the core, he shouted.

"It's finished! Father, into your hands I offer my spirit."

Closing his eyes, his head dropped forward.

And he died.

Everything stopped, and I was aware of nothing else, apart from Jesus's lifeless body, his face now at rest. We stood mute, gazing at his broken body, until a deep rumbling under our feet shattered our silence, and the ground shook, splitting rocks in two. People cried out in terror, screaming and stumbling as they ran. Soldiers turned to run away before being halted by their Centurion. Jesus's mother screamed and collapsed to her knees. John fell next to her in tears.

People from the surrounding areas, including Bethany, said they experienced the earthquake which split the curtain in the Holy Place of the Temple from the top to the bottom. God was now available to all; the ultimate sacrifice had been paid. When the earth was still once more, the Centurion stood at the foot of Jesus's cross, gazing at his face and shaking his head in amazement.

"Who do you think he was?" one soldier asked the Centurion.

"Perhaps he was an innocent holy man and their God is angry because he's dead."

"It wasn't our fault, we were just following orders," the soldier replied, and they nodded in agreement. These men, whose career was death, recognised the uniqueness of this one individual death amongst the many thousands they encountered. The priests, now assured Jesus was dead, walked back into Jerusalem, leaving Jonas behind. John and Johanna helped Jesus's mother to her feet, but her legs gave way under the weight of her body and she clung to them.

"I'll take her back to the upstairs room," John said.

"Jesus's burial will need arranging, so we'll stay and watch what they do with him," I said.

"Mary, do you want to come with us?" he asked my sister.

With her eyes red and swollen, Mary replied, "No, I'll stay." Like our brother, adversity was maturing her.

Huddled together for warmth and comfort, we watched as the unnatural darkness lifted. The crowd drifted away now the main spectacle was over, disappointed that there had been no miracle that day. A soldier ran past with a message for the Centurion, overtaking two well-dressed men, their clothes marking them out as members of the Sanhedrin.

Not wanting to see them I turned my back. "More of them coming to gloat."

"I recognise the older one," Miriam said. "He's one of the Sanhedrin who visited Jesus a few times. He only came at night, because he was afraid someone would recognise him."

The Centurion read his new orders. "It's from Governor Pilate. We're to make sure we finish these three off before nightfall. Something to do with their Jewish religion, they don't want any of these bodies still up here on their Sabbath." He dispatched the soldiers to break the legs of the two criminals, a further injustice, but at least it quickened their suffering to an end.

Pointing to Jesus he said, "Make sure he's dead."

The soldier nearest him took his spear and pushed it under Jesus's ribs at the side. Blood gushed out followed by a clear liquid which looked like water.

"He's dead all right," he confirmed.

The older of the two men approached the Centurion with another written order from Pilate. After a discussion between them, the soldiers took Jesus's lifeless body down from the cross and threw it like a sack of rotten vegetables at the man's feet. Two servants came forward and bent to pick up the body.

"Careful! Pick him up gently," the older man said to the servants. One picked Jesus up under his arms and the other by his feet, and they placed him on a handcart.

I expected no member of the Sanhedrin to treat Jesus with respect, either alive or dead. The younger man looked at us and nodded, recognising that we were with him. We followed the cart down the hill towards the nearby tombs and stopped at a newly hewn tomb in the rock. The servants took the body inside and placed it on the stone ledge and left. Wanting to finish by nightfall and the start of the Sabbath, the men hurriedly wrapped Jesus's body in linen. The sweet smell of myrrh and aloes wafted from inside the tomb where they enclosed these spices between the folds of linen.

"I thank God for these two men and their kindness to Jesus," I wept.

Johanna replied, "Yes, now we know where the tomb is, we can return the day after the Sabbath on Sunday and prepare his body as we should."

The two men, now finished, bent as they vacated the tomb. Solemnly nodding to us again, they left the two servants to push the stone into place. Jesus was alone and lying dead in a stranger's tomb.

Leaning against the wall, Jonas waited for us, picking his teeth. There was no other way but to walk past him. I covered my head with my scarf and looked at the ground instead of his smug face. He followed us through the city walls; I sensed his presence behind me, but when I turned around, he was heading towards the Temple.

Our journey back through the streets to the upstairs room past as if in a dream, or a nightmare. We were in shock as were the disciples when we arrived. With empty eyes and vacant faces, they stared at us. John had told them everything, and I was glad because I couldn't have recounted the details. It was far too traumatic. All I wanted to do was lie down, and as I lay quietly in the dark, images of the day came jumbled and unbidden into my mind.

Jesus had said, "It is finished" and it was. It was over.

CHAPTER 11

Grief hung in the air, heavy and dark as midnight. All of us in the upstairs room were in shock and distraught at having lost the most important person in our lives. It was the loss of everything we held dear. Each one of us had suffered loss and mourned a loved one in our past; I had lost parents, husband and brother, though Jesus had returned Lazarus. But nothing compared to the collective grief and sorrow we felt that day. Not just the heartache of the loss of our leader, rabbi and friend, but the hope which we cherished that Jesus was the one to free his people. That hope lay shattered like the cooking pot I broke on the first day I met him.

Saturday dawned, and we awoke to face a Sabbath without Jesus, and unable to walk back to Bethany on the day of rest, we stayed in the upstairs room. It was not only because of this, but because I recognised that the disciples needed us, as much as we needed them. Normally enjoying the Sabbath rest from chores and work, this day dragged in silence and no one had any appetite for food. Simon sat mute on the floor by the wall, but at least he was no longer facing it. When they did talk, the men bickered and disagreed between themselves as each tried to come to terms with his loss in his own way.

Fear compounded grief. Fear of reprisals and a loud knock on the door and the Temple guards or Roman soldiers bursting in and arresting everyone to share a similar fate to Jesus. We kept the door securely locked and barred, not that this was much protection against the boot of a determined soldier.

I was glad when the sun set to end the Sabbath, and we could go to the market to buy spices. The two men at the tomb had wrapped Jesus's body hurriedly, but we needed to lay him to rest with the dignity he deserved. Hiding our faces in our scarves, Miriam, Johanna and I left the upstairs room and walked to the market through the streets becoming busy after the Sabbath.

Miriam held her scarf over her face and said, "Martha, can you do the talking at the stall? It may arouse suspicion if Johanna and I speak, but you have a local accent." I was walking next to her lost in my own thoughts. "Martha, did you hear me?"

"Sorry, Miriam, did you say something?"

Placing a reassuring hand on my arm she said, "I suggested you should ask for what we need as you are local."

Without the energy to protest and the headache which I had been suffering from since Thursday evening still not improved, I nodded. I took my friends to a stall which I had used before and asked for what we needed.

"I'm sorry for your loss," the burly stallholder said.

Stood at my side, I sensed Miriam tense. "Why do you say we've lost someone?" I asked.

"You wouldn't be buying aloes and myrrh so late if you hadn't. Terrible news at Passover when we need our family and friends around us." He shook his head and handed over the spices.

Johanna gave him the money as I offered my thanks and turned to walk away. The stallholder looked to see if anyone was watching.

"I've seen you with Jesus," he whispered. "Crucifixion is a cruel way for anyone to die, let alone an innocent good man. I heard him speak in the Temple and agreed with what he said. There's a little extra in the package for him." He handed Johanna the money back with a smile. This kindness, shown again by a stranger, made me weep.

Voices raised in anger met us when we returned. "I can't stay here any longer," James cried. "I'm going home tomorrow morning. Who is coming with me back to Galilee? John, we've neglected our fishing business for too long. We can pick it up again." There were murmurs of agreement.

"What have we left to keep us here?" John's voice was bitter with failure. "We might as well go back to our old lives as though nothing has happened these past three years."

"That's decided then, I'm leaving at first light." James looked around. Everyone was nodding.

"No!" I shouted, surprising even myself. "No, don't go. Not yet, wait a couple more days."

"What's the point of staying any longer?" James asked.

"Don't you remember what Jesus said? That he could rebuild the Temple in three days, and you know he was talking about something other than the actual stone Temple."

John opened his arms and sighed. "What do you think will happen? Yesterday I stood alongside you and we watched him die. Do you expect him to turn up and knock at the door?" I'd never heard him speak with such sarcasm and bitterness.

"I don't know what will happen, but give it time," I pleaded through my tears and with a faith I didn't have myself. "Lazarus was dead for four days."

"That's different. Jesus was there to bring him back to life. Who will bring Jesus back to us? Admit it, Martha, he's gone, and the dream is over. Finished! Go and prepare his body in the morning and leave him in the tomb for ever. Then take Mary and Lazarus and go home to Bethany." His words stung.

"I know Jesus is dead, and he's not coming back. He promised something would happen, but I don't know what. Wait a day, just one day, please."

John and James looked at each other, before John shrugged his shoulders. "All right, but only because of our friendship. We go home on Monday."

* * *

Sunday morning dawned, and my sister shook me awake after another fitful night's sleep. This was the third day in a row and my head felt as if it was being crushed from the inside. I groaned as I remembered what I had to do that day. Lazarus opened the door and Johanna, Miriam, Mary and I left in silence before he locked it behind us. The sky was lightening with the promise of a new day, but it would not herald a new dawn for us. I didn't believe my own words to John but wanted him to stay another day. Just in case. But the tension in the depth of my stomach, and because we were carrying spices to anoint his dead body, told me I believed it was an ending, not a beginning.

I walked behind the others in silence with a grave headache and a worse temper. Johanna took my hand and, without speaking, we continued the short walk to the tomb. A wave of nausea hit me when in the slow creep of light, I saw the place of execution. I held onto the city wall to stop myself from falling and tried to blot out the memory of Friday, knowing I could never forget. When we approached the tombs, Miriam stopped.

"We've forgotten something," she said.

"We have the spices and water," Johanna answered.

"No, not that. We've forgotten that the rich men had servants to roll the stone back into place. It's too heavy for us to move on our own."

"I will return to get help to move it," Johanna turned to leave.

Mary had walked ahead, then she halted before running back to grab me. "There's somebody here," she gasped.

"Stay here with Mary," Miriam whispered, and she and Johanna went to investigate.

A minute later they beckoned us to join them. Johanna pointed to the campfire, the embers still glowing. Discarded cloaks and bags surrounded the fire.

Despite her fears, Mary bent to pick something up. "Here's a dagger." She held a short-handled dagger favoured by Temple guards.

"Put it down," I urged.

"No, give it here," Miriam held out her hand. "I don't want to leave it lying on the ground." She slid it inside her bag slung across her shoulders. "There have been soldiers here, but something made them leave in a hurry."

"They must have been guarding the tomb in case someone tried to steal Jesus's body. Jonas will have reported where the tomb was," Johanna answered.

"But why would anyone steal his body?" Mary asked.

"Jesus's claim that he could raise the Temple in three days will have worried the authorities. Maybe they thought he referred to his body or wondered whether we might take his body away," Johanna answered.

Horrified at the prospect of soldiers, I looked around. "Where are they now? Guards don't leave their post, otherwise they face the death penalty."

Mary walked up the slope towards the tomb. "Look!" she shouted, pointing to the entrance. "Someone has rolled the stone to one side."

Without hesitation, I ran towards the darkness of the open tomb. It took a few seconds for my eyes to adjust to the gloom and I saw the shelf where the men had laid Jesus's body was bare. Folded linen strips showed where his body had laid, and lying separately, the cloth which had covered his head.

"Someone has taken him away from me. Why did they have to do that?" At this final ignominy to Jesus, my legs gave way, and I crumbled to my knees putting my head on the shelf where I'd last seen his body. I'd given everything and didn't even have a place to mourn. Sobs racked my entire body and my fists banged the shelf in despair. Broken like my pot, there was nothing left to give.

An unexpected brightness filled the emptiness of the tomb as if lit by the brilliance of the noonday sun. Johanna gripped my shoulder, gasped and fell beside me. In dazzling luminous robes stood what looked like two men, but these were not human. Recognising them as heavenly beings we sank to our knees. One of them spoke, in a thunderous yet gentle voice.

"Why are you here?" No one dared answer. "Why are you here in a tomb when you are looking for someone who is alive? Remember he said he would die and be raised to life on the third day. He is not here, because he is alive."

My heart thumped loudly within my chest, echoing in my ears. Jesus asked me three times to believe him and three times I replied that I did and then failed. And here I was looking for his dead body in a tomb.

With my voice faltering, I said, "Yes, I remember and now fully believe."

As abruptly as they appeared, they vanished, once more shrouding the tomb in darkness. I blinked as my eyes readjusted to the dark and we held our breath, looking at each other in astonishment. The only sound was the beating of our hearts as, speechless, we took in the significance of their words.

"We must tell the others." Mary dashed out of the tomb and ran down the slope.

"Wait," I shouted after her, "we need to go together."

Mary stopped and cried, "Hurry!"

We ran back to the upstairs room, excited to tell the good news. Mary rushed up the stairs ahead of us and burst into the room.

"He's not there," she shouted. "There were two angels who said he's alive."

Open-mouthed, the disciples looked at me for confirmation of Mary's story.

"Yes, that happened. Jesus is not dead he's alive," I panted, trying to catch my breath.

"Did you see him?" James asked.

"The angels said he's alive," Mary answered. "The strips of grave linen are lying folded on the shelf."

"But did you see him?" James asked again.

"No," I replied, "but I now believe I will."

John bolted out of the room. Simon rose from the spot on the floor where he had sat for three days and ran after him. The sound of their footsteps was heavy as they bounded down the stairs and out into the street. Miriam turned and followed them.

Jesus's mother approached me. "Is this true, he's alive and not dead?" Her eyes glistened with tears. I put my arms around her and told her everything that had happened. A short time later John and Simon returned.

"John got there first and stood at the entrance but didn't go inside." It was good to hear Simon's voice again. "I pushed past and crept in and he followed. Just as you said, we found it empty, except for the grave linen and cloths. But there were no angels. We looked around the campfire and there was no one there."

"Is it true?" John said more to himself than anyone else. "Is he alive? If he is, where is he? I want to see him to be certain. He was definitely dead. Roman soldiers don't make those mistakes; they wouldn't have taken the body off the cross and given it to the two men unless they were positive."

"Did you see Miriam?" I asked.

"Yes, she said she wanted time on her own," Simon replied.

Miriam could look after herself, but I was glad when a knock at the door announced she was back. A different woman returned from the one who left a short time before. Her face glowed, highlighting the tears cascading down her cheeks. As I clasped her shaking hands in mine, she smiled, and her eyes shone.

"I saw him," her voice barely more than a whisper.

Simon took her hands. "What happened Miriam?"

By then her whole body was shaking, and she grabbed hold of him to steady herself. He guided her towards a chair and asked for a drink, telling everyone to move away. After a few sips, Miriam calmed down enough to talk.

"When John and Simon left, I felt lost and returned to the tomb where I met the two angels again. 'Why are you crying?' one asked. 'You told me Jesus is alive but where is he? I need to see him.' I replied.

"The air in the tomb was stuffy, and I walked out into the sunshine past a man with his back to me. I thought he was the gardener who looks after the tombs. 'Who are you looking for?' he asked. 'Have you taken Jesus's body away? Where have you put him? I need to find him,' I said, and when he didn't answer I turned to leave.

"'Miriam!' That's all it took for me to recognise him. That one word. My name. I ran and flung my arms around him, but he told me not to cling and to go back to you with this message, that I have seen him and he's alive. I have seen Jesus, and he's alive! Jesus is alive!"

She jumped out of her chair, laughing and shouting. "I have seen him. Jesus is alive, and I've seen him!" I joined in the laughter and hugged her, as did my sister. Johanna embraced Jesus's mother, and they both cried with happiness. Impassive, the men watched, silent at Miriam's news. Even Simon and John who had seen the empty tomb were unconvinced, their faces lifeless.

Realising that we had not eaten for three days, we prepared a meal for everyone. After eating, there were long arguments as to the events of the morning. Many of the disciples were still sceptical even after Miriam's account. Amongst them Thomas, who insisted that Jesus couldn't be alive. Thomas had family living in Jerusalem and left to visit them, saying he would return later. The lamps were lit, and the discussions continued into the evening. Engrossed in our conversation we didn't notice someone appear inside the locked room until a voice spoke in greeting.

"Peace to you!" It was a voice we recognised and loved.

At once the conversation stilled; all was silent apart from a stray dog barking outside. I turned to the sound of the voice, and there he was, standing in front of us as if nothing had happened. It was an indescribable moment. No mere words of mine can adequately express what I felt. I forgot to breathe until, breaking the silence, Matthew whispered.

"It's Jesus's ghost."

"Why are you frightened of me?" Jesus looked at the open mouths. "You still don't believe the evidence of your own eyes. Why did you not believe Miriam? Or Martha, Johanna and Mary when they said they had seen an empty tomb and gave you the angel's message? Look at my hands and feet." He showed us his wounds, still scarred from the executioner's nails. "Touch me and make sure I'm no ghost." No one moved. "James, pass me that dish with the leftover fish."

Without taking his eyes off Jesus, James held out the dish and Jesus picked up a piece of fish and ate it in front of everyone. James reached out a trembling hand and touched Jesus's arm and, squeezing, found it was solid. This was no phantom.

"This isn't a ghost, he's real." The dish in James's hand shook.

At that, everyone crowded around talking all at once and reaching out to touch Jesus. Everyone except Simon, who slunk back to the wall, fear etched on his face.

John left Jesus's side to fetch his friend, and said, "Come and see Jesus." Simon shook his head.

"Where's Simon?" Jesus asked. John dragged him towards Jesus.

"I'm sorry for the things I said about you on the night of your arrest," Simon mumbled,

"Look at me," Jesus said, but Simon continued to stare at the floor. "Simon, look at me." When Simon raised his head to meet Jesus's eyes, he grabbed hold of him. "I forgive you, Simon. We'll talk more about this soon."

The disciples parted as Johanna brought his mother to him. Jesus stretched out his hand and wiped a tear from her cheek with his thumb; no words were necessary between mother and son.

He turned to me and said, "Thank you, Martha, for keeping everyone here today."

Rushing to him, I grabbed his hands in mine and felt his warmth, now believing I had him back again after losing him to death. This was now the second time I had someone dear brought back from the tomb. His face, which I had last seen wearing the grey mask of death, was transformed like the rest of his body. Ruddy cheeks glowed, his lips flushed red, and the spark of life had returned to his eyes.

"I'm sorry I lost faith in you again."

Jesus held onto both my shoulders and smiled. "I forgive you," he said.

All shame of my unbelief left, and a giggle started in my stomach. When I could contain it no longer, it erupted from my mouth. Soon everyone was laughing along with me. Once we had all touched and spoken to Jesus, he taught us as he had done many times before.

"You won't have me with you like this for long, but I'll see you a few more times before I leave."

After this, he left as suddenly as he appeared and, excited, we talked all at once, until a knock at the door silenced us.

"Thomas!" James said after he had opened the door. "You've just missed him."

"Missed who?" Thomas asked with a scowl.

"Jesus!" shouted James with a laugh.

"You are as bad as the women this morning," Thomas scoffed.

James opened his arms wide. "I wouldn't joke about this. Jesus isn't dead, and he's been here this evening."

"I'll only believe if I see him with my own eyes, touch his hands where the nails have been, and put my hand in the wound the spear made." With that Thomas slung his bag on the floor.

"He promised he'll come back," James said. "Then you can do just that."

"Jesus promised to return the first time we met," I said to Thomas. "He came back to me then and he'll come back to you."

CHAPTER 12

It was with lighter hearts and clear heads that we slept that evening. All thought of going back to our old lives was forgotten. In the morning, Lazarus asked if he could stay in the upstairs room, to which John agreed, while I returned to Bethany with the women. The following days at home were quiet and we remained inside, resting after the trauma and excitement of the previous week. Every day two of us walked into Jerusalem to take food and check on the disciples, who stayed in the safety of the upstairs room. They discussed Jesus's life and teachings in the light of his death and resurrection, and the things he taught during his visit on Sunday. Together, they read the Scriptures and sang psalms and songs. Lazarus was excited to hear everything and asked many questions.

"It's important," Lazarus explained one morning when I was in the upstairs room, "that we remember accurately what Jesus has said. Not only in Bethany, but in the other towns and villages too. The time is coming soon when we need to pass on his teachings, and we have to be ready." I detected a new seriousness in my young brother.

Each morning, Johanna and Miriam offered to collect water so Mary and I wouldn't meet either Jonas or Rebekah at the well. One week after Jesus's death they had gone into

Jerusalem when I noticed that the pitcher was empty. I thought I might risk a trip to the well during the quiet of the afternoon when most people were resting indoors. Making sure no one was by the well, I ran out of the gate, filled my pitcher and returned the short distance to find a grinning Jonas leaning on the wall. With no way to avoid him, he waited for his chance to pounce.

"Well, well, look who it is. Have your precious Messiah's cronies run back to where they came from with their tails between their legs?" He laughed. "You backed the wrong man. If you'd taken up my offer, you'd be safe. But it's too late, my brother is now married and won't be here when you need him to protect you. Admit it, you've lost."

Realising I was no longer afraid, I met his eyes. "On the contrary, Jonas, I have lost nothing. In fact, I've gained everything I need."

Jonas shrugged his shoulders and looked surprised that I should stand up to him. "Jesus has gone, and you'll never see him again."

After the events of Sunday, this comment struck me as ludicrous, and I began laughing.

"What's so funny?" He asked.

"You'll never understand that no one can get rid of a man like Jesus. No matter how hard you try."

"There's one less in his gang now because one of his closest disciples betrayed him."

"You're not telling me anything new."

"I bet you don't know he took money to betray him. It was me who approached him first and introduced him to the Sanhedrin when he agreed to their deal. He sold his Messiah for thirty silver coins and was desperate to get his hands on the money. Then being filled with remorse after Jesus got what was coming to him, he flung the coins back at the Chief Priest. Not being able to take the shame of what he'd done, he hung himself yesterday. Stupid man. If you'll betray a friend for a reward you should at least enjoy it." Jonas finished his story with a shrug and then stepped aside to let me pass.

This news was upsetting, and we discussed it over the evening meal. We stayed at home during the Saturday Sabbath and on Sunday morning returned to Jerusalem together. I'd arrived at the upstairs room and taken my bag off my shoulder when a young man approached with Lazarus.

"Martha, do you remember Stefanos?" It took a moment to place him, but then a loud laugh and the large frame of Barnabas reminded me they had escorted Mary, Miriam and Johanna to our home. They introduced another man with them as Philip.

This young man was a friend of Stefanos and Barnabas who had followed Jesus alongside them. He was an intelligent and caring man, ready to do anything asked of him.

"We've stayed with my family here in Jerusalem, but when we heard about Jesus's appearance last week, decided that we should come here today," Stefanos explained.

"I've unsettling news," I told everyone, "and I'm not sure what to make of it. Jonas told me that the Sanhedrin paid Judas thirty silver coins for information about Jesus which led to his arrest."

"Judas looked after the money given to aid our ministry, and I suspected he took a percentage for himself. When I mentioned this to Jesus, he said he already knew and told me not to say anything," Johanna added.

"He was always more interested in how much money we had in the purse than anything else." Matthew's voice was bitter with hurt. "Where is he now? Cosying up to the Temple priests I suppose."

"No, far worse than that," I said. "When he found out Jesus was dead, he threw the money back in their faces, and then …" I struggled to say the words, "then he hung himself."

There was an intake of breath, before Andrew said, "Good, he deserved to die, and better at his own hand after what he did to Jesus."

Simon shook his head. "I feel sorry for Judas. What's the difference between him and me? I betrayed Jesus too."

Andrew disagreed with his brother. "You didn't give the Sanhedrin any information they could use against Jesus."

"And you didn't steal from us," Matthew added.

"But I refused to acknowledge I'd even met Jesus and, to my shame, even cursed him. Why didn't Judas come back here? Jesus would've forgiven him as he forgave me, and he could still have been one of our group."

Mary screamed, "Jesus is here!"

We turned away from our conversation to see him standing there, and in our excitement we talked all at once.

"Where's Thomas?" Jesus asked. A stunned Thomas came forward. His mouth moved, but no words came out. "Come here, Thomas. Look at my hands. Can you see the marks where the nails were? Put your finger there and feel it. See my side and the hole the spear made."

Thomas found his voice and, falling in front of Jesus, said, "I'm sorry Jesus. You are my Lord and my God." Jesus helped him to his feet and, with his arm around Thomas's shoulders, looked around at everyone.

"Do you only believe because you've seen me? It will be far better for those who believe I'm alive without seeing me. Come, Thomas, let's sit and talk together."

* * *

After being cooped up in the upstairs room for three weeks, the men travelled to Galilee. Normally so active, their enforced stay in the stuffy room had not done their health or their friendships any good. Johanna returned home to see her family, and the days for us were quiet. Our lives reverted to the sedate pace they had before I met Jesus. At first, I enjoyed the peaceful reflection, but I soon tired of this and yearned for the busyness of being with Jesus and the disciples.

One week later, a knock on the gate announced their return, and they tumbled into the courtyard, tired and dusty after their journey from Galilee.

Miriam greeted them with a smile. "You look well. The walk has done you good."

A hint of red in the cheeks replaced their pale faces, and the exercise and fresh air after the stale air of the upstairs room had revitalised them. As many times before, they relaxed as Mary brought out wine and water, and drank deeply to refresh themselves after the long journey. Simon sat in the shade and closed his eyes, appearing more his usual self than he had since the evening of Jesus's arrest.

James took a cup from Mary. "We met with Jesus, but I'll leave Simon to tell the story."

Dusk arrived and, as the early summer heat dissipated, we sat in comfortable companionship, reminding me of the many times we had sat under the grapevine arbour with Jesus. The loss of his presence was huge, and with a pang, I missed the times we spent together in this courtyard. When Simon was ready, he began his story.

"I was despondent," he started.

James laughed. "Despondent! You were in a pit of depression."

It was good to hear Simon laugh again. "Yes, I'd fallen into a pit of depression, but with good reason. I couldn't forget my denial of Jesus, and was incapable of forgiving myself, even after he forgave me. The news of Judas's suicide hurt and only reminded me we'd both betrayed him. Inconsolable, I wondered whether death could be a way out for me too. I've always had far too high an opinion of myself, but I was knocked down by my own arrogant behaviour, and felt unworthy to be called a disciple.

"The old family boat lay on the lakeshore and, still feeling low, I longed to be out night-fishing on the water again. Andrew and I pushed the boat into the water as the others jumped in. After three years away, it was fabulous being back on the lake in the moonlight as the wind caught the sails. I hadn't forgotten how to fish, except that we couldn't catch even the smallest tiddler. The sky was lightening when we gave up and returned home. Then John saw a man on the shore standing by a fire. 'Have you caught anything?' he called out.

"Disgruntled that a stranger should shout out, I called back that our nets were empty. He suggested we throw our net on the other side of the boat. Cold and hungry, I was in no mood to do what the stranger suggested. But, ever the optimist, James threw the net over the other side and almost at once it filled with fish. The net was so full we couldn't haul it into the boat and had to row to shore with the net still over the side.

"John shouted that it was Jesus. Excited, I couldn't wait for the boat to get to shore and dived overboard to swim the short distance to where he stood on the beach. I ran to him and warmed and dried myself by the fire, hungry with the smell of the breakfast he was cooking. Once the boat was on the shore, Jesus asked for fish. I ran back, helped to haul in the catch, and took fresh fish for Jesus to put over the fire. He gave us the fish he had already cooked, along with bread, and it tasted fantastic. The best breakfast I've ever had. Soon, feeling full and warm, we sat by the fire, talking to Jesus.

"Loud enough for everyone to hear, Jesus asked, 'Simon, do you truly love me?' I replied that I cared for him and he told me to look after of his lambs. After a short silence, he asked again, 'Simon, do you truly love me?' and again I said I liked him. He replied, 'Take care of my sheep.' This was the strangest conversation I've had with Jesus.

"For a third time he looked directly into my eyes and asked, 'Simon, do you like me?' It upset me he should ask three times whether I loved him. This time I replied, 'Jesus, you know everything, and you know how much I sincerely love you.' Jesus told me again to feed his lambs. He then said, 'Listen, I'll tell you the truth. When you were young, you dressed yourself and decided where to go. But when you become old, someone else will dress you and take you to where you don't want to go. Just follow me.'

"Not understanding, I asked what would happen to John. Jesus replied that it was nothing to do with me whether he should live a long life. What I had to do was follow him. After this Jesus disappeared, and we were alone again. Later, James counted the catch, and we'd caught one hundred and fifty-three large fish without a single tear in the net. I've been fishing all my life and never caught so many. We gave the fish to our families which will bring in enough money to feed them for a while. The following day we returned here."

Quiet for a moment, we considered Jesus's words to Simon, until John spoke. "We discussed it on the way back here and wondered what Jesus meant."

"You had good ideas. Tell us what you thought," James said to his brother.

"Three times Jesus asked how much you loved him," John stood and walked over to Simon. "Tell me, how many times did you say you didn't know Jesus the night of his arrest?"

Simon closed his eyes and whispered, "Three."

"He knows your love for him is sincere. But it was three times by the fire in Caiaphas's courtyard, you denied him, so by the fire on the beach he asked you the same question three times. He gave you instructions to feed and care for the sheep like a shepherd looks after the flock, and how Jesus looked after us." John raised Simon to his feet. "What Jesus is saying is that you are still the man you no longer consider yourself to be. You are now our leader and we will follow you."

With tears in his eyes, Simon shook his head. "No, no I'm not your leader. John, you're a much better choice, I'd follow you."

"Jesus didn't say this to me," John replied. "He said it to you. You are his choice."

"I cannot do this."

"Yes, you can, and we'll help and support you," John said to murmurs of agreement.

Simon didn't look as convinced as the rest of us that he was Jesus's choice for our leader, but everyone agreed with John. This reminded me of my own lack of faith. I'd said I believed three times and, like Simon, had failed three times. Simon had a new role; would Jesus have a plan for me too?

* * *

One morning a few days later, I arrived at the upstairs room with bread for the day ahead. Deep in conversation, Jesus's mother sat holding the hands of two young men whom I didn't recognise. With their heads close together, they listened with serious expressions and nodding heads. When Mary saw me, she beckoned me over.

"Martha, I want to introduce Jacob and Joseph, my sons."

Mary had told me of her children's antagonism towards Jesus, and I was surprised to meet two of his brothers. Jacob stood when I approached.

"Thank you for looking after our mother," he said. "She has high regard for you and your family and has told us how well you care for her."

"It's a pleasure," I replied, embarrassed by Mary's praise.

Mary patted Jacob's arm, her eyes bright. "After hearing of Jesus's death, and worried for my safety, my sons travelled to Jerusalem to find me. But as they can see, I'm well cared for and happy."

"We intended to take our mother back home to Nazareth, and we were arguing about this when ..." With a shake of the head and outstretched arms, Jacob paused, not sure how to continue.

"... when our brother appeared in front of us." Wide-eyed, Joseph filled in for Jacob. "It wasn't what we expected when we arrived."

Jacob continued, "Mother claimed Jesus was alive and that everyone here had seen and spoken to him several times. Not believing her, we supposed you were suffering from delusion or mass hysteria when he ..." Jacob shrugged, "he appeared and asked us to sit and talk with him. Dumbfounded, this time we listened instead of arguing."

"We didn't understand when Jesus left home to be a wandering preacher," Joseph said, "and dismissed the tales of his teaching and miraculous healings as make-believe. His responsibility as the eldest son was to care for our mother and the family business. Jesus was shirking his obligations, and I took every opportunity to tell him so. By last year the family agreed he was going insane and refused to speak to him further. There was no chance I could accept what he was saying, as mother did."

"That's now changed." Mary glanced into the faces of her two sons and squeezed their hands.

"Shocked is the only word to describe how we feel now," Jacob said. "What we have just seen has turned our beliefs upside down and we need time to consider what has happened."

John approached. "You're welcome to stay here and take as much time as you need. There must be many questions which we'll try to answer."

Jacob and Joseph stayed in the upstairs room for three days before returning to Nazareth, leaving their mother once more in our safekeeping.

* * *

Just after dawn in the cool of the morning, we arrived at the Mount of Olives. Jesus told us to meet him there and people made their way along the path from Jerusalem. He had appeared to all of us over the previous six weeks since that first Sunday we saw him alive after his death. Over five hundred people saw him alive, and many gathered together in anticipation that morning. I'd brought breakfast and gave it out as they arrived, excited and chatting as if it was a festival. A figure waved at me from the path and I took a moment to realise that it was Lazarus, who seemed to have grown in stature.

"Martha," he shouted running up the hill, "I met with Jesus last night and he took me to one side and said he saved me for a reason. Whatever the future holds and whatever happens to us, we are to keep our faith in him. We mustn't forget all we've learned, because when the time is right, each one of us will become teachers and leaders in the new faith. Where's Mary? I must tell her." Lazarus ran off towards Mary, calling her name.

"He's a special young man." I turned around to see Barnabas stood with Stefanos.

I smiled at his praise of my brother. "He has his moments, I suppose."

Barnabas patted me on my shoulder. "You can be proud of him and his sister."

"He's here!"

Simon's voice echoed above the noise we were making. At once we hurried towards Jesus and gathered around the rocky outcrop where he stood. With the scars of the nails still on his hands and feet, his face now shone with life. Our mutterings ceased when he spoke.

"I don't want you to leave Jerusalem for the moment, stay where you are and wait for the promise the Father will give you. Soon the Holy Spirit will fill you to overflowing. Wait here in Jerusalem because this will happen soon."

Simon raised his hand to touch Jesus and shouted, "Is it time to restore God's rule on the earth? Are you going to kick the Romans out?"

We cheered, expecting the same as Simon. To see this would be glorious.

Jesus shook his head. "Simon, it's not for you to know the time or date the Father has planned for these things." Opening his arms, he looked around at everyone assembled on the hill. "When the Holy Spirit comes, he will give you the power to do the tasks which my Father will give you. Each of you is an eyewitness to my death and resurrection and you are to tell everyone the good news of the salvation I offer.

"Start here in Jerusalem, then go to Judea, into Samaria and finally spread out to the ends of the earth. You're to go to every nation in the world to make new disciples and to baptise them in the name of the Father, the Son and the Holy Spirit. Remember to teach them everything I've taught you. Don't stress or worry in case you are not good enough because I'll always be with you wherever you go."

As he finished these final words, a cloud descended and hid him from us. Shielding my eyes with my hand, I gazed to where I had last seen him. Lost for words, no one spoke until a voice behind caused us to turn around. The same two heavenly beings I had met at the tomb, stood on the hill.

"Why are you still looking into the sky?" one asked. "Jesus has now gone to heaven. One day he will come back in the same as way as he has left." With that, they too disappeared.

I then understood I would never see Jesus's face again until I joined him in death. We remained on the Mount of Olives, discussing everything in hushed tones until dusk. When the skies darkened, we returned home to wait as Jesus had commanded us.

We waited for Jesus's promise to arrive. This was no futile wait in the hope of something we could barely expect. Like a pregnant woman, we waited in anticipation for the day it would arrive. No longer behind locked doors, but out in the open of the Temple precincts, we prayed and worshipped in expectation of the promise.

CHAPTER 13

I've always had little patience. I consider waiting a waste of time and become frustrated when I must wait for something, especially when I don't know why I'm waiting. Many others were growing impatient too and wondered how long we had to wait for Jesus's promise, and I was chief amongst them.

The dim light of the early dawn caused me to open my eyes, and the loss of Jesus's presence was palpable that morning, as every morning since his death. On his last day, Jesus promised to be with us, but there was still an emptiness inside. I shed a silent tear as I stared at the familiar ceiling because I wouldn't see him that day. Whatever Jesus had promised could never match up to being with him. I'd lost something precious and didn't even know where to search for it.

It was the morning of the festival of Pentecost, and we were to go to the Temple to thank God for the harvest. Without waking anyone, I wiped my eyes, dressed and prepared breakfast. Miriam and Johanna were staying in Bethany with us and as the sun rose, we walked into Jerusalem. I followed them, watching our shadows shorten.

"Martha, you're doing it again," Miriam observed.

"Doing what?" I asked.

"Staring," laughed Johanna, "just walking and staring."

"I'm not just staring, I'm thinking."

"She shouts at me when I say that, then tells me to stop daydreaming and get on with my work," said Mary.

"But I am thinking." I joined in with their laughter. "Today is ten days since Jesus left. He promised us a gift, and I'm impatient to know what the gift is and when it will come."

Miriam stopped beside me. "I was with Jesus once and he told a story about a father and his family. His son was playing outside in the street one morning and by lunchtime became hungry. The boy ran home to find his father and asked him for a piece of bread. Now, the boy's father was a good man who loved his children, and Jesus asked us whether he would give him a stone instead of bread."

"If he did, his son's teeth might break," Mary said.

Miriam continued, "And a stone is not filling for a hungry boy. Now, the father also had a daughter, and one morning, she skipped up to him and asked for a fish for lunch. Would her good father serve up a live slithering snake on a plate?"

Mary shivered. "I'm glad my father never gave me a snake."

Miriam smiled. "So, if our fathers know how to give us good gifts, think how much more our Father in heaven wants to give us even better gifts."

"Do you remember, Martha," Mary asked, "whenever our father went on a trip, he always brought us back a gift? We couldn't wait for him to return."

"Mary and Lazarus used to watch from the roof and shout when they saw him coming. Then we ran downstairs and would pick up our sewing or pretend to cook and look busy when he arrived home. He'd always make us wait patiently for our treat until he'd eaten. If Jesus called his

Father Abba, then his gift must be far better than a stone or a snake."

"You're still no better at waiting, are you?" Mary asked taking my arm.

"No! I wish he would hurry."

Continuing our journey, we arrived at the Temple courts and pushed our way through the throngs of people to meet with Lazarus who had stayed in the upstairs room. It had become our habit to meet each day in the Temple or the upstairs room and that morning, we gathered together in a large group of over one hundred and twenty. I've often visited the Temple, and that day was like the many others before it. People congregated in small groups and, talking loudly or shouting, they conducted business deals or bought sacrifices. From around the Roman Empire, pilgrims and local Jews gathered for the morning prayers.

It was still early when this normal festival day at the Temple shifted abruptly, and heaven's door opened. It started as a soft barely audible whisper, the sound of a gentle breeze wafting through the branches of an olive tree. Puzzled, I looked up, because there were no olive trees in the Temple.

"Where's the wind coming from?" Mary said, looking up and holding onto her headscarf.

By this time the sound was so loud, Johanna had to shout. "What is happening? There is no wind, and nothing is being blown around."

Mary let go of her headscarf and it didn't move. People around us were holding onto their scarves and robes as if scared they would blow away, but there was no wind. The noise reverberated around the walls of the court, increasing in volume until it became a crescendo. Still no clothing or litter blew around the court. Without warning, the sound stopped; the quiet was as deafening as the noise.

With the sound ringing in my ears, a tingling sensation coursed through my body and I knew God had touched me. Equally stunned, everyone looked at one another for reassurance. Seconds later a brilliant flash of bright light and flames appeared above our heads. Everyone in the court looked up at the swirling mass of light and flames above us.

Mary tried to look up into the light. "It's so bright." She shielded her eyes with her hand and screamed as a flame of fire and light fell on her. With a jolt, it hit me.

"Martha," Johanna shook my shoulders, "Martha, breathe!"

In between gasps, I said, "My heart is bursting open."

"Mine too. God has filled it. Jesus is here!"

Birthed in the pit of my stomach, a giggle rose through my chest and I held my hands over my mouth trying to keep it in. When I could no longer contain it, a hearty laugh escaped from my mouth. I had felt the physical touch of Jesus.

"I've not laughed since the day Jesus left," I giggled.

Johanna wasn't listening, she was on her knees next to Mary who was standing with her arms up to heaven. John and James were holding onto each other to stop themselves falling over and Simon was crying and calling out the name of Jesus. A crowd surrounded us, trying to look over one another's shoulders, some laughing and pointing at us, others open-mouthed in surprise. I approached a woman standing nearby, hoping to explain who we were, but the words came out wrong. With intent, she listened and nodded her head, but I was totally unaware of what I was saying: it wasn't Hebrew or Aramaic, neither was it Greek, which I knew a little of. Two men near me sniggered, and one imitated holding a wineskin to his mouth and glugging it, staggering as if drunk. His friend laughed and pointed to us. Ignoring them, Mary grabbed my shoulders, and we embraced, both of us laughing and crying.

She shouted above the noise, "I've felt Jesus again, he's come back."

Deep in conversation, Simon, Miriam, John and James huddled together, and Miriam called me over.

"Why me?" Simon asked.

"It's got to be you, Simon," John told him.

"Because you have the biggest mouth," James laughed.

"What my brother means is you have got the loudest voice."

Miriam took Simon's arm. "Jesus appointed you as our leader, and he's now filled you with his Spirit."

"Simon," I said, "look around you. Everyone is straining their necks to see us because they want to know what's happened this morning. There's never been a better time to speak to them."

With a hand on Simon's back, John pushed him forward in front of our group. "Besides, you do have the loudest voice."

"Friends," Simon coughed and looked back to John who nodded again. "Friends, take note of what we'll tell you this morning." The crowd became silent, craning their necks above those in front to get a better view. He took a deep breath and continued.

"Don't think for one moment we're drunk, because it's only nine o'clock in the morning. There hasn't been time to drink that much, besides the wine stalls aren't even open yet." The crowd laughed, warming to Simon. "No, what's just happened is that God has visited us, to fill us with his Holy Spirit, and now his very presence is with us. God said long ago through our prophets that one day he'll pour his Spirit out on ordinary men and women, and that's what you saw this morning."

Simon had spent three years listening to Jesus and observing him teaching, and now it was his turn. The crowd listened to him as intently as they had listened to Jesus. John looked over and smiled, proud of Simon and his new ability to speak to the crowd with boldness. There weren't many people in the Temple that day who hadn't either seen Jesus themselves or heard about him. The manner of his death and rumours of his resurrection had spread, and the events of that morning had made many afraid.

"Everyone here knows about Jesus from Nazareth, and many of you were here when he taught and performed miracles in this Temple. Some of you saw him crucified and killed in a cruel and degrading way. But what you may not know is that this wasn't a mistake but part of God's prearranged plan. Jesus didn't stay dead, and everyone in our group here today and many others saw him afterwards. He walked among us, not as a ghost, but a real person, and now he has filled us with his Spirit. I'm telling you now, so you will know for certain, that God has made Jesus both our Lord and Messiah."

The crowd gasped, and a man's voice shouted out, "If that's true what do we need to do now?"

"Each one of you must search within yourself and say sorry for your wrongdoing before God. Turn your face towards him and ask his forgiveness. Then we will baptise you in the name of Jesus our Saviour and he'll fill you with the Holy Spirit as you have seen happen to us."

The crowd shouted and surrounded Simon, saying they wanted to do just that. There was great excitement, and the large number of people responding to him overwhelmed us. They shouted out and asked to join our group as followers of Jesus. Simon had spoken with confidence, the shadow of the man he became after he betrayed Jesus now gone, never to return. For the rest of the morning, we talked to people, praying and baptising them in many of the pools surrounding the Temple.

By midday, it was time to leave and, in small groups, we returned to the upstairs room. Johanna covered her face with her scarf and elbowed me as we arrived at the passage to take us out into the street. Lined up along the wall were four Temple priests standing mute with pursed lips and narrow eyes.

"They do not look happy." Johanna took my elbow and hurried me through the tunnel.

I looked back as they huddled together and pointed towards Simon and John who were still in the Temple court.

"Do you think they saw everything?" I asked.

"They would have to be blind and deaf to miss it," Johanna said and then laughed. "I feel sorry for them."

Surprised at her comment I asked, "Why do you say that?"

"Because they thought they had done away with Jesus at Passover and then seven weeks later at Pentecost, we turn up and cause trouble again. I wonder what they will do now?"

We mused on this on the way back to the upstairs room and soon everyone returned, excited to talk about that morning. By then it was past the time of the midday meal and we were all hot, tired and thirsty. Over a meal, the talk turned to the events of the day.

John slapped Simon on the back. "Well done Simon, you delivered a powerful speech, and I'm proud of you speaking to such a large crowd. Jesus was right, you now have no reason to feel ashamed."

"What a day." Simon sighed and drained a large cup of wine and water. "There has never been a day like today in the history of our people."

James helped himself to a drink. "This day is unique, and when I saw the flames coming down, I thought we'd die. I was so awestruck; I didn't look at what was happening with anyone else."

"We were talking on the walk back here," I said, "about the story of our people, when God freed us from slavery in Egypt. He led Moses and the people through the desert by a pillar of cloud during the day and fire during the night. That is how Moses knew where to lead his people."

Simon agreed. "I hadn't made that connection between the fire and God's leading. Jesus has filled us with his presence and will lead us as he always has."

John said, "Yes, Simon, and we can all agree this is the gift Jesus promised to send us."

"Who's disappointed?" James asked.

"Not even Martha!" Mary shouted.

"I'm not disappointed at all. It's the best gift I've ever had."

Simon shrugged. "The only question is, what do we do now?" No one spoke because, along with Simon, no one had any thoughts on how we should carry on God's work.

John spoke up. "We've had a busy, exhilarating yet tiring day. Why don't we agree to meet tomorrow at the Mount of Olives where we can decide what to do next?"

Agreeing with John to meet in the morning, we left to return to Bethany, and Lazarus came home with us. After a hectic day, a calm descended upon us and we were happy to walk together in companionable silence.

CHAPTER 14

Something was different. Awaking from a deep sleep, I noticed my breathing and listened to the silence. No longer weighed down by loss and despair, something had changed, and I realised it was me. I was changed by the experience of the day before. Jesus was more real at that moment than I had known at any other time. Looking at the patterns the light made on my ceiling and the dust motes shimmering and dancing, I giggled as if someone had told me the funniest joke.

"Martha, what's so funny?" Mary turned over and opened one eye. "I was asleep."

I replied, "I don't know why I'm laughing. It's as if something is bursting out of me!"

"Can't it burst somewhere else?" Mary said before she laughed along with me. "Now you've started me off."

"We must get up because today will be busy and I want to get an early start." I rolled over, and tried to rise out of my bed, but fell again, giggling helplessly.

"What is happening in here?" Johanna stood in the doorway, smiling at us.

"It's Martha's fault, she's giggling, and I couldn't help but join in."

For once Mary blaming me was amusing. I stopped laughing long enough to pull the bed covers to one side. Tears fell onto my cheeks, unbidden but welcome, and I wiped them away with my hand. I tried to speak again.

"I cannot explain why I'm laughing so much. This happened yesterday."

Johanna nodded. "You are right, I woke up feeling the same as yesterday. Perhaps this is permanent."

"If these giggles don't subside soon, I won't get any work done."

"And what is wrong with that, Martha?" Johanna laughed.

Still giggling, Mary crawled on the floor to find her clothes, and continuing to chortle, I dressed and went downstairs with Johanna laughing behind me. In between fits of laughter, in which Miriam and Lazarus now joined, we prepared food and drink and carried them to the meeting place. The plan was to meet under the olive trees before the sun heated the land.

I placed the heavy bag of food on the ground. "We're the first here," I said.

Miriam looked up at the blue sky. "I'm glad we agreed to meet early. There's hardly a breeze today." She wiped her forehead on her sleeve.

"They're coming!" Mary spotted the others arriving and ran down the hill with Lazarus to meet them, walking back with Barnabas and Stefanos. After greeting one another they agreed with Johanna that the feelings from the day before had not gone away.

When we were all assembled, Simon stood on a rock and had to clap his hands to get everyone's attention. "Hush, can we have quiet please?" When everyone stopped talking, he continued. "I know the events of yesterday are very exciting and we are trying to work out what happened. But having three thousand people join us in one day has created rather a problem. To be honest, I'm not sure what to do next. How are we going to incorporate so many new people into our group?"

John stood beside Simon. "You have all been invited here this morning because you are disciples and saw Jesus's resurrection. We need a plan to help the new believers learn more of Jesus and his teachings and become part of our family." Looking around at the group of nearly fifty people he continued, "A decision has to made today so we can continue our work."

After Simon prayed, we debated many ideas of what we could do and after an hour we broke for refreshment. Then John called us together again.

"After a good discussion earlier, we must now make a decision. Martha, you've said nothing yet." Surprised, I stared at him and wondered why I should have anything to contribute. "We were with Jesus many times in your home. Can you remember back to those times and think of how that could help us?"

Thinking for a moment I said, "Well, we always shared a meal, and this is important because that's what families do. After we had eaten, Jesus called us together, and we sat around him while he taught us."

"John, I know what else we did." Mary wanted to add her thoughts. "Jesus always prayed, and we sang psalms and songs together. I want to carry on singing our songs and we could write new ones."

"We read the scriptures too," Lazarus shouted.

Simon summarised the discussion. "We have no pattern except that taught us by Jesus. Martha, Lazarus and Mary are right in what they say, and we have all experienced the things they describe. There's no reason we should do anything different. We will continue to meet at the Temple and in the upstairs room and any larger houses we have, such as Martha's in Bethany.

"When we meet, we will share a meal, then pray, sing, read the scriptures and teach the things we heard from Jesus and tell his stories. We will share bread and wine as Jesus did at our last supper together on the evening before he died. In these ways, we will continue to imitate Jesus in everything we do."

There were murmurs of approval at the wisdom of this decision, and we departed to our homes in excitement at the thought that this was the beginning of an adventure. However, it was one far bigger than we could have understood that morning. Each day we gathered in the Temple and spoke to any who would listen. Daily, our numbers increased as people from Jerusalem and Judea, and pilgrims from throughout the Roman Empire became believers. Many gave money or sold properties to help feed those who were in need, including Barnabas, who sold a field which he owned. We started to refer to Simon, John, James and the other closest disciples as apostles. We knew that Jesus had commissioned them as his envoys and sent them to tell everyone the good news. They were his apostles to the world.

Several new believers gathered in my home, and as agreed, we continued to eat communal meals and share our food with those who were hungry and in need. During our meals, we remembered Jesus's death and resurrection by sharing the wine and bread. We prayed and sang psalms, read our scriptures and discussed Jesus's teachings. My life was changing in ways I didn't understand, and I felt like a chick flapping my wings on the edge of her nest. Soon I would have to jump and hope I flew and did not crash to the ground.

* * *

There was a continual flow of people through our home and the group continued to grow as new friends and family members joined. We met in the courtyard or the inside room and John or one of the other apostles would share Jesus's teachings. One afternoon towards the end of summer, a familiar voice from outside the gate announced Barnabas's arrival.

"John asks whether you, Lazarus and Mary would lead the group this evening?" he asked as he sat down in the shade.

"I don't think I can do that!" Dismissing the idea, I passed him a cup of wine.

"Martha, you have as much knowledge and understanding of Jesus's teaching as any of us."

"But what … what could I say? Surely someone must be available. Besides, others are better at speaking than I am," I objected.

Barnabas laughed. "John thought you might say something like that."

"You are here now, so you can do it."

"You and your brother and sister knew and loved Jesus as much as any of us. He sat in this courtyard many times, sharing the scriptures and teaching you wonderful things about God, and now is the time to pass this on to others. Jesus raised Lazarus from the dead, and Mary showed her love for him by pouring oil on his feet. You were there at the crucifixion and the first at the tomb. Never doubt, you have many things to say. Besides, John, Simon and the others are busy speaking to the many groups around Jerusalem and it's time for those who knew Jesus to share their stories. We need you to do this."

The gate opened, and Mary and Lazarus returned from the market where they had bought supplies for the meal. Mary put down her heavy bag of vegetables from off her shoulder.

"Are you here to talk this evening?" She asked.

"John wants us to do it," I informed her.

She looked at me, then at Lazarus and Barnabas, her expression showing the same objections I had. "We can't do that." Mary shook her head.

Barnabas walked up to Lazarus and, putting his arm around the young man's shoulders, said, "You have an experience that none of us has. Jesus raised you from the dead, and that's quite spectacular. That's something worth saying." He slapped Lazarus on the back.

Lazarus brushed Barnabas's hands off his shoulders. "I don't enjoy talking about it. People always want to know what happened when I was dead, not that Jesus gave me back my life."

Not accepting no for an answer, Barnabas continued, "You can say what you want, and describe what happened from your perspective. Don't worry, I'll stay and help plan something. First, do you remember the day the Holy Spirit filled us? God gave us his Spirit to empower us to do all the things that Jesus did." We nodded in agreement and he continued, "We'll pray and ask the Holy Spirit what we are to do this evening and then plan it. John has no doubts you'll do a great job, and neither do I."

"I'll prepare the meal while you talk," I said and picked up the bag of vegetables.

Barnabas stood in front of me and there was no way around him. "Martha, sit down." His voice had a sternness I hadn't heard before. Raising his eyebrows and with a slight smile at the corner of his mouth, he pointed to the seat I had just vacated. "There's plenty of time to make the meal, and we'll help."

Open-mouthed, I had no choice but to sit and with Barnabas's encouragement was soon enjoying planning the evening. Afterwards, everyone helped to make the meal, singing together as we chopped vegetables and stirred pots, which I had to admit, was more fun than doing it on my own.

Later that evening, when everyone had assembled in our courtyard, Lazarus took the bread, tore it in half and blessed it, as he had seen Jesus do many times. After the meal, he shared a scripture reading from the prophets showing how Jesus is the Messiah. Then Mary talked of the night she anointed Jesus's feet and her love for him, kneeling in the place where it happened. She stood and sang a psalm, at first quietly by herself, but by the end, everyone joined her in praise. Her voice filling the air, calm and assured.

"It is good to give thanks to the Lord,
to sing praises to the Most High.
It is good to proclaim your unfailing love in the morning,
your faithfulness in the evening,
accompanied by a ten-stringed instrument,
a harp and the melody of a lyre.
You thrill me, Lord, with all you have done for me!
I sing for joy because of what you have done."

After we sang, I explained how Jesus called God "Abba, Daddy" and what that meant to me. At first, I was nervous and kept looking over at Barnabas, who smiled and nodded at me to continue. Gaining confidence, I was soon speaking the words I heard Jesus say. There were many questions from the group which we answered, and after Lazarus gave a final blessing, they dispersed to their homes. I closed the gate behind our final guest and looked over at Barnabas.

"Well done, you worked well together," he said.

Mary came into the courtyard. "That was exciting, I loved it when everyone joined in my song."

"I recognised the words of the psalm, but not the tune. Where did you get it from?" Barnabas asked her.

"Lazarus and I came up with it on the way back from the market. Did you like it, Martha?"

"I liked it very much," I answered. "We must sing it again, now we know the tune."

"John is waiting for me to report back so I'll leave now and tell him how good you were."

"Thanks for encouraging us," Lazarus said to him.

Barnabas opened the gate. "It won't be so hard next time."

"Your nickname is the Encourager, but I've got a new one for you," I said.

"What's that?" he asked.

I pushed his large frame out of the gate. "The Bully!" I shouted.

Barnabas's deep laugh echoed across the street. It was half in jest, that I'd called him a bully. But he had to be forceful to make me step out of the familiar role of provider into a new life as a teacher. It was a role into which the three of us entered increasingly as the weeks and months passed by. Lazarus became more confident as he spoke daily, and I watched Mary come alive and her face shine when she talked. These were exciting times, with wonderful things happening every day. Our numbers kept growing, and we felt that nothing could stop us.

CHAPTER 15

"Miss, can you spare any money?" With his bent legs under him, a beggar cried out from the ground by our feet.

Mary and I stood by the Temple gate waiting for our friends. "Do you see Miriam?" Mary tried to peer over the heads of the people rushing past.

"She's coming with Simon and John, and we agreed to meet here."

"Do you have anything to spare for a poor beggar?" The beggar's voice was barely audible over the noise.

"Martha!" I turned around at the sound of Miriam's voice. "Simon and John are behind me. It's so noisy here, let's go in and wait for them inside."

Ignored, the grey-haired beggar continued to shout out to passing worshippers, "Please have mercy on a lame man."

Turning to walk through the gate, we discussed the latest news until Simon shouted to us. Mary waved at him and he waved back before disappearing into the crowd. Wondering where he had got to, I wandered back and saw him and John crouching on the ground by the old lame beggar, whom I had ignored. Sometimes I threw a few coins into the begging bowls, but with no second thought of who the beggars were. The beggar smiled when they stopped to speak to him.

"I've seen you here before my friend," Simon said to him.

"My family bring me here every day to beg."

"What's your name?"

"Elias." The man smiled and held out his hand.

"Why are you here?" asked John.

"Why do you think?" He lifted his tatty cloak to show thin bent legs unable to take his weight. "I can't walk so I can't work, and I've no choice but to beg. This is my spot where I've sat for forty years since I was a small child."

"Elias, what would you like us to do for you?" John asked. Elias replied by holding out his begging bowl.

Simon shook his head. "We've no money on us."

The beggar tutted as if talking to our friends was a waste of his time. He turned his head away, looking up to the next person passing.

Simon put his hand upon his shoulder. "But we've something far better to give you." Elias was interested again. "Did you know Jesus who often came to the Temple?"

"He passed by, but never gave me any money. Sometimes one of his followers would throw me a few coins. I heard they crucified him, and there's a rumour he came back to life."

"Yes, Elias he did. We'll pray for you that you will be healed."

Elias looked at Simon and laughed. "Don't be daft! Jesus could heal people, but who are you?"

"We are Jesus's friends and followers," John told him.

They prayed for the beggar and, taking hold of his hands, lifted him to his feet.

Elias gripped tight hold of their hands and screamed, "Don't let me go, I can't stand."

"Look at his legs," Mary shouted.

Elias looked down and gasped as his ankles became strong, and muscles grew on his thin legs. He let go of

Simon's hand and stood up straight, revealing a tall man. By this time a large group stood by the gate, blocking the entrance, and cheers and shouts from the crowd brought more people running. Red, glowing cheeks replaced Elias's sallow complexion and his eyes shone as he rubbed his legs. First, he lifted one foot into the air and laughed as he stood on one leg. Hopping from foot to foot he jumped and punched the air with his hands.

This was the first time anyone from our group had prayed and healed anyone, but we couldn't have done it ourselves. It was only through Jesus's name that this happened. My heart beat quickly at seeing this and I wondered what else was possible now.

Simon took hold of Elias's elbow. "Let's get you inside. Don't be afraid, you can now go in." Elias looked up at the gate his disability had prevented him from going through, but now he was free to enter.

"Hallelujah! Praise God." He ran through the gate screaming and drawing an inquisitive crowd desperate to know what the noise was about. We caught up with him and stood together as the crowd gathered around us.

"Simon," Miriam put her hand on his arm, "speak to everyone as you did at Pentecost. They're ready to listen."

Simon held up his hands, and the crowd fell silent. "Friends, most of you recognise Elias the old lame beggar, but now you can see him standing and walking. In fact, he has never stopped jumping since." The crowd laughed as Elias jumped and shouted again. "There's nothing special about us, and we're not good enough to heal him ourselves. But it's only because of Jesus that he can now stand whole before you. This is the same Jesus who many of you saw arrested and killed only a few months ago. We can confirm that the rumours of his resurrection and being alive are true because we saw him. God wants everyone to turn to him, to have our wrongdoings forgiven and to receive new lives."

"Out of the way. Get out of my way," an angry voice shouted. Temple guards pushed people aside and forced their way towards us. The Captain of the Guard marched up to Simon and stood facing him, their noses almost touching.

"It's you again, peddling your falsehoods that Jesus rose from the dead. That's impossible." He spat into Simon's face.

Unflinching, Simon replied, "We are witnesses to this and we are willing to swear in a court of law that what we say is true."

The Captain sneered. "I can arrange that, and I've got a nice cell for you while you wait." He beckoned to the guards who grasped Simon and John by the arms. "Him too," he pointed at Elias.

"But what have I done?" Elias cried.

"Let the beggar go. He's done nothing wrong, and you've got us," John shouted at the Captain.

"Take them away."

In silence, everyone watched as the guards took Simon, John and Elias away. Worried for our friends, Miriam, Mary and I held onto each other. Jesus was executed the morning after his arrest, and we were fearful that this would be their fate.

"We must run to the upstairs room and tell everyone to pray," Miriam cried as she ran towards the Temple gate, followed by Mary and myself.

* * *

With eyes filled with sleep, we huddled together throughout the night, praying. Until streaks of morning light lit the upstairs room, where the air was heavy with our prayers. I startled as, without warning, there was a knock on the door. James ran to open it.

"Barnabas! Is there any news?"

"We stood outside the jail all night and kept watch. Then at first light, the Temple guards took John, Simon and the beggar to the High Priest's house. As I left, members of the Sanhedrin were arriving, and we can only assume it's for their trial."

James groaned. "A trial before the Sanhedrin? I'd hoped to see them released this morning. That's what we've prayed for."

"James, we must be strong and continue to pray for their release." Andrew took hold of his friend's shoulders, both shedding tears of worry for their brothers.

Barnabas held both men in his large arms. "Stefanos and Philip are still watching outside whilst I rushed here to tell you where they are. I'll go back now and keep you updated when anything occurs."

"Be careful," I told him as he opened the door to leave.

"Don't worry, we are being careful. It's too dangerous for the apostles to go outside, and the three of us are not as well-known as they are." Barnabas closed the door behind him, and for a big man, his steps were light down the stairs.

We continued praying that whatever happened through the trial, the Holy Spirit would fill our friends with courage and wisdom. An hour later, footsteps echoed on the stairs outside and I recognised John's voice. Mary ran to open the door and in walked Simon and John as if returning from the market, followed by Barnabas, Stefanos, Philip and Elias. James held John tight as if they were about to be separated again by the guards.

John prised himself away. "No need to worry, we are safe."

"Here they are, safely back home after being released by the Sanhedrin, and we've brought Elias back too." Philip stood beside Elias who looked around the large group, blinking rapidly.

With his hand on Elias's back, Simon drew him in front of us and introduced him. "This is Elias. He's the man who yesterday couldn't walk, and now Jesus has healed him through our prayers. He has been with us throughout our trial, if that's what you call what has just occurred with the High Priest." Elias looked down and rubbed his legs as if he still didn't believe he could walk. "Yesterday he was a lame beggar at the Temple, and this morning he walked up our stairs." We broke into applause and gave thanks to God for their release and Elias's healing.

"Welcome Elias," I said to him. "Come and sit and I'll get you a drink." He murmured his thanks and returned my smile.

As they ate breakfast, which I insisted they had, Simon began his account of the preceding few hours. "After Elias's healing, the Captain of the Temple guard arrested us, and we spent the night in the cells. It was still dark when the cell door opened, and the guards who arrested us ordered us to follow them. As dawn broke, we entered the High Priest's courtyard, passed the place where I sat by the fire and said I didn't know Jesus. This time, I prayed that I would have the strength not to do the same again."

"And he didn't," interjected John. He looked around at us and said, "Simon was brave and answered their questions truthfully."

Simon smiled at John before continuing. "The guards took us into a large room to stand before the High Priest Caiaphas and the Sanhedrin. When John saw them dressed in their fine robes and turbans, he whispered to ask whether they had risen early to dress in their finery or if they'd been up all night. Trying to intimidate us, they murmured and jeered as we walked in behind the guards. It almost worked because they terrified me. Sunlight hadn't yet lit up the dark room and oil lamps still burned, their smoke filling the room. Caiaphas sat in his ornate gold chair, and when he rose the room fell silent. Smoothing out his blue robe he pointed at Elias who stood next to us as if he was also on trial and asked, 'By what power and in whose name, did you heal this man?'

"My mouth was dry, and to be honest, at this point I felt scared, but as I spoke, I gained more confidence. No one could deny Elias had been healed. Everyone knows he's been a regular beggar in the Temple for decades. I said if they call us to account for his healing, then they should know it occurred because of Jesus. The same Jesus who stood before them, as we did."

John laughed. "That upset them. They'll do anything to stop the news of Jesus's resurrection spreading, but it's too late for that. Ignoring Elias, they manhandled us outside while they deliberated on what to do with us. Do you want to tell us what they said?" he asked Elias, who looked at Simon for assurance.

Simon nodded, "Go ahead."

"Err, well," Elias continued to rub his legs. "The priests ignored me, so I stood at the back by the wall. They were angry, and many shouted that they must stop you from telling the crowds that Jesus is alive."

Elias stopped and looked at his feet until I refilled his wine cup. "You're safe here, please continue."

"What's the name of the man in the blue turban and the fancy chair?" he asked.

Simon answered, "That disagreeable man is Caiaphas, the Chief Priest."

"Well, whatever he's called, he doesn't like you." Simon's laughter helped Elias to relax and continue. "He mocked Simon and John and said they're uneducated nobodies from Galilee who don't understand the scriptures and pose no threat. Some of them wanted Simon flogged, but two men stood up for him. They talked for a long time before the man in the turban made his decision."

Pleased to be asked for his account, Elias gave us a shy smile, and I wondered whether anyone had asked him for his opinion before.

"They called us back in," John continued, "and the Chief Priest tried to look stern as he pointed to us and said we were never to talk about Jesus again. Simon looked him straight in the eye, and I saw Caiaphas flinch and look away. Simon said Caiaphas should judge whether it was right to obey him rather than God because we cannot help but talk about everything we've seen. They threatened us further with flogging or worse if we did it again. Not knowing what else to do with us, they let us go."

James hugged his brother again. "Thank God for your release without harm, it's over now."

"I don't think it's over," John shook his head. "It could be just the beginning. We need to pray for boldness and strength for the future."

John stood and prayed for us all, and after he finished the room shook, and I felt as I had on the day in the Temple. This time I knew what to expect as the Holy Spirit again filled us as John had asked. Despite this, I was still anxious about the threat of flogging or worse still. Our small group was without power or influence amongst the Jerusalem elite. The Sanhedrin conspired to have Jesus killed, and they could threaten and squash us as easily as I could kill a fly buzzing around my food.

CHAPTER 16

"Stop fussing Martha." Lazarus crossed his arms. "Stefanos and I are meeting at the Temple this morning."

"I don't like you going there after what happened to Simon and John." The smell of the freshly baked flatbreads was still strong as I placed them in a bag for Lazarus to take to the upstairs room.

"That was two weeks ago, and the Temple guards have ignored us since."

"That doesn't mean they're not watching."

Lazarus slung the bag over his shoulders. "I owe Jesus everything. The life I now lead is only because of him and I'll not stop talking about him."

"We'll never forget what Jesus means to our family and I respect your decision to go. But Jesus warned us that the Sanhedrin know about you, and will be keeping a note of who is there." I straightened the strap of his bag to make it more comfortable. "Please be careful."

Lazarus laughed and put his arms around my shoulders. "I promise to be careful and to stay near Barnabas. He's big enough to scare anyone."

"Yes, his presence can intimidate, but once he caught a mouse in the courtyard and then released it in a field, rather than kill it."

"But they don't know that!" He laughed and, opening the gate, walked into the street.

Putting my hand on his face I felt stubble and had to stretch on my toes to kiss his cheek. My little brother was growing into a man and was no longer the boy who needed my protection, but that didn't make it any easier to let him go. I was so intent on watching Lazarus turning to wave, and praying for his safety, that I didn't hear someone sneak up behind me.

"If your brother is off to the Temple to cause trouble, he'd better be careful."

Alarmed, I spun around and fell against the wall as Jonas pointed his finger into my face. I hadn't seen him for a while and had almost forgotten his opposition to us.

"The Temple guards are on high alert and keeping watch on your group. The next time they arrest your friends they won't get away so lightly with a reprimand. Let me tell you." Rebekah came out, and when she saw Jonas talking with me, she scuttled back inside. "There's still an outstanding warrant for Lazarus's arrest. Don't forget that," he sneered.

Letting out a breath, I tried to quieten my beating heart, and looked him straight in the face. "Nothing will stop us proclaiming Jesus's message, and if you thought killing him would solve the problem, you're wrong because that was part of God's plan, and whatever happens to each one of us, is also part of his plan. So, we won't be afraid, and we will not stop."

As I spoke, I became more assured of the words I was saying, and my fear for Lazarus dissipated. With as much confidence as I could find, I walked past him. "Good day Jonas, please give my regards to Rebekah."

After closing the gate and leaving Jonas standing alone in the street, I looked over at the brush and the dusty courtyard.

"Mary!"

"Don't shout, I'm coming to do the sweeping now." With a frown she walked towards the brush.

"Do you want to go to the Temple instead this morning? You can do the sweeping later."

Mary's eyes widened, and a smile creased her face. "What changed your mind?"

"Jonas has helped me reassess our priorities."

Mary looked confused at my statement, but within five minutes Mary and I followed Lazarus towards Jerusalem. We were turning the corner by the upstairs room when our brother ran down the stairs, talking to Stefanos and followed by Miriam.

Miriam greeted me with a kiss. "I didn't expect to see you today. The others have already left, and we're meeting in the colonnade as usual."

"Martha," Lazarus called, "are you coming to the Temple with us?"

Mary took Lazarus's arm. "She needs to keep her eye on you." Lazarus pulled a face, but Mary didn't see it as she was looking at his friend. "Shall we go to the Temple together, Stefanos?"

When he returned her smile, Mary looked at the ground. Lazarus thumped him on the shoulder and they both laughed. Miriam and I followed behind and the similarity of the two young men struck me again. Stefanos, an inch taller and his curly hair a shade lighter than Lazarus, chatted to Mary, walking in between her brother and his friend.

Miriam looked pensive. "Have you noticed Mary and Stefanos together lately? They seem fond of each other, and I wonder if there's anything else in it?"

"No!" I was emphatic. "They're just young people. Besides, Mary is too young to think about boys."

"A seventeen-year-old girl is old enough to think about boys, and Stefanos is certainly old enough to think about girls," she replied.

I hadn't considered the possibility of this before and at once dismissed the idea. "I'll keep it in mind and have a word if they become too close."

By the time we arrived at the Temple, a crowd had gathered around the colonnade where Simon was already speaking. He was answering a man's question concerning a prophecy from Isaiah. Simon had matured into a confident public speaker since the Pentecost festival and the crowd was listening intently, eager to hear what he was saying. Mary wandered off with Lazarus and Stefanos to see who was in the crowd. A tap on my shoulder caused me to spin around, fearing Jonas had followed me.

An elderly woman wiped her eyes with her scarf. "Excuse me, I hope you don't mind but I remember you. You were at the crucifixion when Jesus died weren't you?" Taking her hands in mine I waited for her to speak again. "I was there too when they killed my son next to him," she sobbed. "He asked Jesus to remember him after they both died. Jesus was kind, especially so near his death, and I keep thinking of what he said."

"I remember your son, what was his name?"

"Joshua, and he was my last surviving child."

"Jesus said they would be together in heaven. I know Jesus well, and never once have I heard him tell a lie or a half-truth. Whatever he said, you can believe it's true."

"Thank you. Thank you so much." She turned to go, so I held onto her arm.

"I'm Martha, what's your name?"

"Esther. I'm a widow and I've no one left alive now."

Steering her towards a seat we talked about Jesus, and I was pleased that Jonas's words had the opposite effect upon me to that he intended. Without being at the Temple, Esther may not have received comfort for her grief.

Daily, we continued to attend the morning and afternoon prayers at the Temple, meeting in the colonnade and speaking to the worshippers. Elias and Esther often met us there along with many other new members. I knew from my own experience that as a widow with no surviving children, Esther was in a difficult position with no one to support her. I invited her back to Bethany, where she soon became indispensable in our home. I relied on her to cook and bake the bread as I was increasingly busy teaching in Bethany and to other groups around Jerusalem.

But, as Jonas had said, such proceedings didn't go unnoticed. From a distance, the Temple guards stood and observed us before reporting back to the Sanhedrin. They would not leave us alone for long.

* * *

It was one afternoon in the Temple that they came for us. Being in our regular place in the colonnade we were easy to find. Loud shouts caused me to stop my conversation, and I looked around as Temple guards parted the people surrounding us. To get to John, a guard pushed me in the chest. I screamed and bumped into Lazarus, and we toppled to the floor. Barnabas lifted us up and silently pulled us away. The apostles came together in a group to stand between us and the guards. The Captain fingered his sword, looking at the angry crowd.

"Who do you want?" Simon was the one to speak first, his calm voice echoed in the now silent Temple courts.

The Captain looked at the crowds of people, who jeered at him. He coughed. "We have a warrant for the arrest of Simon and John of Galilee, known associates of Jesus of Nazareth."

170

Simon and John walked forward and were flanked by guards. Then, to the Captain's surprise, James, Andrew and the other apostles followed. Even though the warrant was only for John and Simon, the men who had followed Jesus from the start would face the consequences together.

"Why are they all going?" Mary asked Barnabas.

"We knew the Temple authorities wouldn't ignore us for long," he answered, "so they agreed that when the time came, they would go together."

"Why get themselves arrested?" Lazarus asked.

"They thought as they had all followed Jesus, they would face arrest and any further punishment together. Also, they wanted no one else placed in danger."

Barnabas led us away and there, standing under the gate which led into the street, was Jonas with his arms folded. Knowing he wouldn't approach me while I was in a large group, I ignored him. Upon returning to the upstairs room we continued in prayer, and in the darkest hour of the night, a quiet tap on the door announced the men's return.

Mary ran to greet them. "Praise God. We've prayed for your early release but didn't expect you so soon."

"You will not believe this, but it's true," James smiled, eager to tell the story. "Once away from the crowds, the guards became more confident and roughed us up a little before shoving us into the same cell where Simon and John were last time. After they locked and secured the door, they left us for the night, and we decided the best thing to do was to pray."

John interrupted. "Always a good idea."

James wished to tell us himself and continued before his brother could say any more. "The guards took their lamps when they left, leaving us in the dark. Suddenly a light shone as bright as the noonday sun. So much so that I had to close my eyes against the glare. I heard the voice before my eyes adjusted to the light and then, there was what I can only describe as an angel, standing in the middle of us. Imagine if you can, an angel giving us a message direct from God. Ever since Martha and the others met the angel at the tomb, I've wanted to see one myself."

"Please get on with the story!" John tried to encourage James who pulled a face at him.

"The angel stood in the centre of the cell and told us to go back to the Temple and continue to talk about Jesus. He disappeared as abruptly as he arrived and with a soft click, the prison door swung open. Creeping out we passed the deserted guard post and walked out of the jail unopposed, through the empty streets to here."

We cheered and clapped our hands at the good news. "What will you do now?" I asked.

"Why not run to our home in Bethany while it's still dark and hide out there?" Lazarus suggested.

John patted Lazarus on his arm. "No, there'll be no more hiding. We will do what the angel said, and they will find us in the Temple when it opens for morning prayers."

Esther took a lamp to illuminate John's face where a cut was visible over his left eye. "Let me tend to that cut before you go."

She washed and bandaged John's wound and, after breakfast, they left the safety of the upstairs room. Only Barnabas, Stefanos, and Philip followed behind and kept their distance. Forty minutes later Stefanos returned with news. He was silent as he came into the room where we waited.

"We entered the Temple behind the apostles where a large crowd waited for us to arrive. News of their mysterious escape from prison had spread, and people were keen to see another spectacle. Simon addressed them as before. The crowd was in no mood to see the guards and jeered and shouted when they approached. Even with a drawn sword, the Captain looked afraid of a riot.

"Simon opened his arms, as he'd seen Jesus do at his arrest, and the guards set upon him and bundled him away. With no resistance, the rest of the men walked after Simon, followed by the guards. At this, the crowd erupted in anger and threw food and continued to shout as they took them away. We followed them directly to the High Priest's house, where we think the Sanhedrin is now meeting. I must get back." Stefanos was eager to return and turned to the door.

"Wait," I said, "I'm coming with you."

Stefanos nodded and relaxed. "Thank you."

"Do you want anyone to come with you?" Miriam asked.

I shook my head. "It will be better if there are fewer of us waiting at the High Priest's house."

"I don't care what you say, I'm not letting you go on your own." Lazarus's voice was firm. "Not you, Mary. As Martha says, we don't want a crowd there."

Everyone knew Mary for her bravery, and even for such a young woman, she hadn't flinched at the horrors of Jesus's death. But this time she saw the sense and agreed with her brother. We walked through the busy Jerusalem streets as its citizens and visitors piled out of their homes or inns to conduct business or buy food. Everyone was getting on with their lives, unaware that for us today held significance. Barnabas stood on the corner by Caiaphas's house, talking with Philip. He smiled when he saw me.

"I'm surprised to see you, Martha, but I'm glad you're here."

"Is there any news?" I asked.

He shook his head. "No one has been in or out for about an hour."

Two large gates stood open at the entrance to the High Priest's house. Cool white walls surrounded the open courtyard where his household now assembled. With the air of a holiday, the servants gathered in one corner, pleased to have time off work even if only for an hour. Two guards stood sentry by a closed door and several more stood around laughing. They parted to reveal Jonas standing in the middle telling a joke.

"Your neighbour suffers from the affliction of having too high an opinion of himself," Barnabas sniffed.

Before I could reply, the door opened, and a young well-dressed man walked through. When Jonas saw him, he broke away from the guards.

"Saul!" he shouted and ran up to him.

Saul turned his head away as Jonas spoke to him. I couldn't hear their conversation, but with a disdainful look, Saul spoke little. After a minute, he shooed Jonas away. He bent his head and went back to the guards.

The Captain strode out and called for the guards to escort our friends to stand in the centre of the courtyard. They were followed by a group of men, who by their dress and bearing held themselves above the apostles, in their ordinary travel cloaks. I'd never seen the High Priest before but recognised him from his description. Two men whom I recognised stood at the back of the group, and with a gasp, I remembered where I'd seen them.

"Those two men at the back, they're the ones who took Jesus's body and put him in a tomb. Do you recognise them?"

Barnabas shook his head. "I don't know who they are. Do you see the Captain over there? He looks more confident than he was at the Temple when he made the arrest."

The Captain stepped forward, holding a clay tablet from which he read, "These men are known associates of Jesus of Nazareth and are found guilty of blasphemy. They are sentenced to thirty-nine lashes each."

Lazarus grasped my hand and squeezed it tight until I could no longer feel it. I didn't believe what my ears told me and shook my head. Six guards dragged three men into the centre of the courtyard and knocked them to their knees. It was Thomas, Matthew and Andrew and we watched helplessly as the guards ripped open their cloaks and stretched out their arms. The others stood behind with their heads high, mouthing silent prayers. I'd seen the effects of lashes on Jesus and had no desire to witness this up close.

Three guards raised their barbarous lashes above their heads for maximum effect, and with a slap, the whip bit into each man's back. At the sound of their screams, I took hold of Lazarus and buried his head into my quaking shoulders, not wanting him to see this degradation and pain inflicted on people we loved. Behind me, Barnabas retched and vomited in the gutter. Ashen faced, he looked at me, pleading for help.

"When this is over, we have to get each man back to the upstairs room and cared for," I said with a strength I didn't feel. I made him face me and listen as I gave instructions. "Listen to me, Barnabas. I'm going back to get help."

Grabbing hold of Lazarus, I dragged him with me, glad to have him to hold on to as I didn't trust my legs to support me. Miriam was waiting in the street and I fell into her arms and told her about the floggings. She helped me upstairs, where she sat me on a stool.

Miriam now took control. "We will need to gather supplies to tend their wounds. Esther, can you make a poultice?" When she nodded, Miriam continued, "What do you need?"

"Herbs, spices and honey," she replied.

"Miriam, give me a job. I need to help," Lazarus told her.

"You and Mary, go around the homes of believers and ask for men to go to the High Priest's house to help get them home. Then, Lazarus, go back and tell them that help is on the way. Mary, bring back supplies of spices, healing herbs, honey and cloth." Lazarus and Mary stood listening to Miriam.

"Go!" she shouted to them, and they dashed out of the door.

"Esther, collect fresh water and put a large pan on the fire to boil. I'll make up the beds,"

She nodded to Miriam and lit the fire. No longer able to think clearly, I was glad she was giving directions. Soon, many believers assembled to help, and the room filled with the smell of the herbs from Esther's poultice. Clean water was boiling on the fire while we ripped sheets to make strips of linen to bind their wounds. Singing from the streets, announced that they were approaching.

"Are we ready?" Miriam asked. We nodded, apprehensive of what we were to experience.

I went outside to meet them and groaned when I saw the state of my friends. Unable to walk on their own, each man needed the help of two others. Lazarus and Stefanos, their cloaks stained with blood, carried James who had his arms around their shoulders dragging his feet.

"Help him please, Martha," Stefanos cried.

"Take him upstairs as gently as you can. Miriam will tell you where to put him and someone will attend to him. Don't worry, we have everything under control." I tried to sound calm and believe my own words. Panicking now would help no one.

I repeated the same to Barnabas who carried Simon in his arms, and then greeted each person with the same message.

Many onlookers, attracted by the singing, watched as they passed. Some looked out of upstairs windows while others offered their help. Many people supported us even if they were not open members, particularly now the apostles had stood up to the authorities and come off worse. Counting each one up the stairs, I followed the last man and entered the room, now filled with the groans and moans of the injured. Each lay on the bed prepared for them as Esther and Miriam directed help to each one.

John sat on a bed, and I went over to him. "John, please lie down and I'll tend to the wounds on your back."

"Are we all here?" he tried to speak through his pain. "James?"

"Yes, you are all accounted for. We've left no one behind."

"Help the others."

"They are being attended to and now it's your turn."

Lazarus and I laid him on his stomach, and I recoiled from his exposed back. Torn skin and open flesh showed the tracts of the whip and I wondered once more how anyone could inflict such pain on another person. I had seen the effects of Jesus's flogging when he struggled to stand and carry his cross, but John's pain seemed so raw up close. I cleaned his wounds with strips of cloth and warm water. My tears mixed with the water stained red with his blood.

Many others gathered outside in the street to sing and pray. Sadly, their singing couldn't cover the cries of pain as we cleansed deep wounds. My sister worked tirelessly, replacing dirty blood-stained cloths and bowls with fresh water and herbs, and handing out linen to bind wounds. After washing their backs, we bandaged them with Esther's poultice to reduce swelling and risk of infection. Each one drank an infusion spiced with poppy seeds which helped to diminish their pain and induced sleep. By midnight most of the apostles were resting or asleep.

Miriam bundled the blood-stained cloths into a bag, and it was then that she took in what had happened, and she put her hand over her face.

"Martha, how terrible," she sobbed when I put my arms around her shoulders. "They'll have the scars for the rest of their lives." I held onto Miriam as her tears joined with my own.

I wiped the tears from her cheeks along with mine. "You've done well this evening," I told her, "we couldn't have done it without you."

The rest of the evening passed quietly as I dismissed the many helpers so the apostles could rest. There were occasional moans of pain, and we comforted each as needed. My eyes must have closed, and I slept upright until Barnabas shook my shoulder and whispered my name. Sunlight crept through the shutters and I realised how tired I was. Without complaint, I allowed Barnabas to lead me to a place to lie down, and as he blew out the lamps, I fell asleep.

CHAPTER 17

"I insist you rest and stay here!" Miriam raised her voice to Simon who sat on the bed where we had placed him the evening before. It was the morning after their flogging and Simon insisted he was well enough to go to the Temple. Wincing with the pain, he tried to put his cloak around his shoulders.

"Martha! Help me!" he shouted.

"You must listen to Miriam." I remained stationary and refused to help. There was no way he was strong enough.

Miriam stood firm. "If you cannot get dressed without help, how are you going to walk to the Temple, let alone stand and preach?"

"Miriam, you go too far."

"I'm not going far enough," she retorted.

"I don't want to let Jesus down." The frustration showed in Simon's voice. Breathing hard and with his skin ashen and clammy, he tried to stand but fell back onto his bed.

Miriam bent in front of him and with a gentler voice said, "Simon, you aren't letting him down. But for your health's sake, you need to rest today. Your wounds will open long before reaching the Temple. Look, blood is seeping through already, and these will now need re-dressing."

Ignoring her, and with great effort, he stood, holding onto the wall to steady himself, screeching in pain. He stretched out a hand towards Barnabas.

"Help me with my cloak," he panted.

Barnabas approached Simon, but instead of assisting as he expected, Barnabas placed both large hands on his shoulders and pushed him back onto the bed. Simon was too weak to resist.

Firmly Barnabas said, "You must stay here for a few days and regain your strength."

Simon shook his head in disagreement and clasped Barnabas's arm. "We can't give the Sanhedrin the satisfaction of thinking they can scare us into silence."

Barnabas continued. "Don't worry, we will have a presence in the Temple this morning. A few of us are going there now."

Simon nodded before resting his head in his hands, his elbows on his knees. The door opened and in walked Mary, Lazarus and Esther, arriving back from the market.

"Where do you want the flour?" Lazarus asked, taking the heavy sack from off his shoulders.

"Put it by the oven please, I'll make the bread straight away," Esther said taking off her outer cloak. "How are they this morning," she whispered.

"Your sleeping draft has done a good job, helping them to sleep and dulling the worst of the pain. Simon is now insisting he needs to be at the Temple, but Miriam and I disagree." Simon was sulking, trying not to wince as Miriam unwrapped his blood-soaked bandages.

Esther turned to him and like a mother talking to her petulant small boy, said, "Don't be silly. You need to listen to Miriam and Martha; they have your best interests at heart. I'll make breakfast and I want everyone to eat it up." Despite his protestations, Simon meekly accepted this.

"Are you ready?" Barnabas asked Lazarus.

"You aren't going!" I told Lazarus as they headed for the door.

"Barnabas and I are meeting Stefanos and others in the Temple," he explained.

Trying Miriam's line, I said, "I insist you stay here today!" but to no avail. Lazarus kissed me on the cheek and saying nothing, walked out of the door. I could no longer tell him what to do.

Before leaving, Barnabas said, "You know we need to be there because we cannot show we are frightened into not talking about Jesus. We won't preach openly, just attend the morning prayers and talk with whoever wants to. Don't worry, I'll look after Lazarus."

I prayed for protection for my brother and the others at the Temple, resigned that no matter what I said they would go. We spent the rest of the morning nursing the apostles, re-dressing their bandages and helping them to eat. Despite my anxieties, it was not long before Lazarus returned and reported back to Simon.

* * *

Shadows flickered on the walls from the lamps still burning. Simon, James and John were still awake and finishing their meal which Esther had left. Miriam and I sat at the table with a lamp and talked in hushed tones. I was writing on a wax tablet when a tap on the door caused us to be quiet. Not expecting anyone at this late hour, we looked at each other, wondering who it could be. Supposing anyone who wished us harm wouldn't knock so politely, I opened the door a crack to see two well-dressed older men. After a moment's surprise, I remembered where I had seen them. These were the men who had taken Jesus's body. They were members of the Sanhedrin and responsible for the apostle's flogging and their present pain.

"Please accept our apologies for calling at this late hour, but may we see Simon and John?" the older of the two men asked. I looked behind me and John nodded so I stood aside to let them enter. Simon, too, looked surprised and tried to stand.

"Please don't get up, you must be in a great deal of pain. We are sorry for this, and that is why we are here," the younger man said.

Simon indicated two vacant stools and Miriam helped the older man sit before lighting an extra lamp. I gave them each a glass of wine and we stayed to listen to what they had to say. I asked myself why Simon and John would allow them to enter the upstairs room and put us in danger?

John put down his plate. "Martha, Miriam, may I introduce you to Nicodemus and Joseph of Arimathea? Both are members of the Sanhedrin. They spoke with Jesus several times and have great respect for him and his teachings."

The two men nodded at us, and I could not understand why they should visit Jesus. Not only that, but why Jesus would speak to those who ultimately convicted him. However, rich or poor, a person's social standing had never mattered to him.

"Martha and Miriam are valued members of our community and you may talk freely," John said.

With a neat white beard, Nicodemus was the older of the two, but his age and walking stick belied his still sharp mind. Joseph of Arimathea was taller, still retaining black flecks in his greying hair and beard. Both their clothing and speech showed them as belonging to the upper echelons of Jerusalem society.

Nicodemus studied his hands in his lap before saying, "We have come here this evening to inform you that our position on the Sanhedrin is no longer tenable. Earlier today we resigned and are no longer members."

"We tried to remain on the council in an effort to smooth relations between yourselves and the Chief Priest, which we now realise is no longer possible," the younger man agreed.

All was quiet, except for the hiss of the lamps until Simon said, "Nicodemus, do you remember the first conversation you had with Jesus?"

Nicodemus nodded. "Yes, I remember it very well. I came at night, more afraid of being seen and reported back to the Sanhedrin, who had already set their mind against Jesus, than seeking the truth. After hearing reports of his miracles and healings, I needed to find out for myself whether he was from God. I have often thought about that evening, and the other times I saw him. Though contradicting many of my old beliefs, I have realised that he was, or as I should say, he is from God. On that first meeting, he told me there must be a rebirth. Not believing it was possible for an old man to be reborn from his mother who had died twenty years before, he explained to me that this is a spiritual birthing. I cannot rely on being a Pharisee or member of God's special nation, I have to choose it for myself."

"Do you now choose this spiritual rebirth?" Simon asked.

"Yes, I do," he replied.

"Joseph, do you choose the same rebirth?"

"Yes, I do too," Joseph replied.

Simon nodded his head in agreement. "Jesus said no one can serve two masters as you will love and serve one and hate and despise the other. You must choose who you will serve." Wincing, he leaned forward. "Who will you serve?

The self-seeking interests of the Sanhedrin or the sacrificial love of Jesus, our Saviour?"

"This is the reason we are here because we wish to serve Jesus." Nicodemus bowed his head in deference to Simon, who looked at the younger one for his answer.

"Yes, we have already made this decision, and our families are in agreement," Joseph nodded.

Simon, James and John now smiled at the two men and grasped their hands in welcome.

"Tell us what's happening with the Sanhedrin. We need to know what their plans are," James said, now that everyone was more relaxed.

"Yesterday was a trying day for the Sanhedrin," Joseph said.

"It wasn't much fun for us either!" James cried.

"Sorry, I appreciate that," Joseph apologised. "I mean to say, they were unsure how to handle you. Nothing in their experience has helped them to understand this. When you were first arrested a few weeks ago, they thought warning you never to speak of Jesus again would silence you. They expected you to run away frightened back to Galilee and presumed that they would never hear the name of Jesus of Nazareth again. Then you were back the following day, and every day since. In their eyes, you are common working men, uneducated, and unschooled in theology and you should not be telling them what to do or what to believe. You needed teaching the lesson that you can defy them no longer."

"Not watering down your message at the trial did not help," Nicodemus continued. "In fact, Simon, you were blunt." Simon smiled at this description. "Telling them they had Jesus killed was not the best defence, especially when your life depended upon their verdict."

"I told them the truth," Simon said, "and I don't care how blunt I need to be. We may appear to be uneducated and not recognise their narrow version of theology, but what we know from Jesus we will tell."

"Caiaphas wanted you dead," Nicodemus continued.

"Dead!" Miriam shouted. "They wanted to kill them?"

I grasped Miriam's hand. "I thought being flogged was awful, but it could've been much worse."

Nicodemus turned to us and explained. "Yes, Caiaphas wanted them killed because, in his eyes, Simon had spoken blasphemy."

"To be truthful, I half expected the death penalty when the soldiers brought us back into the room after the verdict. What changed their mind?" John asked.

"Gamaliel spoke up for you."

"I've heard of that name, who is he?" James asked.

"Gamaliel is a well-respected and esteemed member of the Sanhedrin, and his wisdom is held in high regard. He advised careful consideration and suggested leaving you well alone. He argued that if Jesus and your movement is from God, then nothing can stop it, and the Sanhedrin could find itself fighting against God. However, if it is of human thought and origin, then it will fizzle out anyway. That persuaded the Chief Priest against the death penalty, reducing it to flogging. Besides, he worried that executing you could lead to a riot."

We were silent for a few moments, taking in what Nicodemus had said. Everything we were doing was from God, and as Gamaliel had wisely said, nothing could stand against that.

"Who was the young man sat next to Gamaliel taking notes?" James asked.

"That is Saul, his scribe," Joseph answered.

"I saw him in Caiaphas's courtyard talking to my neighbour, and I didn't like him," I said.

"I don't like him very much either. He spent the entire trial with a sour look on his face as if we were a disease he is afraid of." James pulled his face.

"That is exactly what he thinks, you are a disease which needs eradicating."

"Then we must pray he catches it," James smiled, but I was not smiling.

"He approved of your punishment and stayed to observe it being carried out. Saul is a very zealous and dangerous young man who needs watching. Come, Joseph, it is time we were leaving, these men need to rest and recover from their ordeal." Miriam helped Nicodemus to his feet, and he squeezed her hand. "Thank you, Miriam. You and your friends are brave young women. To be present at Jesus's death and when we interred him in Joseph's tomb took great courage. How blessed you are to see him alive, and it is an honour to meet you." Miriam smiled and patted his hand.

"Excuse me, could you see to the delivery of this letter?" I handed Nicodemus the wax tablet.

"Who are you writing to?" asked Simon.

"To Mary and Jacob," Miriam replied. "We've asked Jacob whether he will come to Jerusalem and help us until you are feeling better. You won't be able to do anything for a while and we need help."

I expected Simon to argue that they could cope, but he simply nodded his head.

Nicodemus put the wax tablet into his bag. "I will send someone first thing in the morning."

As they were leaving, Joseph turned to Simon and said, "Everything we have is now at your disposal."

Struck afresh by the seriousness of our situation, I closed the door behind them. Troubled by the acquaintance of Jonas and Saul, I considered how perilous our lives were becoming and what this could mean for our family.

CHAPTER 18

It was a relief when, three days later, Jacob arrived and with great skill set about organising and managing our groups, while the apostles recovered from their flogging. We took up their teaching responsibilities and spent most days with one or other of our groups. Gradually, the apostles recovered and were able to take on more tasks, and after six weeks, Jacob returned to Nazareth to see to his carpentry business. Two months later we were as busy as before. Since our last dealing with the Sanhedrin, they had left us alone, but none of us believed they would ignore us for long.

The afternoon sun was pleasant for an early spring day, and I was returning home from Jerusalem after a busy morning. Mary and I had visited Stefanos's house to teach a group meeting there. We were visiting the group for the first time and spoke about the morning of Jesus's resurrection. Those attending were Greek speakers which meant that Stefanos translated our Aramaic into Greek. Mary then stayed behind in Jerusalem to help Miriam pack and distribute the food parcels to those in need.

Enjoying the quiet of being on my own, I contemplated what had happened over the past few weeks. Though many of us still attended prayers at the Temple, we'd scaled down our open preaching there. Now, the growing network of believers' homes became important centres for our teaching. Though Esther took over the running of my home, I still returned to Bethany to the group meeting there. We met in the evening when the villagers had finished work in the fields, and they arrived tired and hungry, both for physical food, which we provided, and for the spiritual food also on offer. New believers brought family and friends, squeezing into the already full rooms and courtyard.

When I reached the outskirts of Bethany, I noticed a familiar figure up ahead. It was Rebekah singing a song I recognised. Now too busy to worry, I had forgotten about my neighbours. She turned around when I called her name.

"Was that one of our new songs?" I asked.

"Sorry." She stopped singing and looked away.

"Don't be sorry, I'm just surprised. I don't think I've ever heard you sing, and you have a lovely voice." Not only had I never heard her sing, but I'd also never paid her a compliment.

"Jonas doesn't like me singing and says I sound like a cat being strangled. And he doesn't know I often sit on the roof and listen." I stood still, looking at her in surprise. "The stories about Jesus are the best and I'm proud he used to stay at your house next to mine."

I put my hand on her arm. "You would be welcome to come in anytime."

"No, I couldn't do that," she shook her head. "Jonas wouldn't approve. But is it all right if I still sneak onto the roof and listen?"

"Yes, of course, you can."

She continued looking at the floor. "I … I must confess, I used to listen to Jesus whenever he was with you."

Laughing out loud at the thought of her listening secretly, I said, "You can listen anytime. Why don't you light a lamp when you're on the roof and put it on the wall where I can see it? That will be our signal you are joining with us even if you cannot be there in person." Rebekah smiled before turning to run inside her home.

That evening, whilst Lazarus was talking to the group, I glanced up and saw a light. Rebekah was on her roof listening to every word and joining in the best she could. At last, I was beginning to understand her as Jesus's mother had advised. Far from the village gossip, as she presented herself, she was a sad and vulnerable woman. As I was no longer in Bethany as often as before, I asked Esther to speak to her and help in any way she could.

* * *

Miriam was always choosy when it came to figs. They were her favourite and she took the time to choose the best. The stallholder offered her one to try, and with a nod, she agreed which ones she wanted.

Handing the money to the stallholder she turned to me and said, "The amount of work each of the apostles is doing worries me. They're busy the entire day and on into the evening and not getting more than a few hours' sleep per night. Especially Simon and John."

"They've recovered from their flogging, but they are looking tired," I agreed.

Miriam picked up our bags, heavy with figs and vegetables. "James fell asleep when Simon was talking last night. Simon had got to the important part of his talk when John had to nudge James to stop him snoring."

"I wish I'd been there to see Simon's face!" I joined in Miriam's laughter. "Apart from the snoring, their relationships have become strained lately, with bickering and arguments between themselves."

"There's only so much we can do to help, and we're busy too. You're looking tired, Martha." She smiled as she took my arm.

"No more than you. All of us need a rest, but I'm not sure when we'll get it. It's exciting talking about Jesus and meeting new people, but it's exhausting."

On the way back to the upstairs room, we found Barnabas sitting on a stone in the street, leaning forward with his head in his hands.

"Barnabas are you all right?" Miriam asked, knowing he was not.

Leaning back against the wall he looked at Miriam. "James and I have been arguing and I walked out before I hit him."

"Whatever were you arguing about?" I asked.

"Nothing important, just what to do with a small amount of money someone has given us. Let me carry those bags upstairs." He took the bags and carried them inside, passing James on the stairs.

"Can I talk with you?" he asked Barnabas.

"Wait for me outside. I'll take these in and come down," he replied.

Watching James and Barnabas I whispered to Miriam, "I can't believe Barnabas would ever hit anyone, and I've never even heard him raise his voice. We must do something soon because they're ready to break. Everyone is under enormous pressure and we need help from somewhere."

"I don't know from where," she answered, "but I'll speak with John, he might suggest something."

James's laugh drifted upstairs. "It sounds like they've made up," I said.

John and Simon soon arrived back from seeing to the food given out to people, and we took the opportunity to speak with them. They agreed they were far too busy and needed support, otherwise their health would suffer. Miriam suggested discussing the matter with everyone over the evening meal. Esther was due to help with the food preparation but arrived late, flustered and out of breath. Accompanying her were two young women who helped to carry her bags.

"I'm sorry I'm late, but Martha can I have a private word with you?" she asked.

"Is there is a problem?" I followed her outside.

"I don't know if it is my place to say." Esther looked around and lowered her voice to a whisper. "Being a widow is difficult, especially when you don't have children to look after you." Both Esther and I understood how easy it was for a widow to become destitute. "Today, I've been with different widows across the city helping to distribute the food parcels. One group this morning said they haven't received their food parcels and not for the first time. They're grumbling and asking whether we love and help each other or just say we do."

"Who is getting missed out?" I asked.

"Mainly the Greek widows. Even though we're all Jewish, they said, as recent immigrants to the city, they're being overlooked and think we're showing favouritism to the Aramaic groups. I know I'm only a new member, but this problem needs resolving or there'll be a falling out amongst us."

"Thank you for telling me, and I'll bring it to John's attention." I didn't look forward to talking to him about this, being worried in case it put even more pressure on him.

When we returned upstairs, the two women had unpacked Esther's bags. "Would you like us to chop the vegetables, Esther?" The older of the two asked.

"You must be Martha," the other woman said grasping my hand. "I've heard so much about you. I'm Lydia, and this is my older sister, Helena."

"You are very welcome. Where do you live?"

Helena approached and kissed me on my cheek. "Our family belong to one of your groups and we have helped Esther this afternoon."

"They are a great help, and I'm glad I met them," Esther said.

"Is that Simon in the corner reading?" Helena asked pointing to Simon.

I left Esther introducing the two women to others in our group. These two smartly dressed women were aged somewhere between me and Mary and were of a friendly disposition, offering to help everyone. They stayed for the evening, helping to serve the meal before leaving to return home.

After the meal, we sat together and outlined the problem of how hectic we'd become, and how this was obstructing our main purpose of talking about Jesus. I asked Esther to say what she'd told me earlier. At first, she didn't think it was her place to speak in front of the apostles, but with encouragement from John, she reported what the Greek widows were saying.

To finish, she stood in front of everyone and said, "These ladies who have no family here in Jerusalem would be destitute without the help we give them. They are now our family and our responsibility and it's very important we show Jesus's love in this way."

John stood. "Thank you, Esther, I agree with you. Our numbers are increasing every day, and this is fantastic, but it raises certain challenges. One problem is how we distribute the food parcels, and I acknowledge we've missed out the Greek widows."

"This isn't deliberate, but because we're so busy," I agreed.

"Yes," John nodded. "The best thing to do is for us to pray and come up with a solution. Miriam and Martha, I'd like you to join us, and Esther too. You have insight into this problem which would be useful for us to hear."

Miriam and I rose to join them, but Esther remained seated. "I don't think John meant me," she said.

I looked around the room. "Is there anyone else here called Esther?" When no one answered, I smiled and took her hand. "It must be you then."

After a short discussion, we had a plan. The Greek-speaking groups would be asked to appoint seven leaders who were trustworthy and who would act with impartiality. Their task would be to organise the food distribution across the city and surrounding villages. In addition, we sent a letter to Nazareth to ask Jesus's brother, Jacob, whether he would return to Jerusalem to help the apostles.

* * *

Two weeks later, we assembled as many of the believers as possible. I thought I'd arrived early, but a crowd congregated outside the upstairs room, talking loudly and singing. No one was rushing to go inside on such a warm summer evening and, pushing passed people on the stairs, I forced my way in. The room was full of many people I didn't recognise and I heard a mixture of languages being spoken.

"Martha!" I heard my name above the babble of the crowd. Mary's hand shot up in the air and with difficulty I made my way towards her. "What a fantastic turnout," she shouted.

"What did you say?"

Mary shouted into my ear. "I said, there's a lot of people here tonight."

Two familiar hands appeared on my shoulders from behind and squeezed them tight. I turned around to see Lazarus and Stefanos, with his arm around a thirteen-year-old boy's shoulders.

"Hello, Martha," the boy said. "Do you remember me? I'm Lucas, Stefanos's brother, and we met when you came to my house."

"Good evening Lucas, I've not forgotten you."

Stefanos laughed. "Once you've seen Lucas, you can't forget him." He tousled his brother's hair before Lucas pushed him away.

Struck by how similar the two brothers were, I asked, "Are you here with your family?"

"Our parents are standing over there." Lucas pointed to a group of people talking and laughing together. A woman waved at him. "Come on Stefanos, mum wants us."

"I'll see you later." Mary smiled at Stefanos and he and Lucas turned towards their family.

Lydia and Helena stood in a corner of the room and talking with their heads together, pointed out people in the crowd. When they saw Mary, they waved and came over to us, and I was pleased for Mary to have friends of her own age.

"Are your family here?" I asked.

"Yes, they are here somewhere," Lydia replied.

Helena looked over Mary's shoulder. "Is that Stefanos?" she asked.

Mary turned around to look at him and on looking back at Helena, said, "Yes, Stefanos is my friend." I noticed her emphasis on the word 'my'.

"Could you introduce him to us?" Lydia asked.

A loud voice over her shoulder spared Mary from an answer.

"Can we have quiet please!"

We turned as Andrew stood on a table and clapped his hands trying to get everyone's attention. When the room quietened, he spoke.

"Good evening and thank you for coming on this important occasion. As you are aware, we've been extremely busy over the past few months, running around like a dog chasing his tail." Everyone laughed at Andrew's fitting description. "Everything we have done is essential, but it has taken us away from our central commission from Jesus. We've taken steps to rectify this and tonight we are appointing seven people into roles which will help us in spreading the message. I'd like to introduce a man whom many of you will know. Jesus's brother, Jacob, has returned from Nazareth to help us in administration. Something we greatly need." We cheered as Andrew helped Jacob onto the table.

They both jumped down as Simon climbed up and the room quietened again. "Esther brought to our attention that some Greek-speaking groups have missed out on the food distribution, and we apologise for this oversight. To make sure it never occurs again, we asked you to bring us a list of seven people, full of the Holy Spirit and wisdom. This you have done, and we approve of each person mentioned and I'll now introduce them to you."

Seven people came forward as Simon called their name to cheers from their families and friends. They included Stefanos and Philip, who stood together as the apostles laid their hands on their shoulders. Once again, the Holy Spirit filled and appointed each one into his new role. Cheers echoed around the room as they were acceptable to all as being filled with faith and wisdom. Afterwards, we broke into small groups to congratulate them.

I walked over to John, who took a deep breath and sighed. "You look relieved," I said.

"It feels as if someone has lifted a heavy load from my shoulders. They're a great group and I look forward to seeing what they will achieve."

"And with Jacob here, your workload should be lighter," I shouted as the noise in the room intensified again.

"He only arrived yesterday and has already been an enormous help. In just one day he's identified problems and seen how he can help us, even organising this evening."

"So, you can now lie on your bed and rest during the day," I joked to him.

"I don't think there's much chance of that! I'm not sure what Simon would say if he saw me. But it gives us the space to do what we should be doing. Thank you for bringing this to our attention and your wisdom in knowing we needed to ask for help."

Philip wanted to speak with John, so I left them together. The air in the room was stuffy with so many bodies and I released my scarf from my shoulders. Deciding to go outside where it was cooler, I forced my way downstairs and walked into the street. Heads together again, Lydia and Helena were walking away on their own without their family. Lazarus and Mary were with Stefanos and his family, and as I watched, his mother took Mary's hand in hers. A look passed between Mary and Stefanos reminding me of the conversation I had had with Miriam.

Unsure of what to do about their growing friendship, I wondered whether John could help, as we were now a new family. Lazarus was not in a position to negotiate marriage terms with his friend's family, and I would never consider approaching Uncle Ephraim as our only other male relative. He'd only think their family was not good enough and sell

Mary to someone else. I decided to bring it up with John in the next few days when we had a quiet moment, but quiet moments were hard to find.

John was right, the apostles were given the time and opportunity to preach and teach and we saw continual growth. No one was hungry and there was unity again between the groups. The apostles increasingly relied on Jacob and came to depend upon his quiet wisdom. It should have been a good time for us, and in many ways, it was.

Yet, as the word of love spread, so did the words of evil. Lurking just behind my shoulder was a persistent threat of opposition and I was afraid it would catch up with me soon. Nicodemus, who still had friends in the Sanhedrin, warned us they were still looking for ways to prevent us from speaking about Jesus. Saul was becoming more prominent and his antagonism and hostility rose towards us even as our numbers grew.

CHAPTER 19

Stefanos and Philip grew into their roles and then far surpassed them, gaining reputations as men of God's grace and power. Coordinating daily with Jacob, they ensured no one went hungry, and they continued to work with Greek-speaking Jews throughout the city, and not just the believers. One morning, two months later, I was in the upstairs room and musing upon Mary. I still hadn't spoken to John because we were both busy and had no opportunity to do so. If I truly intended to, I could have found the time, but I kept dismissing the thought of Mary being in love as a youthful indiscretion on her part. I tried to limit the times she accompanied Stefanos and Lazarus but that morning she had followed them out before I could stop her from going. Two hours later they returned to the upstairs room and fell giggling through the door.

"Martha," exclaimed Mary, "Stefanos is teaching us Greek."

Lazarus followed her in. "Greek is such a difficult language to speak because there's so much to remember. I already have the basics, but I need to keep practising because it's spoken throughout the world and we only use Aramaic here in Judea." He tried to say a phrase in Greek before Stefanos laughed at his pronunciation and corrected him.

Mary repeated the phrase to which Stefanos replied, "Well done Mary, that was excellent." Mary's smile was wide with his praise.

"What does it mean?" I asked.

"Jesus is the saviour!" she replied. "I will learn Greek and then I can help Stefanos."

"The person you can help most now is Esther because I need you to return home with her and get everything ready for the meeting tonight," I said, more sharply than I intended.

Stefanos picked up his bag. "Philip is waiting for me, so I'll see you tomorrow."

We said goodbye to Stefanos, and Mary returned home with Esther. Later in the afternoon, I walked home from Jerusalem with Lazarus. I remembered the day Mary bought the expensive perfume with her dowry to anoint Jesus's feet. She said she wanted to marry a man who loved Jesus as much as she did, and Stefanos fitted that category. Stefanos would be a suitable husband for her, and it was a good match for them both. My two younger siblings had always been confederates and Lazarus would know what his sister was thinking. Struggling to find the right words to bring it into the conversation, I said it outright.

"Is Mary in love with Stefanos?"

Lazarus stopped walking and looked at me open-mouthed, unsure how to answer, "She comes along with us sometimes. There's nothing more in it, they're just friends."

"Are you sure that's all? A young woman of Mary's age shouldn't spend so much time in the company of a young man."

"Don't worry about that, I'm always there and act as a chaperone, though Mary wouldn't thank me for saying that."

"What about Stefanos? Do you know what his intentions are towards her?"

Lazarus blushed, which he always did when he was hiding something. "He likes her."

"In what way does he like her? Does he love her?" Lazarus was quiet, looking at the ground. "Look at me!" He lifted his head to meet my eyes. "Has he spoken about marriage?"

"No! He hasn't mentioned marriage, and I know he has never spoken to Mary about it."

Knowing my sister well, I was sure she couldn't remain silent if Stefanos had asked her to marry him. We entered the village and I had to leave the conversation there as I wanted no one to overhear us. When we arrived home, Mary was sweeping the courtyard, smiling and humming to herself.

* * *

Having spent longer on her appearance than usual, Mary rushed her breakfast. The reason for her eagerness to get to the upstairs room became clear when we arrived. Much to her disappointment, Stefanos had left five minutes earlier with Philip. When they returned two hours later, they explained how they had been with a group of Greek Jews who were ex-slaves and had resettled in Jerusalem. Stefanos was excited because they had invited them back to continue the discussions the next day. He asked if one of the apostles was free, but none was available, so Barnabas agreed to go with them.

The following morning, Mary hurried me over breakfast again to make sure we arrived in good time to meet Stefanos, but she almost missed him. We met him with Philip and Barnabas as they walked down the street from the upstairs room. Mary skipped when she saw him.

"Good morning Martha, Lazarus, Mary." Stefanos lingered over Mary's name.

"Good morning Stefanos," she replied.

"When your Greek is better, Lazarus, you can come along with us. Keep practising!" Stefanos smiled and waved to Mary before turning the corner.

"Come on Mary, let's go upstairs." I had to pull her arm to move her away from the street.

The day continued as normal, except that Mary walked around the room in a daze and couldn't concentrate on any task. So, I sent her on an errand with Lazarus. Everyone was out, and I was enjoying being on my own and humming to myself when Philip dashed in. His cloak was ripped and scratches were visible on his shoulder.

"It was a set-up. They only pretended to want to meet with us again and were lying in wait to drag Stefanos away to the Sanhedrin."

This attack on Stefanos shocked me. I was not expecting it and couldn't speak. Philip looked at me for help, and I didn't know what to do.

"Where's Barnabas?" I asked.

"It was Stefanos they wanted, but someone made a grab for me and I ran off. Barnabas has gone with them to support Stefanos and told me to run back here. He thought it might be dangerous for me to go because I was with him yesterday."

To my relief, the door opened, and Miriam, James and Jacob walked in. I told them what Philip had said while he recovered his breath.

"On what charges?" James wanted to know.

"They were shouting and calling him a blasphemer as they dragged him away." Philip was angry and crying now. "They told lies and misrepresented what he said, saying he had spoken against Moses and the Temple, but I was there and heard everything. I tried to tell them, but they wouldn't listen. Do you think I should go back and speak up for him?"

Philip stood to leave, but Jacob shook his head and held on to Philip's arm. Intent on listening to Philip I didn't hear Mary and Lazarus enter. Mary screamed, and I ran to her and put my arms around her.

"He'll be all right Mary. Barnabas is with him," I said, trying to comfort her.

Jacob spoke. "I'll go to the Sanhedrin and find out what's happening. James, can you go to Nicodemus and ask what influence he still has? Miriam and Lazarus, I want you to run to Stefanos's family and tell them what's happened. Then, Lazarus, go to the homes of the believers and pass the word around for people to pray."

Philip stood up. "What do you want me to do?"

"I want you to stay here," Jacob replied before turning to run out of the door.

The room was quiet after they left and, hoping to keep Mary and Philip calm, I gave them a drink. Soon, people arrived and we prayed for Stefanos that whatever was to befall him, he would face with courage, boldness and faith. Pacing the room, I felt helpless, not knowing what to do. When Esther arrived, I asked her to sit with Mary and left the upstairs room.

Reminiscent of the day of Jesus's death, the shouts and noise rose the nearer I got to the Sanhedrin. A woman screamed and pulled her child to a wall as a wave of angry men advanced toward her. I did the same pressing my back against the wall as they ran past with shouts of 'blasphemy' and 'heresy'. Dragged along in the dust in the centre of the pack, were two sandaled feet. I closed my eyes against the threatening scene, and didn't see someone grab my arm, pulling me away from the wall.

"Martha!"

With relief, I opened my eyes at the sound of Barnabas's voice. Lazarus's hand found mine and along with Jacob, we ran behind the mob.

"Where's Stefanos?" I shouted.

Dread filled my stomach when they didn't answer. Out through the city gate, we ran after them. The mob pushed someone to the ground and moved away from him, their noise finally silenced. With a shudder, I saw the kneeling figure of Stefanos.

"Blasphemer!" A chill ran down my back. It was Jonas. Again, in a place to harm those I loved. "What do we do with blasphemers?" Gull-like, his voice was a high-pitched screech.

"Stone him, stone him," the mob shouted.

Stefanos stood up, the least frightened of us.

"No!" Lazarus ran forward. "He's innocent." Barnabas caught his wrist, and he spun around.

Stefanos looked towards heaven, his face shining and at peace. With a loud voice heard by everyone he spoke, "Lord Jesus, I'm yours. Don't hold this against any of them and bring them to you." With a thud, the first stone hit his back, and he fell to his knees. "Forgive them," he shouted.

"Let me go!" Lazarus held tight in Barnabas's big arms screamed, "We have to help him."

"We cannot stop this, you'll only get yourself killed," Barnabas shouted above the baying of the mob.

"Stefanos!" Lazarus beat his fists into Barnabas's shoulders. "No!"

Lazarus's shouts quietened as the noise from the mob intensified, and the thud of the stones hit a now lifeless body. Holding my hands tight over my ears, I tried in vain to block out the hideous and vile screams of the men throwing the stones. Still encircling Stefanos, the mob's stones floated through the air, and a bloody rock rolled towards my feet. Paralysed with shock I was unable to move my shaking body, and the cries of the mob seemed to reach me from far away. Someone shook my shoulders and, taking a gasp of air, I awoke as from a nightmare. It was James. Still holding a now limp Lazarus, Barnabas sobbed and sank to the ground.

"I'm sorry James, there was nothing we could do," Jacob explained, his voice breaking.

"Did you try?" James yelled back.

"They were intent on his death. We ran after them, but nothing could have stopped this." Jacob lost control and, beating his chest, sank to the ground.

The deed now done, the mob lost its intensity, and gazed at Stefanos's lifeless body, as if shocked at their part in his death. Three men ran out of the gate, and Stefanos's father ran to him and collapsed on the ground in a silent scream. Picking up his son's body, he cradled and rocked it as he once had done long ago.

With his hands covered in his son's blood, he cried, "Stefanos! Stefanos wake up, please wake up." He buried his head on Stefanos's chest and wailed.

Kneeling next to the lifeless body, Simon closed the young man's eyes in death.

"John, John!" Nicodemus, who had just arrived, shook John's arm. "We must take Stefanos's body home."

John's pale face turned to look at him. "How do we tell his mother?"

A figure with a familiar stride approached us. "Now you know what becomes of those who turn away and blaspheme," Jonas smirked.

John squared up to him. "Do you even know what that means?"

"It means he deserved to die, just like your leader."

"You have taken away the life of a beautiful young man, and now I have to tell his mother." He grabbed hold of Jonas's cloak. "I should drag you with me and then you can see the result of your afternoon's work."

Jonas didn't take to being challenged and pulled himself away. "It's your fault, putting dangerous ideas into gullible and impressionable young minds."

He sauntered back to speak to a man who had observed the proceedings. This man, who wouldn't bloody his manicured hands by throwing a stone, straightened his smart cloak. His look told me this short, lean man considered us beneath him. Saul looked at me with cold dark eyes, shrewd and devious. Without a word he turned to walk away, followed by a scuttling Jonas.

* * *

Numb with shock, I returned to the upstairs room with Lazarus and Barnabas, wondering how I would tell Mary. I'd wiped my eyes on my scarf before entering but couldn't disguise the sorrowful news. Every head turned in my direction and their shocked looks mirrored my own. Mary rose from where she was sitting next to Esther and covered her mouth with her hand.

"No, No, No!" She shook her head, trying to dismiss the thought.

I wanted to go to her, but my feet, as heavy as iron, refused to move until she fell, and I ran to catch her. Kneeling beside Mary, I cupped her cheeks in my trembling hands, and her eyes pleaded with me to tell her it wasn't true. With hands clasped tight against her stomach, she rocked backwards and forwards on her knees. Esther laid Mary's head on her lap, making soothing noises and stroking her hair.

Mary grabbed my hand. "Stefanos is not dead. Tell me it's a mistake, and he's not dead."

"Martha!" Lazarus called. I went to him and he allowed me to smooth his face as he had as a child. "They killed Stefanos. My friend is dead, and I saw them kill him." Those I loved most were grieving, and I didn't know how to comfort them.

Jacob stood in the centre of the room and wiped his eyes with the heel of his hand. "Stefanos is dead, stoned to death only an hour ago. Simon and John are taking his body back to the family and the funeral will be at the tombs later this evening."

"I want to go," Mary's frail voice rasped.

"We'll go together." Lazarus lifted her up and, united in grief, they embraced.

People began to leave and as they passed, many touched my shoulder or kissed Lazarus and Mary. Even in grief I felt surrounded by their love and hoped Stefanos's family would feel this too. Unaware of how much time passed, Mary, Lazarus, and I lay on the floor, until the elderly figures of Nicodemus and Joseph appeared. With his face as pale as a blanched almond, Nicodemus laid a hand on Lazarus's shoulder, his stately presence reassuring.

"How is the young man? He has had a terrible shock, as indeed we all have," he said.

"What happened in the Sanhedrin?" I was becoming angry and wanted to know who to blame for the death of this exceptional man, who could have become my brother-in-law.

Joseph said, "We discovered that Saul has connections with the group which tricked Stefanos into going back this morning. He deliberately misrepresented what Stefanos said as blasphemy. The Chief Priest and the other members did not say much, leaving it to the mob. They may not have passed the death sentence, as they cannot under Roman rule, but they are complicit in this viciousness. The guards did nothing to stop the mob, they stood there and let them pass."

I shook my head. "Saul never bloodied his hands by throwing a stone."

"No, but the responsibility for Stefanos's death lies upon his shoulders, as much as the man who threw the first stone."

Spitting out the words I said, "Saul stood smirking with his arms folded, while he let others like Jonas do his dirty work. How can anyone stand there and let a young man die so horribly?"

"There is collusion here. It is nothing short of murder," Nicodemus agreed.

A deep sigh came from the corner of the room and Barnabas's shoulders sank, "What can I say to his parents? This is my fault because I encouraged him to go back this morning. I should've stopped them stoning him, but I was too frightened."

Jacob squatted near him, putting his arms around Barnabas's head. "The Sanhedrin knew that, once unleashed, such mob violence is unstoppable and they let it happen. Nothing we could've done would have prevented this."

* * *

The summer heat still radiated from the ground as the procession passed through the gate and out of the city. We walked beneath thin clouds turning pink by the setting sun, and oblivious of our misery, the birds chirped in the trees and took food to their young. Distraught at losing their eldest son and brother in such terrible circumstances, Stefanos's family followed the wooden funeral bier, carried by the apostles. Faint with grief, his mother buried her head in the shoulder of her husband, and Lucas walked between his two sisters. Following behind, we sang Stefanos's favourite songs and psalms, in praise of his God and Saviour, and many priests, angry at what had happened, joined us.

Simon led the prayers at the entrance to the tomb then John and James carried the body, wrapped in linen strips, into the darkness. This was so different from the person full of life and vigour, who turned, smiled and waved goodbye in the morning sunshine. His mother screamed, beat her chest and called Stefanos's name as the stone slammed shut. His father ripped his cloak and Miriam held a hysterical Lucas, who adored his brother.

I wanted to scream at God for the waste of a good life cut short by evil men with sinister motives. As much as I tried, I couldn't dispel the image of the bloody stone by my feet or the smirk on Saul's face. I prayed that Stefanos's parents would find comfort in the knowledge their son had died as he had lived, in the love of God, and that one day they would meet again.

Wrapped in anguish we cried together in our bitter lament. Mary's body shook, and I held her and Lazarus to my chest. Miriam returned to Jerusalem with the family and I asked Barnabas to stay with us. Preoccupied in helping Lazarus and Mary in their sorrow I had forgotten he was in shock and grieving too. As Stefanos's close friend and mentor, he helped him to become the man of God he was and felt responsible for his death. Sometimes the encourager needs support and encouragement themselves. He readily accepted my request and in the evening's quietness, we turned to walk home. When Mary stumbled on the path, Barnabas picked her up and, like a small child, carried her home.

CHAPTER 20

"Stefanos, Stefanos, I can't find you," Mary cried out. "Where are you?"

Sitting on the edge of her bed, I smoothed her hair away from her tear-stained face. Still crying, she grabbed hold of me, and with panic in her voice and a pounding heart, held onto me.

"Martha, I keep dreaming Stefanos is calling and I cannot find him. I'm searching through the tombs and I can hear him crying but the night's too dark, and I have no light."

I gave her another drink of Esther's sleeping draft, which helped her sleep but did nothing to prevent the nightmares. Laying her down again, I covered her with the blanket and, leaving the lamp burning, I lay next to her and closed my eyes. With no expectation of doing so, I slept, and awoke as the sky was lightening and, seeing that Mary was sleeping, I went downstairs. Outside in the courtyard, a motionless figure sat hunched under a blanket in the hazy dawn light. It was Lazarus.

I sat next to him taking his cold hand in mine. "How long have you been here?"

"I couldn't sleep, so came outside to wait for the dawn."

Rubbing his hand in mine I said. "Oh, Lazarus, your hands are cold. Come inside and sit by the fire." I helped him inside and lit the fire to prepare breakfast. He was not inclined to talk, so I carried out my tasks in silence, knowing he would speak when ready.

"Why did God let him die?" There was no answer to the question I'd asked myself many times during that long night. "Was there anything we could have done to stop it?"

"No matter what we did, we couldn't have changed the outcome. Once started, violence like that is unstoppable."

"Even when I close my eyes, I can still see the rocks thumping against his body and hear his cries of pain. I can't stop thinking about it. Stefanos was such a good man. Why him and not me?"

He buried his head in his hands, trying to block out the images, and allowed me to stroke his hair as I used to when he was a child. Lazarus and Mary would recover, but their pain was real, and this hurt would take longer to heal than any grazed knee.

Still huddled under the blanket, Lazarus said, "Stefanos was brave, even forgiving his attackers as he died. If he could say that, then we should try to do so."

A voice behind me said, "Yes, I suppose we should." It was Barnabas who leaned against the courtyard wall. "That's what Jesus taught, even giving us the example by forgiving those who crucified him. But I cannot easily forgive the way they butchered Stefanos, and the sneer on Saul's face as he watched." Barnabas took a seat. "He was excited about going back to the group and was sure they would become believers. I shouldn't have encouraged him to return. Philip might be dead too."

"No one could've known, so don't blame yourself." Lazarus put his hand on his friend's shoulder.

Esther appeared with Mary and, trying to sound her cheerful self, said, "Look who I found awake."

Barnabas made room for Mary to sit, and together we held a quiet breakfast. No one had much appetite for food let alone conversation. After breakfast, Barnabas took his leave and returned to Jerusalem, and Mary and Lazarus went back upstairs. I moved to tidy the breakfast away.

"You must rest too," Esther said.

"I'll be fine." Turning away, I removed a plate.

She took the trembling plate from my hand. "Martha, let me care for you so you can care for Mary and Lazarus."

Taking hold of Esther's hand, I said, "It was terrible, and I hope to see nothing like that ever again. The worst thing was the blood." I put my hand over my mouth to stifle a cry. "Blood splattered through the air as a stone hit Stefanos's head and a blood-soaked rock rolled by my feet and stayed there. I wanted to kick it away but dared not touch it." Esther drew me to herself and at last the tears flowed. "Stefanos was so full of life, only to have it snuffed out like a lamp. Lazarus talked about forgiveness, but how can I forgive Jonas and Saul now? Stefanos would have made the perfect husband for Mary."

Safe within Esther's embrace, I let go of my grief, and I too found healing. Still missing my mother, I found in Esther someone to turn to for comfort when I needed her most. She helped me see that I too needed help and there was no shame in baring my emotions.

Mary spent most of the day in bed, refusing to eat, while Lazarus walked around the house, not settling on any occupation until I gave him the job of sorting the bedding. When I found him a while later, he was asleep on top of the blankets. I covered him and left him sleeping.

* * *

There was an almost imperceptible tap on the gate. Lamp in hand, I stood in the centre of the courtyard and listened. Everyone was in bed and, as always, I was checking the house was secure before retiring myself. It happened again, a little louder the second time, matching the pounding of my heart. I opened the gate a crack and John put his finger on his lips to silence me. Behind him stood Philip with a group of people, one being carried. It was Stefanos's family who the day before had buried their son.

"Let's get inside," John whispered.

Everyone crept inside the house and Lucas winced as Philip helped his father put him on a chair. Dark blood oozed from a large gash in his leg and I retched as the image of his brother's blood came unbidden into my mind.

"What's happened?" I asked, at a loss to explain why they had arrived so furtively when it was dark, not normally a time to travel on the roads even so close to Jerusalem. Esther, who always appeared at the right moment when there was a need, fetched a bowl of water and bandages. Helped by Lucas's mother, she attended to his leg.

John watched Esther tend to Lucas and said, "Saul has been busy today, going from house to house and rounding up many of the believers. There must be at least twenty-five people in prison, and maybe more since we left. Jacob is trying to keep an account of who is where and we're helping those most vulnerable to escape."

"How can things deteriorate so swiftly?" I asked.

"Nothing Saul does will surprise me, and his hatred towards us is limitless," he replied.

"Are you in any danger?"

John rubbed the scars on his shoulder. "Not for now at least. The target of Saul's vehemence seems to be the Greek-speaking believers. He has singled out Stefanos's family for arrest and we must get them away from Jerusalem as soon as possible."

"What's the plan?"

"The plan was to bypass Bethany, but we had to stop here because Lucas couldn't walk any further."

Lucas cried out as Esther bandaged his leg. "How did he get this gash?" she asked.

John replied, "I was helping Stefanos's family collect a few belongings when Lucas ran in shouting. On the lookout for Saul, he spotted him with the guards, and we rushed out of the house just in time. Lucas slipped and gashed his leg on a wooden crate as we were rounding one corner a second before Saul appeared around the other. I got them out of the city gates before they closed, and we hid behind some rocks until dark and we could make our escape. The plan is for Philip to take them north into Samaria where he has friends."

Lazarus who appeared with Mary said, "You did the right thing in bringing them here, and we'll do everything possible to help."

Mary embraced Lucas's mother. "You are welcome to our home," she said.

"How is he, Esther?" John asked.

She shook her head. "The wound is deep and has bled a lot, but the bleeding is now stemmed, and I've bandaged it. If he puts his weight on it, the wound will reopen. He can't walk tonight." Lucas pulled a face and squeezed his mother's hand.

Lucas's father stepped forward. "In that case, I want to get my wife and daughters to safety. Philip, can you take my family and continue as planned?"

"No!" his wife cried.

Philip nodded. "We need to leave as soon as possible."

"I don't want to put you and your household in further danger, but if it's all right, Martha, may I stay here with Lucas and continue the journey tomorrow night?"

"We are pleased to help in any way we can," I assured him.

Lucas's mother held onto her son. "We cannot separate our family, and we must stay together!"

"It will be safer for you and the girls to leave this evening. You must think of them."

"Yesterday I lost one son and I won't lose another."

John took her hand. "I understand you want to keep the family together and your desire to be with Lucas, but your husband is right. It will be far safer for your daughters to be away from Jerusalem. Philip will take you to the rendezvous point and Lucas and his father will follow tomorrow night after he has rested his leg." John's wisdom persuaded her it was the right course of action, even though she feared for them.

Her husband kissed her on her head. "We will be together soon my love. Don't be afraid, and trust in God."

Smiling through his tears, Lucas tried to reassure his mother. "Don't worry mum, we'll be safe here in Martha's house, and I'll see you soon."

She stroked her son's face and let go of his hand before kissing him on the head. "What have we ever done to Saul that he should do this to our family? Instead of being in mourning as we should be, we have to leave our home and scatter like birds as he hunts us down."

Stefanos's father embraced his daughters. "Be brave girls, and look after your mother." They kissed their father, then took their mother towards the door.

He shook Philip's hand and, out of his wife's hearing, said, "If Lucas and I are not at the rendezvous the day after tomorrow, go on without us. My wife won't like the idea but make her go and we'll find you in Samaria." Philip nodded.

We tiptoed into the courtyard and I slid the bar off the gate. Opening it, I looked around at the deserted street before letting them out into the night. Keeping close to the walls they crept out of Bethany towards Samaria. I made beds up in one of our upstairs rooms and John stayed the evening.

* * *

The following day, we instructed Lucas and his father to stay quiet and away from the windows in case someone saw them. Lucas's leg was still bleeding, so Esther made a poultice and packed the wound, whilst his father held onto him. Trying to keep their spirits up, Mary and Lazarus stayed with them through most of the day. In the afternoon, another sudden knock alerted me to more visitors. Esther opened the gate to Miriam, Barnabas and two young women, who rushed in. After we closed the gate and moved inside, the two women removed their scarves from their faces.

Lydia ran to me. "Oh, Martha, it's terrible."

"Help us please." Helena fell into Lazarus's arms. He looked unsure how to comfort her.

"Saul imprisoned all our family this morning when we were out, and I'm afraid we'll be next," Helena said between her sobs.

Lydia left me and hugged Mary. "We must reach our Aunt who lives in Antioch, where we'll be safe."

Miriam said, "I thought the safest way was to escort them here in daylight as if we were simply visiting friends. They'll leave for Samaria this evening with Stefanos's father."

"I'll be glad to help you," Stefanos's father reassured them.

"It has only been two days since Stefanos's murder. What's happening in Jerusalem that so many have had to flee?" I asked my friend.

"Jerusalem doesn't feel the same city as it did just a few days ago," Barnabas explained. "It's too dangerous now for many of us to leave our homes even at night, and there are people hiding out all over the city. Jacob and the apostles are doing what they can, keeping everyone calm and helping those with family members in prison."

"Has Saul been to the upstairs room?" I asked.

Miriam shook her head. "No, and we must be thankful for that."

"He could send the guards."

Barnabas answered, "He knows he can't scare us, so he prefers to pick off individuals. It causes more fear that way."

Lazarus voiced the fear which was in my heart. "Barnabas, you are one of the Greek speakers, are you in danger too?"

"There are others in more urgent need to escape than I am. But don't worry about me, I'll leave if necessary. This morning, they released many of those arrested yesterday. Saul interrogated everyone and warned them against our so-called blasphemous teachings. Some received a beating or a flogging to teach us what happens if we continue to preach Jesus. Standing outside the prison yesterday, I tried to get word to those inside and could hear singing. The guards are asking them to sing our praise songs, but Saul is furious!" Barnabas laughed at the irony.

"Snake-like, Saul is full of venom, and I don't know why he hates us so much." Miriam's voice was bitter.

Barnabas continued, "If only I could get him in a room with just the two of us, then I could have a chat with him."

Mary asked, "What would you say?" Barnabas raised his eyebrows.

"It would be to tell him how much he's loved I hope," Lazarus said.

"I may tell him that," Barnabas smiled, "eventually."

"We need to pray for him, that he sees Jesus as the Saviour and Messiah as we do."

Barnabas took a deep breath and then breathed out. "I admire your faith Lazarus, but it's not likely to happen anytime soon. However, as much as I don't like to admit it, you are right, and Simon has said something similar. But this is a hard thing for us to pray because he's hurt too many of us."

"Jesus never said this was the easy road to travel."

"You are wise Lazarus, far beyond your years." Barnabas patted his friend on the back. Soon it was time for Miriam and Barnabas to return to the upstairs room.

"I'll come with you," I said getting my cloak.

Miriam held onto my hand. "No, we want you to stay here because we may need your home again to help people escape. Besides, it's dangerous."

"Then it's dangerous for you too. I feel so helpless here doing nothing. Please be careful."

I prayed for their safety as they left and for the safety of those who remained in my home. Later that evening after it had turned dark, Lucas, with his leg heavily bandaged, limped out, supported by his father, and Lydia and Helena slipped behind them in silence.

* * *

Resting the full pitcher of water on the rim of the well, I wiped the sweat from my face. Too lost in my thoughts for Stefanos's family, I was unaware of someone behind me. Startled by a tap on my shoulder, I turned and glared at Rebekah.

"Martha," she whispered and looked back towards her house, "there's something I have say to you. Last night, Jonas saw you letting people out of your house in the dark: there was a man, two women and a boy limping."

My heart plunged into my stomach. "What does he intend to do?"

She looked behind her again and fiddled with her scarf. "He doesn't tell me everything, but he's going into Jerusalem later to report you to Saul. Jonas has a high opinion of himself and thinks he's Saul's compatriot, both working together to uphold the law of Moses. But he exaggerates his importance because he's nothing. Full of jealousy as always, he laughed at what he saw. He's been waiting for a chance to get one over you since he said your husband swindled him out of money."

"That's not true. Nathan stopped working with Jonas because he stole from him."

"That's just like Jonas, to turn the facts to his advantage and believe what he wants to believe. His greatest interest is himself and that's all he cares about. In his opinion, the world is against him and owes him something. I know how dangerous my husband is when crossed, and he was angry when you refused to marry his brother. Please be careful."

There was a moment of solidarity which I hadn't felt before when she placed her hand on my arm. "Thank you for the warning, and I'd be grateful if you have any more information."

Hastily she filled her pitcher before Jonas knew she was missing. Perturbed, I walked back knowing I had to do something quickly. Lazarus didn't want me going into Jerusalem on my own and agreed to go with me. Within forty minutes we'd entered the city gates. The door to the upstairs room didn't open when Lazarus pushed it, he looked puzzled and knocked. Since Pentecost, it had remained open during the day.

"Who is it?"

"It's Martha and Lazarus."

James unbarred the door. "Miriam said you weren't coming today."

"There's important information I must tell you."

James let us in before barring the door again behind us. Barnabas and Jacob were sitting at a table piled high with coins and leather purses, and a wax tablet lay in front of Jacob. I recounted what Rebekah had said at the well. Jacob rubbed his forehead and heavy lines showed how long he had been working without rest.

He said, "You've come at just the right time because we were about to send another family to you, and the plans will need changing now. Saul is still on the rampage and his ardour doesn't seem to slow down."

"What about the Roman authorities?" I asked. "Surely Pilate doesn't want this level of unrest in the city."

"We think he's leaving Saul and the Chief Priest alone for now. From their point of view, if we're fighting amongst ourselves, then we're not fighting them."

"I feel sad for those families who have to leave everything behind." Looking at the table I asked, "What are you doing with this money?"

Jacob sighed. "These are to give to those who need to flee the city. It's not much for losing home and business and to start again in a new place, but it's something to help their journey and pay for travel." A bag of purses sat on the floor. "Miriam and Simon are collecting these to hand out later. Barnabas keeps insisting he'll take them, but he has to stay inside now."

Barnabas folded his arms. "They're exaggerating the danger, my name hasn't appeared on any lists."

James lost his temper. "They're arresting people whether their name is on a list or not. Everyone knows you, and your size makes you unmistakable."

Jacob saw me looking at what he was writing. "I'm keeping an account of those who have had to leave and where they intend to go. Families are being split up and it will help to reunite them later. So much has changed since you were last here."

"What about you, Martha, do you think Jonas means you harm?" Barnabas asked.

"Jonas has wanted to harm us for a long time," Lazarus said curtly. "This is just the latest excuse."

"If the situation deteriorates, we'll get you out of Bethany before he can do any harm," Jacob insisted. "We are good now at making people disappear."

Trying to assure myself as much as the others I said, "Everything will be fine. Don't worry, he's just full of bluster and I know how to deal with him."

James was serious. "Be careful. I worry about you in Bethany. If you have a problem, we are too far away to help."

"I've always lived in Bethany and don't intend to live anywhere else."

Worried about Mary and Esther, we returned home, and as we passed Jonas's house my spine prickled as if a spider was crawling up it. Feeling Jonas's eyes watching, I resisted the urge to look up at the window. The night was quiet with no sudden visitors and I rested the best I could, but my thoughts kept returning to Jerusalem and my friends.

CHAPTER 21

"Has that dough offended you?" Esther asked.

She had seen how restless I was since my visit to the upstairs room the previous day and to occupy my hands had asked me to make the bread. Agitated, my thoughts kept straying to what was happening only a short distance away in Jerusalem. Not knowing what Saul was up to was worse than being there.

"What do you mean?" I threw the dough down and gave it a hard punch.

"Do you imagine it's Saul and what you would like to do to him?"

"No, but not a bad idea! I feel so useless here!"

Kneeling by the herb patch, Mary pulled out the weeds which had grown since the weather warmed. On hearing a knock on the gate, she opened it.

"What's happened?" Mary gasped.

Wondering what the matter was, I walked into the courtyard as a woman entered, hiding under a scarf. Rebekah took off the scarf to reveal a bloodshot eye surrounded by black and purple skin.

"What's the matter with your eye?" I asked.

"Oh, nothing, I just fell on the stairs."

Esther wiped her hands on a cloth. "I've seen far too many women with a black eye who claim they've fallen at home," she said.

"That's not important now. I can't stay long. Jonas has gone into Jerusalem and I had to come and tell you." She grabbed a tight hold of me and sobbed. "Terrible news, I can hardly speak. Jonas said with such glee that Lazarus is on the list for the next round of arrests." The news stunned us into silence. "He was keen to arrest him this morning, but Saul said others were more of a priority today."

"What's that about me?" Lazarus walked into the courtyard when he heard his name.

Mary ran to him. "Saul is going to arrest you!" She clung onto his shoulder. "We must leave right now." She ran to pick up a bag and threw things into it.

"Mary, calm yourself, and we'll decide what to do," I shouted to her.

Rebekah squeezed my hand. "There's more. Jonas insists that he'll arrest you alongside Lazarus." Mary dropped the bag. "Because you've aided and abetted known criminals."

"What known criminals?" I asked, thinking of robbers and bandits.

"Helping members of your group evade justice."

"We aren't criminals," Lazarus shouted.

"Be quiet Lazarus, we don't know who is listening," Esther told him.

"Is my name on the list?" Mary whispered.

Rebekah shook her head. "No, but Jonas has an ulterior motive in arresting Martha. What he wants is the seizure of your assets which he can then buy cheaply."

"Not my house and farm?"

"Yes, both yours and Lazarus's. That's what he's wanted for a long time and thought he would get his hands on them when he planned for you to marry his brother." She rubbed her face. "He was cross when Lazarus reappeared after his death and you snubbed him. I must go, Jonas might arrive home any minute now." Rebekah turned to leave.

"Before you go, how long do we have?" Mary asked.

"It could be tomorrow."

"Thank you for coming, you may have saved Lazarus's life." I squeezed her hand before she turned and ran home. We stood still and looked at one another, dazed and frightened.

Esther put on her cloak. "It will be too dangerous for any of you to go to Jerusalem, but no one takes notice of an old woman. Jacob will know what to do. While I'm gone, pack a small bag each and be ready to leave."

I looked around my lovely home where I'd always felt safe, and it didn't seem possible I had to leave. Putting my hand on the table, I remembered the times we had sat around it. Meals with Nathan, and how Jesus had sat there, talking, laughing and teaching. How could I bear to leave anything behind?

"We're ready." Mary and Lazarus appeared, each with a bag slung across their shoulders. "Martha is your bag packed?"

I came out of my reverie. "It's only been five minutes since Esther left."

"That was an hour ago," Lazarus informed me. "What have you been doing?"

I realised I'd been daydreaming and couldn't think of living anywhere else other than within these walls.

"We've packed a spare set of clothes and our valuables. What money do we have?" For once my younger sister was being level-headed and sensible, whilst I couldn't think straight.

"Esther has returned." Lazarus noticed her entering the courtyard with Barnabas. "Is there any news?"

Esther took my hand and led me to a chair. "Let's sit and I'll tell you." She was talking as if in the distance, and her words confused me.

"Martha, did you hear what Esther has just said?" Lazarus asked.

"Sorry, can you repeat it? I can't seem to take anything in."

"When I arrived at the upstairs room everyone was in, and I told them what Rebekah had said. The news was upsetting, and Barnabas has volunteered to take you to safety in Cyprus."

"Cyprus is so far away from Bethany. How will we get there?" Mary asked.

I looked at her. "You aren't going."

"Of course, I'm going with you."

"No, the journey will be long and dangerous, and you will be safer here."

Mary looked to her brother to help. "Mary will be safer coming with us," he said. "It's not Saul who worries me, but Jonas. He'll never stop trying to get his sordid hands onto our property. The most important thing is to be together."

Mary ran to me and held my hands. "Martha, we have to stay together, and I'll have no argument because I'm leaving with you."

I kissed her hands. "You are still too young for such an arduous journey."

"I'm nearly nineteen years old, and you were already married to Nathan at my age. Stop treating me like a little girl."

"I promised mother to look after you, and that's all I've tried to do."

Lazarus joined us. "You've done a good job so far. But now we're adults and can make up our own minds and I agree with Mary that we all go to Cyprus."

I looked at Barnabas who said, "We assumed Mary would go with you, but we'd support her if she wanted to stay."

"That's decided then, I'm leaving with you. There's no reason for me to stay now Stefanos is dead. Besides, my bag is packed and I'm ready."

That was it, I had no choice but to accept Mary's and Lazarus's decision.

Lazarus was more excited than frightened. "Barnabas has told me Cyprus is an island in the middle of the Mediterranean Sea and a long way by ship."

"Where will we live?" Mary wanted to know all the details.

"Barnabas's family live in a town on the south coast of Cyprus and have a business making and selling cloth," Lazarus answered.

Barnabas said, "We can work out the details on the journey, but don't worry because my family will care for you." Seeing me protest he continued, "Martha, you have looked after everyone else, now let us look after you."

"When do we leave?" Mary asked.

"This evening under the cover of darkness. Pack a small bag, with a change of clothing and your valuables. Caesarea is a three-day walk and you must only take what you can carry."

"Johanna lives in Caesarea," I said as if in a dream.

"A messenger is already on the way there. We are to go to her home and wait for a ship bound for Cyprus."

Having seen the looks on the faces of those who had to flee, I never thought we would join them. Incomprehensible as it was, my mind was making sense of what we needed to do.

I took a deep breath. "We must decide what is important to take and pack our bags together," I said.

* * *

My hands found the hardness of the wood, and I removed the jewellery box from under the bedding. As special as each piece was, I was prepared to sell them. We needed to buy passage on a ship, accommodation and a new livelihood in Cyprus. This was no time to dwell on precious memories and I placed each one in a cloth purse and replaced the box. Keeping focused on the task helped me not to become sentimental at leaving the box given to me by Nathan or his possessions still left in the house.

Only packing what we could carry and leaving space for food and water, our bags were ready an hour later. Barnabas advised us to rest as the journey to Caesarea was long and arduous. Unable to sleep, I lay on my bed and listened to the familiar noises of the village. The sounds of children playing, neighbours arguing and laughing drifted through my open shutters. Every person known to me and who I would never meet again. A commotion in the street disturbed me, and surprised to hear John's voice, I peered out of the shutters, but the gate obscured him.

"Good afternoon Jonas," he said with a forced light-hearted tone.

"What are you doing here?" Jonas demanded.

"As you've followed us since the city gates, I think even you could work out this was our destination," John replied.

Alerted by the noise Barnabas rushed out. "Jonas!" he shouted, followed by Jonas's high-pitched scream. "Up to more mischief?" he asked.

Simon squared up to Jonas. "Why we are visiting our friends is none of your concern, and neither is it Saul's."

"How is Stefanos's family?" Jonas asked with mock interest. I entered the street to see Jonas now pinned to the wall by Barnabas, who had lifted him into the air.

"Barnabas, please put the man down." Simon touched his shoulder and Jonas dropped to the floor.

"Leave them alone, they have suffered enough." Barnabas's whispers were more threatening than many man's shouts. Jonas coughed and clung to his throat.

"Welcome, come inside for refreshments," I said ushering Miriam, Simon, James and John into the courtyard. "Good day Jonas," I smiled, trying hard to appear that this was a normal day.

"Go away!" he screamed. Little did he know this is what we planned.

Once inside I ran into Miriam's arms. "I thought I would never see you again," I cried.

"Nothing could stop me from saying goodbye. We are here to create a cover for you to leave, but we must be careful what we say and do outside, he will be listening."

"Leaving would be so much harder if I hadn't seen you one last time."

"Cyprus is not that far that we cannot see each other often," she said pretending to be brave.

Simon rounded on Barnabas. "What were you thinking Barnabas? If you were trying to intimidate Jonas, then you succeeded. We're here to provide cover for your escape, and you nearly ruined it."

"I'm sorry, but I became angry when he mentioned Stefanos's family and the hurt he has caused them."

Simon said, "We stick to the plan now."

Barnabas nodded and hung his head. Refusing help in making our final meal, Esther insisted I rest and talk to Miriam. She stroked my hand, and we reminisced about old times, while Lazarus sat outside with the men, talking loudly, sure that Jonas was listening. Prepared especially for our leaving, we ate one last hearty meal of chicken and lentil stew. Enjoying each other's company as of old, the laughter and noise of our conversation disguising our real intention.

After the meal, we withdrew from the courtyard for our final goodbyes. I asked for a pen and ink and, taking the deeds for the house, unwound the scroll and signed my name and handed it to Simon.

"My house and farm are now yours to do with as you see fit. I ask one thing, that for as long as you use it, Esther stays as the housekeeper."

Esther took my hand. "Martha, you are too kind. You invited me into your home and now you are asking me to stay. Thank you so much."

"In the few months we've known each other, you have become a mother to us, and I'll miss you." She kissed my head as mother used to do. "Say thank you to Rebekah and keep a lookout for her, she may need your help."

"Don't worry about your house or Rebekah, I'll take good care of them."

"I couldn't leave them in better hands."

"John, can you arrange for the sale of our family home and farm?" Lazarus asked. "When you sell it, you may take a percentage and pass the rest onto us to help set up home in Cyprus."

"We've had little time to decide," Mary joined in, "but we agree on what to do with our homes."

Simon shook Lazarus's hand. "We'll do as you wish and look after your properties."

John pulled four purses out of his cloak and handed us one each.

"I don't need these," I said trying to give it back. "We have money for the journey. Give it to others who need it more than us."

John refused to take the purses back. "Please accept these from us, they are but a small token of our love and appreciation for you. Besides, how could I explain to Jacob that you've refused them?"

I smiled my thanks to him. "Tell Jacob, thank you for the gifts, and we accept them with the love and grace in which they are offered."

"I'll miss you, Martha," Simon said. "I'll miss your wisdom that often sees the answer before the rest of us have thought of the question." I tried to return his smile. "Our shared experiences bind us together, both the happy and the sorrowful. Too many tears of laughter, sorrow and heartache have flowed and mingled together which none will forget."

John stood. "The sky is now dark, and it is time to go into the courtyard."

Our travelling bags and cloaks were ready, out of view of Jonas's house, and we sang and shared bread and wine. With a nod from Simon, James opened the gate and looked out. A final squeeze of Miriam's hand and the four of us crept out into the street. To avoid passing Jonas's house, we skirted the village, and I resisted one last look back at the home I had shared with Nathan. The sounds of the singing died as we left the village and turned onto the road to the coast. The night was dark and the road quiet.

* * *

Each step took me further away from Bethany than I'd ever travelled. I realised that it wasn't the place you live which is important, but the people you share it with. I was taking the most important things with me, my brother and sister, and nothing else mattered. The most precious things I left behind were my friends, and you don't truly leave them because you carry them forever.

The direct route to Caesarea passed through Samaria, but it was one little used by most Jewish people. A series of events many centuries before caused a rift between our peoples which had never healed. If Saul was in pursuit, we hoped he would take the much longer route via Galilee, assuming we had done the same.

Barnabas led us through Samaria and, like a good travel guide, pointed out places of interest which kept us occupied. Having travelled with Jesus through Samaria, he regaled us with many stories. The sun was setting on the first day of travel and we entered the outskirts of a small Samaritan village. Two scraggy goats nibbled grass around the well and chickens pecked at the dust. The houses were poor and ill-kept, and the quietness was disconcerting. Our water bags were empty, and Lazarus peered over the side of the well hoping to find a bucket to draw water.

"Be careful Lazarus," I warned, "the well looks unstable."

He stood up suddenly as a stone dislodged and fell with a splash.

Mary looked around. "Can we go somewhere else? I don't like this village."

Before I could reply a woman came out of a house with a pitcher on her shoulder.

"Go inside, where your friends are waiting for you, and I'll bring you a drink. The water from our well is always cool. Jesus once asked me for a drink from this well." I wondered what surprised me most, that she gave water to Jesus or we had friends here.

A man rushed out of her house. "Barnabas! Lazarus!" he cried. With relief, I saw it was Philip.

Barnabas lifted his friend off the floor. "Jacob instructed us to stop here, but I didn't know it was your rendezvous place as well."

Stefanos's mother greeted us by the door. "I can tell from your face Martha, that you too have had to flee. I'm sorry if we caused you any problems."

I shook my head. "The problems stem from our neighbour and his greed which goes back several years. I'm glad we could have been of help to you."

In the interior's gloom, a boy limped towards the door. "Lucas, how's your leg?" Mary asked.

"It's much better now and the lady here is almost as good as Esther at looking after me."

Lydia kissed my cheek. "We've stayed here an extra two nights to give Lucas's leg time to heal. Sara and the rest of the village are very kind."

"Did Jacob not tell you we were passing through here?" Philip asked.

"He's being careful with what he says to everyone," Barnabas replied.

"Why is that?" Stefanos's father asked.

"Because we have information that Saul has spies within our groups, and the less everyone knows the better. It's for everyone's safety."

Helena looked around our little group. "Surely he doesn't think any of us are spies," she laughed.

The woman called Sara entered and poured me a drink. The water was as refreshing as she had said.

"You met with Jesus?" I asked.

"One afternoon I went out to fetch water when it was quiet because the other women used to call me names. You see, I had many lovers, and they said wicked things about me. Jesus sat by the well and asked for a drink. This was very unusual because I could tell he was a Jewish man who would usually cross the street rather than talk to me, a poor Samaritan woman. I couldn't believe it when he told me about my life and what I'd done, and he still wanted to talk with me.

"Jesus drank a cup of water and then said everyone who drinks from the well will become thirsty. But he's the water that brings life, and after we've drunk from him, we'll never be thirsty again. I ran to my neighbours to tell them who I'd met, wondering whether he was the Saviour. After talking to him they asked him to stay and tell us more about God. For two nights he and his followers stayed right here in my house. Stories of his death and resurrection came to us and many of my neighbours still believe in him."

That evening, several villagers came to meet with us and Mary and I gave our eyewitness account of how Jesus died and the events of the following Sunday morning. After a simple but welcome meal, we taught them a song and shared the bread and wine before retiring. In the dark, I listened to the unfamiliar sounds of the village, but after a day with little rest, I soon slept.

Awaking at first light, we had a quick breakfast because Barnabas was eager to be on the road. Hanging back in the house, Lazarus was talking with Lydia and Helena.

"Sara, you have our thanks and Jacob sends you this." Barnabas took a purse out of his bag and handed it to her. "There will be others following."

With a smile, she took the purse. "Thank you, we'll help anyone we can."

Lazarus came out. "Lydia and Helena have asked whether they can come with us to Caesarea instead." He beckoned the sisters over.

Lydia touched my arm. "It would be easier to find a ship in Caesarea to take us to our Aunt in Antioch."

"Please say yes, Martha," Mary pleaded. "We'll be sailing in that direction, and we can go together."

"Yes," I said and Helena ran to hug me. "It will be good to travel with you both."

Philip wanted to speak with Barnabas before we left. "I've spoken to Sara and agreed to stay behind in Samaria," he said. "Jacob asked that if the opportunity arose, I should stay here to be of help to those travelling through. I can also to be of use teaching in the surrounding villages."

After a brief farewell to Stefanos's family and Philip, we left the village with Lazarus and Mary walking ahead with Helena and Lydia. I followed behind with Barnabas.

* * *

That night we slept under the stars, with Barnabas telling us of his travels around the Mediterranean Sea by ship. The thought of sailing away from the land was terrifying, but I didn't show my fear in front of my brother and sister. Sleeping better than I imagined I would out in the open, I awoke to a vivid dawn which gave way to another fine day. Barnabas claimed it was a good day for travel and led us by the back paths, helping us to stay away from people and to travel in safety.

The day progressed without incident and we stopped at midday for a rest. Barnabas looked behind himself and scanned the road. With squinting eyes his eyebrows came together in a sombre expression. I made sure the others couldn't overhear and approached him.

"Do you think we are in danger of being followed?" I whispered.

"That's a possibility, but I don't think anyone will be on this back road," he answered.

"Then why the serious face?"

"Look in the distance, what can you see?"

I scoured the horizon and squinting in the sun, noticed a thin brown line creeping over the landscape.

"Is that what I think it is?" I asked in horror.

He nodded, "We'd better find shelter quick."

Mary saw my anxious face. "Is Saul behind us?" she screamed.

"No, but we are in danger. We need somewhere to shelter immediately. There's a dust storm heading this way."

Dust storms were a danger which happened every few years. At home, we rushed around the house bringing everything inside and closing all the shutters and gates. Inside the house we were safe but what worried me most was being caught out in the open.

"Lazarus run up that hill and see if there is any house or barn for shelter," I shouted.

Helena followed him saying, "I'll go with him, I've got good eyesight."

They searched around for what seemed like minutes, and with increasing anxiety, I looked up and shouted, "Can you see anywhere at all where we can shelter?"

Lazarus looked down and shook his head.

"There!" Helena pointed. "There's a roof behind those olive trees."

By the time they had run back and we had collected our bags to run across the open fields towards the building, the looming wall of dust was almost upon us. The wind whipped our clothing and scarves, pressing them into our bodies.

"How far, Helena?" Barnabas shouted over the sound of the wind howling in our ears. "We've little time."

She pointed towards the trees, and in the growing gloom I made out stone walls and a wooden roof of an old barn. It didn't look secure, but it was the best we had to protect ourselves from the imminent storm. No matter how we covered our faces with scarves and clothing, the sand and stones swirled around and stung our eyes. The storm filled our mouths with grit making breathing difficult, as if someone had thrown bowls of sand in our faces. Mary screamed when a large branch fell off an olive tree and landed at her feet, its leaves and branches adding to the churning dust. Barnabas stood behind her and pushed her across the field.

Helena was the first at the barn and determinedly rattled the door, Lazarus joined her, but it wouldn't budge until Barnabas gave it a mighty whack. The door banged against the wall, almost taking it off its hinges. Once inside, I found the bar to close the door behind us, but the groaning wind kept knocking the door away. With great difficulty, we managed to secure it and instantly felt more shielded by the stone walls, but we were far from safe, the full storm hadn't yet reached us.

Lazarus found an amphora and looked inside. "There's water here, give me your scarves."

He took Lydia's scarf. dipped it in the water and wound it around her face. We copied and found breathing easier. The wind buffeted and shook the small barn, blowing dust through even the smallest gap between the stones, and making the roof timbers creak. Searching through the rest of the old farm equipment, I found a barn door.

"That roof isn't safe. Lydia get those stones and make a pile there," I screamed to make myself heard over the howling gusts. "Barnabas, get the door!"

Together, we made a small wall with the stones, and Barnabas picked up the door and flung it across them to lie on the floor at an angle. He pushed us under just in time before the timbers flew off the roof, and we cowered as each stone and piece of debris hammered onto our makeshift covering. With no breath to scream, we gripped onto each other as if afraid we would blow away. How long we lay buffeted I'm not sure, but gradually the wind ceased. The door above our backs was heavy with stones and rocks.

"Lie still and cover your heads," Barnabas croaked and heaved the door from our back, sending yet more stones into the air.

I tried to speak, and with my throat itchy with dust, gasped, "Is anyone hurt?"

We examined ourselves, but apart from a few cuts and bruises, we had come through the dust storm unscathed.

Lazarus coughed. "Thank God Helena found this barn, and for your idea of the door."

Choking and coughing, we tried to dislodge the dust from our stinging throats. Miraculously, the amphora of water was still intact, and taking our scarves, we washed our faces, removing the grit from our eyes, ears and noses. We covered our mouths once more with a wet scarves and surveyed the damage to the now roofless barn. Debris littered the ground, and someone's sandal, picked up by the wind, lay amongst wooden timbers, roof tiles and torn branches. An olive tree rested at an angle, suspended by the stone wall. It had only just missed us. Even with the door for protection, the tree would have crushed us to death.

* * *

Tired from the exertion of surviving the dust storm, we refilled our water bags and resumed our journey towards the coast in silence. Dust continued to swirl in the air for the rest of the day and we lay down wearily to rest and sleep that night. In the morning, the birds renewed their singing in a greeting of the dawn as if nothing out of the ordinary had happened the day before. And like the birds, we shook off the trauma and the four young people chatted together as they walked.

"When did Jesus first come to Bethany?" asked Lydia.

Mary sniggered and said, "It was nearly three years ago when Martha invited him in for lunch and had to hide the sweeping brush behind her back."

Walking next to Lazarus, Helena asked, "When did the gatherings in your home begin?"

"Ours was one of the first groups set up for the new believers to gather and worship," he answered.

"Does Simon teach there?"

"Sometimes, but it's usually one of us now, and we go around to the other groups to teach."

I noticed Lazarus's use of the present tense. These events were now in our past, and I felt sorrow at leaving them behind, but I was also pleased that we had achieved much in our home. Helena was an inquisitive young woman who, walking with Lazarus, continued to smile at him and ask many questions.

"How many people worship with you?"

"It varies. Sometimes only ten, but we've had up to fifty people crammed into our courtyard."

"Do they all live in Bethany, or do some travel from Jerusalem?"

"They're mainly from the village, but we've had visitors from Jerusalem and even from the rest of Judea."

Helena touched his arm. "What does Simon say about the Temple?"

Lazarus continued to walk alongside Helena for the rest of the morning, answering her many questions.

Since leaving the Samaritan village, Helena had sought Lazarus's company, and he delighted in the attention. I detected a growing intimacy between them, more noticeable from Lazarus's side. Having avoided confronting Mary over her relationship with Stefanos, I determined not to make the same mistake twice. After a stop for a frugal lunch, I pulled Lazarus back to walk with me behind everyone. Helena turned back to us.

"Helena, stay with Lydia and Mary. I want to walk with Lazarus for a little while," I shouted.

Lazarus was blunt. "What do you want, Martha?"

I tried the direct approach. "I want to talk with you about Helena." He looked away. "When we arrive in Antioch, they will leave us to join their family and I'm worried that you are becoming too attached to her."

"I'm not attached to her, no more than to Lydia. They've both suffered a great deal, with their family in prison."

"Have you met their family?"

"No, but I think Stefanos did. He met with most of the Greek-speaking groups."

"Barnabas hasn't met them, and he went with Stefanos most of the time."

"If you want to know more about their family, why don't you ask them yourself."

"I've tried and they don't give many details."

Lazarus sighed. "It's upsetting to talk about them like it upsets me and Mary to talk about Stefanos."

I put my arm around his shoulders. "You are still grieving for your friend, and I don't want you hurt further when we have to say goodbye."

He shrugged my arm away. "Leave me alone, Martha. You don't understand how I'm feeling." His words stung; I was too well acquainted with grief to miss it in others. "We're glad they're here, and the four of us are comforting each other. Besides Antioch is only a short sail from Cyprus if we want to meet again. Helena!" she turned around. "Wait for me."

Lazarus left me standing on the path and ran to Helena, who smiled and took his arm. Certain that Helena wouldn't make a good wife for my brother, there was little I could do, except pray that he wouldn't be too disappointed. Lazarus avoided me after this conversation and took every opportunity to spend time with Helena.

On the morning of the third day after leaving Bethany, Barnabas stopped on a rocky outcrop and pointed into the distance.

"Mary, come and look," he shouted and held out his hand to pull her onto the rocks.

She stood open-mouthed. "What's that?"

"That's the Mediterranean Sea." Barnabas made room for me as I climbed up. "What do you think, Martha?" he asked.

I shielded my eyes from the glare of the sun and looked out towards the sea. "How far does it go? It's huge."

"The sea stretches way beyond the horizon for many miles."

"Where's Cyprus?" Lazarus asked.

Barnabas laughed. "We cannot see Cyprus from here, it's much too far away."

Helena and Lydia stood together whispering, until Lazarus took Helena's hand. "Come and look at the sea. Have you seen it before?"

"No, we haven't, we've spent most of our lives in Jerusalem."

"Do you like it?" he asked.

She smiled at him. "It's beautiful."

From that first glimpse of the sea, it held a fascination for me. As tired as I was after three days of walking, rough sleeping and the aftereffects of the dust storm, the sight was invigorating. I felt the cool breeze gently skimming my face, relieved to be near Caesarea after our journey, and I looked forward to meeting Johanna again.

"Is that a town?" Mary pointed to a settlement at the coast. "There are roads and buildings."

"That's Caesarea."

"Look! Ships are sailing in and out of the harbour," Lazarus shouted. "Will we be sailing on one of those?"

"Johanna and Chuza will arrange passage on a ship sailing past Cyprus. There'll be no problem, I've done it many times. Can you see those larger ships in the centre of the bay? That's the Roman Navy."

"Won't it be dangerous with the Romans here?" Mary asked.

"Caesarea is one of their main bases because the harbour is deep. Having the Navy stationed here helps to protect the cargo ships from pirates."

Lazarus stared at him. "Pirates and the Roman Navy. Now there are two more things to worry about."

CHAPTER 22

No building can compare to our Temple, but the grandeur of the buildings and monuments in Caesarea could not but impress. Excited, we looked around, and while the streets in Jerusalem were narrow, here we walked along wide avenues with shops and storerooms on either side. Full of the same bustling crowds I was used to, but these people were more cosmopolitan, many of whose language, dress and appearance I didn't recognise. Helena and Lydia hung their heads and covered their faces.

Lazarus walked with the sisters. "Don't be afraid, we'll be at Johanna's house soon and then we'll be safe."

"Stay close," Barnabas instructed.

I didn't need to hear that as I was too frightened of losing him and then I would never find Johanna. Grabbing hold of Mary, I held her tight, until she slipped from my grasp.

"Barnabas stop!" I shouted as loud as I could. "I can't see Mary."

We retraced our steps and found her staring at a large building with marble columns and wide steps, watching people coming and going.

"Mary, you must stay with us," I chided.

Without looking at me she continued. "What's that building? There's an enormous statue in front."

Barnabas explained. "This is the Temple of Caesar Augustus. When Herod the Great arrived here, there was only a small fishing village. In a few years, he had built one of the largest ports in the world and rebuilt the town as you see it today. Then to ingratiate himself with the Emperor, he renamed it Caesarea in his honour."

"Is Herod the Great the father of Herod Antipas whom Chuza works for?" Lazarus asked.

"Yes, that's right."

"Why is there such a large statue of the Emperor in a temple?" I asked.

"Herod dedicated the temple to him because the Emperor expects every Roman Citizen to worship him as a god."

"But the Emperor is just a man. Herod is Jewish. Why would he dedicate a temple to a false god?" Mary asked.

Barnabas took hold of Mary's arm. "Not so loud Mary," he whispered. He looked around to see if anyone was listening, but the passers-by were too busy to take notice of six tired and dusty travellers. "The Roman Emperor only allows Herod to be king; he would exile or even kill him if he displeased him. Not far to go now, but we must keep moving." He dragged us away from the temple. "We will follow the aqueduct, to the Palace."

"Why are we going to the Palace?" Mary asked, suddenly afraid.

"Where do you think Johanna lives? Chuza needs to be near Herod when he calls for him. Now, stop asking too many questions and hurry." Barnabas was becoming annoyed in his anxiety to reach safety.

We followed the aqueduct to an area of town where grand houses lined both sides of the street. A woman stood by a gate in front of a guard with a sword. She looked elegant in a crimson dress tied with a blue belt. Her scarf, a deep yellow, covered her braided hair under a gold circlet. Bracelets on her arm jangled as she waved in our direction. I turned around to see who she was waving at.

"Martha! Mary!" she shouted and ran to us. It was only when she was in front of me I realised who she was.

"Johanna, is it really you?" I hadn't recognised my friend in her rich clothes and jewellery.

"You have had a long journey to reach us, come inside my home and rest. Jacob's message arrived two days ago and we are expecting you." Johanna looked up the street before leading us into a courtyard garden, and once inside, we relaxed.

"I see you have fellow travellers," Johanna said as Helena and Lydia followed us in, and Lazarus introduced them.

Helena began crying. "Saul has arrested our parents, and we had to run away from Jerusalem. Martha is so kind in allowing us to travel with them."

Lydia grabbed Johanna's hands. "We have to sail to Antioch to our Aunt, please help us."

Johanna patted her hand. "You are welcome here, and we will do all we can to make sure you arrive there safely."

"Johanna, where do you live?" Lazarus asked, looking around at the opulent garden.

"Welcome to our home, please rest and relax." She squeezed my hands and kissed me. "I was so worried when I heard there was a dust storm in Samaria."

Lazarus was about to answer, but Mary butted in. "We sheltered in a barn and the roof blew off, but we hid under an old door. It was very exciting."

The sound of a fountain splashing on marble was refreshing after the dusty roads. Mosaics and tiles covered the ground, showing peacocks and exotic birds I had never seen. I turned around when a boy of seven years ran into the garden.

"Mummy, is this Martha, Mary and Lazarus?"

"Yes, darling, these are my friends who are visiting us for a few days."

"You must be Jesse," I said to him.

"How do you know my name?"

"Your mother has told me all about you and your sisters." Jesse looked up at Johanna and smiled.

Two girls entered holding hands. The younger one ran to Johanna. "This is Susanna," she said and taking hold of the older girl's hand introduced her, "and my eldest child, Abigail." Turning to her she said, "Can you arrange refreshments for our guests?"

"Yes mother." She turned and left the courtyard. Tall for her ten years of age, she had the same grace and poise as her mother.

Susanna touched my cloak. "Your clothes are all dusty and dirty," she said.

"Don't be rude, Susanna, but yes, they have walked a long way and now need to rest." Johanna led us to benches around the fountain. Abigail reappeared holding a jug of wine followed by two servants with silver trays of drink and food. Setting them upon on a table, they bowed and stood to one side before being dismissed.

Lazarus mouthed to Mary, "Johanna has servants."

"Lazarus, don't be shy. Please eat and drink."

The others helped themselves, enjoying the food after our sparse rations. Here was a different Johanna in her opulent home with servants to command. She sat next to me and took my hand.

"Martha, I am the same Johanna as I am in Bethany in your home, but here I am the wife of Herod Antipas's chief steward." Leaning towards me, she whispered, "But I prefer your home because you have always made me welcome. You have taught me so much with your generous hospitality." I cried at the mention of my home in Bethany. "I am so insensitive to mention your home, forgive me."

"Don't hold me, you'll get your nice clothes dirty," I said.

Ignoring me she continued to sit close and stroked my hand. "You look exhausted after your long journey, but you will feel better once you have rested."

I allowed Johanna to serve me a drink and a plate of food. When we had eaten, she showed us to bedrooms where we could wash and rest.

* * *

The room was full of bright sunshine and I awoke refreshed and feeling better after a good night's sleep in a bed. My clothes were lying clean and folded on a chair, and after dressing, I joined Johanna, Mary and Susanna in the courtyard garden.

"Good morning, Martha, or should I say good afternoon," Mary giggled.

"How long have I slept?" I asked.

Johanna indicated a seat next to her. "It doesn't matter how long; I am only pleased you have had a refreshing sleep."

A servant brought my breakfast which I ate, not realising how hungry I was. Sounds of laughter echoed around the fountain where Mary played with Susanna and her doll.

"Where is everyone?" I asked.

"Barnabas and Lazarus are still sleeping, and I've sent a servant up with their breakfasts."

"Where are Lydia and Helena?"

Mary answered. "They're in their bedroom, talking together as usual. I wonder what they find to talk about so much."

"What do you know of them?" Johanna asked.

"Very little," I answered. "They became believers two months ago along with their family. Saul arrested their parents the day after Stefanos's death." Mary tensed, and I immediately regretted mentioning Stefanos. "You spent time with them on the road, Mary, did they say anything?"

Mary looked up from playing with Susanna. "I've never known two people talk so much and say so little." I laughed at her succinct description of the sisters.

"Why do you ask?"

Johanna looked serious. "It is just a feeling that I recognise them. Did they mention a connection to Herod's Palace in Jerusalem? Perhaps as servants there?" Mary shook her head. "Never mind, it is probably nothing. Chuza apologises for not meeting you yesterday, you were asleep when he arrived home last night, and he had to leave early this morning. He intends to see you later today when he can get away."

Helena walked into the garden. "Did you have a good sleep, Martha?"

Lydia followed her. "It's so lovely here Johanna, I wonder how you can bear to leave home to travel to Jerusalem so often."

Barnabas and Lazarus entered behind them and stretched after their sleep. Helena went to stand by Lazarus's side.

"You look refreshed after your sleep, Lazarus. It's so nice to sleep in a proper bed. I've missed mine," she said.

A servant entered and spoke to Johanna. "Send him in please," she instructed the servant. "Any news, Thomas?" she asked when a man wearing street clothes entered.

"There is good news," he nodded. "I met a captain of a ship sailing to Cyprus on the early morning tide and booked your passage with him. You need to be at the jetty by midnight tonight."

"So soon. I'd hoped we could spend a few days with Johanna before we left," Mary pleaded.

"I would like longer too, but we need to leave as soon as we can," I told her. A silent tear fell as I took in the finality of our leaving. There was only one more day with my friend and it was possible we may never return to our homeland.

"Who have you booked our passage with?" Barnabas asked.

"The ship is called the *Minerva*."

"That's good news indeed. I've sailed on the *Minerva* with Captain Marcus and his crew many times."

"Are you Martha, Mary and Lazarus?" Thomas said. "Johanna has told many stories about you and it is an honour to meet you, and Barnabas too."

Lazarus tried to encourage Mary. "Imagine sailing on a ship on the sea, it will be such an adventure, Mary."

"We are not safe even here," Barnabas explained. "Saul's influence stretches throughout Judea and maybe even beyond our borders. There are spies in Caesarea, and the sooner we leave, the safer we will be. John instructed me to make sure you are safe, and he was most insistent that we sail as soon as possible."

Johanna took my arm. "I will have food and water sent to the ship this afternoon to save you carrying it this evening. Come, Martha, let us have one last day together and talk of old times."

Talking with Johanna led me to a more positive frame of mind. I decided if God was leading us into a new life in another country then I would gladly go. Jesus had offered his all for us and Stefanos had given his life. If I was being asked to leave my home, then so be it. Lazarus and Mary had such a positive attitude and were looking forward to their new life and new challenges. It was only a few days since the death of their friend, but I saw their healing from the grief and hurt was beginning.

* * *

I paced the room, trying to decide whether to be angry or worried about their safety. Two hours earlier, we discovered Helena and Lydia were missing. They told Mary they had shopping to do before going on the ship. Annoyed at not being asked to go with them, Mary only mentioned it after they had left Johanna's house.

Mary tutted. "What's so important that they couldn't buy it in Antioch? Unless it's a present for their Aunt."

Lazarus ran to the door. "I'm going out to look for them."

"No, you are not, you are staying right here," Barnabas blocked his way.

Lazarus tried to push him out of the way. "You can't make me stay here."

"I think you'll find I can," he said, refusing to move.

Lazarus found trying to shift Barnabas's considerable bulk an impossible task. He gave up and sank on a chair with his head in his hands. A minute later the door opened and Johanna and Chuza appeared with Thomas and another man.

"We have looked all over the town and cannot find them." Chuza's face was red, and I wasn't sure whether it was from exertion or anger.

Thomas shook his head. "Julius and I walked up and down the main street where the shops are, and there was no sight of them."

"No," Julius added, "we didn't ask any of the shopkeepers if they had seen them, because we didn't want anyone to know who they are."

Thomas introduced his friend. "This is Julius. He works at the harbour and has helped many people to escape."

"Anything could have happened to them," Lazarus cried. "They could have been attacked and lying injured or worse."

"Don't be dramatic, Lazarus," I shouted, but that possibility had occurred to me too.

"I'm not leaving without them."

Chuza stood in front of him and folded his arms. "I had strict instructions from John and Simon to ensure your safety. You will be on that ship this evening, even if I have to drag you there myself." Chuza's sheer personality was enough to quieten Lazarus.

Johanna tried to offer him comfort. "Try not to worry, Lazarus. If they miss this ship, we will take care of them and ensure that they get to their Aunt on the next one. Now, dinner is served, and we should eat."

"We'll go out and look again," Thomas said and left with Julius.

We shared a final meal which we determined to enjoy rather than be sad. I sat next to Johanna with Chuza on the other side of her. Chuza was tall with short black hair, greying at the temples, and a cropped beard in the Roman style. He wore a Roman toga when he arrived home, which he changed out of for the meal. His commanding presence and intelligent face had ensured his rise to a place of trust in Herod Antipas's household. Johanna and Chuza told us what they were doing to help believers escape from Saul.

"Many have passed through Caesarea," Chuza explained, "and we help to arrange safe passage to wherever they need to go."

"Where are they going?" Mary asked.

"Many leave to stay with relatives settled across the Roman Empire. Three families have crossed to Cyprus, so you may find friends already there. Others go to Greece or even as far as Rome."

Johanna's assurance to look after Helena and Lydia had calmed Lazarus. "Do you remember the last time we saw Jesus before he left?" he asked. "What did he say would happen?"

Mary answered, "He said we would talk about him first in Jerusalem, then in Judea, Samaria and finally out to all the earth."

Lazarus leaned forward on the table. "That's exactly what's happening. First, we spoke about him in Jerusalem and Judea. Philip has stayed in Samaria with Sara, and we are spreading out over the Roman Empire. We may not like it and it may be hard, but I'm sure this is part of God's plan."

Mary laughed. "Saul will never win because he's acting as God's agent, even if he doesn't know it."

"Know it yet! I'm praying he will one day," Lazarus replied.

"I admire your faith Lazarus," Chuza said, "but I cannot see that happening soon. I met Saul three months ago in Jerusalem when he went to see Herod. A rodent-like man with a perpetual scowl, thoroughly unlikeable in every way."

"That describes the man," Barnabas agreed. "What did he want with Herod?"

"He wanted to enlist his help in chasing down and capturing the believers."

"Is Herod going to help him?" Lazarus asked.

"No, Herod is far too concerned with strengthening his kingdom and appearing strong to the Romans to worry about what he sees as theological disputes. But I was listening when Saul let slip his intentions. His persecution would have happened anytime, and Stefanos was just the one who gave him the excuse to start. Before returning to Caesarea I met in secret with Jacob, John, James and Simon."

The news surprised Barnabas. "I didn't know that, did you, Martha?" I shook my head.

251

"No one other than us knew because we had to keep it secret. That was one reason Stefanos's death upset John so much, he wondered whether we could have prevented it."

Johanna touched her husband's arm. "Nothing could stop Saul, but together you have saved many lives."

Chuza took her hand. "It gave us time to put plans into operation. Jacob is an intelligent man with great foresight, and together we put into place a network of safe houses, like Sara's house in Samaria. Johanna and I developed routes to safety going through Samaria, west towards Damascus, the land route north to Antioch and here in Caesarea. When Stefanos's family left Sara's, she would tell them where to go next. For everyone's safety, no one knows the whole set up."

Intrigued to discover more I asked, "What happens when someone arrives here?"

Johanna explained. "Jacob gives each person escaping via Caesarea instructions of where to go. We meet them and take them to one of our safe houses. There they wait for a ship sailing in their direction and then slip onto it, usually under cover of darkness."

"Saul has spies here and we are trying to find out who they are. Some may even have infiltrated our group. We realise the danger of what we are doing, and we are careful not to endanger any of us. Our group is small, but we are doing what we can." Chuza said.

"You are both very brave," Mary said to Johanna.

"No, we are not brave. People like you, leaving their land and families, are the brave ones," Johanna answered.

"But your position in Herod's household might put you in danger." I looked at Chuza and he nodded.

"Does Saul suspect you are one of us?" Mary asked.

"Not yet, hopefully!" Chuza laughed. "I am trying to keep it that way. Herod has a volatile nature, with terrible mood swings and no one is safe." He lowered his voice to a whisper, "There is a saying that it is safer to be Herod's pig than his son. He may not be a good Jew, but he never eats pork and keeps his pigs as pets. However, he has murdered his own son whom he accused of betraying him. Don't worry, I have worked for him for a long time and know how to placate him. Our friends who run the safe houses are in a more dangerous position than we are."

A knock at the door caused Chuza to put his hand up to silence us. "Come in," he shouted. A servant entered followed by Thomas. The servant bowed and closed the door behind him.

Lazarus ran to him. "Have you found Helena and Lydia?"

"No, sorry, we've looked everywhere we can think of. Julius has left for the harbour. He has work to do this evening."

Chuza stood and Thomas whispered something into his ear. "Damn it! They have spotted Saul in Caesarea. Tell us what you know, Thomas."

Thomas nodded as Chuza offered him a cup of wine. "Our contacts saw Saul entering Caesarea with one other man and two guards, travelling south from Galilee."

"Will they come here?" Mary cried.

"No, you are safe here," Johanna assured her.

"We followed them to the harbour where they booked lodgings at an inn."

"How will we get to the ship?" It was Lazarus's turn to cry out.

"Sir, I had an idea on my way here. Can I discuss something with you?"

Chuza left with Thomas and returned five minutes later. "There is a slight change of plan, and you will leave a little earlier. It is only nine o'clock and you will not need to leave for two hours. Please rest and I will call you when it is time. Barnabas, may I take your cloak? Yours too, Lazarus."

Barnabas shrugged his shoulders and handed over his cloak along with Lazarus's. Chuza nodded to Johanna who left the room with him.

* * *

"I'm not going without them," Lazarus reiterated.

I was becoming cross. "We've been through this, and you are getting on that ship. You can decide whether to walk on your own or Barnabas can throw you on."

"What if Saul has arrested them?"

"It's their own fault for leaving Johanna's house," Mary scoffed.

Lazarus wiped his nose with his hand. "He could take them back to Jerusalem to be killed like Stefanos."

Chuza appeared with Thomas. "I have checked with my contacts, and it does not appear that Saul has arrested them." He put a reassuring arm around Lazarus. "There must be a reason for their disappearance, and when we find them, we will keep them safe here."

Thomas handed cloaks to Barnabas and Lazarus. "It's time," he said.

Johanna placed my cloak around my shoulders and held it in place. "The weather has been mild, and you should have a good crossing." She pretended that this was just a short journey and we would return in a few days, but we both knew we may never see each other again. "I want to know how you settle in with Barnabas's family. There will be no problems if they are all as cheerful as he is. Write me a long letter detailing everything."

"We look ridiculous!" Barnabas put on Chuza's longest cloak which had the straps extended to tie around his neck and the end of which didn't reach his knees. Lazarus was wearing another cloak which Johanna had shortened. Despite the seriousness of what we were facing we laughed at them.

Lazarus grumbled, "I don't see why we couldn't wear our own."

"Because we need them," Chuza explained again. "It is of vital importance you keep your hoods up and your faces covered. Be as quiet as possible from the moment you leave here because someone may be watching. Thomas will lead you to the harbour, and I will send a message to Jacob as soon as you sail safely away."

Despite promising myself not to, I held onto Johanna. "Kiss your children for me," I cried as she wiped my eyes and smiled.

Unable to utter a goodbye, I turned to leave and for the second time disappeared into the night. Thomas led us by narrow darkened passageways towards the harbour but stopped on the corner by the safe house. He peeped around the wall.

"There are men outside. Something's wrong." Bending his head he looked around the building again, then breathed out in relief, "Oh, it's only Julius."

Laughter echoed around the walls and I gripped Thomas's arm to stop him from moving and in alarm shook my head.

"What is it?" he mouthed.

"That's Jonas, my neighbour who has followed us here. He works for Saul."

Thomas stopped breathing. "Julius?" he asked, and I nodded realising who the infiltrator was. Recovering himself, he whispered, "This way."

We followed him into a deserted warehouse where we hid behind sacks of grain.

"Thank God he left before I came up with the plan. Stay here until I give the signal," he said. "When I say run, you run along the jetty, as if the devil is at your heels, to the ship at the end and don't stop for anything."

Thomas disappeared and despite the warmth of the night and our cloaks, I shivered. Mary's fingers dug into my arm and her beating heart echoed my own. Two minutes later we heard voices outside the warehouse.

"Which ship are they heading towards?" It was Saul. He'd found us.

"The *Minerva*, that's the ship on the end." I recognised Julius's voice from earlier. "They'll never get there, we can stop them anytime we like."

"I don't want any mishaps. I need to have all three arrested and I'll have them at last." It was Jonas again.

"Don't you mean four?" Saul asked.

"Well yes, but the three from Bethany are important."

Saul was angry. "You are fixated on Martha and her house, when stopping this erroneous teaching from spreading is our main priority."

Jonas muttered something I didn't hear.

"There you are," Julius laughed. "I wondered where you'd got to."

A woman joined in with his laughter. "Giving Chuza the runaround, brother!"

"They never suspected you?" he asked.

"No, they're too trusting and stupid, and we've lied to them since Jerusalem." She changed her voice into one more pleading. "Oh please help me, Martha. Sob, sob, sob." I closed my eyes in the realisation we had taken spies into the heart of Johanna's and Chuza's network and endangered people I loved.

"At least, you didn't have to pretend to like Lazarus. I almost gagged." They all laughed. "Next time, you're the one to fall in love."

Hidden next to me, my brother crumbled, and his shoulders shook.

"Guards, there's Barnabas. Don't let them get away," Saul shouted.

"Lazarus, too. I want him caught," shrieked Jonas. Barnabas held on to Lazarus's arm to prevent him from darting out from our hiding place. Their footsteps disappeared around the corner and Thomas beckoned us forward.

"Quick, run up the jetty towards the ship at the far end. The one with the torch on the bow." From our hiding place we ran onto the jetty.

"Thomas, what's happening?" I asked breathlessly.

"Decoys in your cloaks have led them away. Hurry, it won't be long before they realise. Once you're on the ship, you'll be safe. I must run to Chuza and tell him Julius has betrayed us."

"Before you go, it's not only Julius but Helena and Lydia too."

"I heard everything. Now run!"

He pushed me forward and I ran, holding Mary's hand, feeling exposed in the torchlight. The jetty stretched far out to sea, and I wondered if we would ever reach the end before being caught.

"You idiots!" Saul screamed. "They are decoys. To the jetty, quick." The sound of Saul's shouts mixed with their running steps as they followed us onto the jetty. Mary dropped her bag and ran back to retrieve it. Thomas whose way back was now blocked had no choice but to follow us. He ran onto the jetty, picked up Mary's bag and pushed her forward.

"Run!" he screeched. The lights of the ship appeared no nearer, and my lungs hurt as I breathed in, trying to get more strength to push my legs to run quicker.

Barnabas pushed me, and Lazarus ran with Mary. The footsteps and shouts of Saul's guards became louder, and I dared not look around. Lazarus tripped and fell over his cloak, rolling along the ground until Barnabas picked him up onto his feet again. A strong hand grabbed my arm and yanked me aboard a ship, followed by Mary and Lazarus. Barnabas shouted when a guard grabbed his cloak which ripped as he pulled it away. The ship rocked as he pushed Thomas and jumped on after him. Armed with swords, daggers and a bow primed with an arrow, the crew stood between us and Saul.

The man who had pulled me aboard stood in the bow. "Take one step onto my ship and I'll kill you." A quiet voice with a menacing edge, which didn't need a sword to be threatening.

Malice flashed in Saul's eyes. "Hand over the fugitives."

"Who are they to you?" the man I later knew as the captain asked.

"You are harbouring dangerous criminals and we have orders to arrest them," Jonas spat out the words.

"They don't seem dangerous to me. Or are you afraid of a little girl?" The crew laughed, but the captain stood unflinching.

"In the name of the Lord God of Israel, hand them over," Jonas shouted.

"I don't recognise your God."

"Then hand them over in the name of Herod Antipas who personally gave me a warrant for their arrest. Or we will call his soldiers." Saul was bluffing but would the captain realise?

"King Herod has no authority on board my ship. So, piss off until you have a platoon of Roman soldiers standing behind you." The captain nodded to a crew member who jumped onto the jetty, let the rope loose and the ship drifted away.

"Thomas," Julius shouted, "how will you get to Chuza before us to warn him?"

The two girls laughed, and Helena blew Lazarus a kiss. I was proud of my brother who stood looking at her impassively until they turned to walk back down the jetty.

I breathed again.

CHAPTER 23

With his hands on his knees and breathing hard, Barnabas gasped, "Thank you, Captain. That was close."

"You can thank me by paying me." He pointed to Thomas. "He said six, but now there are five. Did you leave someone behind?"

"No, unless you mean the women who betrayed us."

The captain looked at me. "That's what women do well."

I went to protest, but Barnabas held my arm.

Thomas grabbed the captain's shoulder. "I must get off this ship as soon as possible."

"I'll tell you when you can get off." The captain folded his arms.

"We are betrayed," Thomas pleaded, "and I have to unmask the traitor, or the lives of our friends may be in danger. We agreed on a fee for six passengers, which we will honour but now there's only four. Or do you want more money?"

"Traitors are evil scum who deserve what they get. The coast is too rocky to let you off before the next port, which is ten miles away. We'll be there by dawn."

"I'll pay more if you can get there sooner."

"We can only go as quickly as the wind or tides allow."

He walked away and shouted to a member of the crew. "What are you doing with that rope? You know what to do. Do it, man."

Lazarus, with blood oozing from a cut on his forehead, heaved, and leaning over the side, was sick.

The captain sneered. "Make sure you're sick over the side boy, or you'll mop the deck yourself. Don't get under our feet. Sailor, get that sail unfurled before we lose the wind." Striding the length of the ship, he continued to bark orders.

Barnabas led us to the stern where we could sit before my legs gave way. Under the dark sky, we sat on the deck leaning against the side and regained our breath and composure after the flight along the jetty.

I held onto Lazarus's head and said, "Let me see to that cut." Lazarus swatted my arm away and hit his head with his hands until I held his wrists. "Don't do that, you'll hurt yourself."

"I can't hurt any more than I do now," he cried. "How stupid I must be to think she liked me, but it was just an act to get me to tell her stuff." He allowed Mary to wipe his head with a cloth she found in her bag. "I hope I didn't tell her anything important that might put people in danger." Sniffing, he wiped his nose with the back of his hand.

Barnabas put his arm around him. "Don't worry, we've all been taken in by a pretty face, I bet even the captain has in his time."

"It wasn't only you, they fooled all of us," I said.

Thomas sat with his head in his hands groaning. "I trusted Julius."

"How long have you known him?" Barnabas asked.

"We've been friends for two years. He said he had sisters, but I never met them. Why would anyone work for Saul after what he's done to us?"

"Motivated by money like most traitors," mused Barnabas. "Jesus understands betrayal because it happened to him. Judas was one of his most trusted followers who turned against him for money."

"Did you know Judas?" he asked me.

"Yes, he stayed at my home many times and shared meals with us. No one could have predicted what he would do."

"What was he like?"

Remembering Judas sitting in my courtyard I said, "I liked him, but with hindsight there were signs. He kept the purse and paid for their food and lodgings when needed. The truth came out later that he'd pocketed cash for his own purposes and took money Johanna and Chuza donated. Did you hear the story of Mary anointing Jesus's feet after he raised Lazarus from the dead?" Thomas nodded. "He spoilt the wonderful occasion by saying it was a waste of money."

"If it happened to Jesus, it should be of no surprise when it happens to us. If I run, I can be home by midday. But what if Julius has told lies and said I'm the betrayer? How will they believe me and not them?"

"What if I tell you something that only Johanna and I know? Then they'll believe you," I said.

"I know," said Mary. "Jesus helped Johanna to grind the corn to make flour, and then made bread for our breakfast. They'll never guess that because it's something no other man would do."

"You didn't mention that to Helena and Lydia, did you?"

"No, they asked what Jesus said in our home, but I never told them that story."

"Good, have you got that Thomas?" He nodded. "Ask to speak to Johanna and Chuza in private, then tell them what Mary and I told you and they'll believe you."

"One thing is bothering me. Where did you find two men who resembled me and Lazarus?" Barnabas asked.

"Believe it or not, they're brothers who hang around the harbour looking for odd jobs and will do anything for money or a flagon of wine. Their job was to lead Saul away from the jetty, but they were too slow and were caught sooner than I expected."

Barnabas smiled. "You should've told them not to drink the wine beforehand, and now they have our cloaks to wear. Let's get some rest, especially you Thomas, you have a long walk back to Caesarea in a few hours."

Underneath our cloaks, we lay on the deck, and despite the unfamiliar movement of the ship and the tiring day I soon fell asleep. I awoke when I felt the ship change course and, stretching, discovered that the captain had made good time and arrived two hours before dawn. We said goodbye to Thomas and after he jumped ashore, the captain ordered the ship back out to sea. Unable to get back to sleep I watched the dawn from the deck of a ship for the first time.

Barnabas tried to comfort Lazarus who was sick again. "You'll soon be used to the motion of the ship. This often happens to first-time sailors."

Lazarus wiped his mouth with the back of his hand. "I want to get off. Can we walk?"

"Jesus walked on the water of Lake Galilee and Simon managed a few steps before almost drowning. But I wouldn't recommend you try it."

"Why aren't Mary and Martha sick?" he groaned.

Barnabas handed him a cup of water. "Not everyone gets seasick. Have a drink or you'll soon dehydrate."

Far too excited to suffer from seasickness, I watched the crew hoist the sails and turn the ship into the wind. "It's amazing how the whole crew knows what to do and each has a job and they do it well."

"This ship has a crew of seven men, two of whom are slaves and the rest freedmen, all experienced sailors. Captain Marcus is stern but fair to his men. He's a good sailor and always steers his ship safe to harbour."

"That's good to know, but he's always shouting orders to the crew."

"Don't let him disturb you, he's like a dog who barks loudly but never bites."

"I've heard ships have names, and they call this one the *Minerva*. Is that a Roman goddess? There were shrines dedicated to her in Caesarea."

"Minerva is the goddess of commerce and wisdom. Captain Marcus thinks she'll bring him luck with the sale of his cargo," Barnabas explained.

"He'd do better to trust in the Lord, and I don't enjoy sailing on a ship dedicated to a goddess."

"There's no need to worry, I've sailed on this ship many times, and we'll be fine."

Lazarus was sick again. Two sailors laughed but fortunately, he was too ill to hear. With my arm around him, I leaned on the rail, staring at the country of my birth sailing passed. Captain Marcus strode up to us and clasped arms with Barnabas.

"Welcome aboard, it's good to see you again." I could see the respect the two men had for one another. "I thought that was you trying to run up the jetty."

"I haven't run that fast for many years," Barnabas shared his joke, "and I'm pleased to sail with you on the *Minerva* again. God is good to us."

"You trust your God and I'll trust *Minerva*; she's never let me down yet. Who are your travelling companions?"

"Captain Marcus, I'd like to introduce my friends. This is Martha, along with her sister Mary and brother Lazarus."

I smiled in greeting. "Captain Marcus, thank you for pulling us to safety last night and for not giving us up to our pursuers."

"Who would pay for your passage if I'd let them take you? Welcome aboard Lady. Stay out of the way of my sailors and they won't bother you. Son, you'll soon feel better. Look straight ahead and keep your eye on the horizon."

Lazarus let out a grunt as the captain slapped him on the back, and for the first time, I saw him smile. He then turned away to shout at a crew member. Captain Marcus was younger than I thought a captain would be. He looked in his early thirties, but the effects of the wind and rain may have made him look older than he was. A head full of dark brown hair reached his shoulders, and he kept his beard cropped short. Like the rest of the crew, he wore a short tunic, but unlike those of the sailors, his was clean. His shrewd dark eyes missed nothing, and he was in command of his vessel. I could see why Barnabas trusted him.

* * *

The *Minerva* was a sturdy cargo ship, designed for sea travel with two masts. The taller central mast had a square crimson sail which billowed when it caught the wind. A smaller mast reached out from the bow and sailors unfurled a small crimson sail when the captain ordered more speed. To the stern was the one cabin where the captain slept. On top of this was an upper deck from which two rudders steered the ship. One of the crew told me that the *Minerva* carried one thousand amphorae of wine and five hundred amphorae of olive oil. Captain Marcus hoped to sell these in various ports between Caesarea and Athens. At each port, he picked up cargo and sold it on at the next for a profit.

Everyone apart from the captain slept under the stars. So, on the second evening, we erected a tent, nothing more than a simple covering over part of the deck allocated as our sleeping area. The following days at sea passed without incident and I was pleased to rest after the turmoil of the previous few days' travel. We made our food in the galley after the crew had made theirs and slept under our tent. Lazarus never got used to the motion of the ship and was constantly sick. Even during the night, he retched and heaved, getting little sleep. Unlike my brother, the rocking had a calming effect on me. Despite the worry of what was happening in Jerusalem and Caesarea, I slept well each night.

The ship sailed north following the coastline and on the morning of the second day I took my last glimpse of Judea. The land looked the same, and I wouldn't have known we were sailing past Syria if Captain Marcus hadn't told me. This didn't grieve me as much as I supposed it would. Not that I had become resigned to the fact of leaving my homeland, but something stirred within me. A feeling that I couldn't figure out.

On the third day, we sailed into the port of Seleucia, near the city of Antioch, where Captain Marcus was to do business. Standing on deck he shouted orders to the crew and the small tugboats rowed by slaves, which directed the ship to rest onto the quayside with a small bump.

Captain Marcus nodded his head. "Now get the cargo unloaded," he instructed.

A gangplank shot onto the quay and I followed Lazarus, who ran down it and collapsed onto the solid ground in relief.

Captain Marcus shouted after me, "You can spend the night at an inn but be here by dawn tomorrow or I'll leave without you, Lady!" I turned to face him. "If you want my advice, I'd take an inn away from the docks. Or you may hear a knock on your door asking how much you charge."

The sailors laughed, but Barnabas rounded on him. "There's no need for that Marcus."

Laughing, he waved Barnabas away. "I'll be there myself tonight if you want to join me."

A man pushed past onto the gangplank. "What've you got for me today, Captain Marcus?"

They shook hands. "What about fifty amphorae of Judean wine? Only the good stuff. Come aboard and I'll give you a taste."

We walked away from the *Minerva*, past the warehouses and towards a more reputable inn for the night.

Mary pulled a face. "I don't like Captain Marcus," she said. "His shouting frightens me."

"Don't be afraid of him, he's lived around sailors all his life, and it's just his way with everyone." Barnabas tried to defend his behaviour.

Disgusted by his comment about the inn, I said, "I've met men like him before, who delight in disturbing you with their coarseness. It's best to ignore them. Nathan would never speak like that to a woman. I wanted to ask you about him but didn't want to onboard in case he overheard. He's younger than I expected."

"When I first met him, he was the first mate, to the old Captain Antonius. How old he was when he first walked onto the ship, I don't know. But he's spent a lifetime aboard the *Minerva* and knows every plank and wooden peg of his beloved ship. He may be young for a captain, but the crew respect and obey him," Barnabas explained.

Intrigued to know more about him, I asked, "When did he become the captain?"

"Captain Antonius spent his life at sea, never marrying or having children. When he retired three years ago, he offered the ship to Marcus who's still paying off his debt to him."

That explained his need to get as much money out of us as he could. We found an inn up the hill from the port which didn't look too filthy. Lazarus was just glad to be away from the constant motion and would have slept on the quayside. That evening I pushed a chair against the doorknob of the bedroom I shared with Mary and got little sleep.

* * *

Terrified of being left behind I made sure we were at the quayside in time to buy provisions before we boarded. An outcry erupted from the *Minerva* and Captain Marcus shouted at a member of the crew and pushed him down the gangplank.

"Get off my ship," he shouted.

The man I recognised as one of the ship's slaves, stood on the quay.

"Who are you?" the Captain cried.

"My name is Alexus," his voice rang clear.

"Are you a slave or free?" the Captain asked.

Alexus punched the air. "I am a freedman!"

"What do you want?"

"To be a free member of your crew."

"You better come aboard."

Alexus stepped on the gangplank to the cheers of the crew.

At a loss to explain what I saw, I asked Barnabas, "What's happening? That man is a slave."

"I've seen this once before with Captain Antonius. When a slave has worked for ten years, he's given his freedom.

He's pushed off the ship and must ask to join the crew as a freedman or walk away, but most decide to re-join."

Captain Marcus tossed a coin to Alexus and slapped him on the back. The crew stood around congratulating him until the captain shouted.

"You! Freedman!" He pointed at Alexus. "Get below deck and make sure the new cargo is stored safely."

"Yes, Captain." Smiling, Alexus climbed down the ladder into the hold.

"Good morning, Lady, I trust you slept well." He made a mock bow and grinned. "I hope there were no untoward disturbances during the night."

Determined to show that he couldn't mock me, I replied, "Mary and I slept well, thank you, Captain."

He laughed. "The ship at the end of the quay is sailing to Caesarea on the tide. Can you write?" I nodded. "Send a letter to the friends you left behind in your hurry to get aboard my ship. Make sure they know who the real traitor is."

"Thank you, but I have no writing tablet or parchment."

"There's parchment and ink in my cabin. Don't take more than five minutes, because I'm seeing its captain before we leave."

The door was low and I had to bend to enter. Not expecting his cabin to be so tidy, it surprised me to see scrolls neatly stacked in shelves around the small room. Folded on top of a sturdy wooden chest was a good crimson tunic and cloak. But apart from the few clothes and his comb and razor, there were no other personal items. A wax tablet lay on a small table which doubled as his desk. Displayed in neat and legible writing was the cargo he had just bought and sold and for what cost and profit. A chart of the sea lay open and I read the names of ports we had visited. I saw the word Cyprus but did not understand how to read the chart. In the absence of a chair, I perched on the edge of his bunk. Taking a scrap of parchment, I picked up his pen, dipped the sharp nib in the ink and wrote:

My Dear Johanna and Chuza,

I am writing from aboard the Minerva and have arrived safely at Seleucia. By now Thomas will be back in Caesarea, and I hope that the story I sent about the morning Jesus ground the corn has convinced you he was telling the truth. On arriving at the quay, we found Julius with Saul and Jonas and he is the one who has betrayed our network. Helena and Lydia are his sisters and were Saul's spies even when in Jerusalem. No one met their family, and we now believe the story of their arrest was a lie. They pretended to escape with the sole intention of finding out information to use against us. Please forgive me for bringing danger into your home. Write as soon as you can, I am desperate for news of your safety.

Regards,

Martha

Sealing the scroll with wax, I left the cabin to hand the letter to Captain Marcus and gave him a coin to pay for its delivery. "Thank you, it has eased my mind to write to them."

"We'll be in the open sea for the next three days and it can get choppy. Would you and your sister prefer to stay in the cabin? It will give you ladies more privacy."

I stared at him. "Thank you, Captain."

Not liking how the men looked at Mary, I gladly accepted his offer. As young women, we would be vulnerable without

Barnabas's presence and the captain's warning we were not to be molested. With three strides he was off the gangplank and heading for the other ship.

Barnabas stared open-mouthed. "Well, I've never known him to give up his cabin. You must have made an impression."

"I'm sure it's nothing I've done, and I wasn't expecting this courtesy from him."

Before turning away to make breakfast, I watched Captain Marcus talk to the other captain. Shouting from the quay made me turn around to see him arguing with another man. Handing him money, he took a boy from his side. The man shouted something I didn't hear, and he fell as Captain Marcus hit him on the jaw. Then the captain took the boy by the arm, dragged him to the ship and pushed him up the gangplank.

The man wiped the blood from his nose and shouted, "Give me back my slave."

Captain Marcus stood on deck. "I gave you the price you asked, and now he's mine."

"I demand you hand him back."

Sprinting, the captain ran onto the quay and the other man withdrew backwards.

"He's useless anyway, you'll soon regret buying him," the man with the bloodied nose cried.

Captain Marcus glared at the man who turned and walked away. He strode back on board and up to the boy. "Alexus! Get him a new tunic and by Minerva, give him a wash, he stinks."

Alexus soon appeared with the smallest tunic he could find, but it was far too big for the scrawny child.

"Give me the tunic," I said to Alexus, "I'll alter it."

I took the boy to one side, where he watched Barnabas's spoon move from the bowl to his mouth. Barnabas offered him a chunk of bread, which he grabbed, stuffed into his mouth, and swallowed without chewing. Mary cut the old tunic and sewed two new ones, and, afraid that he might choke, I gave him small pieces of bread one at a time. Blood seeped from a gash above his eye.

Worried at the anger I'd witnessed from the captain I asked, "Did Captain Marcus hit you?"

With terror-stricken eyes, he shook his head. His ragged filthy tunic was ripped to show a skinny body covered in old bruises. Mary wanted to hug him, but he backed away in fear. Taking a cloth, I gently washed his body and shaved head and placing the new tunic on him, took him to the captain.

"What's your name?" he growled, but when the boy didn't answer, he shouted louder. "What are you called?"

In a gentler tone, I asked, "What did your old master call you?"

"Stupid," his whisper was only just audible.

Captain Marcus folded his arms. "That's not much of a name. I'll call you Gallio."

I turned to him. "You can't just invent a new name for him."

"Why not? Because I'm not calling him Stupid. Gallio," he called more quietly than before, "how old are you?"

His entire body shaking, the boy swallowed. "Twelve, I think," his small voice uttered.

"He's small for twelve," Captain Marcus said to me.

"His ribs are sticking out of his chest and he's covered in bruises."

"Gallio, you're my slave now. You'll address me as Captain and do what I say. See him," he pointed at Lazarus, "he'll be sick in a few minutes, and when he is you clean the deck." Gallio nodded, too scared to say anything.

CHAPTER 24

From the safe confines of the port, we headed away from the coast and out into open water. Before long the land disappeared, the waves became larger, and I prayed for Lazarus that he wouldn't suffer much. Unable to keep anything down, not even water, he continued to retch over the side. Afraid of displeasing his new master, Gallio hung around Lazarus, with buckets of seawater at the ready to clean up after him.

With the salt spray in my face and the wind blowing my hair, I stood in the bow as the ship rose and fell with each wave. Feeling free and invigorated, I was becoming stronger as poor Lazarus became weaker.

"Lady!" Captain Marcus shouted. "Look to starboard." By this time I knew this meant the right side of the ship.

He joined me and held onto the small mast in the bow. With loud splashes, creatures like large fishes jumped in and out of the water.

"What are they?"

"Dolphins, Lady."

"Are they dangerous?"

Laughing at my lack of knowledge, he said, "No, they bring a sailor good luck. Dolphins enjoy swimming with ships and often lead us to shore."

One dolphin jumped high out of the water, and I clapped and cheered when it landed with a huge splash, wetting my cloak. "For all of my life, I've lived surrounded by arid land and fields and never knew such wonderful creatures existed."

Too soon they dived, and I leaned over the side to catch one last glimpse before they disappeared once more into the sea.

"I thought you'd like to see them," and with that, the captain walked away.

The evening of that first day away from land, I made a simple meal from the ingredients bought in Seleucia. Mary, Barnabas and I sat on the deck, and I tried to tempt Lazarus with a piece of bread.

"Just try," I pleaded, "you need to eat, or you'll become weaker."

He took the bread and examined it as if I'd given him something poisonous. Breaking off a small crumb he put it inside his mouth, pulled a face and tried to swallow. Gallio watched, opening and closing his mouth as if he ate the bread. I broke a chunk off and handed it to him. He snatched it and hid behind the mast, stuffing it in his mouth, staring around him.

Mary pulled a face. "He eats like an animal!"

Captain Marcus joined us. "He's probably been a slave all his life and if you're treated like an animal, you'll become one." He looked at what we were eating. "It looks like you have a feast."

"Martha is famed for her hospitality and the standard of her food. We bought this in the port," Barnabas explained.

"My cook never gets such good food when I send him."

I put bread, olives and pickled vegetables on a plate. "You're welcome to share what we have."

He took the plate and ate the bread and olives. "Thank you, it tastes as good as it looks. If you were staying on board any longer, I'd ask you to buy the supplies."

Despite his appreciation of the food, he left half. "Gallio, finish this for me."

The slave approached the outstretched arm and took the plate back to his hiding place. When he finished, he pushed the empty plate, devoid of crumbs along the deck towards me.

"Did you enjoy that, Gallio?" I asked.

Staring at the deck, there was an imperceptible nod, and he returned to his place by the mast.

* * *

There was a hint of dawn, but it was still to arrive. I stood on deck holding onto a rope to steady myself and closed my eyes to remember better. In Bethany, I would be awake now, picking up the pitcher, perhaps a 'good morning' to the chickens before a walk to the well. I thought of grinding corn, kneading bread, sweeping the courtyard and all the small details of my life before. Before I had to flee, before the *Minerva*, before whatever lies in front of me.

Like good food in the mouth, I savoured each detail and gave my body to the gentle rhythm of the waves. Trying to lose myself in the mundane. Wherever I should travel, I knew I would never reach the limit of where God could find me. He had travelled before me and was there waiting. The words of a psalm came to mind, and I started singing.

> *"O Lord, you have examined my heart*
> *and know everything about me.*
> *You know when I sit down or stand up.*
> *You know my thoughts even when I'm far away.*

You see me when I travel and when I rest at home.
You know everything I do.
You know what I am going to say even before I say it, Lord.
You go before me and follow me.
You place your hand of blessing on my head.
Such knowledge is too wonderful for me,
too great for me to understand!

I can never escape from your Spirit!
I can never get away from your presence!
If I go up to heaven, you are there;
if I go down to the grave, you are there.
If I ride the wings of the morning,
if I dwell by the farthest oceans,
even there your hand will guide me,
and your strength will support me.
I could ask the darkness to hide me and
the light around me to become night,
but even in darkness I cannot hide from you.
To you the night shines as bright as day.
Darkness and light are the same to you."

Taking deep breaths of refreshing sea air, I slowly became aware that I was not alone, and opened my eyes to find Captain Marcus, arms folded, leaning on the side of the ship. His face, a mask, hiding his emotions, he stared at me.

Disturbed, I asked, "How long have you been here?"

"Long enough to listen to you sing that beautiful song. Is it Aramaic?" I nodded. "Tell me what it means."

Struggling to translate the song into Greek, I wondered whether to wake Barnabas, then dismissed the idea. But I couldn't make the words as beautiful as before.

Captain Marcus stroked his beard. "How can your God be both where you've been and where you're going?"

"Because he's not limited to one place at a time."

"I've heard you talk about this man Jesus, who visited your house and ate your food."

"Yes, many times."

"You think he's God too?" I nodded. "If that's true, why did he die? I've seen crucifixions, and it's a cruel way for even a slave to die. If I was a god, I wouldn't choose that." Silent again, he looked out to sea. "Did you see his ghost?"

"No, Captain Marcus, not his ghost."

I told him of the morning Mary and I went to his tomb and found it empty and the stories of Jesus's resurrection. Of how solid his body felt and how he ate the fish. He looked at me as if he thought I was talking nonsense and I suggested he speak to Barnabas. The captain may think of me as a foolish woman, but he respected Barnabas.

"The crew are waking up, and I must relieve the man on the rudder." With a curt nod he walked towards the upper deck.

* * *

Squeezed into Captain Marcus's bunk, I struggled to sleep with Mary snoring in my ear. I swung my legs over the side, enjoying the cool wood under my toes. The night was hot and the air stuffy in the cabin and I took a sip of water. Throwing my cloak over my shoulders, I walked out barefoot onto the deck and took a breath of fresh air.

"Can't you sleep, Lady?" Captain Marcus was at the rudder, steering the ship even during the watches of the night. "Come on up and talk to me."

Steps led to the upper deck above the cabin. This was somewhere I'd not been because I was afraid of getting in the way of the sailors and the captain.

"There's not much room for two in that bunk is there?" he chuckled.

Choosing to ignore his teasing, I said, "There's a good view of the ship from here."

"This is my favourite place. Up here on my own at night, with just *Minerva* and the moon and stars for company."

A silver streak shimmered on the waves, reflecting the moon's light, and I breathed in deeply. "It's beautiful here at night," I agreed. We stood side by side in silence until I asked a question I'd wanted to know since I came aboard. "I understand how you steer the ship in the direction you want to travel by the sun's position during the day. But how is it done at night?"

Captain Marcus pointed to the sky above his right shoulder. "Do you see that bright star? Come and stand next to me, so you can see where I'm pointing." I moved to stand in front of him, and followed his finger. He put his hand on my shoulder. "That's Polaris, or the Northern Star, which tells me where north is. It's the end of the tail of the Little Bear constellation, or *Ursa Minor* to give its correct title. Now I want to sail in a south-westerly direction, so the Northern Star has to be just there where it is now."

He flashed a smile which I guessed he thought was charming, and I wondered how many women had fallen for his winning smile. It did not impress me, and my name would not be added to that list. I stepped away from him and he placed both hands on the rudder, moving his body in time with his ship. A movement so natural to him, he was one with his beloved *Minerva*.

"Who taught you to sail?" I asked to break the silence.

"Captain Antonius taught me all I know. The names of the constellations, and how to steer during the day and night. To read the wind and tides, and how to listen when she speaks to me."

Wondering who she was, I asked, "Who speaks to you?"

"Listen," he whispered.

It never occurred to me that he would refer to the ship as a woman. By this time, the creaks and groans were familiar, but I never thought of this as her way of talking to her captain.

"He taught me much more: to read and write and keep accounts, how to do deals and how to be a man. When Captain Antonius retired three years ago, he sold me the ship for which I'm still paying," he stroked the rail, "and she's worth every denarius."

"How long have you sailed with her?"

"Eighteen years last month. I was twelve years old, nothing but a scrap of a lad like Gallio. Standing on a jetty at a small port, I asked if I could join the crew. The sailors laughed and told me to go away." He laughed. "Those weren't their exact words, but I won't say them in front of a lady. But Captain Antonius took one look and told me to come aboard. Best decision I've ever made was to climb up that gangplank but, to be honest, I'd have sailed on a leaky tugboat to get away from there." He sighed. "That's enough about me, tell me about yourself."

"What do you want to know?" I shrugged my shoulders, hoping his questions wouldn't be too personal.

"Barnabas tells me you're a widow."

"Nathan, my husband died three years ago."

"You couldn't have been married for long."

"Just two short years together."

"Was Nathan a good man?"

"The best," I laughed. "I couldn't have prayed for a better husband and we were very happy together. He was a landowner who farmed olive and lemon groves on the hills near Jerusalem. The farm was profitable and well kept, and he looked after his labourers well."

"Did he have a temper?"

I'd witnessed Captain Marcus's temper on the quay at Seleucia and wondered why he should ask such a question.

"Did he ever beat you?" he asked again.

"No, never once was I afraid of him. We were partners and he often asked my opinion on the running of the farm. When he died, he left me the entire estate."

"You were lucky."

"Yes, I know how fortunate I was. You had the pleasure of meeting my neighbour the evening you pulled me aboard."

"The rodent or the one with bad breath?"

I laughed at his descriptions. "I can't tell you about the rodent, but the one with bad breath often hits his wife."

Pulling his face, he turned away to check the position of the Northern Star. "Men who beat women are scum. Does he have children?"

"No, they don't."

"That's some consolation, no poor child is being beaten for no reason."

In silence, he stared out along the deck, and I thought it best to change the topic. "Do you carry all kinds of cargo?"

"Anything I can do a deal on. Grain, wine, olive oil, foodstuffs, timber, and if you can name it, I'll buy and sell it for a profit."

"All legal and honest?" I asked with a smile.

He returned my smile and chuckled. "Most of the time, but I'm not above an embellishment or two to sell something. I'll sell everything except one. It was always a rule of Captain Antonius and I agree."

"What's that?"

"Human cargo." He screwed his face in disgust. "I've seen them lined up at ports. Men, women and children, chained together like cattle. I'll have no part in that trade."

"But you have slaves on board."

"Only one sailor now, and when he's freed, there'll be no more."

Aghast at what I heard, I said, "You bought a child slave in Seleucia."

To my surprise, he laughed. "I did, but I didn't intend to do so, it just happened, besides he's better off with me."

"It was a child who you bought and then you beat his master in an unprovoked attack."

His laughter was so loud I thought the crew might wake up. "Is that what you think? I don't have to explain my actions to you."

Certain that my silence would make him talk more, I leaned on the rail and looked out to sea.

He tutted. "If you want to know, I'll tell you. He owns a warehouse at the port, one I won't use because he's always angry and handy with a stick. When I left the other ship, he was whipping the boy. It riled me, so I asked to buy him. I punched him in the face because he suggested that the reason I wanted a boy was for use on a long voyage. Are you shocked?"

"You may consider living in a small village sheltered, but all of humanity's evils lurk behind closed doors. I'm sorry, Captain."

"What for?"

"Since coming aboard in Caesarea, I made a hasty opinion and have misjudged you."

He nodded his acceptance of my apology. "Dawn won't be far off and you should get some sleep. Warn your brother that tomorrow the sea will be rough."

"How can you tell what the weather will be like tomorrow?"

"The wind is picking up and has blown clouds in to obscure the stars."

"Good evening, Captain." I turned to leave.

"Good morning, Lady."

I left him swaying at the rudder and, preferring to sleep in the open, I collected my blanket from the cabin and took it to where Lazarus and Barnabas were sleeping. Captain Marcus's bluster and swagger was just a mask he wore, which he'd let slip that night. Closing my eyes, I tried to make sense of him, and found him a man hard to read. Before long, *Minerva*'s gentle rocking lulled me to sleep.

CHAPTER 25

Captain Marcus was right, and the clouds rolled in on the morning as he'd predicted. By midday, they had turned the bright blue sky to shades of black and grey. The *Minerva* rose and fell on the swell of the waves, causing Lazarus to lean over the side.

"You should get into the cabin, Lady," Captain Marcus said, "and make sure Mary and Gallio are safe. The deck will be no place for women and children."

"What can I do to help?" I asked.

"I appreciate your offer, but the sailors know what to do."

With calloused hands and tense muscles, he gripped the rail of the upper deck, examining the sky and taking in the ferocity of the wind. I examined his face, which in contrast to the previous evening, was now taut, and with brows pulled together, he focused his eyes on the sea and sky.

"Leave both sails up until I tell you. We'll use the wind until it's too strong. But be ready to take them down."

"Yes, Captain," a sailor nodded.

"Alexus," he called, "get in the hold and secure the cargo."

"I'll go with him," I said, desperate to help.

"Good. Take Lazarus with you, it'll keep him out of the way. Make sure he's not sick in the hold. Barnabas, I could use your strength."

Barnabas nodded. "Ready to help, Captain. Is it going to be bad?" A thunderclap answered his question.

Captain Marcus nodded, his lips tightened into a thin pale line. "By Jupiter, it will. *Minerva* will get us through this, trust her Barnabas. But pray to your God and Jesus too, we will need all the help available. Make sure the cargo is lashed tight."

Angry that some broken amphorae should worry him, I said, "Why are you concerned about your precious cargo at a time like this?"

"Do you think I care about a few broken pots? If they come loose and roll around in the storm, their weight will roll to one side of the hull, maybe even cracking it and sinking the ship. Is that a good enough reason for you?"

I ran to get Lazarus and followed Alexus into the hold as the first drops of rain fell. Alexus uncoiled the ropes used for lashing the cargo and threw one end to me.

"Tie that on the hook at the side," he said.

"Here, Martha." Lazarus took the rope and tied it to the hook with a knot. Alexus pulled the rope, and the knot opened.

"Not like that! Here let me show you." Lazarus watched intently as Alexus showed us how to tie the knot so it wouldn't come undone. He took the other end and lashed it around the amphorae before tying it onto another hook.

"Pull it tight," shouted Alexus. "Let me see." He examined the knot. "Well done. Tie the other cargo in the same way."

I took the rope and a sudden swell caused me to fall over and land on a sack of grain. Lazarus took my hand and helped me up, but by then standing was difficult as the waves buffeted the ship, tossing us back and forth. Anxious that all the cargo should be secure, Lazarus fumbled to tie the last of the sacks of grain to the hull. Before he finished securing them, the ship tilted to the other side, and Alexus screamed as a sack came loose, pinning him to the hull. I then understood the captain's concern that each piece should be secure. Lazarus tried to free Alexus, but the rolling of the ship made it difficult. Together we released him. He was holding his left hand.

"Let me see your hand," I said.

"Leave it, for now, it's not important. Time enough to worry later."

I took his hand and his grimace told me how much it hurt. Seeing his middle and ring finger pointing back I realised why.

"Lazarus secure that sack of grain, and make sure it will not move," he instructed, "and Lady, if you can do anything, do it quickly because I'm needed on deck."

Searching around the hull in the growing darkness I found a piece of wood and sacking. I broke off a small slip of wood and ripped the sacking. A sudden flash of lightning lit up the darkened hull, followed swiftly by a loud peel of thunder, telling me that the storm was upon us.

"I'm sorry, Alexus, but this will hurt."

He screamed as I pulled his fingers back and placed the wood between them and, wrapping the sacking around them, made an improvised splint.

With a grimace, he said, "Let me check everything before we go back up."

Assured that everything was secure, we climbed the ladder out of the hold. I'd only been in there ten minutes, but a different world awaited me. The calm sea, which had been my companion for the voyage, took on a malevolent tone, screaming with its wrath.

With water running down his face, the captain shouted, "Secure the hold door, we don't want water in there or we're lost."

The sail on the main mast was furled and Barnabas tied the rope, straining to make sure it didn't come undone.

"Furl the small mast," the captain screeched over the force of the wind.

Barnabas and two sailors ran to the bow and took down the sail. Drenched by the rain in a matter of seconds after coming up from the hold, my cloak stuck to my legs and the wind took my breath away. The horizon had now vanished behind a wall of rain.

"Martha, get to the cabin, quick." Lazarus pushed me towards shelter.

In their evil intent to come aboard, the waves pounded the hull, and the sea simmered and boiled in a fit of unforgiving anger. A sailor lost his footing on the water sodden deck, knocked into me and I fell on top of him. Gaining my footing I tried to stand, but it was impossible against the wind, and the heaving and rolling deck. Panic on the sailor's face caused it to rise in me and I gave way to it and cried. Arms pulled me to my feet, and the only one not in open panic was Captain Marcus, but I could see the fear written on his face. He and Lazarus helped me to the cabin. I opened the door to a scream from Mary and pulled Lazarus in with me. Mary and Gallio sat on the bunk, their eyes wide in fear.

"I can't stay here, I need to help." Lazarus darted out before I could object.

Tossed from side to side, we huddled on the bunk, while the raging waves rocked the *Minerva*, praying that the storm would still, and we would be saved. After a time, I could not guess how long had passed, the violence began to cease, and the storm quelled. Apprehensive at what I might find, I opened the door and Mary followed me out. Searching the tired, alarmed faces of the crew, with relief, I found Lazarus holding onto the mast, with Barnabas's arms around him. Splintered wood showed where a section of the port side was missing, a gaping void like a broken tooth.

The ship rocked and an unforeseen wave rose as high as the mast and slammed its ferocity upon the deck as if to break us to splinters. Taking Lazarus, it dragged him away, towards the break in the side. I ran and held onto his hand as others grabbed him and pulled him to safety. If the sea couldn't have Lazarus, it wanted another. Knocking Mary over, it pulled her feet first towards the gap. Panic etched on her face, she held out her hands for help. Captain Marcus slid along the deck but was too slow and crashed into the side of the ship. No word escaped, no gasp or shout came, as my sister slipped into the boiling sea.

Solid and immovable, my feet became part of the deck. Quick to recover, Captain Marcus tied a rope around himself and, knowing what he intended to do, Alexus tied the other end to the mast.

A crew member attempted to untie the knot. "Captain, she's gone. Don't waste your life on a silly girl." The captain pushed him away.

Alexus dug the sailor in the chest. "If she was your sister, you'd want her rescued."

"When I tug the rope, pull us in." The captain looked at me, took a deep breath, then dived into the water.

I ran to the side and, grasping onto the rail, searched the waves for any sign of my sister. She struggled to stay on the surface, fighting against the pull of the water dragging her under. Battling against the rise and fall of the waves, the captain swam away from the ship. His head bobbed on the surface looking around for Mary until he too disappeared. In a desperate attempt to survive, Mary's hand rose heavenward until grasped by another.

"Pull!" Alexus shouted.

We ran to the rope and together pulled them back. Straining against the weight, Barnabas held the rope tight as Lazarus and I ran to the gap and pulled Mary on board. Another hand clutched the deck and Alexus dragged the captain over. Mary lay on her back not breathing, her lips turning purple as Lazarus's did on the day he died. I couldn't believe that I would lose her now. Alexus knocked me out of the way and turned Mary onto her side. He slapped her back hard and when nothing happened, he put his ear by her mouth. Looking up at me in horror, he shook his head.

"Do it again," I shouted.

He slapped her once more.

"Again," screamed Lazarus.

Mary spluttered, and I cried in relief. Water gushed from her mouth and with a gasp, she breathed again. On his hands and knees, Captain Marcus retched up water and vomit. I ran to fetch fresh water and gave him a drink. I wanted to give my thanks, but couldn't speak. Sitting Mary up, she leaned on me and I gave her sips of water.

"Martha!" she cried and held me tight.

The waves abruptly ceased their crashing and became benign once more, and a ray of sunlight lit up the deck. Captain Marcus got to his feet assessing the damage.

"Are we all here?" He counted heads. "Thank Jupiter."

A sailor sighed and laughed. "There was a point there, that I thought we were done for." Others joined in with his relief, except for the captain who stood grim-faced.

"No, no, it's not over yet." His face white and breathing hard, he looked into the sky.

We followed his gaze up to a blue sky, but all around in every direction, black menacing clouds swirled.

"I've heard about this, and we will go through all that again, very shortly. There's nothing we can do except pray and trust *Minerva* will run the storm herself. Now everyone do exactly as I say. Martha, take Lazarus and Mary into the cabin with Gallio and don't come out for any reason, no matter what you hear."

Barnabas picked up Mary and carried her to the cabin. I passed the captain and touching his arm said, "Thank you, Marcus, but I'll see to the injured sailors first."

He took my hand in his. "No time for that, Martha, the storm will be upon us in less than five minutes. Now, promise me you'll stay in the cabin?"

I nodded, but he was already giving orders again. He cut ropes from the sails and tied each crew member to the ship. As I closed the cabin door, the deluge started, and the wind surged once more. Marcus tied Barnabas to the mast and with the last knot lashed himself next to him. With both men tied to *Minerva*'s mast, I prayed she would run the storm and keep us safe.

* * *

A deep rumble, either from the depth of the earth or the highest heaven, I knew not, echoed around the ship. Lightning lit up the dark cabin where Gallio folded himself, whimpering, into a tight ball with his head on Mary's knee. Lazarus held her shuddering body as if afraid she would slide into the sea once more. All around us men shouted and prayed to whichever god they believed in, but Barnabas's voice rang out over them. Praying that Jesus who stilled the wind would see us through this storm.

Why had God brought us the many miles from Bethany, just to perish along with the crew of a cargo ship in the middle of the sea? I thought of the Sanhedrin, who thought they had killed Jesus, but they were wrong. Who, along with Saul, tried flogging, stoning and arrests to stop us, but this was in vain too. Jonas who would do anything to get my house, and Helena, Lydia and Julius who had betrayed us. We had escaped them all. The dust storm in the desert had not harmed us, and Marcus had rescued Mary from the tempest. Yet here we were at the mercy of the angry sea.

I took a deep breath and, despite the circumstances, felt Jesus's presence in that tiny cabin on the small ship surrounded by the vast ocean. Stretching out my hand I touched Lazarus's head, then Mary's and Gallio's, praying for peace. I began to sing the song I had sung in the bow which Marcus had listened to. Hesitant at first, Lazarus and Mary joined in.

"Sing louder. Sing as if our lives depend upon it," I shouted, and we sang. From outside, Barnabas joined us, and his deep sonorous voice mixed with ours. The wailing of the men stopped, and they cried as they listened. Trying to drown out our song, the winds screeched and moaned, but we continued.

> "I can never escape from your Spirit!
> I can never get away from your presence!
> If I go up to heaven, you are there;
> if I go down to the grave, you are there.
> If I ride the wings of the morning,
> if I dwell by the farthest oceans,
> even there your hand will guide me,
> and your strength will support me."

* * *

Felt more than heard, the ship's creaking intensified, and *Minerva*'s sounds, which only the day before were comforting, now sent shivers through me. Her screeches and cries of pain tore at my nerves. From deep within the ship a loud crack caused me to flinch and move towards the door, as the mast smashed into the cabin. Lazarus screamed and moved away as it cut through the bunk where he was sitting and split the deck into the hold.

"Lazarus, are you safe?" I searched over the mast.

"We're all here," he called.

"The mast missed us. What about you?" Mary shouted.

"The roof has gone," I screamed.

Once more drenched with the unrelenting rain, I tried to squeeze beneath the mast to where they lay, but there was not enough room. The mast shielded them from the storm, but I had nowhere to go. Now exposed to the elements, the wind blew my hair and ripped at my clothes, flinging water into my face and causing me to close my eyes. I remembered that Marcus had lashed Barnabas and himself to the mast and was afraid for their safety. Over the screeching wind and splitting wood, someone called my name, indistinct and far away.

"Martha! Martha!"

With water churning around me, I crawled towards the sound. The ship lurched over the crests and fell headlong into a trough, surrounding us with walls of water, too high to penetrate. An arm grabbed me and pulled me to him. Still lashed to the bottom of the shattered mast Barnabas and Marcus held me safe. One a man who followed Jesus, strong and gentle, who loved, encouraged and helped everyone. The other one I'd known only a few days, a course, rude man who talked of brothels, shifty deals and fights. One who bought a slave to save him from a beating, who disliked traitors and deplored violence to women, and who risked his own life to save my sister. Both men I would trust with my life; both held me safe through the dark night.

* * *

The sun warmed my back and relaxed my stiffened fingers. After the maelstrom, the silence was notable, not even a bird screeched overhead, and the wind returned to its gentle blowing of my hair. With a groan, Barnabas took his arms from around my shoulders, where he held me tight. Marcus's right hand still gripped me, his left arm limp on his outstretched legs.

He rested his head on mine. "Are we still alive?" his voice came out as a grunt. "Thank *Minerva*."

"Thank God," added Barnabas.

My weak legs refused to stand. "Mary!" I shouted.

In the daylight, the damage to the cabin was horrendous, and I crawled and stumbled towards where I'd last seen it. The mast had smashed through it into the hold, strewing what now resembled firewood across the deck.

Mary's weak voice responded from deep within the ship, "We're here."

"Gallio?" Marcus croaked.

"He's here!"

Further relieved to hear Lazarus's voice, I sighed, and three anxious faces looked up from the hold.

"Stay there, until we can get you out," I instructed.

"Martha." It was Marcus. "Help me untie this knot."

Using only his right hand, he tried in vain to undo it, and I struggled with both of mine until a jolt of pain made me cry out. Unbeknown to me a large splinter had embedded itself in my upper left arm. Marcus moved to pull it out.

"No, leave it in, I must be able to stem the flow of blood when it's removed. What about your left hand?"

"I think I've got a broken arm," he groaned. "The ropes have tightened with the saltwater and will need cutting. Get my knife. It's behind my back."

I stretched behind him and pulled the knife from his belt. With my good right hand, I cut through the rope to release him and then cut Barnabas free.

Marcus rolled over onto his knees and one good arm. "Can you help me stand?" I put my good arm under him and pushed him onto his feet.

He surveyed the damage. "My ship. Look what's happened to my beautiful *Minerva*," he sighed.

The upper deck and cabin were destroyed, and debris lay scattered around. It was a miracle that the four of us had escaped with our lives. A gap in the side showed where Mary had slipped into the sea and part of the front port side was now missing.

"No!" he ran to the gap in the rail and looked over screaming and kicked the side of the ship in frustration.

"Alexus has gone," he cried.

A sailor released by Barnabas joined him. "We'd all be gone Captain if you hadn't reacted so quickly."

"I'd only just freed him from slavery, and he was so happy."

"He died free, and that's more than many of us achieve."

Lazarus helped to lift Gallio and Mary from the hold before being pulled out himself. Gallio ran to his new master and, sobbing, flung his arms around his waist. Surprised, Marcus didn't know how to react and rested his good hand on his head. The captain in charge of his vessel now came to the fore, and he surveyed all the people looking at him.

His left arm hung limp at his side. "I want a damage report," he said. "First, what injuries are there?"

One man remained sitting on the deck, his leg crushed, others had wounds to their heads or limbs. None of us had escaped injury, except those in the hold. I'd found a piece of sacking amongst the wood and tried to take Marcus's broken arm.

"See to the others first, that includes yourself," he ordered.

"I'm not a member of your crew that you can order around, now stand there until I've put this sling on you."

Not used to being told what to do he stared at me as I took his broken arm and wrapped the sling around him and tied it behind his neck.

"Thank you. Now, see to your arm, please."

Mary, who now seemed to have recovered from her ordeal, found Marcus's clean tunic in the remains of the cabin and used the knife to cut it to make bandages. She ripped the sleeve of my tunic and pulled the splinter out, quickly wrapping a bandage around it to stem the bleeding.

"Barnabas, help me with the man with the broken leg, it's at a bad angle," I said.

The sailor screamed and passed out when we pulled his leg into place. Using two planks we made a splint and bound it to his leg with sacking. Men were busy with orders from the captain, so we went around each one to tend to their wounds, finally bandaging the gash on Barnabas's head.

I peered into the hold, where Marcus paddled, knee-deep in water. Taking great care, he examined the hull for leaks. With sadness I thought of Alexus, working with us to stash the cargo. Deftly, Marcus climbed the ladder one-handed.

"How does it look, down there?" I asked.

"Not as bad as I'd feared, there are no cracks and we are watertight. You and Alexus did a good job before the storm, and everything is still in its place."

Marcus called everyone together and stood with Gallio by his side. He tried to speak, but lost for words, he closed his eyes and swallowed.

"Not one of us has experienced anything like this before, and I've only heard about storms of this nature from Captain Antonius. My greatest sorrow is losing Alexus, a fine sailor and, we'll drink to him and mourn him later. Before doing anything else, I've asked Barnabas to thank his God for his protection."

In the bright sunshine and with his hands up to heaven, Barnabas prayed. "Thank you our Father, for leading us through the storm. Though the winds battered, and the waves pounded, you held the *Minerva* in your hand. Thank you for the life of Alexus, a good man, now in your care. We ask for your strength to support us in our time of need, and to lead us safely to shore."

After the prayer, Marcus explained that we were far from safe. "The only good news is that the hull is sound, but it's waterlogged and our main priority will be to bail it out. The sacks of grain are waterlogged and will need throwing overboard, and this will help to lighten the ship. We have one rudder and the small sail, and once I have discovered where we are, I can plot a route to the nearest port or land."

He paused before delivering more bad news. "Two of the water jars stored under the cabin have cracked and are full of seawater which leaves us with only one jar. For now, the water will be rationed and let's hope we reach land soon."

Splitting us into work teams he tasked two sailors with checking for further damage and hoisting the small sail in the bow. Another sailor helped Marcus make sure that the one rudder was in working order and in the correct position. The rest of us threw the grain overboard and bailed out the hold. I found three buckets and tied a rope to each one.

Mary, Gallio and I climbed into the hold and filled the buckets with water. Barnabas and Lazarus raised them and threw the water over the side.

"Mary," Captain Marcus called down, "last night was distressing for you, come up and recover first."

She looked up at him. "No, Captain, I feel better helping."

He nodded. "Good, we need all the hands we have."

After an hour, Marcus called us up, and three men took our places and he took over from Lazarus. Gallio took the drinking water around, with each person rationed to one cupful. Sailors tied the mainsail over the hole made by the mast, in case it rained again and for shelter. To prevent more loss of life, they fastened ropes across the gaps in the side. Mary and I found the food supplies and, as the sky darkened, we served a meal to the crew, now in a more positive mood. The night was clear, and the stars sparkled enough for Marcus to read.

"Do you know where we are?" I asked.

He nodded. "I think we're north of Cyprus, so I'll sail south hoping to reach the north coast."

"Are you familiar with that area?"

He smirked. "Oh, yes, but it's one I normally avoid."

CHAPTER 26

Exhaustion and trauma lulled me into a shallow sleep and, startled, I awoke from a nightmare. This time, it was not Mary but me who slipped into the raging sea and sank to the depths of the ocean. Under the water, I called Marcus's name, but he didn't hear. When I awoke my clothes were wet once more, but this time with sweat. The night was still dark, and I stretched, hoping to shed the images of the dream.

"Can't sleep, Lady?" Using one hand, Marcus was again at the rudder during the night. "I'm surprised any of us can sleep after that storm without having a nightmare."

"When did you last sleep, Marcus?"

"There'll be time for sleep when we're safe in a port and can begin the repairs."

"If you don't sleep, you'll not be in a fit state to get us to a port, and you don't know how long it will take."

"I estimate the day after tomorrow. The drinking water should last until then, but not much longer."

"Can you stay awake that long?"

He shrugged his shoulders. "I can't sleep yet. Something else might go wrong."

"This wasn't your fault, you understand that, don't you?" He looked away to view the stars. "You are not responsible for what happened to the *Minerva*."

He closed his eyes and shook his head. "I'm the captain and I'm responsible for everything and everyone aboard my ship. It was me who tied Alexus to that part of the ship and it's my fault he drowned. Every time I close my eyes, I can see him laughing and smiling on the day I released him from slavery. He was a good man. The whole crew, you and your family, and little Gallio could be dead too. Mary ..." he left the sentence unfinished.

"Marcus, we're not dead, and that's only because of your skills as a good sailor and captain."

"If the mast had fallen a little to one side, it would have crushed you to death."

"But it didn't, and the sea would have swept me overboard like Alexus if you hadn't held me tight through the rest of the storm."

He stared at me. "You're the most extraordinary woman I've ever met, Martha." This time I looked away. "Barnabas and Lazarus have told me everything you did for Jesus. How you followed and stayed with him until the end at his crucifixion. Few women could do that with someone they loved. How you supported friends through dangers, even at the risk of arrest and death yourself. You're fearless."

"Now you're mocking me, Marcus, please stop."

"I wouldn't mock you," his voice dropped to barely more than a whisper. "Last night, you were the only one who didn't give in to their fear. That's bravery, knowing why you should be afraid, but not giving in. After I'd tied myself to the mast, I shook in fear, men were crying and calling out to any god they knew to save them. But you sang, and you gave me hope. I've known men jump overboard in madness and fear, but no one would do that after your singing inspired us."

"I've cause to be thankful for your bravery. You dived in to rescue Mary, and you'll always have my gratitude."

"I realised that it was more foolishness than bravery the moment I hit the water and could see nothing. The waves were too high to see where she was, but somehow she grabbed my hand."

"She says it was you who grabbed her."

"Whoever it was, you can thank your God who saved her."

"Not only my sister, but I'm thankful he saved you too."

"You can't be more thankful than I am," he laughed. "Your brother and sister are both brave and you are a remarkable family. Lazarus took orders and helped the crew during the storm and Gallio said how Mary helped him not to be frightened. Poor lad, just days after I save him from a master who starved and beat him, he's almost lost at sea. Now you know why sailors say that the sea is a cruel master."

Wincing, he rounded his shoulders and cried out as a spasm of pain hit his broken arm.

"Does your arm hurt?"

"Hold the rudder for me, and for Minerva's sake keep her in a straight line."

With dark rings under his eyes, he handed me the rudder and rubbed his left shoulder with his good hand.

"Let me do that for you. I handed the rudder back and stood behind him to massage his shoulders.

In between groans, he said, "That feels better."

A movement behind caused me to turn around, and a crew member who I'd seen on the rudder was awake. I beckoned him over.

"You must relieve the captain because he needs to sleep."

He looked at the captain, unsure of an order coming from anyone but him. Marcus nodded and gave him the rudder with instructions to sail south, then dragged himself to the bow. Sinking to the deck he laid his heavy head on his arm.

"Tell everyone, that unless there's a dire emergency, the captain is to sleep for at least four hours, more if possible," I told the sailor at the rudder.

"Yes, Lady," he replied.

I undid my cloak and used it to cover Marcus's curled up body, then returned to try to sleep myself.

"So, you're in charge of the ship now, are you?" Barnabas whispered.

"Yes, and you'll call me Lady!"

* * *

As Marcus predicted, by midday two days later the coast of Northern Cyprus came into view, and we sailed towards a finger of land stretching out into the sea. Even without the ravages of the storm, to call the place we landed a port would be to stretch the imagination. Dilapidated houses huddled around a run-down stone jetty and, stranded on the shore where the storm had abandoned them, were four fishing boats. The village seemed deserted. I would have expected the inhabitants to be mending their homes and fishing boats, but I could see no one.

With just one rudder, Marcus brought us alongside the jetty with a scrape which made him cringe as if it was himself who was being dragged along. Within minutes sailors secured the ropes, tying us alongside. Lazarus was first off, and I breathed in relief to join him on solid ground, which still felt as if we were moving with the waves lapping the stones.

Marcus joined us on the jetty. "There may be an inn or somewhere you can stay in the village which will be more comfortable than the open deck."

Gallio jumped onto the jetty and trotted after his captain.

"Have you been here before?" Mary asked.

"Just the once, and that was a long time ago, and I'd no money to stay anywhere other than under the sky."

"What are your plans now we are here?" Lazarus asked.

"I won't be able to get a new mast, but hopefully there will be wood to fashion another rudder and its mountings and to mend the gaps in the rail. With luck, we can buy rope for the rigging. The less time we spend here the better, it's a miserable place. We'll do the main repairs and winter in Paphos after I've dropped you off in Larnaca. I don't want to sail away from the coast until I've taken the *Minerva* into a dry dock and checked her entire hull."

"While you and your men are seeing to the repairs, would you like us to purchase supplies and see to the water?" I asked.

"Thank you, that will be a great help."

Six unkempt houses stretched along the bay, nothing better than fishermen's homes. One acted as an inn and served wine to the inhabitants and any passing ships, though I doubted many stopped. The innkeeper showed us an upstairs room where we could stay, saying we were lucky that the roof hadn't blown off. Mary pulled a face when she checked the beds, which were nothing more than filthy straw mattresses on the floor. A floorboard creaked when Barnabas walked into the centre of the room.

"I think I'd better keep to the sides," he laughed.

"I'm not laughing, it's disgusting here." Mary stuck out her tongue.

"Let's make the best of it, at least it's not moving," Lazarus added.

Leaving the room, we bought a few vegetables from the innkeeper, at an exorbitant price, but I'd haggled him down from an even higher one. They took advantage of our desperation, but they needed the money. Taking the stores to the ship, I passed sailors on the jetty, already sawing and fashioning wood to replace the damaged pieces. Marcus was wasting no time.

That evening Barnabas stayed with a sulking Gallio to guard the ship, while the crew, carrying the man with the broken leg, went to the inn to drink to Alexus's memory. The innkeeper couldn't believe his luck when Marcus gave him enough money to keep the flagons of wine coming all night. Upstairs, I pulled the blanket back from the mattress and screamed as a cockroach dashed out. Refusing to stay the night in the dirty room, I found Marcus sitting at a table with the crew. With his arms folded, his head drooped onto his chest.

"Captain," I shook his arm. "Marcus!" He awoke with a jolt. "We're going back to the *Minerva* because I'd rather sleep on the deck than in a filthy bed."

With a scowl Marcus peered into a flagon of wine. "I don't blame you; I've paid more for this sour slop than an amphora of the good Judean wine I've on board."

"We could open one of those tomorrow night, Captain," a sailor suggested.

"Let's see how much work you do tomorrow, first," he replied.

We left them swopping stories about Alexus, the laughter growing the more they drank. Later that night they came aboard singing lewd songs, and I was glad Mary was asleep.

* * *

Two days later we sailed on the morning tide. The mast remained in the smashed cabin and upper deck, but we'd cleared the debris away and made repairs to the gaps in the rail. The rudder, which Marcus fashioned from a plank, was not up to his usual high standards, but it would do the job alongside the other one. As soon as the crew completed basic repairs, we sailed out of the port with the small front sail hoisted and left the village behind. Without looking back, Marcus stood on the remains of the upper deck. He took a deep breath and, breathed out in relief, his shoulders relaxing.

When Marcus was alone at the rudder, I joined him. "What is it about that village you are so eager to leave?"

"Do you remember me telling you about joining the *Minerva* as a boy of Gallio's age?" I nodded. "Well, it was on that jetty that I first saw this ship."

"Were you a runaway?" I asked.

Shaking his head, he said, "I wasn't a slave if that's what you mean, but I had to leave my home."

"What could make a twelve-year-old boy run away from their home?"

He kept his eyes on the horizon. "The way you ask, I can tell you've always had a happy home and never been in danger."

I remembered the tussle between Uncle Ephraim and Jonas about my house and farm, and who would get to decide what to do with my possessions and my body. "And I can tell that you've never been a woman at the mercy of a male relative who wants to sell you like a slave to an unknown man as his possession."

Deep in thought, he stroked his beard. "True, I've never been a woman," he smiled, "or in danger of being sold. But I've been on the receiving end of a strap wielded by a monster of a stepfather who beat me daily. That I didn't mind as much as him hitting my mother, but I was too young and powerless to make him stop."

A member of the crew walked past, and he became silent. His story was for me only and I would keep his secrets.

When we were alone again, he continued. "One day he threw me out of the house and told me to never go back. My own mother didn't stop him; she let him push me out of the door with not so much as a piece of bread."

"Don't blame your mother for what he did to you. She was as powerless as you."

"When my father died, I was only ten years old, and he left us with just each other. We were poor farmers, living about twenty miles away from that dump we've just left. As young as I was, I did my best to keep the farm running, but six months later my mother remarried, without a thought for her dead husband."

"I understand that you want to blame her, Marcus, but we women have little choice in these matters. She would've needed a man to look after the farm and provide you with a measure of security."

"Well, she should've made a better choice," he mumbled.

"If it hadn't been for Jesus raising my brother from the dead, I'd be little more than a domestic slave for my uncle. Either that or married to a man I'd never choose or could ever hope to love."

We looked at one another, beginning to understand each other's suffering. The pain of the twelve-year-old boy was still written on his face.

"By the time the brute threw me out, he'd given her another son, so I wasn't needed any more. I walked for two days until I reached that dump of a port, stealing food to feed myself on the way. Then a miracle happened, and it was the *Minerva* tied at the jetty."

"Have you ever gone back?"

"What's the point in going back? But if I did, I'd strangle the life out of him. I don't regret how my life turned out because I've got a good life now. Better the life of the captain of the *Minerva*, even in as dilapidated a state as this, than a poor farmer scratching at the dry dirt."

"I can't imagine you as a farmer, and I won't be able to think of you anywhere other than on the deck of the *Minerva*."

He flashed me a smile. "So, you'll think of me after you've left?"

Returning his smile, I replied, "How could I ever forget you and what we've been through together?"

* * *

"Lazarus, come and look," Barnabas shouted. "Mary, Martha, we're almost there."

Two weeks had passed since leaving the port on the north coast, a journey which should take half that time. But with one sail and only one good rudder, it took twice as long. Life settled into a routine based upon the tides and winds, the sun and stars and daily conversations with Marcus at the rudder. Though he kept it well hidden from others, he revealed his warm and amiable side when we were alone together. I'd never been at ease with another man, apart from Nathan.

Despite the differences between the two men, which appeared large at first, I realised how similar they were. Marcus was a good captain who loved his ship and kept it to the best of his abilities. He was an experienced sailor and looked after his crew. Our farm in Bethany was equally well kept by Nathan, a good farmer who paid his labourers well and provided them with decent accommodation.

Mary clapped her hands. "I can see white buildings. Is your home visible from here?"

"Not yet, but by the time we dock, you'll see our warehouse," Barnabas laughed, excited to show his hometown.

Lazarus leaned on the rail and groaned. "This journey has been too long. Even though I'm not as bad as at the beginning, I still feel sick all the time. Don't let me step one foot on a ship ever again."

"What do you think, Martha?" Barnabas asked.

I smiled, and he continued to talk about the town and harbour, until Marcus appeared, with Gallio like a shadow by his side. Since arriving on board, Gallio had transformed from the scared slave with wild eyes, to a boy who ate his food with the crew and spoke when addressed. Since the storm, he had followed his new master around, and Marcus had to give him jobs with the crew to get him away from his side. Knowing Marcus as I did by that time, I could tell he was secretly pleased. In time, Gallio's scars, both the visible and invisible ones, would heal.

"It may have taken longer than expected, but I've got you to Larnaca," Marcus said.

Barnabas took out his purse. "Then, it's time we paid you. The journey has certainly been more adventurous than usual." He counted coins out into Marcus's hand.

"Thank you, Captain Marcus, despite everything that's happened you've got us here in one piece," Mary said.

Marcus looked at his arm, still in a sling. "Some of us are in one piece, and by this time next year, the *Minerva* will look brand new."

With his good hand, he led me to one side and held me under my elbow. "How do you like Larnaca, Martha?"

By then, we were so near I could pick out individual buildings. "Barnabas has told us so much that I feel I know it already," I replied.

"You'll be glad to sleep in a bed, rather than on the wooden deck."

"Yes, it will be more comfortable, but I shall miss the motion of the ship which I've found soothing."

"The journey has taken a while with only one sail, but I've been in no hurry to arrive."

"Neither have I." I looked at the deck.

"I must supervise the ship's docking," and with a nod he left me standing alone.

Mary took my arm. "I can't wait to see our new home. I've seen it in my imagination so many times, and I can't believe we are here at last. There's so much to say in a letter to Johanna."

I watched Marcus shouting orders and wondered what I would miss out in my letter to her. Impatient to be off the ship, Lazarus waited for the sailors to slip the gangplank onto the jetty, then ran down it. I followed at a slower pace, with Marcus and Gallio behind me.

"Gallio!" he ordered without looking at him, "Help the crew with the sail."

"Yes, Captain," his quiet voice replied.

Searching in my bag, I pulled out the purse from Jacob and handed it to Marcus. He tried to return it and put it back into my bag, but I refused.

"This is for your repairs," I insisted.

"Barnabas has paid me already, and more than we'd agreed at the beginning. That's enough."

"This is not our fare, it's my gift to you as a thank you. I can never repay you enough for saving Mary's life and for holding me safe in the storm." I folded his hand over the purse and kept it between mine.

He shook his head. "There's no debt between friends."

"Don't argue with me, Marcus, because I don't want that to be our final conversation."

"Martha, hurry up!" Mary shouted.

"I'm coming," I replied over my shoulder.

Still, with his hand in mine, he said, "Could I see you again when I'm passing? It won't be difficult to find where you live."

My pounding heart told me that more than anything I wanted to say yes but knew that it was not possible.

"No, Marcus," I sighed. "I still have a responsibility towards Lazarus and Mary, to make sure they are secure in our new life. I don't need any ..." I struggled to find the right word, "... distractions."

His face was as serious as when he watched the storm approach and my heart softened.

"But if you're in the market and see me," I continued, "we may meet as friends. You can tell me how you're doing, all about your cargo and how Gallio is faring."

"And if you're passing the jetty," he said, "and see the *Minerva*, you may come aboard and talk to me."

"Goodbye, Captain."

"Goodbye, Lady."

I walked away, but unable to resist the urge to look back, I turned and saw him walk up the gangplank and pause at the top to look towards me.

"Come on, Martha," Mary shouted.

I turned around and before I'd caught up with the others, Marcus was barking orders once more. Barnabas understood and putting his arm around my shoulders, led me to my new home.

CHAPTER 27

Surrounded by Barnabas's family, and their enthusiastic greeting, I should have felt welcomed into their home. But the joy of life on the *Minerva* evaporated, and there was a tangible feeling of loss. I knew there was no other way but to leave Marcus on the jetty and build a new life for us in Cyprus, and this I determined to do. Because of the delay, two letters awaited our arrival, one from Miriam and another from Johanna. Waiting until I had a quiet moment, I opened Miriam's letter first and savoured each detail.

"Dear Martha, Mary and Lazarus,

I hope that this letter finds you well and settling into Larnaca and that your journey was not too arduous. The days have been long since you left, and I miss the times we spent together talking long into the night.

The evening of your departure was difficult, and it was hard to carry on pretending we were a happy group after you left. I even called out "Goodnight, Martha" when you were by then miles away. An hour after dawn, Jonas demanded admittance to see Lazarus. Simon told him that Lazarus was ill, and he could not enter. Together, we waited knowing he would return, but we wanted to give you as much time to escape as we could.

Two hours later he arrived with Temple guards who forced their way in and searched the house. Jonas was furious when he discovered you had flown and demanded to know where you were heading. Refusing to tell them, we were all, including Esther, taken into custody.

For the rest of the day, Saul interrogated us and, considering Esther would be the easiest to break, slapped her several times. Esther regards herself as your mother, and Saul should have known a mother's love is impossible to crack. When she refused to speak, Saul and Jonas left for Caesarea, rightly assuming you would head there. Hoping to overtake you, they took the route via Galilee while you were already well on your way through Samaria.

Everyone in Jerusalem sends their fondest regards. James says he misses your lentil stew and asks you to send some back with Barnabas. I cannot wait until you write telling me every detail.

Miriam."

I closed my eyes, angry at Saul for hitting an old woman. Esther may appear to him as the weak one amongst my friends, but someone who has both suffered and loved so much is strong, something Saul would never understand. Eager to learn what had happened in Caesarea since our flight along the jetty, I tore open the seal of Johanna's letter.

"Dear Martha,

This must be a short letter written in haste, and I promise a longer one will follow, but I must tell you about the events after your leaving. An hour later, a knock at the gate alerted our servants, and a tearful Helena and Lydia burst through with Julius. He said he had seen Thomas leading you into a trap and after a fight and despite the dangers to his own safety, led you to the ship. As before, Helena ran to me crying and said they had become lost at the market and robbed of their money. Disorientated, they could not find our home and were relieved to see Julius, who led them back here. Something about their story did not seem true, and we began to suspect them.

We had become certain that Saul had infiltrated our group but because of lack of evidence could suspect no one in particular. Chuza hoped that Saul would overstretch his hand and bring the spies to light. So, pretending that we believed their story, we kept them close in the house. The next morning, Thomas arrived, and when Julius saw him, he hit him, saying that he was the traitor, and we should not listen to anything he said.

Chuza made as to interrogate Thomas in private, and he told us the story of the morning Jesus ground the flour. This was enough to make us sure that his words were true. I remembered where I had seen Helena and Lydia before. Their family owned a fish stall at the port, which had gone out of business last year. Thomas told us they were Julius's sisters, and we realised that he had recruited them to Saul's cause.

Saul spun his web of deceit many months ago, even before Stefanos's death, and his spy network stretches far. Chuza was for throwing the girls out of the house, but I had another idea to use them to spread a little deceit of our own. To make Julius think, we believed him, we threw Thomas out shouting that he was a traitor and not welcome any more. We informed Julius that he should then escort Helena and Lydia to Alexandria where we have a new network of safe houses, which, as you know, we do not. We hope that this subterfuge will keep Saul busy for a while.

I have sent a letter to Jerusalem to inform Jacob of the extent of Saul's infiltration and to recommend the closure of the route via Samaria. I will not write any more details in case this letter is intercepted.

We miss you and, do not fear, I will write again soon.

Johanna."

It seemed so long since we were together, and Jerusalem and Caesarea were so far away. I missed my friends and would have given anything at that moment to open my heart and tell them things hard to write in a letter.

Barnabas's family welcomed us into their home, and as Johanna had said, his family were like him in their warmth and generosity to us as refugees. They gave us shelter and a family when we had neither. Barnabas's grandfather had left Judea to start a cloth merchant business, which his father then built into a thriving industry. The family produced and sold linen and wool across the Roman Empire, from Rome to Britannia and North Africa. Soon, we became proficient in spinning and weaving, and Mary and I spent many hours in their workshop, working and enjoying conversation with the family. Our stories found ears eager to hear first-hand accounts of the life of Jesus.

I've never lost my love of the sea since that first glimpse from the hill overlooking Caesarea. As Marcus said, it is a cruel master, and from bitter experience, I know how ferocious it can be, but also how it can bring hope and life. Each day I walked across the bay to the port and along the jetty; the windier the day the more I loved it. Taking down my scarf I would enjoy the wind and salt spray and remember Marcus standing at the rudder, swaying in time to the movements of his beloved ship.

Sometimes the memories were so vivid, I thought I heard the knock on my gate in Bethany, announcing Jesus's arrival, or smelled the bread he baked. I would be taken back to my courtyard to sit at Jesus's feet, and to talk together once more, or to the upstairs room, working with the others to spread the message of love.

Remembering Esther, who had both suffered and loved, I realised I could say this of myself. My strength too came from suffering and loving; sometimes it was difficult to see where suffering stopped and love began, or whether the loving came first. They have become woven together to create the tapestry of my life and story, and they are what made me the woman I had become. Someday I knew I would return, I would sail across the sea, and back to Bethany once more.

HISTORICAL NOTES

"We proclaim to you the one who existed from the beginning, whom we have heard and seen. We saw him with our own eyes and touched him with our own hands. He is the Word of life. This one who is life itself was revealed to us, and we have seen him. And now we testify and proclaim to you that he is the one who is eternal life. He was with the Father, and then he was revealed to us. We proclaim to you what we ourselves have actually seen and heard so that you may have fellowship with us. And our fellowship is with the Father and with his Son, Jesus Christ. We are writing these things so that you may fully share our joy."

John wrote these words in the introduction to one of his letters written to the early churches (1 John 1:1-4, *New Living Translation*). The real women and men in this story, like Martha, were eyewitnesses to the events as outlined in the New Testament. As John says, they saw him with their own eyes and touched him with their own hands.

I have based *Leaving Bethany* upon the Biblical accounts and traditions of the early church, with a big chunk of imagination, interweaving this creatively to create a fictitious story of their lives. Martha, Mary and Lazarus appear three times in the New Testament, Luke 10, and John chapters 11 and 12. I have, as according to tradition, placed them in a central role in the death and resurrection of Jesus, and at the formation of what would become the early church.

Martha acts as the mistress of her house by inviting Jesus into her home. She is the most proactive of the family, which is why I have given her the position of the eldest of her siblings, followed by Lazarus and Mary as the youngest. There is no mention of their parents, so it is feasible to assume that they had died, which is the reason the unmarried Lazarus and Mary lived with Martha. However, a household of three single siblings would have been quite unusual. Lazarus would be the male head of the household which is why the sisters were in such danger with no living guardian after his death.

There is no mention of Martha having a husband or children in any of the accounts, and some traditions suggest she was a widow. I have chosen to portray her as a childless widow, and it would be possible that she may have inherited the house and farm. Though unusual, a father or husband could sign their property over to a woman. This would give her the necessary funds to support Jesus. The story of her marriage, childlessness and home are purely fictitious on my part.

It is an Eastern Orthodox tradition that Martha, Lazarus and Mary had to flee from Saul to Cyprus after the death of Stefanos. Tradition also suggests that Paul, the Latinised version of Saul, appointed Lazarus the first Bishop of Kition, modern-day Larnaca. The Church of St. Lazarus in Larnaca now stands on the spot where, in 890, a tomb was found with the inscription, 'Lazarus the friend of Christ'.

Mary was a popular name in first-century Judea, and there are several scenes of five women, three of whom are called Mary. So, to avoid confusion, I have called Mary Magdalene by her Hebrew name, Miriam. She is perhaps one of the most misunderstood women of the first century AD. The belief that Miriam was a sinful, fallen woman and prostitute originated in the sixth century. Confusion between her, Mary of Bethany and the unnamed woman, described as immoral, who anointed Jesus's feet in Luke 7:36-38, led to the three women to be seen as the same person. This idea is now discredited because it is unsupported by the Biblical texts, but literature and films to this day abound with this enduring opinion of her.

This story has tried to show her as a strong and courageous woman, healed, saved and loved by Jesus in her own right. It was to her that Jesus first showed himself after his resurrection. There is no mention of her in Acts and we know little about her after the resurrection. But tradition has it that she remained in Jerusalem to assist the leaders and was called 'apostle to the apostles' showing her leadership role in the early church.

Luke tells us the names of three women who followed and supported Jesus. These are Mary Magdalene, Susanna (who I have not placed into the story), and Johanna, whose husband was Chuza, Herod's steward or manager. Luke's gospel mentions that Johanna went with Miriam to Jesus's tomb and witnessed the resurrection. It is thought that Chuza and Johanna were the sources of the material of the stories of Jesus's trial with Herod and the Sanhedrin.

For many centuries, Jesus's female disciples have been written out of the history of the early church. This is not supported by the Gospels, Acts or Paul's letters, where they play a central role. I have hoped to address this imbalance within *Leaving Bethany* by giving Martha, Mary and their female friends a pivotal role in the story.

CHAPTER NOTES

Chapter 1

Martha's first meeting with Jesus occurs in Luke 10:38-42.

Jesus's prayer for blessing the bread is from the Jewish Virtual Library: http://www.jewishvirtuallibrary.org/the-blessing-over-bread-hamotzi

Mary mimics her father, telling Martha that women should not study the law. This saying is found in the Mishna, a collection of Rabbinic laws. The Mishna was written down in the second century AD, after previously existing only in oral form. It is often cited as a source of information about Judaism in the first century.

Chapter 2

In chapter 8:1-3, Luke tells of the women who follow and support Jesus, one of which was Johanna. Luke tells us that Jesus healed her, but does not give us the illness. I have described the symptoms of diphtheria, reported in the eastern Mediterranean in the first century AD.

Jesus's teaching as he makes the bread is from John 6:35-40 and Matthew 6:25-34.

In Flanders Fields

In Flanders fields the poppies blow
Between the crosses, row on row,
That mark our place; and in the sky
The larks, still bravely singing, fly
Scarce heard amid the guns below.

We are the Dead. Short days ago
We lived, felt dawn, saw sunset glow,
Loved and were loved, and now we lie,
In Flanders fields.

Take up our quarrel with the foe:
To you from failing hands we throw
The torch; be yours to hold it high.
If ye break faith with us who die
We shall not sleep, though poppies grow
In Flanders fields.

by John McCrae

One small flower has touched
the lives of millions.

Thank you for helping today's
Armed Forces community.

ROYAL BRITISH LEGION

Chapter 3

Lazarus's death and resurrection are found in John chapter 11.

Simon Peter said he believed Jesus was the Messiah in Matthew 16:13-20 and Mark 8:27-30. Martha is the only other person in the Gospels who directly says this of Jesus, but her confession is often overlooked in favour of Simon's.

Chapter 5

We can find Jesus's statements about his death and resurrection, which John quotes, in Mark 8:31-33, 9:30-32 and 10:23-34.

Jesus's teaching about the vine and branches is from John 15:1-17. John places this teaching in the middle of the Last Supper, but I have placed it at Martha's courtyard, five days earlier.

John tells us the story of Mary anointing Jesus's feet in chapter 12:1-11 of his gospel and identifies that it was Mary. Matthew 26:6-13 and Mark 14:1-7 describe a woman who anointed Jesus's head in Bethany, but does not name her. This should not be confused with the unamed woman who is described as sinful and who also washed Jesus's feet in Luke 7:36-39, in the home of a Pharisee.

Chapter 6

Jesus's entry into Jerusalem, often called the triumphant entry, is found in Matthew 21:1-11, Mark 11:1-11, Luke 19:28-40 and John 12:12-19.

We find Jesus clearing the Temple courts of the money changers in Matthew 21:12-17, Mark 11:15-18 and Luke 19:45-48. John places this incident at the beginning of Jesus's ministry in John 2:13-17.

Jesus and the disciples stayed in Bethany in the week between his entry into Jerusalem and his crucifixion, and it is often suggested that they used Martha's house as a base. Mark 11:11-12.

Chapter 7

There is no mention in the Gospels of Joseph after Jesus is lost in the Temple at about age 12, in Luke 2:41-52. So it is commonly assumed that he died before Jesus began his public ministry.

Luke followed up his Gospel by writing about what happened in the next thirty years in the Acts of the Apostles. In Acts 14:12, Barnabas and Saul (called Paul, the Romanised version of his Hebrew name, by this time in Acts) in Lystra, and the local people call him Zeus and call Paul, Hermes. The Greeks often portrayed Zeus, the king of the gods, as a tall well-built man, suggesting that Barnabas was also built this way.

There is no mention of Barnabas in the Gospels, but certain traditions suggest that he was one of the seventy sent out by Jesus. He is called an apostle which would suggest that he was a witness to the resurrection.

Mark 3:21 refers to Jesus's siblings misunderstanding his ministry and thinking he is out of his mind. Mark 6:3 gives us the names of his brothers, James (called Jacob in the story), Joseph (sometimes referred to as Joses, Judas and Simon, but his sisters are not named.

Luke introduces us to Mary Magdalene, whom I call Miriam in the story. In Luke 8:1-3, he says that Jesus healed her of seven demons. The story of her life and healing is purely fictitious and based upon her suffering from a mental illness. We can find Jesus healing many people in Capernaum in Luke 4:40-41.

Jesus's teaching about forgiveness is from Matthew 18:21-22.

Mary's stories about Jesus's teaching in the Temple are taken from Matthew 22:15-22 and 34-40.

Chapter 8

The last meal Jesus spent with his closest disciples, often called the Last Supper, and his arrest happen in Matthew 26:17-56, Mark 14:12-52, Luke 22:7-53, and John 13:1–17:26.

Mark's Gospel recounts a young man who ran away naked during Jesus's arrest. Many names are suggested as to the identity of the mysterious young man, notably Mark himself. Nick Page in *The Longest Week* suggests that this may have been Lazarus, which would explain why there are calls for his arrest when the disciples are left alone. From the story, we know that the Temple authorities already wanted him arrested.

Chapter 9

Jesus's mother, Mary, recounts the day of Jesus's dedication as a baby in the Temple, which is found in Luke 2:22-40.

Matthew 26:57-68 and 27:11-31, Mark 14:53-65 and 15:1-20, Luke 22:54, 66-71 and 23:1-25, and John 18:12-14, 19-24 and 19:1-16 tell us of Jesus's trial and torture by Pilate.

Chapter 10

Jesus's death is described in Matthew 27:32-61, Mark 15:21-47, Luke 23:26-56, and John 19:16-42.

Each Gospel lists the women who were present at the cross and tomb on Sunday morning. However, they each list slightly different names and add that other unnamed women were present. For literary reasons and to aid the telling of the story, I have condensed these lists to five women. Miriam (Mary Magdalene), Jesus's mother and Johanna, and added Martha and her sister Mary. The Gospels do not mention Martha and Mary as being present, but various traditions say that they were witnesses to both the crucifixion and resurrection.

Chapter 11

The events of the resurrection take place in Matthew 27:62–28:15, Mark 16:1-20, Luke 24:1-49, and John 20:1-23.

Chapter 12

Judas's betrayal and suicide can be read in Matthew 27:1-10, Mark 14:10-11, Luke 22:1-6 and Acts 1:18-19.

Jesus's appearance to Thomas is found in John 20:24-29, and the appearance to the disciples in Galilee is in John 21:1-25.

Saul, or Paul, lists the witnesses to the resurrection as over 500 people, many of whom he said were still alive at the time of his writing. See 1 Corinthians 15:3-8.

The ascension is found in Matthew 28:16-20, Mark 16:15-20, Luke 24:50-53 and Acts 1:1-11.

Chapter 13

Luke tells us in Acts 1:15 that there were about 120 people in their group which met together before Pentecost, and he lists many by name. He does not mention Martha or her family, but tradition suggests they were involved in the events described in Acts.

Acts 2:1-41 tells us of the occasion when the disciples were filled with the Holy Spirit at Pentecost. It is often said that this occurred in the upstairs room; however, in *Kingdom of Fools*, page 22, Nick Page suggests that this could have been in the Temple courts. Luke in chapter 2 of Acts uses a different word for the venue than the one he uses for the upstairs room in chapter 1. This seems to be a public event and there is no clear change of scene between the filling of the Holy Spirit and Simon's speech. Therefore, I have situated this within the Temple.

Chapter 14

Acts 2:42-47 tell us that the new groups met together in the Temple and homes where they continued Jesus's teaching, shared meals, took the bread and wine and prayed. They shared their goods and possessions so that no one was in need. Acts 4:36-37 says that Barnabas sold a field and took the money to the apostles.

Mary sings from Psalm 92:1-4. In keeping with the contemporary language of the book, I have used the *New Living Translation*.

Chapter 15

The healing of the beggar who could not walk and the subsequent arrest, trial and release of Simon and John is in Acts chapters 3 and 4.

Chapter 16

The second arrest of the apostles, their release from prison, recapture and flogging are told in Acts 5:17-42.

Chapter 17

The Gospels mention Nicodemus and Joseph of Arimathea as Pharisees and members of the Sanhedrin, but also as secret believers in Jesus. See Matthew 27:57, Mark 15:43 and Luke 23:50-56. Nicodemus visited Jesus at night, John 3:1-21, and in John 7:50-52 he stood in defence of Jesus in front of the High Priest.

In Acts 22:3, Paul describes himself as a student of Gamaliel but there is no evidence that he attended the Sanhedrin as his assistant or scribe. This is a fictitious invention of mine to introduce him into the story.

Chapter 18

Acts 6:1-7 describes how the Greek-speaking widows were missed out of the daily food parcels. One solution to prevent this happening again was to appoint seven people to oversee the food distribution. This included Stefanos and Phillip. Rather than use the Anglicized name Stephen, as common in English Bibles, I have chosen to use the Greek name Stefanos.

The Gospels tell us that Jesus's brothers and sisters were initially antagonistic towards Jesus, blaming him, as the eldest son, of abandoning their mother. It was only later that they became believers. To avoid confusion with James, John's brother, I have called Jesus's brother by his Hebrew name, Jacob. Acts tells us that his brother, James, became the leader of the fledgling church. It is not known when he took up his role, and it is my suggestion that he was in Jerusalem at this time.

Chapter 19

The arrest, trial and stoning of Stefanos are found in Acts 6:8–8:1.

Chapter 20

Just a few verses in Acts 8:1-3 record Saul's antagonism leading to the persecution of the believers. He went from house to house to arrest men and women. This results in the scattering of the early church, as many escaped Jerusalem. Saul aimed to destroy the faith, but the opposite happened they told about Jesus and proclaimed the gospel wherever they went. It was mainly the Greek-speaking believers who were the target of his persecution, rather than the apostles or other Aramaic Jews.

Chapter 21

Though Saul's anger was directed towards the Greek-speaking Jews, it is a church tradition that Martha, Mary and Lazarus had to flee Jerusalem after Stefanos's death. The Roman Catholic tradition suggests that they went to France, but the Greek Orthodox tradition says they went to Cyprus. As Barnabas is from Cyprus, I have chosen for him to take them to his family.

Martha and the group rest for the night at a Samaritan village. The woman who greets them is the woman whom Jesus met at the well in John 4:1-42.

Chapter 24

Martha sings from Psalm 139:1-12, from the *New Living Translation*.

Chapter 27

Barnabas's family business as cloth merchants is fictitious, based upon the common products of Cyprus at the time.